THE MAFIA AND HIS ANGEL

PART 1

Tainted Hearts Series

By Lylah James

THE MAFIA AND HIS ANGEL

Limitless Publishing, LLC
Kailua, HI 96734
www.limitlesspublishing.com

Formatting: Limitless Publishing

ISBN-13: 978-1-64034-998-8

Dedication

To my parents for always believing in me.

Prologue

Alessio

"We've got a problem," a harsh voice said through the phone. It was my second in command.

"I'm coming," I told him. I didn't like his tone. I could tell it was something really bad. His nervousness made me nervous. Viktor was a crazy bastard, and if something had him this riled up, then it was something big. Something I really wouldn't like.

I walked out of my office and found a few of my men standing in the hallway, lined up and on guard. They bowed their heads in respect as I walked by.

As I stepped into the dark hallway that led to the soundproof basement, my body tensed. The air around me was stale and my steps were hard against the silence as I prepared myself for the worst.

When I opened the door, I saw Viktor leaning against the wall, his head cast down in defeat. My entrance didn't even faze him, he was so lost in his own thoughts. I cleared my throat and he glanced up.

His expression conveyed horror and disgust. "It's bad," Viktor said, pointing toward the room. I nodded, then walked farther inside, leading the way while Viktor fell into step behind me.

Stomping forward, I found a bloodied man strapped to a chair. The basement room was empty except for the chair in the middle and a table at the back. Four of my men stood around him. They were my right-hand men.

I didn't recognize the captive, but when he looked up at me, his eyes were filled with terror. As I got closer, his already pale face twisted in pain. He pushed back against the chair when I stopped in front of him.

"What the fuck is going on?" My voice boomed around the room. I didn't take my eyes off the man, but when I saw him flinch, satisfaction coursed through my body. The fucker better be petrified.

Viktor walked around me to stand behind the man. He grabbed the captive's hair and pulled hard until his neck snapped back painfully. The man screamed and thrashed.

I lifted my eyes from the battered captive to meet Viktor's disgusted gaze.

"The fucker betrayed us. I heard him talking. The fucking Italians. He's working for them," Viktor growled.

I looked down at the man and his eyes were closed. He refused to look at me. The anger that took over my body was indescribable. He fucking betrayed me. *Me*. The. Fucking. King. The person who owned his life.

Nobody betrayed me and got away with it. I trusted all my men. They were my family, but when one of my own betrayed me, they paid the ultimate price. Death. Very *painful* death.

Taking a deep breath and schooling my features, I stepped away from the strapped man.

"Bring me a chair," I yelled. I saw one of my men scrambling back, doing as I commanded.

"Here you go, Boss," Phoenix said a minute later. He placed the chair behind me and slowly stepped away.

I sat down and faced the motherfucker. He opened his eyes and stared directly at me. My temper flared. Leaning forward, I snarled into his face. "Why?"

His body shook in fear but he refused to answer. I looked up and signaled Viktor. He let the man go and walked toward the table at the back of the room, only to come back with a cutter in his hand.

I smiled almost maliciously and leaned back against the chair, crossing my arms over my chest.

"Enjoy," I said, nodding at Viktor.

As he got to work, the man's screams filled the room. Blood dripped all over the floor, but I kept my gaze fixed on him the whole time. When he started to lose consciousness, I raised my hand. Viktor instantly stopped his torturous ministrations.

Leaning forward again, I asked, "Why and who?"

I laughed when he glared at me. Viktor leaned forward and punched him. "Show respect."

"I will ask one last time. Why and who?" I said menacingly as I took his face in my hand. My fingers pressed hard into his cheek until blood oozed badly from his wounds.

When he still wouldn't answer, I let his face go and stood up, pushing my chair away. I wasn't going to get my hands dirty this time. But the man strapped against the chair in front of me forced my hand. The rest of my men needed to see me kill. They needed to see the consequences of betraying me.

They needed to see the worst of me. How brutal I could be. It appeared they had forgotten.

I was feared by all and nobody fucking betrayed me.

Walking toward the table, I picked up the pliers. As I turned, all the men took a step back. Viktor smiled sadistically and shook his head. "Fuck, yeah. Now you're talking."

Viktor held the captive's head against the chair. I stood in front of him and roughly grabbed his chin, not caring if I hurt him. I forced his mouth open and held the pliers to his teeth.

The man tried to scream, but I never gave him a chance. It took me hours to be satisfied.

And when I was done, he was no longer breathing.

May this be a lesson learned.

***

Ayla

Run, keep running, I told myself.

Escaping wasn't easy. I had planned it for years

but never found the courage to actually do it.

But tonight I had to escape from the nightmare I'd been born into.

My father never cared. It didn't matter that I begged him to listen. He always turned a blind eye. My father only cared about his profits. After all, he was the Boss. The Italians, the *Famiglia* respected him. He was the feared leader.

And I was just a pawn in the cruel game.

I had no choice, no will. No respect. No love.

I had nothing.

My engagement to my father's second in command hadn't been my choice either. After all, what choice did I have at sixteen?

At twenty-three, after all the years of torture I went through by Alberto's hands, I decided to escape. For years, I wished my father would put a stop to the violence against me, but it never happened. Alberto did whatever he wanted with me.

I was just a toy for pleasure and for pain.

After he left me bloodied and beaten up from yet another torturous night, I crawled out of the bed and climbed out the window. No matter how much I thought of it and planned for my escape, it wasn't easy. Nothing was ever easy.

But I still ran for my life.

Whatever was left of my sanity depended on it.

"Stop!"

I heard yelling behind me, snapping me out of my thoughts.

"No. No. No," I gasped, panting. I was almost off the property, my legs burning as I ran.

Run, keep running.

I just needed time, but the men were closing in on me.

"Miss Ayla. Stop. Stop," I heard one of them yelling behind me.

Shuffling deeper into the forest, I forced myself to move quicker. I pushed hard, running until my body felt like it was breaking. I was already bleeding badly.

Everything hurt, but I kept going. Only my escape mattered.

I kept running into the darkness until the screams of the men faded away. When I couldn't hear them anymore, I stopped and leaned against a tree.

My safety wasn't guaranteed yet, but I had to rest. My heart was pounding and my legs were shaking too hard for me to continue.

But when I heard a noise to my left, my eyes widened and I pushed myself from the tree, taking a few steps away. The sounds got louder.

Without sparing another glance in that direction, I turned away and started running again, praying that I would find someone who could help me. There must be a good person left in this cruel world.

When dawn approached, I was too tired to keep going. I was no longer in the forest, but at the side of a deserted road. I knew my father's estate was on the outskirts of New York City. He'd said something about one day ruling the whole city. But for now, it belonged to someone else. Someone more powerful than him.

Limping along the side of road, I continued until I came across houses.

A sigh of relief escaped my lips. I was safe.

Someone would help me.

I walked over to one of the houses and knocked softly at the door. An old woman opened the door and gasped at the sight of me. Before I could say anything, she slammed the door in my face.

My eyes widened and I stared at the closed door in shock. *What?*

My fist came up to knock again, but I saw something else from the corner of my eye.

Alberto's men. They were walking around, looking for me.

With my heart in my throat, I quickly hid behind the house. As I tried to figure out my next plan, lights flared around the corner. I looked to my left and saw a black vehicle slowing to a stop.

I stood still as a large man stepped out of the car. He was wearing a black suit, similar to what Alberto and my father wore. I couldn't see him well, the darkness hiding his face. He went inside one of the houses.

Looking back at the car, I made up my mind. After making sure that Alberto's men were not looking, I quickly walked away from my hiding spot and ran toward the car. I pulled on the handle of the back door.

The door opened. Tears of relief blinded my vision and I hiccupped back a sob.

I looked on either side of me, making sure nobody saw me. My path was clear when I climbed into the car and closed the door behind me.

My body folded into itself as I crouched down between the seats, trying to make myself as invisible as possible. My eyes closed as I tried to calm my breathing.

After a few minutes, the door opened and the man sat down. I jumped slightly when he slammed the door shut. My stomach twisted in knots as my breathing slowed. My hands shook in fear.

I heard some shuffling noises and then he started talking. "Viktor, I'm coming home. Get everything prepared."

My body was strung tight with tension but when the car suddenly lurched forward and the man began driving, I let out a sigh of relief.

I was safe. For now. And that was all that mattered.

Chapter 1

My body trembled with tension during the drive. The man was silent but the air surrounding him was intense and brooding. When the car finally came to a stop, I froze.

My heart skipped a beat when he opened the door. I waited for a reaction from him. But he only stepped out of the car and the door closed behind him.

Then, utter silence.

I breathed out a sigh of relief, my body sagging against the back of the car seat. I was safe. After waiting for a few more minutes, I climbed to my knees and stared outside through the tinted window.

I gasped, my eyes widening in shock. The beauty beyond the window took my breath away.

There was a long circular driveway lined with pine trees and tall red glass garden stakes. Beautiful shrubs surrounded a gigantic fountain in the middle of the driveway. The central fountain was mesmerizing, made of glazed ceramic tiles and surrounded by flowers.

I could see trees in the distance, which continued down the long driveway toward the main gate. This place was serene.

When I felt sure I was alone, I quickly opened the door and stepped out. When I had left my father's estate, it was still dark, dawn just slowly approaching, but now the sunlight was bright. I winced and had to blink to get used to the glare.

Turning around, I was speechless.

This estate seemed much bigger than my father's. There were white marble pillars around the entrance to the mansion. The towers were topped in silver domes and intricate stonework decorated the walls. A large wooden double door probably cost more than I could imagine.

My father was wealthy, but I had never seen anything like this. The mansion I lived in was much smaller compared to this one.

Sudden realization came crashing down on me and it occurred to me that this man was much wealthier than my dad, and possibly just as dangerous—if not more so.

I had learned my lesson. Rich people were blinded by their power and they stopped acting like human beings. They had no emotions. And I wasn't going to take the risk with this stranger.

Taking several steps back, I bumped into the car. I swallowed and then closed my eyes. I had to go. I had to find somewhere safer.

I turned away but my eyes widened in shock when I saw two men striding toward me. They were looking at each other, away from me. Taking the chance, I quickly hid behind the car.

My body was shaking with fear and I felt myself sweating.

I had to leave. Now! But my safety was compromised. When the men entered the mansion, my body dropped forward in relief, but tension still coiled tight inside me. Fear lodged deep in my gut and my stomach cramped. As I turned back toward the main gate, I froze again.

There was no escape. It was impossible.

For the first time, I noticed four men standing at the main gate, guarding it. Nobody entered or left without them noticing. It was the same way at my father's estate. There were always guards on the ground, making sure there weren't any impending attacks.

I swallowed and looked behind me. My heart stopped beating for a moment when I saw the doors open. Going through the main gates wasn't an option anymore. And I wasn't familiar with the grounds.

Tears of frustration blinded my vision as I tried to think of a way out.

I took a step toward the opened door, my heart beating hard and fast against my ribcage. I could go in. I could hide in there and most likely nobody would see me. I would be safe for some time, until I had a plan.

Before I could take more steps toward the door, a shout came from behind me.

"Hey!"

I froze and turned around to see two of the guards running toward me at full force.

"Stop right there!" one of the men shouted, his

expression furious. I saw both of them taking their guns out and pointing them at me.

My heart stuttered and my vision turned blurry with panic. Without a second thought, I turned around and ran toward the opened door.

I felt them behind me. They were closing in and their steps sounded hard and angry.

My pulse drummed in my throat. My breath came out in short pants and I smelled it—fear. Fear surrounded me.

The doors were so close. I was almost inside the mansion.

They came close, their heat at my back. Feeling a touch on my arm, I let out a small scream and increased my pace until I passed through the door.

I ran blindly. Between sofas, chairs, a table, and then the stairs. I didn't pay attention to where I was going. I just ran.

When I reached the second floor, I tripped over my legs and almost went down in a heap. Saving myself in time with the help of the banister, I continued running.

All I heard were furious shouts. Even when several men came from different directions, I didn't stop running.

The halls were big and filled with many doors. When I heard distant screams, I blindly moved toward one door and opened it. I ran inside and slammed it behind me.

My body prickled with tension, like thousands of pointy knives piercing my body. My heart was beating as fast as the thrumming wings of a caged bird. It sounded like drums to my ears. It was the only thing I could hear.

I closed my eyes and leaned heavily against the door.

The mansion was too big. It would take them some time to find me. I slowly slid down until my butt met the floor. Pulling my knees toward me, I hugged them tight to my chest. I placed my head on them and tried to calm my breathing.

When I could finally breathe normally, and my gasps no longer filled the room, I looked up. Noticing that I was in a bedroom, I stood on shaky legs and moved away from the door.

The room was massive. There was a king size bed in the middle of the room and a nightstand on either side. A bench sat in front of the bed. I walked closer and pressed my hand into the soft cushions.

Looking to my left, I noticed a chest against the wall. I turned around to see a sitting area. There were two couches and a coffee table in the middle, facing a fireplace.

I looked to my right and saw that instead of walls, there were big paneled windows framed by intricate draperies. The room was welcoming, but *dark.*

My breath picked up when I heard someone at the door. The knob moved and my eyes widened in panic. My heart pounded faster. *No. No. No.*

I searched the room for a place to hide. The bed was the closest to me, so I crawled under it.

I lied down on my side. Bringing my knees to my chest, I wrapped my arms around them and closed my eyes tightly, praying that whoever was at the door wouldn't find me.

13

Chapter 2

Alessio

I opened the door to my bedroom and slammed it behind me. Viktor had been busy with the clubs' problems, to make sure all our *businesses* were running smoothly, so house check-ups fell on me. That was Viktor's job and I didn't trust anyone else to take care of it. So I went myself.

Shifting my weight on my feet, I jerked at my tie hard until it came undone and I pulled it off my neck. As I was taking off my suit jacket, my phone vibrated in my pocket.

Taking it out, I saw Phoenix's name flashing on the screen.

"What is it?" I growled into the phone.

"Boss," he said, sounding panicked and out of breath. I *almost* rolled my eyes.

"What is it?"

"Boss…"

I didn't hear the rest of his sentence, instead tuning him out.

My eyes widened when I noticed a white cloth extending from beneath my bed. I walked closer, the phone still at my ear.

When I reached the cloth, I crouched down and touched it.

As I lifted the covers around the bed and looked down, my mouth fell open at the sight, then anger coursed through me. I could feel my eyes narrowing into slits.

A girl. A dirty-looking girl was hiding under my bed.

"Boss, boss, are you there?" Phoenix yelled through the phone.

"What?" I bellowed, as I kept my eyes on the little intruder.

She jumped at my tone and started shaking, her chin trembling and tears forming at the corners of her eyes.

I bared my teeth at her and she tried to scoot away from me, but I didn't give her a chance. Grabbing onto her white, shredded, dirty dress, I held her still. She wasn't going anywhere.

I fisted the material in my hand and pulled until she was no longer under the bed.

"Boss! Someone broke into the estate," Phoenix screamed through the phone, sounding frustrated.

I smiled. The girl kept her knees against her chest, then wrapped her arms around her head as if to protect herself from me.

I laughed at the thought. Poor girl. She didn't even know what she'd gotten herself into. Breaking into the house of the Bratva's boss—the *Pakhan*—and then hiding under his bed.

"Boss?" Phoenix said, sounding confused.

"I got this," I growled through the phone, glaring at the intruder. I ended the call before he could answer.

Putting it back in my pocket, I grabbed her arm and pulled her upward. She whimpered painfully and her sniffles filled the room. She kept her head down, her hair falling like a curtain around her face, shielding her from me.

When I tried to pull her close, she resisted and tried to twist away. I tightened my hold on her small wrist, and I knew I was hurting her. Her wincing told me so, but I didn't let go.

If I wanted to, with barely no effort, I could break her hands in half.

I let her go and took a step back. She did exactly what I expected. She ran straight toward the door.

I smirked, pulling my gun from the back of my pants. I pointed it at her and spoke calmly.

"Another step and I'll shoot you."

She stopped. Her body trembled badly and I knew it was from fear. What she didn't know was that I fed on fear.

I laughed and it sounded harsh to my own ears. She jumped but didn't run for her life.

"Turn around."

She didn't turn around.

Red hot anger coursed through my body. Nobody dared to ignore me. Yet, this girl….

"Turn around," I shouted at her back.

My little captive jumped again, but this time she swiveled around quickly. She kept her face down.

I wanted to see her.

16

I blinked at the sudden thought. *What?*

Shaking my head, my brow furrowed as I watched her. What was she doing here? Why was she here? By the look of her, she didn't belong in a place like this. Not in a Mafia house. Especially not in *my* house.

"Look at me," I said before I could stop myself. My fingers tightened around the gun as I waited for her to do as she was told.

She took longer than I expected. If she was one of my men, I would have already shot her for disobedience. But I couldn't bring myself to move.

For some unknown reason, the way she covered her face with her long dark hair, looking so childlike, made my chest hurt.

What the fuck?

"Look at me," I said again, this time my voice grating. She slowly brought her head up and I saw doe-like eyes peeping through her hair. I sucked in a breath and took a step toward her.

As she continued to lift her head, I saw a tiny round nose and then pink full lips that had dried blood on them. Her cheeks were round, but obviously bruised. I couldn't see her face properly, it was so covered with dirt and bruises.

She was hugging her arms around herself, her body shaking with silent tremors. The little intruder was obviously frightened. She was a tiny girl and I felt my heart twisting at her fragile state.

Taking a step forward, I saw green eyes peeping up at me under her long lashes. She blinked away tears as she saw me approaching, my gun still pointed at her.

When I was close, I slowly brought the gun down and glared at her menacingly. When she flinched, I felt my resolve slipping.

She took a step back and I growled, "Don't move."

She flinched again. My heart was beating fast in my chest. *What the fuck is wrong with me?*

I moved closer until our chests were almost touching. I felt her tremble against me, and she whimpered in fear. She hugged her body tighter and folded into herself, as if she was trying to hide from me, even in plain sight.

I brought my empty hand up to her face. She winced but didn't move. Silent tears streamed down her cheek and I touched a drop, thumbing it away. She froze and I felt her suck in a breath.

I froze too. Something was wrong with me.

Before I could stop myself, my hands went to the strands of hair hanging over her face. I slowly moved her hair to the side until her whole face was visible to me. Maybe my heart stuttered for a moment. I didn't know.

She slowly lifted her gaze until she was staring at me with glassy green eyes, the color of the rain forest.

I swallowed hard, slowly moving my thumb over her soft cheek. When she winced in pain, I let her go, taking several steps back.

A wave of emotion ran through me. First sadness, then tenderness, and finally anger. I decided to hang on to the anger and let it consume me.

There was no place for tenderness in my life.

Tenderness made you weak. Any emotion other than anger made you weak.

And I couldn't be weak. I had thousands of people behind me and I had thousands to lead.

So, I grabbed on to the anger and let it course through me until my body was shaking.

Red hot anger. I glared at her and pointed my gun at her again. Her eyes widened and she let out a cry, her hand coming up to her chest.

She shook her head repeatedly, her mouth opening and closing silently as if she wanted to say something.

"Who the fuck are you and why are you here?" I growled at her, my voice low, but my tone dangerous. It spoke volume and it was obvious the girl understood it.

If she didn't give me an answer that I was satisfied with, I would shoot her without a second thought.

Chapter 3

Ayla

I stared at the man standing in front of me, my body shaking with indescribable fear. When he pulled me from under the bed, I didn't notice his face. I was too scared to look at him.

But when he ordered me to look up, I was surprised. He took my breath away. For a minute, I stopped thinking that he was about to shoot me. I stopped thinking that I was supposed to run away.

All I could do was stare into the bluish-steel eyes that reminded me of the midwinter sky.

When he took a step toward me, my heart stuttered. His steps were powerful and hard. He moved confidently. I tried to take a step back, but he stopped me with his gun.

His presence was one of a leader. A dangerous leader. The air around him felt frigid.

As he came to a stop in front of me, our chests almost touching, my body trembled both in fear and in anticipation. I should have been screaming and running, but something about him caused me to remain immobile.

His touch felt electric. My body hummed in response and I no longer felt cold. His warm hand caressed my cheek and I wanted to rub against his palm like a kitten craving attention.

I realized how big he was. Compared to my small size, he was gigantic. My head only came to the middle of his wide, muscled chest. I felt fragile and small next to him.

But for some unknown reason, my body was warming up in his presence. Even though fear coursed through my body, I didn't mind him being near me.

I hated when Alberto was near me. My skin was always crawling in disgust and fear, but with this strange man, I only felt comfort. Even with his gun pointing at me, I felt oddly safe.

But that changed when his face turned hard and then angry. I jumped in surprise as he took a sudden step back. His whole body tightened and he pointed the gun back at me. My eyes widened and my heart beat faster.

Was it all a game? Did he act like he was softening up to me, just to calm me down so he could shoot me?

Tears fell down my dirty, bruised cheeks.

His eyes were trained on my tears. His gaze followed the drops. When they reached my chin, I saw him smile. His mouth quirked up to the side, but his smile looked dangerously malicious.

Oh God. This man was going to kill me.

"Who the fuck are you and why are you here?"

he growled deeply, his voice low but the tone dangerous and angry. I knew that tone.

Alberto used it when he was about to kill someone. He used it on me too, whenever he took me against my will…every single night.

I shivered in terror, my distress likely evident on my face and the way I was trembling. I felt my pulse beating in my ears, blocking out all other sounds except my gasping breath.

I felt myself growing colder. His hard eyes were penetrating mine and I had to lock my knees together to stop myself from taking a step backward. I knew if I moved, he would shoot me.

He took several steps backward, the gun still pointed at me as he waited for my answer. When he reached the couch, he sat down and crossed his right foot over his left knee. The gun was still pointed at my chest.

"I…I am…my…" I stuttered, finding it hard to talk. Alberto and my father had many enemies. What if he was one of them?

"I won't repeat myself, so you better start talking. You have thirty seconds," the man said. He was losing patience. It was evident in the way his face twisted angrily with each word.

"Ayla. My name is Ayla," I said in a rush, my voice raspy.

"Ayla," he whispered, my name rolling off his tongue as if the word itself had been laced with molasses. His voice was deep and it vibrated throughout my body.

"Ayla," he said again. I hated to admit it, but I liked how my name sounded when it came from him. I liked how he said it, almost gently.

Get yourself together, Ayla. This man is about to shoot you. Stupid, Ayla. Stupid. Focus.

"What is your last name, Ayla? And why are you here?" he asked, this time slowly as he continued to stare at me.

I sucked in a deep breath, trying to figure out how much I should tell him. His gaze never left mine, and when I didn't answer quickly enough, he sat forward angrily.

"Now, Ayla. You are very lucky that I am being patient. But I won't ask again."

I nodded, but he continued.

"Let me introduce myself. I'm sure you've heard my name. Alessio Ivanshov," the man stated, his tone low.

My body froze. I stared at the man sitting in front of me, speechless, as my body started to go numb. *No. It couldn't be.*

My heart drummed in alarm as I stared into his unmoving, cold eyes. *Oh God. Please, no.* It couldn't be him.

"Does it ring a bell?" he asked.

My stomach twisted painfully and my vision blurred. I felt myself stumbling forward. Quickly, I righted myself before my face met the floor.

Oh, it definitely rang a bell. Dread and horror filled me. I thought I ran away from dangerous men, but this man sitting in front of me was more dangerous than any of them. He was feared by all.

But most importantly, I was trapped because I was his biggest enemy. My family was his biggest enemy. The Italians. The Abandonato.

The Russians and the Italians had been enemies for so many decades. But the Ivanshov and Abandonato, their enmity ran deep.

And I was standing in front of the Boss, who would kill me mercilessly if he found out that I was an Abandonato.

I stared into Alessio's eyes. I ran from a deadly man, and now I was awaiting my fate in front of another. A deadlier and more dangerous one.

I closed my eyes and tried to calm my breathing. *Think, Ayla. You ran from one. You can do it again.*

Opening my eyes, I met his gaze. My body still shaking with silent tremors, I stood up straighter.

"Ayla Blinov. My name is Ayla Blinov," I said slowly. I wasn't ready to die. I ran away because I wanted a better life so I could finally be myself. I wasn't letting this man take away my newly found freedom.

So I lied.

I swallowed hard, and continued. "I have been living on the streets for a few months, and some men found me and wanted me to work at a brothel. I ran away and hid in your car. When your guards found me, I panicked, so I hid under your bed."

The lie rushed out from me effortlessly. My heart was beating hard against my ribcage. This was a big risk, and I hoped, prayed, that he would believe me.

Alessio sat back and uncrossed his legs. "Hmmm," he said, never shifting his gaze from me.

Both of us stayed silent for a few minutes, my body tensing more with each passing second. My stomach cramped in fear.

Alessio moved forward again, until his elbows

were on his knees and his fingers were crossed together. That was when I noticed he didn't have his gun with him anymore.

My gaze moved to his sides, and I saw his gun sat next to his hip, on the couch. I looked back at his face, and he kept staring at me, his gaze more intense.

Did he believe me? Alessio Ivanshov was a man with many secrets. Dark secrets. He was also very unpredictable. "I have a deal for you," he said suddenly. I jumped at his voice, my body shuddering.

"You have three options," he continued, as I stood in front of him trembling. "One: You work for me," he said. His voice was monotone, so I wasn't sure what he might be planning.

"Two: You go back to the streets, unsafe." He paused as my body froze. "Three: Or I shoot you for trespassing," he finished.

My breath went out in a whoosh as he stopped talking. Alessio's lips quirked up in a tiny smile as he waited for my response.

My eyes widened as I tried to think. I brought a shaky hand to my throat and rubbed it gently, a gesture of nervousness and discomfort.

Option three was obviously not an option. I was not even taking it in consideration. Option two meant being homeless, no money, unsafe on the streets, and very easy for Alberto's men to find me. Option one meant that I would have money and probably a place to live. But there was only one problem.

I would be dead if he ever found out who I was.

With my eyes still locked on his face, I thought about my options. But most importantly, I thought about my survival. And only one option could help me.

"One," I whispered hoarsely, as I stared into Alessio's eyes. He seemed surprised, but then his lips stretched into a full smile.

And I just knew.

With that answer, I had signed myself over to him. I was no longer my own. I belonged to him.

Alessio stood up and walked slowly to me, his steps confident. When he was close, he reached out and touched a dirty strand of my hair.

"Good choice, Ayla," Alessio said. The sound of my name coming from him made me shiver again. God, why did his voice have to sound so…intimate? My eyes widened with the sudden thought. *No. No, Ayla. Don't lose yourself.*

"I'm glad that you decided to…work for me." The way he said those words made my body freeze. He stared at me, his eyes intense.

Alessio stepped closer so that our bodies were pressed together. He moved his finger down my bruised cheek.

"I'll make sure that you won't regret this decision," he whispered huskily.

Wait, what? Did he mean…? No, he couldn't. He wouldn't.

Oh, but he would. He was Alessio Ivanshov. Nothing had ever been denied to him. *And I just said yes to his offer.*

My breathing and the beat of my heart was too loud. I was sure he could hear it. Alessio bent down

26

until his eyes were to my level.

"Don't worry. I won't hurt you."

I swallowed and licked my lips quickly. His gaze followed my movement as his blue eyes turned from cold to hot. He licked his own, and then he whispered, "Not unless you want me to."

I sucked in a shocked breath and it made my chest move against his. The friction made my body shiver. Was it apprehension? Or anticipation?

"Umm…what…what did you…mean by…work?" I asked quietly, tripping over my own words.

He took another step closer, forcing me to take a step back. Alessio crowded me, his presence so strong that it made me feel weak and small.

"Exactly what it means…work," he continued in a husky voice.

Oh my God. Please no. Not that. Anything but that.

"What…what work?" I asked again.

Alessio stared into my eyes. Blue to green.

We both stared at each other, unblinking. The tension vibrated around us. But I couldn't understand what type of tension it was. No. I refused to understand it. I refused to *acknowledge* it.

He suddenly took a step back. I breathed out at the movement, and my tensed muscles uncoiled with relief. Alessio stood to his full height, now looking down at me, his eyes hard again.

"My maids need a little help. You'll be helping with the cleaning and cooking," he said briskly.

Huh? He wanted me to clean and cook?

I stared at him in confusion. Alessio must have

been the most perplexing man I had ever met. Confusing, strange, and dangerous.

"You want me to clean…and cook?" I asked in bewilderment. He cocked his head to the side, still looking at me. Then he smiled. The same malicious smile as before.

"Yes," he said as he took a step toward me, crowding my personal space again. "Did you think I meant something else?" he asked quietly, his tone suggestive as he traced a finger lightly up my right arm.

Yes. Yes, I did think you meant something else. I thought you wanted me to be your wh—

I halted the thought. *Don't go there, Ayla.*

I shook my head quickly, my hair covering my face with the brisk action. Alessio brought his hand up and moved my hair away, baring my face to him again.

I swallowed nervously as I waited for his next move. His warm hand on my face was making the numbness of my body fade away. I hated that his touch could do that. I hated that he had such an effect on me. Already, it was clear he could make me tremble in fear one minute and make me feel warm the next. Inside and out.

***

Alessio

The woman standing in front me, with black hair and green eyes, her name was Ayla. I took my hand away from her face and moved several steps back, severing our connection.

I stared at her and smiled. She thought she could fool me.

Such an innocent little girl.

It was obvious her name was not Blinov. She must have not known. I was the *Pakhan*. I knew when someone was lying. I could sense it. And her lies were written all over her face. She was a shitty liar and I couldn't help but scoff at her nerves.

Ayla. That was her name. I knew it because she didn't stutter when she said it. She wasn't lying about that, but the rest…all of it was a lie.

I would find the truth, but that wasn't the reason why I was keeping her.

I stared at her, her arms wrapped around her waist. She looked so small. So innocent.

Poor little girl. She didn't know what she just brought upon herself.

There was one thing everyone knew. What Alessio Ivanshov wanted, Alessio got. And the bruised and beaten up girl in front of me…

I wanted her.

Innocent kitten. I laughed at the thought. *My* kitten. She belonged to me now.

I was going to play her just like a violin.

And she would enjoy it.

Chapter 4

Ayla

When Alessio stepped back, I felt my body warming up under his piercing gaze. It was like my body wasn't my own under his careful and intense attention.

I licked my suddenly dried lips and saw his eyes following the movement. He slowly licked his own, keeping his eyes on mine. He made the action look so sensual that I had to avert my gaze.

Why was he doing this to me? One minute he acted like he wanted to kill me, while the next it appeared like he wanted to kiss me senseless. Was it all a game to him?

I scoffed. Of course, it was a game. That's what he did. I had heard rumors about him. He would play you masterfully, like the notes of a piano. And when he was done, he would cast you out without a second thought. Or kill you.

I was only a pawn to him. And because of that, I had to tread smartly. If he was playing a game, then

I would play one too, because one way or another, I had to get out of here alive.

"Nikolay," Alessio yelled suddenly. His harsh voice snapped me out of my thoughts and I jumped when the door banged open behind me.

I swiveled around quickly to see an enormous man crowding the doorway. The way his feet were planted apart and with his wide shoulder, the man almost took up the whole doorway. His hair was cut very short. A long deep scar ran from the right side of his forehead and down to his chin. It made him look even more vicious. He wore a three-piece black suit, similar to Alessio's. Two guns were attached to his holster.

I felt myself shiver when the man gave me a hateful glare.

"Nikolay, show Ayla the room beside mine. It's hers now," Alessio said in a familiar hard tone. My father and Alberto used the same tone when they ordered their men to do something. It meant they wanted immediate actions, without any questions or hesitations.

"When she's settled, you are to bring her down to the maids. She'll be working with them," he continued. The whole time, Nikolay's face was emotionless. There was not even a twitch. And I was sure he didn't even blink.

When Alessio finished, Nikolay gave a sharp nod and waited for me to move. I looked back at Alessio and saw that he was staring at me, waiting to see what I did.

"Do I need any…umm…what do I need to do?" I stuttered nervously. With two big and powerful men in the room, it made me feel like prey. Maybe I was.

Alessio stepped closer until we were only an inch apart. He leaned down and whispered in my ear. "Anything I tell you."

I stepped back quickly, my heart beating faster at his admission. "Excuse me?" I asked, my tone edgy.

"For now, the maids will tell you what you need to do," Alessio said as he moved a step closer. "But if I want you to do something else…" He left his sentence hanging, his gaze intensely on mine. "Then I'll let you know."

His words did not soothe me in any way. In fact, they made me even more nervous. The way he finished his sentence, it was obvious that I had no say. Whatever he wanted me to do, I had to do it. Without any questions.

"Nikolay, take her away. I've got business to do," Alessio demanded, taking a step away. His gaze was fixed on mine as I felt Nikolay coming closer.

Nikolay stepped so close that I felt his breath on my neck. I trembled and took a step forward, which brought me closer to Alessio. I was trapped either way. Between two vicious men, they made me want to scoot down and hide.

"Come," Nikolay said, his voice jarring to my ears. I stared at Alessio and saw him nod, as if giving me permission to go. Nikolay grabbed my arm roughly and started to pull me out of the bedroom. His hold was tight and I felt my arm going numb.

With all the bruises covering my body, I hurt everywhere. Weakness began to take over my body and I felt suddenly dizzy.

I tripped over my own feet but quickly straightened when Nikolay growled. I swallowed hard and tried my best to walk normally as he pulled me forcibly to the room next to Alessio's.

When he opened the door and pushed me inside, I gasped as indescribable pain took over my body. The room was dark, but all of a sudden, the light was on. And I gasped again, but for another reason.

The bedroom was huge, at least three times the size of mine. But the best part of it was the magnificent view, which overlooked the beautiful back garden. As I walked closer to the window and peeked outside, a sense of peace overcame me. For a moment, I felt liberated.

I wondered how it was possible for something to look so serene when the world around me was crashing down—a clear contradiction to my situation.

"Clean up and then I'll bring you down to the maids. Clothes will be brought to you." Nikolay's voice broke through my thoughts. I turned around to see him standing at the doorway. His arms were crossed over his chest, his muscles bulging.

I swallowed hard against the lump growing in my throat. When I nodded, he stepped back and closed the door.

I sighed in relief when his intense presence was no longer overwhelming the room. I looked around and saw the bed, which took up half the space in the room. A nightstand sat on either side of the bed, a matching wardrobe to my left. In front of the bed was a bench with two pillows on either end, much like in Alessio's room.

I walked over to the bed and sat on it, bouncing a little. The silky comforter was soft under my hands and all I wanted to do was sleep.

My body felt feeble and tiredness clouded my vision. When I yawned, I slowly stretched out on the bed, then snuggled deeper into the soft mattress and comforter until my body went limp. Feeling warm and cozy, my eyes slowly drifted shut.

Just for a few minutes, I thought.

***

I woke up with a start when the door banged open. It slammed against the wall hard, and I jumped off the bed, shaking violently. Swaying to the side slightly, my body felt sluggish.

My eyes were blurry with sleep, and I had to blink a few times to get myself accustomed to the lights. When I could finally see, I gulped hard. Nikolay was standing there, looking dangerously angry.

"You were supposed to get clean," he said through gritted teeth. Nikolay walked inside the room, his steps hard against the wood. "Listen, Boss gives orders and you follow them. Without any problems. Got it?"

I nodded only because I couldn't bring myself to form any words.

Nikolay scared me. He looked like someone who didn't take any nonsense from anyone. Most importantly, he was also a killer. If I wasn't wrong, a brutal one at that. Everyone was a killer here.

There was no innocence in this life.

Without any other words, he pointed to the door at my left. I walked toward it nervously, my body hyperaware of his presence.

I opened the white door, and at the sight of a bathtub, shower, shampoo, and soaps, I felt tears prickling my eyes. When I ran away from home, I thought that I would be living on the streets, trying to fend for myself, desperate for basic necessities.

But I stood in front of a fabulous bathroom, I had a big bedroom with a cozy bed. I had a job and food. Even though it was not my ideal situation, gratefulness filled my body.

As I closed the door behind me, I noticed there were no female accessories. I shrugged and whispered, "Cleaning is all that matters."

I glanced at the mirror and my eyes widened in shock.

I was dirty. Grimy. My face was red with bruises and some parts were already green. My white dress was filthy and shredded. All I wanted to do was soak in the tub but I could only take a quick shower.

I winced as I quickly removed my dress. I looked back at the mirror and noticed scratches on my arms.

I looked horrible. Was I really standing in front of Alessio, looking like *this*? Why wasn't he disgusted? Most importantly, why did he even keep me? I was frightened just by looking at my reflection in the mirror.

Shaking my head, I stepped into the shower. The moment the warm water hit me, sliding down my bare body, warming the numbness, I felt my tense muscles loosening. At first my bruises itched and were aching under the warm water, but after a few minutes, all I felt was warmth.

I sucked in a deep breath as my body went limp. Lifting my face up into the spray, I let the water cascade around me. A feeling of happiness consumed me as I reached up, squeezed out some shampoo in my palm and started to massage it through my dirty hair.

I let the water sluice through my hair. Brown water, leaves, and small twigs swirled through the drain. When the water finally ran clear, I started to wash my body. After I was done, I stayed under the water for a few more minutes, letting the heat penetrate my body.

I stepped out of the shower on wobbling legs, and when the cool air hit my body, I shivered. Grabbing a towel from a nearby rack, I started to dry my hair and then my body. I wrapped the towel around me and went to stand in front of the mirror.

I looked much better. My bruises didn't appear as horrible as they were before. My face was no longer pale. My cheeks were red from the warm water and my green eyes shone brightly. Giving my reflection a smile, I opened the door and peeked outside.

When I saw that Nikolay was not there, I stepped out and walked over to the bed, where a black dress was waiting for me with a pair of underwear.

The cotton dress was simple, and when I put it on, it came down to mid-thigh. It flowed from the hips and fit me perfectly, showing my curves. Putting on the black flats I found beside the bench, I walked back into the bathroom.

I opened several drawers, looking for a hairbrush. When I finally found one, I combed my messy, tangled hair until it was smooth and shiny.

After giving myself a pinch on each cheek and biting down my lips, reddening them further, I was ready. I walked toward the door, my steps confident and my shoulders straight. Opening it, I saw Nikolay waiting for me, leaning against the wall.

When he looked at me, his eyes flared for a moment, his expression one of surprise.

"C'mon," he said after masking his emotions again. His face was hard and he glared at me. *It's probably the only thing he knows.* Glaring, growling, and anger.

Without waiting for my response, he started to walk toward the stairs. I followed him, my steps close behind his.

I was ready for this. Whatever would be thrown at me, I was ready. Because this time, I was going to fight for my freedom.

Chapter 5

Alessio

I was leaning back on my sofa chair, head tilted toward the ceiling, my eyes closed when the door opened. I knew who it was without opening my eyes. Only one person would dare come into my room without permission.

Opening my eyes, I caught sight of Viktor strolling in. He closed the door behind him, leaned against it, and crossed his arms in front of his chest.

"Seriously?" he asked as he stared at me, his face expressionless.

"I need a full background check on Ayla Blinov," I fired back without answering his question. I knew what he was talking about, but I had no desire to discuss that matter. It was none of his business who I decided to keep or not.

I stood up and walked over to the small bar. "I'm sure her last name is not Blinov, but I still want a check, in case you find something."

After I poured some whiskey in two glasses,

Viktor took one from my hand and sipped slowly.

We both stared at each other, the air tense around us. When his glass was empty, he placed it on the bar and turned back toward me.

"What are you planning, Alessio?" he asked, giving me a strange look.

I shrugged. "Why do you think I'm planning something?"

Viktor scoffed and shook his head. "Because you never do anything without a plan. The girl trespassed and you are keeping her. Sounds like a plan to me." He paused for a second and then asked slowly, "Is she a rat? Is that why you are keeping her? To know who she's working with?"

Shaking my head, I glared at him. If it was someone else questioning my decision, they would be on the ground writhing in pain. But Viktor was my second in command.

We were born two weeks apart. His father was my father's second in command. When I took over, it was never a question that he would be my second. He was my *brother*.

"Do you really think I would keep her if she was a rat?" I asked through gritted teeth. He got on my nerves sometimes.

"Anything is possible with you. Why are you keeping her, anyway?"

"None of your business. Do as you're told," I responded harshly.

Viktor nodded and stepped away from the bar. "I'll let you know what I find."

I turned toward the large windows, dismissing him. I heard his feet shuffling and then the door closed.

I looked down at the glass in my hand as I moved it around my fingers.

"Let's see what we get about you, kitten," I whispered, bringing the glass to my lips.

I was intrigued. My body was coursing with excitement.

I would slowly uncover her, layer by layer until I knew everything. Every last detail. And when I was done, I would devour her until nothing was left.

A few minutes later, I was still standing in front of the large windows that overlooked the majestic back garden. My phone rang in my pocket and I quickly took it out, answering the call without looking.

"What?" I barked.

"There's nothing on her," Viktor said. My hand tightened around the phone and I smirked.

I knew it.

"She doesn't even exist in the database," he continued, his voice smooth and calm as if he knew the information wouldn't surprise me.

I let out a small laugh. Shaking my head, I thought about the seemingly innocent girl I found cowering under my bed. The moment I saw her, I knew she was trouble, and instead of taking it out, I invited it.

Why?

Simple. She intrigued me.

"I got this," I said through the phone, and hung up without waiting for an answer.

Well, this is going to be fun.

I walked away from the window and out of the

room.

***

Ayla

As I followed Nikolay down the stairs, I was finally able to look at the house. *Mansion*, I corrected myself.

It had the tallest ceiling I had ever seen, decorated by the most gorgeous crown molding. As we walked down the spiral staircase, I noticed another one to my right. They both led up to the second floor and met in the middle in an imperial staircase style. I held onto the wooden banister and felt how smooth it was under my hand. The mansion was immaculate, with white sparkling marble.

I looked up and noticed a big Venetian-style crystal chandelier hanging from the ceiling, decorated with hundreds of teardrop crystals. It evoked a very vintage, elegant feel.

I was still staring at it when I suddenly crashed into a wall of hard muscles. Stiffening, I stepped away. Nikolay turned around and glared at me aggressively.

"Are you blind?" he barked. I shook my head.

"Then fucking watch where you are going." This time I nodded. He scared me beyond words.

Nikolay gave me a final glare before turning around. We stepped off the stairs and he started walking toward the left corridor.

As I began to relax again, I continued to inspect

the mansion. I lived in a mansion too. My father was wealthy, but our estate was not as big and beautiful as this one. My house was plain, cold, and uninviting.

Whoever decorated this place had good taste and it was obvious they did it with love. Details had been refined and blended. As I followed Nikolay, I was in awe of my surroundings.

When he came to a stop, I quickly halted in my tracks, stopping an inch away from him. My eyes widened and I took a few steps back. I stuck my tongue out to his back and twisted my lips ruefully. I didn't want to get snapped at again. He was a moody man.

"Lena, I have another maid for you," he said, his voice soft. I felt my mouth drop as I stared at his enormous back in shock. Did he just talk softly? Was my mouth on the floor? I hoped not.

"Ohh, dear. How lovely. Where is she, sweetie?" I heard a voice ask.

Sweetie? Had I just been transported to an alternate universe?

Nikolay's back was blocking my sight, so I stepped to the side and my eyes widened. A woman, probably in her early fifties, was standing in front of him, wearing a similar black dress, even though hers was below the knees. She smiled sweetly at Nikolay as she wiped her hands on her white apron.

When she saw me, her smile widened. "Ah, there you are," she said as she walked toward me. "Look at you. Such a beautiful young girl."

Before I could do anything, I was swept away from Nikolay. Taking me by the hands, Lena led me into the kitchen through a brown, modern-looking wooden door.

The kitchen was very similar to ours at home, except larger. The big cabinets were beige and there was a big island in the middle. The shiny counter-tops were made with a mixture of different shades of brown.

There were four high chairs placed in front of the bar and I saw two women standing there, wearing the same dress as mine.

They were definitely younger than Lena but older than me. Both appeared to be in their mid-thirties. They looked up when they heard us coming in. As I got closer, they looked me up and down as if they were inspecting an object.

I felt my palm started to sweat in Lena's hand and I grasped the bottom of my dress with my other hand.

"We have a new maid," Lena announced excitedly.

"We don't need a new maid," the blonde woman said.

I saw Lena opening her mouth to answer but before she could say anything, a voice cut her off.

"Actually, you do."

My back straightened at the sound of his voice and my body tensed. I swallowed hard when I saw the women's eyes widened. They suddenly appeared skittish and quickly looked down.

Lena let go of my hand and swiveled around, hands on her hips as she stared at the intruder.

Not intruder. This was *his* house, anyway.

Licking my lips, I slowly turned around and

made contact with Alessio's blue eyes.

Blue and green, clashing together as we stared at each other silently. I felt my heartbeat accelerate as he kept his unflinching gaze on mine.

My stomach twisted in knots as I squirmed restlessly on the spot. I felt weightless, and a weird feeling encompassed my body.

My stomach twisted again when I saw him taking a step forward, his big body moving smoothly. I sucked in a surprised breath when I realized that it was butterflies I felt.

His presence made me nervous. Scared. And giddy.

"Ayla is going to work here with you. Lena, you can assign her work schedule," Alessio stated evenly. I swallowed several times when I heard his voice again.

His eyes moved away from mine but only because he was looking at my body. I saw his gaze travel down to my waist, hips, and then my legs. My body started to warm up under his scrutinizing stare. His eyes stayed there for a few seconds before he moved back to my face.

The look that he gave me made me stagger back a step. At my reaction, his lips tilted upward slightly into a small smirk that was hard to see. But it was there. That devilish smirk. Sexy devilish smirk.

I shook my head and closed my eyes quickly as I tried to get myself under control.

It was impossible. Without even trying, Alessio Ivanshov had successful taken over my mind.

Opening my eyes, I stared into his. He gave me the same look as before, clearly not trying to hide what he wanted.

Pure unadulterated lust. His eyes were filled with desire and hunger.

Chapter 6

Alessio

As I saw Nikolay walk out of the kitchen, I knew where the little kitten was. He gave me a sharp nod as I walked past him.

When I got to the kitchen, I was instantly transfixed by the sight in front of me. Ayla's back was facing me and she stood beside Lena. The back of her dress was stretched perfectly over her round ass. *What a view,* I thought with a smirk.

Shaking my head after a few seconds, I took in a deep breath. *Get yourself together.*

Looking up, I saw the other two maids staring at Ayla with bored expressions, clearly not happy with another maid joining them.

"We have a new maid," Lena announced excitedly, bouncing lightly on her toes. I couldn't help but smile at her cheerfulness.

Lena had been working for the estate for about thirty years, since before I was even born. She had been one of the first maids my father hired. Lena had shown loyalty over the years and she quickly became our favorite maid—our *mother*.

"We don't need a new maid," Moira said, her tone snarky.

Walking into the light so they could see me, I said, "Actually, you do."

No, they didn't. But that didn't matter. If I said they needed one, then none of them would question me. Questioning me meant losing their job. I wouldn't even think twice before kicking them out.

I had zero tolerance for people demanding answers from me. My words were law.

I walked forward, sending the two maids a glare. They instantly cowered and bowed their heads, avoiding my gaze.

Now, that was better.

Lena swiveled around, hand on her hips as she stared at me. But I wasn't looking at her. I couldn't because the little broken girl standing beside her had my full attention. Her body had tensed at my voice and she moved nervously on her feet.

Ayla slowly turned around and we instantly made eye contact, her wide green eyes staring at me with surprise and shock. I noticed that her body trembled under my unflinching gaze.

She was definitely affected by my presence.

"Ayla is going to work here with you. Lena, you can assign her work schedule," I continued as I kept my eyes on Ayla. She swallowed hard and squirmed nervously on the spot.

My gaze slowly made its way down her body. Her dress fit her perfectly, showcasing her curves at the right places. And her legs. Damn, those legs.

As I stared at her legs, all I could think about was having them wrapped around my waist as I pounded relentlessly into her.

When I felt myself growing hard, I quickly snapped out of my thoughts, moving my eyes away.

I looked back up and saw her suck in a deep breath. She stared at me, her eyes fearful as she took a step back.

My desire for her was written all over my face. I didn't hide it. I let her see what I wanted and then shut down my expression again.

It was all part of the game. Let them see but not too much. Let them feel and then take it away.

I gave them a sharp nod and then started to back out of the kitchen. I saw Lena giving me a suspicious look before turning toward Ayla.

I walked out.

I would give her a week to settle. A week to get herself together.

And then I would pounce.

***

Ayla

When Alessio walked out of the room, I let out a sigh of relief. Lena noticed and gave me a strange look.

"Is everything okay?" she asked.

I didn't know if I should laugh or fall down and cry.

No. Of course everything was *not* okay.

Instead, I said, "Yes," my voice small.

Lena looked at me suspiciously but didn't push. Giving me a small smile, she turned toward the other two maids.

"This is Moira," she said, indicating the blonde, who gave me a blank stare.

I nodded in greeting.

"And this is Milena." The short woman with caramel skin, her black hair tied in a tight bun, waved at me with a smile. I smiled back and felt myself relax.

"Welcome," Milena said softly.

At least there were two people who didn't look like they wanted to kill me.

"Now that introductions have been made, Milena and Moira, get back to work," Lena said in a stern voice.

Both women said nothing before they walked out of the kitchen. Lena grabbed my arms and gently shoved me toward the stools.

"Sit," she said. I did as I was told.

"Did you eat breakfast yet?" Lena asked as she went through the refrigerator.

I shook my head but then realized that she couldn't see me.

"No. I haven't," I replied.

"I thought so." She closed the fridge, her arms full of ingredients. I reached out to help her, but she shook her head.

Sitting back down, I waited for her next instruction.

Lena made breakfast while talking animatedly the whole time. She was excited, as if she hadn't had a chance to talk to someone for a long while.

49

She talked about everything and nothing. Sometimes none of it made sense. She told me about her experience working as a maid. I also found out that I was the youngest maid here, which surprised her.

"Hmm. Alessio never hires young maids. He says they are incompetent."

I didn't tell her how Alessio came to hire me, and she never asked, so I kept quiet. As she continued talking, I felt myself relaxing.

The tense muscles in my shoulders started to loosen and I sagged into my stool. Crossing my legs, I moved my elbows on the bar and placed my chin in my palms, watching Lena talk. Her voice soothed me and I smiled.

She was sweet and adorable and I felt comfortable around her. I don't know how long I sat there and listened to her talk, but she eventually brought a plate to me. Placing it front of me, Lena smiled and nodded toward the food.

"Dig in, hon."

The plate was brimming with toast, scrambled eggs, bacon, fried diced potatoes, and a small bowl of mixed fruits.

She watched me with a soft expression. My nose started to tingle and I felt hot tears at the back of my eyes. I sniffed and looked down at the plate of food.

Nobody had ever made me food like that. Sure, I had maids back at my father's estate and I always had food. But no one ever prepared it with love. Nobody cared if I ate or not. I simply didn't exist. I lived as a shadow.

My heart constricted and I held the fork with a

shaky hand.

As I took the first bite, a tear fell down my cheek. Quickly swiping it away with my other hand, I took a second bite. Then a third. With each bite, it felt like my heart would burst at any moment.

When Lena gave me a gentle pat on the hand, I looked up with red-rimmed eyes. She gave me a sad smile and then nodded, as if telling me that everything would be okay. Lena didn't ask any questions. She just accepted me.

She turned around and went back to filling the other plates. I looked back at the food, then stared at the hand she had touched.

Kindness wasn't something I saw much of. In fact, I had never experienced true kindness in my life.

My days were spent locked in my room and my nights were filled with terrors. I didn't know what kindness was.

But with that simple action from Lena, I saw kindness for the first time. I felt it for the first time.

Chapter 7

Ayla

As I cleaned the smooth surface, I heard Lena ask, "Honey, are you done?"

Leaning away from the bar, I turned toward her. I smiled, waving the cleaning towel in the air. "Almost. I just need to finish wiping down the bar."

"Okay. Hurry up and finish, then you are done for today."

It's been a week since I started working at the estate. I didn't know anything about cooking or cleaning. At my father's house, I had maids who did it all while I was trapped in my bedroom.

But Lena helped me with the transition, and she was always gentle. When she assigned me to work, she made sure I was only doing the cleaning. And I was always with her, so the other maids wouldn't judge me.

Even though I knew the house was filled with people, I was surprised that I barely saw anyone other than a few maids here and there, as if everyone was in the shadows.

Most of my time was spent in the kitchen, helping Lena make the food, and then I would clean when she was done. The first three days were horrible and I was sure Lena had a good laugh at all the messes I made. But I was finally getting the hang of it.

A few minutes later, I was done. Swiping at my forehead tiredly, I sagged against the counter. Most of the time, I was done around seven or eight. But we had guests over, so the estate was really busy. Now it was close to midnight.

After doing a quick check around the kitchen to make sure that I was finished, I turned off the lights and walked out. As I closed the door, I saw Lena coming toward me.

"I'm done," I announced with a quick smile. She came closer and enveloped me in a hug.

"Good job," she said as she pulled back. Lena was a very affectionate woman. In my short time here, she had become a mother to me.

My mom died when I was only a year old. I never knew what it was like to have a mother caring for me, so I hung on to Lena's affectionate side. I let my heart accept the fact that there was someone who cared for me, like the lonely child I was.

Giving her a nod and after saying goodnight, I headed for my room. My legs felt heavy as I walked up the stairs, tiredness overtaking me.

I stopped when I noticed the door of the sitting room open. The sitting room was between my room and Alessio's. I looked around me. No one was there. With a nervous gulp, I slowly made my way toward the room. As I got closer, I saw that the lights were on. Leaning forward, I peeked inside.

There was no one.

I walked in and went straight to the piano next to the large windows. Two days before, I had been assigned to clean the sitting room, which was also a library. When I walked in, the first thing that got my attention was the large piano.

Music had always been my solace. I used to play the piano every day at my father's estate. It helped me forget.

The only way that I could block the memories of what Alberto did to me every night was by losing myself in music. The rhythm. The soft and gentle sounds that came through the keys.

As I got closer to the piano, my heart started to beat faster. I knew I shouldn't have been there but I couldn't stop myself. I stopped in front of the bench and leaned forward, placing my hand gently on the piano keys.

My fingers were itching to play. Just one song.

But I couldn't. I was told not to come into this room, except for cleaning. Softly moving my fingers over the keys, I made sure I didn't press down.

With a heavy sigh, I stepped away, my hand falling from the piano. Giving it a final sad glance, I walked away, my body turning into itself with desolation. Closing my bedroom door behind me, I leaned against it with a sigh and then shut my eyes tiredly. The lights were off, except for the tiny lamp on my nightstand.

While talking with Lena, I also found out that I

was the only maid who didn't live in the maids' quarters. We were both surprised by it, but could I really question Alessio's decision? I didn't think so.

I started to undress, slowly removing my dress, my body languid. Throwing the black dress on the nightstand, I reached blindly for my night shirt on the bed.

Just when I was about to put it on, a deep rough voice came from behind me.

"I have to say, you have a lovely body."

I shrieked loudly and swiveled around toward the voice. I tried to focus on the intruder, but he was effortlessly hidden in the darkness.

I didn't have to see him to know who it was.

I knew that voice. My body knew that voice.

Alessio.

I took a step back in fear, my nightshirt pressed against my body, hiding my nakedness from his eyes. Shaking from head to toe, I swallowed hard and my stomach started to cramp in fear—maybe in anticipation too.

Suddenly, the lights were on. I had to blink a few times to adjust my eyes.

Alessio was sitting in my sofa chair, leaning back comfortably. His left ankle was crossed on top of his right knee and there was a small remote in his hand, which he probably used to turn on the lights.

He wasn't wearing a suit. But he did have his black slacks on and a black linen shirt, which was unbuttoned at the top, to reveal some of his chest.

His hard, muscular chest. I forced away the thought.

Keeping my eyes on him, I saw his gaze

intensely focused on my body. There was no embarrassment. No awkwardness. Alessio was completely calm and confident as his eyes raked over my body.

"Hmm," he muttered, looking thoughtful as he watched me.

He leaned back against the sofa. His muscles were clear beneath his shirt, making him look big.

I forced myself not to fidget, but it was hard. I couldn't show fear. Men like him fed on fear. They used it to their advantage.

My fingers tightened around my shirt. My throat felt heavy and dry. When I started to feel lightheaded, I realized I'd been holding my breath for too long.

I let it out in a loud whoosh and then sucked in a deep breath again, but it was pointless.

His heated gaze traveled all the way down my body. I was speechless and frozen where I stood. When my body started to warm up under his focus, I closed my eyes tightly. But the tingling didn't stop.

When he stood and walked toward me, I shrunk away. His dark presence filled the room, and I suddenly felt hot. Sweat beaded on my neck and between my breasts as he moved closer.

When he stopped before me, I shivered in fear and my body tensed in alarm. Alessio stepped closer until we were half an inch apart, so close that my nose started to tingle with the scent of his cologne and I could feel his breath next to my ear.

My lips were suddenly dry. When I moistened them with my tongue, Alessio's eyes followed the movement. If possible, his already lustful gaze became more heated.

He licked his own lips too, making the action appear so deeply sensual that I had to squeeze my legs together, trying to stop the sudden tingling between them.

What's happening to me?

Alessio leaned his head forward until his lips were hovering over mine. My body froze, my mind went blank for a moment.

Was he going to kiss me?

His hand came up and wrapped around my shirt. He gave it a tug, but I refused to let go of the fabric. He frowned and tugged harder.

I swallowed in fear when his eyes changed and he leveled me with a glare. The shirt fell from my grasp. He took a step back and stared at me. Except for my black bra and panties, I was almost naked. Crossing my hand over my chest, I tried to hide my body from him.

"Move your hands," he ordered, his voice gruff. Shaking my head wildly, I took a step back but came in contact with the wall.

There was nowhere to hide. I was trapped as he moved closer.

Alessio crowded my space and he wrapped his fingers around my wrists, tugging downward until I was no longer covering my chest.

He brought his hand right over my chest but he didn't touch me. I shivered as my body warmed under his scrutinizing gaze. Even though he hadn't touched me yet, my body was already on fire.

When the tip of his finger made contact with my

skin, I jumped and stared at him with wide eyes. He kept his eyes on mine as he slowly dragged his finger down my chest, stopping between my breasts.

My chest heaved, and each time my breasts brushed against his shirt, the tingling sensation in my lower region increased. My body tightened, hyper aware of Alessio's touch.

He brought his other hand up and let it travel down my neck. I was sure he could feel my pulse throbbing in fear—and I hated to admit it, but in anticipation too. My body was reacting to his touch, eagerly awaiting his next movement. No matter how hard I tried to stop my reactions, my body wouldn't listen.

"You have lovely skin. Smooth as silk," he muttered as he softly brushed his thumb over my throbbing vein. "So fucking beautiful." Then he frowned, like he couldn't believe I was attractive to him. Or maybe he was surprised he'd said it.

His face became expressionless, but his heated gaze couldn't be misunderstood. It showed everything he felt.

He wanted me, and my body was reacting accordingly.

As he continued to look into my eyes, the hand that was over my chest moved to my right breast. I was so captivated by his pale and vivid blue eyes, I didn't notice when he moved the cup of my bra downward.

When I felt the cold air on my skin, my eyes widened and I looked down to see my right breast bare. My nipple pebbled and I sucked in a shocked breath when Alessio softly moved his thumb over the tip.

My head snapped back and he was still looking at me, his gaze intensely on mine as he watched my reaction.

He rubbed his thumb over my nipple and I let out a gasp, my eyes slowly closing. When I heard a moan, my body tightened. My eyes snapped back open when I realized that it came from me.

Alessio's lips tilted upward in a smirk, and then he took my nipple in between his thumb and forefinger. He pinched my nipple hard.

Gasping, I shrank away from his touch with a whimper.

Oh God, what was happening to me? I felt myself growing wet between my legs.

"Shhh. Don't be scared, kitten. I'm not going to hurt you."

I let out another whimper when he rolled my nipple around his fingers, teasing the tip until I was shaking my head, my stomach clenching as I moaned again.

Alessio leaned closer until his mouth was next to my ear. He blew on my skin and then bit down on my earlobe. "Not unless you want me to," he whispered harshly in my ears, saying the same words that he had when we first met.

"What…what…what are you doing?" I stumbled over my words, my voice hoarse.

He let out a laugh and pulled back. "What do you think I'm doing? From your reaction, I think it's pretty obvious."

I shook my head and stared at him mutely. No, it

was not obvious. He was playing with me. But why?

I tried to pull away, but Alessio wrapped his arms around my waist, pulling me into his body. My breasts pressed hard against his chest. When my sensitive nipples brushed against the roughness of his shirt, I couldn't keep from moaning.

Oh, God. No. Save me from this.

"Plea…please don't hurt me."

His body shook with silent laughter. "Aww, baby. Pleasure and pain come hand in hand." Alessio leaned forward, and slowly licked down my neck. "Don't you know? The best pleasure comes from pain," he whispered roughly against my skin.

No. I knew pain. I was accustomed to pain and felt it every night when Alberto tortured me mercilessly. There was no pleasure from that.

My body froze, and then I started to struggle against his hold.

"Let me go. Please. Please let me go," I begged as my eyes filled with unshed tears. I was wrong to think I was safe. He was a monster like Alberto. He would take what he wanted and then leave me bleeding and scarred.

"Stop struggling," he ordered harshly.

"No. No. No. Please." I shook my head and pushed hard against his chest but it was like pushing a wall. He didn't even move a step.

"Enough!"

I whimpered and shrank away. He let go of me and I scrambled back to the wall, plastering myself against it.

Alessio stared at me blankly. My harsh breathing

filled the room and I was trembling. My legs were barely holding me up.

He stepped forward, but when I let out cry, he stopped.

"You are scared of me," he said.

I swallowed but didn't say anything. What could I say? He already had me figured out.

"But you also enjoy my touch," he continued. My body went still, and this time I shook my head. His eyes became hard and he walked closer.

"Don't lie to me. If you didn't know already, then let me enlighten you," he said through gritted teeth. "I always know when someone lies. So, you'd be better off if you don't."

I didn't answer. I couldn't. My throat was dry and my tongue felt heavy in my mouth. Alessio moved his hand to my hair and twisted it around his fist. Even though his hold was firm, he gently tilted my head up, making sure he didn't hurt me.

"Now answer me, kitten. Did you like it when I touched you?"

I thought of lying again, but what would it bring me? It wouldn't help my situation. I nodded. It was so small that it would have been easy for him to miss it. But he didn't.

Alessio Ivanshov never missed anything.

At my nod, he smiled and it took my breath away. It was the first real smile that I saw from him. His lips stretched wide and I noticed a dimple on his right cheek.

The smile changed his face completely. He didn't look so scary anymore.

He looked gentle.

My eyes widened as my heart constricted.

"Now, that's out of the way. Let's talk about why I'm here," he said, losing the smile. I swallowed nervously and nodded again.

I tried to move away but his fingers tightened in my hair. When he seemed sure I wouldn't move, Alessio let go. He placed his hands on the wall behind me, one on either side of my face, caging me into his body.

"I want you," he said without any hesitation.

Oh, I knew that was coming, but what I didn't expect was how my body reacted to his words.

My legs weakened and my panties were instantly wet. My lower region pulsed and I bit down on my lips hard to stop the moan that threatened to slip out.

"What?" I asked, my voice shaking.

Alessio leaned forward until his lips were hovering over mine. I saw his tongue slip out and he gently licked my lips. My body tightened in shock.

"Exactly what I said. I want to fuck you."

I didn't want to admit it, but I could see myself doing whatever he wanted me to do. He knew how to play with his words and how to play my body. The only fear I had was that he might hurt me. I suddenly felt sick.

I was exactly what Alberto said. A whore. What kind of woman feels turn on by a strange man who whispers such vulgar words? I had been raped repeatedly by my fiancé. And now I felt turned on by a monster exactly like him.

"What if I don't want it?" I asked, trying to remain coherent as I felt my knees begin to buckle.

Alessio smirked. "Oh, kitten. You want me. I'm turning you on right now, aren't I? I can see it." He was filled with so much confidence and arrogance. I hated it.

He licked my neck again, then bit down. I moaned as he sucked on my tortured skin.

"I can feel it," he murmured against my skin. Shaking my head, I tried to move away but it was no use. "I can smell it."

He wouldn't let me go. I was feeling dizzy and giddy. It was surreal. I wanted him, but at the same time, I wanted to sink down and cry.

He stepped away slightly but not too much, still crowding my space.

"I will never take a woman against her will," he said as he stared into my eyes. At his words, my heart started to calm down. "But, kitten, you want me. I know it and you know it. I will not fuck you until you beg me." His vulgar words went through my body and I trembled.

Alessio leaned close again. I could feel his breath on my lips. "You owe me, kitten. And don't forget. I own you. You do what I tell you. So, it's simple. Do you want me?"

I started to say no, but he brought his finger to my lips. "And don't even think of lying. Lying will just get you in more trouble."

I swallowed hard and my heart was beating hard against my ribcage and my palms started to sweat. My breathing was irregular and I felt like was suffocating. Alessio's blue eyes were fixed on mine.

Blue and green.

We stared at each other with a mixture of

emotions. Desires. Lust. Excitement. Fear. Anticipation.

Oh, dear God, what have I gotten myself into?

Chapter 8

As I stood there, trapped in his arms, I was speechless. What could I say?

Yes meant submitting to him. It would mean I was ready to be his whore. When I ran away from Alberto, I promised myself that I would never be at the mercy of another man again.

Yet, here I was, cornered by Alessio and I couldn't even say *no*.

He stared at me for a few seconds, his gaze intense as he waited for my answer. But I defiantly stayed quiet, pursing my lips together, refusing to utter a response. Not replying was better than replying, right?

That was what I thought. But I was wrong.

Alessio gave me another of his devilish smirks and I swallowed hard against the lump in my throat.

That smirk didn't look nice. Definitely not good.

He leaned in, his lips lightly brushing my ear. "You like testing me, don't you?"

My body was shaking. But even under the layers of fear and anger, my body was responding to him.

His rough, hard voice sent a shiver through my body. I refused to acknowledge what I was feeling. It was wrong. I shouldn't have been feeling that way.

But as much as I wanted to act strong, I felt weak.

Alberto's voice echoed in my head as I stared at Alessio's hard chest.

Weak. So pathetic. Look at you. All broken. You are nothing but a low, dirty whore.

Old memories came to a screeching halt when I felt a hand on my chin, tilting my head up. My eyes snapped open and I looked up at Alessio.

His fingers were firm on my chin, holding my head still as he moved in closer until our bodies were plastered together. So close that it would have been impossible to even push a thin string in between us.

His heat enveloped my body and I didn't feel cold anymore. My heart was hammering in my chest, and I felt sure that he knew.

The rough pad of his thumb rubbed over my full soft lips, and I gasped at the sensation. His touch traveled all the way down to my body and I pressed my legs together.

Why? Why did I feel that way with him?

I inhaled a desperate breath, moving my eyes away from his, looking everywhere but at him. My eyes moved desperately around the room, trying to find something that would keep me grounded.

Think, Ayla. Think.

I felt Alessio shift, his shirt moving against my sensitive skin, and I bit my lips, trying to hide another moan.

He wrapped an arm around my waist, anchoring me to his body while he slowly brought his other hand down.

"So, do we have an agreement?" he asked. Alessio pushed his knee between my legs, slightly pushing them apart.

The thought of him taking me was so demeaning, but even through my disgust, as hard as it was for me to admit it, I also found that thought very appealing.

Alessio overwhelmed me. He scared me, but at the same time, I couldn't stop my body from responding to his words and seductiveness.

What was wrong with me?

Before I could say something, or even think about a proper answer, he bent down and latched onto my nipple. I hissed at his sudden action and then my head fell backward when a moan slipped from my mouth.

He suckled my nipple, pulling at it hard, and then gently swirling his tongue over the tip. I felt the rasp of his slight stubble against my tender skin, and without thinking, I pushed my breast forward.

Oh God, what's happening to me?

Releasing his hold on my hips, he brought his hand to my other breast and teased my pebbled nipple through the fabric of my bra. Slowly rubbing his thumb in circular motion, his tongue followed the same movement on my other nipple.

I moaned and my head moved wildly from left to right, trying to get rid of the sensation that was happening in my lower region.

I tried to squeeze my legs together but Alessio's knee stopped me. "Oh…"

I unconsciously lifted a shaking hand and cupped his cheek as he sucked me. Without even thinking, I gently moved my hand over his cheek, feeling his soft skin under the pads of my fingers. My hand wrapped around his neck as I held him to me.

My body wasn't my own. I didn't know what was happening. It was all going too fast.

My fingers tightened around his neck when I felt his hand move down toward my dripping core. My nails gently scratched at his skin. It was a chaste and slow caress, but erotic. In an instant, I felt him harden against my belly.

He bit down on my nipple and I squirmed against him, but the movement only caused me to grind myself into his hardness.

Alessio chuckled as I felt him push his knee forward, parting my legs more so that his hand had access to move freely between my thighs.

He slowly moved aside my black panties and located my throbbing clit.

"Uh," I gasped as he flicked his thumb over it. Moaning loud, I thrashed against him.

What's happening?

My body tightened hard and I felt my muscles start to cramp. The sensation was intoxicating. He filled my senses.

I started to shake uncontrollably. The muscles in my legs spasmed as Alessio continued to rub his thumb over me.

He pressed his thumb against my bundle of nerves and I jerked, letting out a sharp cry.

"Alessio…"

He glanced up and stared into my eyes for a few seconds. My skin prickled and it was sensitive. I was taut as a bowstring and my body was shaking with a mixture of pain and intense pleasure.

I couldn't describe it. I didn't know what it was. It was something I had never felt before.

My senses were overwhelmed and my vision blurred as Alessio continued his slow, torturous ministration on my body.

"What's happening to me?" I whispered, my voice bewildered.

Alessio's eyes widened and he sucked in a surprised breath.

Then slowly, the corners of his lips lifted upward. He grinned at me wickedly before answering.

"You are about to have your first orgasm, kitten," he said in a husky voice. "Trust me. Just let go. Don't fight it. It will be the most wonderful thing you have ever felt."

I shook my head and tried to move away but Alessio quickly wrapped his arm around my waist, refusing to let me go.

Still keeping his eyes on me, he rubbed his thumb over my clit once before slowly pushing inside. I tensed around him and then moaned, my eyes slowly closing in pleasure.

"Keep your eyes on me," he ordered, his voice rough and harsh. My eyes quickly snapped open and I stared at him.

I clamped down on his finger as he slid inside me. He eased in deeper, plunging through my tight walls.

It was all too much. Every movement heightened the sensation and I twitched uncontrollably. My hips bucked upward when he moved his finger deep and hard inside of me.

I let out another moan as my hand tightened around his neck, as if begging for more.

My body was hyperaware of Alessio's every touch. I felt desperate. Edgy. My skin felt tight and my body was on fire.

"Oh God," I panted, and Alessio chuckled low at my reaction.

I started to feel dizzy and my head fell back against the wall. I couldn't take it.

It was too much.

When Alessio pushed deeper inside of me, I came around his fingers. My screams resonated through the wall of the room as I came, my first orgasm hitting me so hard that my vision blurred and black dots appeared in front of my eyes.

Alessio pulled away and my body swayed as I tried to focus on him. But I couldn't. I was floating, my body so light. All sounds were muted around me and I was numb.

He brought his hand to his lips and licked it clean.

"I'll take that as a yes," he murmured in that husky voice that I was beginning to hate.

And then I fainted.

***

Alessio

As I licked her come off my fingers, I saw her swaying unsteadily on her feet.

Poor kitten didn't even know.

She was mine now.

That orgasm she just had—well, it had marked her fate.

MINE, my head screamed. And I couldn't wait to take what was mine. I couldn't wait until I was fucking her tight pussy. Until she was twitching and moaning underneath me. I couldn't wait until I was making her scream with both pleasure and pain.

My hard cock begged me to do it. *Now. Take her. Use her. Fuck her.*

"I'll take that as a yes," I murmured.

As soon as I said the words, her body tilted forward and her eyes rolled upward.

"Fuck," I hissed, quickly moving forward and catching her in my arms.

Ayla laid limply in my arms. With her eyes closed, she looked so at peace. Serene. Happy. I felt my heart stutter as I stared at her.

So beautiful, a fleeting thought passed through my mind. But I quickly shook my head, trying to get rid of my stupid thoughts.

Wrapping an arm behind her knees and the other around her back, I pulled her up to my chest and walked to the bed. Gently placing her down, I fixed her bra and then pulled the covers over her body.

I sat down on the bed and stared at her. I couldn't take my eyes off her. For a week I tried to stay away. It was the hardest fucking thing I have ever done, when all I wanted to do was fuck her.

But I kept myself away, giving her time to settle, watching her, waiting for the right opportunity. As soon as one week hit its mark, I was there, waiting for her.

Ayla now knew what I wanted. She tried to refuse, but I saw her as clearly as day. She wanted me. There was no denying it.

When I heard her first moan, I knew this was it. There was no going back.

I always got what I wanted, and I wanted her. Nothing and no one was going to stop me from getting what I wanted.

The first orgasm was mine. It belonged to me and I took it. Now, there was no turning back. *Claim her*, my mind screamed. *Take her.*

I didn't even have to put too much effort in it. One flick of my thumb, she'd been coming.

That little orgasm, that was nothing.

As I stared at her sleeping face, I felt myself smile.

Oh, kitten, when you wake up, I'm going to show you the real thing.

Chapter 9

Ayla

My eyes slowly opened. My vision was still hazy from sleep and I closed my eyes again. Turning to my side, I burrowed deeper under the soft covers.

"Hmm…" I groaned when my aching muscles protested.

I needed a break from working.

My bed moved, and knowing it was not from me, my eyes snapped open and I came face to face with Alessio.

He was sitting on the bed, but leaning forward until his face was close to mine.

"Good morning," he said.

My eyes widened and I let out a scream. As I tried to scramble off the bed, the covers twisted around me in my haste and I ended up on the floor in a heap.

I stared up at him, my chest heaving. I was sure I looked frightened, while he seemed ready to pounce.

73

My head spun as the memories of the night before came crashing into my mind like never ending wild waves.

"Oh my God," I whispered, trying to untangle myself from the covers. When I was finally free, I stood up and took several steps away, trying to keep a safe distance between us.

"How could you?" I asked.

Alessio stood up and made an act of fixing his suit. He took his time, as if he was doing it on purpose to get me riled up and extend the suspense.

When he was done, he leveled me with a blank stare. "What do you mean?"

"You…" I stuttered as I tried to find words.

He gave you an orgasm, a voice said in my mind.

Against my wishes, I screamed back, horrified by the thought.

"I what?" His voice broke through my thoughts. I looked up to see him moving toward me, his steps purposeful.

"You…" His body was so close to mine that his heat enveloped me.

"What is it?" Alessio asked as he bent down slightly so we were eye level.

I swallowed but didn't answer.

"Say it," he urged.

Shaking my head, I tried to take a step back but his arms shot out and were instantly wrapped around my waist, pulling me close. "I want you to say it. Tell me. What did I do last night?" he whispered, his lips dangerously close to mine.

Placing both hands on his chest, I tried to shove

him away from me but he didn't even move an inch.

"Mr. Ivanshov, please let me go," I begged, struggling in his arms, desperate to free myself.

His arms tightened around my waist. "Oh, kitten, I think we should leave the pleasantries behind now." Leaning forward so that his lips were next to my ear, he continued, "After what I did to you last night, I think we should stick with Alessio." He finished his sentence with a nip on my earlobe and I jumped at his sudden touch.

"Okay. *Alessio*, please let go of me."

"I will when you tell me what I did to you last night. Say it," he muttered in a husky tone.

He was trying to embarrass me. How heartless could he be? He was a monster.

Alessio leaned his face into my neck and when I felt his warm lips on my cold skin, I shivered and went limp against him. Only his arms were holding me upright.

He placed wet kisses on my neck. Biting and then sucking at the tortured skin.

His lips drew wet trails on the length on my neck.

Shaking my head, I brought my hands to his hair and pulled hard until his face was not buried in my neck anymore.

"Fuck," Alessio swore loudly as I continued pulling.

His head snapped up and he slowly stood to his full height until he was towering over me. He went rigid, his arms like a band of steel around my waist. I let out a small hiss and struggled with slight discomfort and pain.

He brought one of his hands up and grasped my chin, his hold firm and hard as he tilted my head, forcing me to look into his hard, cold eyes. Anger flashed behind the blue irises and I cowered under his seething glare.

"I really don't like repeating myself, but I will one last time," he said, his tone flat and grating. "Tell me what I did to you last night and I'll let you go. It's simple."

"You gave me an orgasm." The words came out of my mouth before I could even think.

The anger in his eyes immediately vanished, but the hard look remained. I played with the wild lion and now I had to pay the consequences. "And did you enjoy it?"

"That was not part of the deal," I whispered, my voice barely audible.

Alessio pulled my face closer as his lips stretched in a small smirk. "Oh, kitten. I make the rules. I make the deals, and I can change them whenever I want. You don't get to make a choice. Understood?"

I nodded mutely and then tried to look down, wanting to escape his intense, cruel stare, but his unyielding hold on my chin stopped me from moving. "Answer me, kitten."

"Umm, I…" I started, but couldn't finish my sentence. How could I answer such a thing? Did I enjoy it when he gave me an orgasm? No? Yes? Even I was confused. I didn't want to like it. I shouldn't have liked it, but I did.

I closed my eyes tightly, unable to believe my own feelings. Something was seriously wrong with me, because this monster held me in his mansion against my will and then gave me an orgasm even though I didn't want it—and I had liked it.

"Ayla, answer me!"

"Yes!" I shouted.

When I was near him, my body wasn't my own. My brain became a chaotic jumble and I couldn't think straight.

He masterfully played my body and my mind.

He held the strings, and I became a puppet.

***

Alessio

She went limp in my arms, the fight running out of her body.

Hearing her admit to her desires had been all I wanted, and it brought me satisfaction. For a little while. She was scared, and I would give her time.

However, my patience was running out because I had given her enough time already, as far as I was concerned. Having her that close to my body made the beast inside me begin to rage.

Her heat and her smell had taken over my senses. All I wanted to do was throw her on her back, spread those long creamy legs, and fuck her hard until she screamed with her orgasm milking my cock.

Even though I wanted her scared of me, I didn't want her to regret what happened. I had never taken a woman against her will and I wouldn't start with her.

Oh, she wanted me, but it was obvious she was terrified. Her confusion was clearly written all over her face.

I would seduce Ayla until she begged me to take her.

Releasing my hold on her chin, I gently moved her hair off her face. I let my fingers linger on her cheek for a few seconds and then slowly moved my thumb over her velvet skin. It warmed under my fingers and a small touch of pink tainted her pale flesh, showing the effect that I had on her.

"See. That wasn't so hard to admit, right?" I stared at her blushing cheek, mesmerized by the color and the softness of her skin.

Ayla tried to step away and I let her go without resistance.

Let's give the little kitten a break.

She took several steps away from me, then placed a shaky hand on her heaving chest. She was trembling, the fear evident.

But why the fuck was she so scared? The fear wasn't just because of me. There was something else, and I hadn't quite figured it out yet.

Ayla was a big mystery to me. She acted like she hated my touch, but she'd moaned in pleasure at the same time.

She fascinated me, captured my attention, and I had no desire to fight it.

She might have been the one to take the first action by hiding under my bed, but now I was in control. I wouldn't let go until I had my fill.

Staring at her, my gaze unyielding, I said, "Now, Ayla. Don't be scared. You have nothing to be scared of. Have I hurt you?"

She shook her head, watching my every movement and reaction. She truly did remind me of a kitten trying to find its way out of danger. Small, skittish, scared. And completely helpless.

I felt my phone vibrate in my pocket, tugged it out, and saw Viktor's number flashing on the screen.

"Yeah?" I answered.

"There's something we gotta tell you. It's fucked up," he replied in a rush. He sounded panicked. Shit.

"Now what?"

"We should discuss this in person, Alessio."

Looking at Ayla, who was now plastered against the wall, I felt anger building inside of me. Viktor had really bad timing.

"I'm busy right now," I said harshly.

"It's important."

"Fine. Meet me in my office," I ordered before hanging up.

I moved toward Ayla, and in three long strides, I was standing in front of her. She folded into herself, her shoulders bunching forward in a protective manner.

She whimpered, as if frightened I would hit her.

"Calm down," I said, my voice surprisingly gentle.

I pulled her forward until she was flush against my body. My hold was light and I leaned down so that my lips were beside her ear.

"I'll be back, kitten. We are not done yet," I whispered harshly, then wrapped my hand in her hair, twisting it around my fingers and pulled her head backward.

Without warning, I crashed my lips to hers. The kiss was hard, fast, and bruising, meant to let her know that she belonged to me. Only me.

Ayla let out a gasp when I licked the seams of her lips. I bit, sucked, kissed, until I was satisfied that she understood.

Leaning away, I stared at her flushed face. She was red and out of breath. It made me want to laugh. I didn't even kiss her properly and she was already reacting this way.

Ayla brought a hand to her swollen lips and touched it gently. I saw her wince as she stared at me with innocent eyes.

Ah, kitten. So innocent.

Giving her a final heated glance, I turned around and walked out of the bedroom, leaving her alone to her thoughts.

I closed the door behind me with a bang and walked straight to my office in the left wing. When I got there, the door was already open. Viktor, Nikolay, Phoenix, and Artur were already there.

Frustration was evident in their expressions. Walking straight in, I growled, "What is it?"

I sat down behind my desk, crossing my arms at my chest as I leaned back. Phoenix closed the door before facing me.

"We found out that someone is spying," Viktor started, his voice rough with anger.

"What?" I yelled. Quickly getting up to my feet, I pushed the chair back.

"Yeah. For the fucking Abandonato. The

bastards knew where we were going to open the next club. They got there first and Alberto said that we should have better control on who we trust." Phoenix's voice came out in a hiss as he tried hard to control his own irritation.

My body shook with fury and my hands tightened into fists until my knuckles hurt from the pressure.

Grabbing my chair, I threw it across the room. Nikolay had to jump out of the way so it didn't crash into him.

"Who the fuck is it?" I roared.

My hands were itching. I wanted to spill blood, and my eyes twitched as I tried to regain control. Whoever betrayed me would have a slow torturous death. I wouldn't spare him any mercy.

"Find out who he is!"

None of them moved.

I saw Viktor swallowing nervously and Nikolay staring at him.

When he didn't say anything, Nikolay sent him a glare and then turned toward me, quickly schooling his features again.

"We think it's Ayla," he said.

Chapter 10

Ayla

Alessio left me standing in a state of shock and walked out of my room without sparing me another glance.

What was that?

My fingers were still touching my swollen, tingling lips. They felt raw. I had never been kissed like that.

Oh, I had most definitely been kissed by Alberto, but with Alessio, it was different. Even though the kiss was possessive and hard, it felt gentle. He didn't kiss me like he wanted to hurt me. Alessio kissed me like he wanted me to feel him, like he wanted me to enjoy it. It was sexy and it made me feel out of control.

I was out of breath and I couldn't understand why. Why didn't I find it repulsive?

I glanced around my room, breathless. I tried to find something, anything, that would ground me and help me understand what was going on. My mind felt rushed and my body tingled from his touch.

The affect he had on me was dangerous. I could easily lose myself in him. I couldn't think straight around him.

He was captivating and demanding.

Ruthless, yet gentle.

Alessio was a dangerous man but when he touched me, my body responded without fear.

Fear was a constant emotion living inside of me. Slowly, I had started to feel nothing but fear. But with Alessio, his touch rid me of that fear. He made me forget why I should be scared.

Slowly, I sank down to my bottom and pulled my knees to my chest, folding my arms over them in a protective manner. Closing my eyes, I took in a deep breath.

No matter how hard I tried to avoid him, he would always find me. I couldn't deny him and I couldn't stop him. If he kept playing me like he was, I would slowly lose myself until I had nothing left. Opening my eyes, I shook my head.

No. I couldn't let this happen.

I stood up and quickly put on a black shirt and the blue jeans that Lena had bought for me. Looking around my room, I felt a pang of sadness. I thought about Lena and felt hot tears prick my eyes. I would miss her. She was the little light in my dark world. And Maddie. But I had no other choice. It was time to move on. I couldn't stay in the estate any longer. I wasn't as safe as I had thought.

Alessio was the new danger. His touch, his voice, his controlling stare.

Before he could break whatever was left inside of me, I had to save myself.

***

Alessio

"What?" I growled at Nikolay's statement.

Viktor nodded and took a step forward. "It makes sense. Ayla is an outsider. Don't you think it's a big coincidence that as soon as she settled in, the Italians started to get information about us?"

Viktor seemed a little conflicted and then shook his head, his expression turning hard again. "We can't find anything about her. We have no idea who she is."

For a second, I wanted to scream in denial. I didn't want to believe that Ayla could be a spy, but when Viktor's words started to penetrate my mind, it made sense.

He was right. We knew nothing about Ayla, and it was too much of a coincidence that she found me and decided to hide in my car. And then a few days later, the fucking Italians were getting information about my plans.

"Fuck!" I screamed as I punched the desk. Raking my aching hand through my hair, I gripped it tightly as rage pulsed through my body. "That bitch!"

Phoenix cleared his throat and I saw him shrug. "It's hard to believe. I mean she looks so innocent, but sometimes the most innocent can be vicious. It's usually the shy one who is the viper."

"They just hide it well," Nikolay added. All four of my men looked forlorn, as if they couldn't believe Ayla could be the spy.

I turned around, giving them my back. Staring outside through my large windows, I let my thoughts wander. I didn't want to believe it either, but if she was a possible suspect, I couldn't overlook it.

As silence fell upon the room, my anger started to diminish, but my tense muscles refused to relax. The little kitten had successfully wrapped me around her finger. I thought I was the master, but clearly she had been playing me.

Suddenly, I felt my phone vibrating in my pocket. I blew out a frustrated breath and took it out.

"What the fuck do you want?" I snapped into the phone.

"Boss, Ayla is escaping through her window."

My eyes widened and the anger was back, full force.

"Get on her," I ordered harshly before hanging up and facing my men. "Ayla is escaping," I told them through gritted teeth. They swore simultaneously. "I want you to go after her," I told Viktor.

"I'll come with you," Nikolay suggested. I gave him a nod and they started to back out. But before they could close the door, I added, "Get her to the basement." My voice was brittle and full of venom.

I saw Viktor sigh, and for a second, his eyes flashed with pity, but it dissipated quickly. I looked at Phoenix and Artur, my gaze unyielding as I ordered them out of the room.

"Get out. Call me when you have her in the basement." They nodded, their faces impassive as they walked out of the room and closed the door behind them.

Placing my hands on the desk, I leaned forward and glared at the door. My knuckles were white with the pressure and my veins throbbed in my throat.

My jaw tensed, my teeth grinding in an attempt to control my fury. I wanted to strike something. Someone.

The beast inside of me was raging, demanding that I kill. Spill the blood of whoever betrayed me. Only then would I feel at peace.

I felt my eyes turned into slits as I continued to stare at the door. Slowly rolling my neck, I tried to release the tension.

Kitten, you might think you have fooled me, but this is my game now. One way or another, doesn't matter how, I will get the truth out of you.

I hoped that for her sake she hadn't truly betrayed me.

Because if she had, there would be no mercy.

Chapter 11

Ayla

My heart thrummed hard like the wings of a bird. I climbed out the window, and when I reached the ground, my legs felt weak. I stumbled for a moment. Looking around me, I didn't see anyone.

Relief filled me and I took off running toward the woods behind the house. It was a long way, and the muscles in my legs burned as I ran full force.

C'mon, Ayla. C'mon. Don't give up. Not now.

Suddenly, I heard shouts behind me and my heart stuttered. Turning my head, I saw a few guards running after me. I looked back toward the woods and kept my eyes focused on my escape.

I was almost into the woods when the steps drew closer, and all of a sudden, someone grabbed my arm. I screamed and tried to escape, but I was dragged down and someone sat on my back. My arms were pulled back and my attacker held on forcefully.

Tears streamed down my cheeks. It was no use.

No matter how hard I fought, they wouldn't let me go. He pulled me upward and I stood on shaky legs. Closing my eyes tightly, I sobbed and begged.

"Please. Please let me go. Please."

My chin was grasped firmly by a rough hand, the fingernails biting into my skin. Whimpering, I tried to move away, but he held on hard.

"If you come with us quietly, we won't have to hurt you. And I sure as hell don't want to hurt you, Ayla."

I let out a cry. I knew that voice. Opening my eyes, I saw Viktor's angry expression.

I made a weak attempt at struggling. "Stop moving," another voice growled in my ears. Nikolay. He was the one holding me.

"Do you understand, Ayla?" Viktor demanded. He always looked so scary, and a dangerous aura surrounded him, just like Alessio and Nikolay.

As he stared at me, I cowered back in fear. He looked murderous, and his voice was filled with fury. "Please," I whispered.

"Ayla, do you understand?" Viktor snarled. Nodding, I let myself go limp in Nikolay's arms.

"Good," he said through gritted teeth as he let go of my chin. My skin was burning and itching where he had touched me. Moving my jaw around a little, I winced at the pain.

Taking a few steps backward, he nodded at Nikolay and started walking back to the mansion. He led the way as Nikolay pulled me forward. My feet were dragging behind and I resisted.

"Fuck, girl. You really don't understand."

He let go of me, but before I could run away,

Nikolay wrapped his arm around my waist. Sending me a fierce glare, his hold was unyielding as he pulled me over his shoulder.

I tried to kick, punch, slap, scratch, and scream, but nothing worked. Nikolay kept walking, his body hard as a rock.

When we got inside, instead of taking me up, they turned to the left and walked down a dark corridor. The air was cold and it was dark. I instantly froze on his shoulder.

A feeling of dread crept up from the pit of my stomach, and a cold wave overtook me as the hairs rose on the back of my neck and my mouth went dry. I was paralyzed over Nikolay's shoulder. A menacing aura gripped me.

We stopped for a moment, and then I heard a door squeak open and I shuddered at the sound. There was the rattling of a metal, it sounded like a heavy chain.

A shiver ran through me as I felt my blood run cold. My hands balled into tight fists and I closed my eyes in terror.

The door banged shut and I saw light underneath my closed eyelids. Slowly opening my eyes again, the first thing I saw was shiny white marble floor. I was placed on my feet.

My head spun at the sudden movement and I stumbled, but Nikolay caught me. Looking up into his dark eyes, I silently begged. *Please let me go.*

But he stared back, expressionless, his eyes cold.

I felt a hand grasp my arm, and then I was being pulled back. I opened my mouth to scream but found that no words came out. My throat closed up and I couldn't breathe. Panic filled me and I went numb.

Viktor pulled me to a chair and pushed me down so that I was sitting. He twisted my arms back. Nikolay walked past me until I couldn't see him.

A few minutes later, I felt something around my wrists, and realized that I was being tied down.

"No!" My screams echoed around the room. I tried to move, but the rope held me immobile. As I struggled, the roughness bit into my skin and scratched until my skin felt raw and hot.

"You are only hurting yourself. If you keep moving, your wrists are going to bleed from the rope," Viktor said behind me. "I suggest that you stop moving."

"Please…"

There were noises behind the door. A moment later, it opened with such force it banged against the wall. Flinching at the sound, I pushed back against the chair, my body trembling with panic.

My body froze in terror. Alessio walked into the room with two other men.

One of them closed the door as Alessio walked toward me.

He wore the same suit as the last time I saw him, but this time his hands were covered with black leather gloves. Slowly bringing my eyes up to his face, I let out a gasp when I met his fierce glare. His eyes glowed with such ferocity that it took my breath away.

His dark presence loomed over me, dread filling me as my spine prickled with unease. The tiny hairs on my arms and the back of my neck stood up straight and my skin itched.

Alessio bent down at his waist so that we were eye level. I whimpered as I stared into his cold eyes.

I had seen him angry before, but this time, he looked deadly. His blue eyes crackled with fury, his face red, and his jaw twitched.

The Alessio standing before me was ruthless, and I could see the killer he truly was—the *monster* I had always heard about.

And there I was, trapped in the lair of the monster everyone feared.

My heart hammered so hard that I could feel it in my throat. My nails dug into my palms and the slight pain brought me comfort.

Pain meant I was still alive, still breathing.

But for how long?

Chapter 12

Alessio

"Boss, we got her in her basement," Phoenix said breathlessly through the phone. I felt the side of my lips tilt upward at the news.

Let's see if you can run away from the truth now, kitten.

"I'm coming," I snapped and then hung up. Throwing on my suit jacket, I fixed my tie and then opened my drawer to take out my black leather gloves.

I always wore them when we had a problem in the basement, just in case I had to get my hands dirty.

Closing the drawer with a bang, I swiftly walked out of my office. Each step I took, I let the anger inside of me build again. It consumed me, and all I saw was red for my betrayer.

My blood roared in my temples and I could feel the veins throbbing. I grasped on the fierce rage inside me and pulled, hard.

My body tensed, my muscles locking as I stomped through the dark corridor. The cold air crackled with my hot fury, and only my footsteps sounded off the walls as the frigid atmosphere became deadly. It sang to me and my body fed on the scent of death.

I wanted to squeeze the life out of someone. I wanted to see the life leaving my traitor's eyes until there was nothing left, just another corpse.

The monster inside of me was raging, begging to be unleashed. I had kept him in for too long and it was time to let him free. And so I did.

As I drew closer to the door, I saw Phoenix and Artur. I pushed the black wooden door open with such force that it banged hard against the wall.

Inside, Ayla had been strapped to the wooden chair. She was folded into herself, sobbing and begging to be released. Her eyes widened at the sight of me and she cowered, terrified.

My monster laughed and fed on it. He wanted *more*.

Keeping my eyes fixed on the frightened kitten, I walked straight up to her, stopping only an inch from her chair. I bent down until we were eye level and she whimpered. Perfect. Just the way I wanted her.

She flinched and pushed back, trying to escape from my cold, angry stare.

She stared at me for a few seconds, her mouth gaping as silent tears streamed down her round, rosy cheeks. Her eyes were red and puffy from crying, and at the sight of her vulnerable face, my heart constricted. Just a little, but it was enough to weaken my resolve.

The monster roared, furious at my show of weakness. He clawed inside me and a blinding rage encompassed me again.

There was no room for weakness in my life. My heart was cold and lifeless, and it had no right to feel. I did not want to feel anything but anger.

I grabbed her chin in my hand, my fingers digging hard into her cheeks. She moaned in pain and thrashed against my hold.

"Please," she mumbled, her face turning red.

"Why the fuck are you spying for the Italian?" I growled, my voice hard.

She stopped struggling for a moment, seeming surprised, a reaction I hadn't expected. After a few seconds of silence, she shook her head and then started crying again, whispering *no* over and over.

"Please no. No. I'm not spying. Please. No. No," she said in a rush, shaking her head left and right, her hair covering her sweaty face in the process.

I expected that answer. Who would be stupid enough to accept their betrayal? They would lie until there was nothing left to lie for. Only when they saw their life flashing before their eyes, just before their last breath left their body, only then would they tell the truth.

Letting go of her cheek, I moved my hand downward, prolonging the suspense before grabbing her neck firmly in my hand and squeezing. She choked, sputtered, and flailed, but she couldn't escape my unyielding grip.

Her cheeks puffed and she emitted a gurgling sound. When I saw her starting to lose consciousness, I let go of her neck. Her head rolled back and she panted. Ayla tried to take a deep breath, but she struggled with it.

Gasping and moaning in pain, she begged again. "Plea...pleas...please. Believe me..." She coughed violently, her chest heaving, drool running down her chin. She shook with wild tremors.

"I'm...te...tell...telling...the...tr...truth." Ayla sobbed. "I...did...I didn't do...any...didn't do...anything."

"Don't fucking lie to me." My voice boomed in the sterile, frigid room.

Shaking her head again, Ayla looked me straight in the eyes. "Please, Alessio. I didn't do it. I don't know what you're talking about." She coughed again, then took a deep breath in, wincing in pain. "Believe me, please. Please, Alessio. I didn't spy on you. Alessio, please believe me." She kept repeating it over and over again, every word growing fainter as she began to lose her resolve.

Her body fell limp against the chair, and she could barely keep her eyes open.

Growling, I raked a hand through my hair. *What if she is innocent?* Could it be?

Is it worth torturing someone who could be innocent? The nagging voice in my head persisted.

My monster argued. He roared. He wanted death. *Kill. Kill. Kill.*

She could be the traitor. Don't let her go.

Confused, I turned my back to Ayla. I couldn't look at her anymore. Her tears. Her pain. Her vulnerability. The begging. Her voice as she said my name. *She* made me weak.

It made my heart do a strange thing. It made me...*feel.*

A sudden pain went through my chest and I hated it.

What's happening to me?

For the first time in my life, I fought against my monster. He wanted to be free, but I pulled him back inside. He fought and roared, but I continued fighting.

Why was I fighting for her?

Looking up, I saw Artur and Phoenix looking at me strangely, their eyes questioning. I glared and bared my teeth at them angrily. Both of them quickly averted their gazes, their faces becoming a mask of impassiveness.

Standing up straighter, I didn't turn around, refusing to look at Ayla. I took a deep breath and walked toward the door. Artur and Phoenix followed me outside and the door closed behind us.

"Keep her here and keep questioning her. She will eventually break down."

"Yes, Boss," Phoenix said.

I took a step forward, but then stopped. Turning around, I faced my men and growled in a deadly tone. "No one lays a hand on her."

If anyone dared to go against my order, then they would die. Both Phoenix and Artur seemed surprised, but then nodded.

My order took me by surprise too. I didn't know where it came from, but all I knew was that I didn't want anyone touching *my* kitten. That admission shocked me too.

Without sparing them another glance, I walked

away, my stomach in knots. I still felt angry at myself for the weakness I had shown.

And then I was angry at Ayla.

I didn't have my answers yet. I wanted to believe her, but could I really? My empire was at stake and she was a possible suspect. It didn't matter what I felt for her, or why her pain was my pain. I still had to get answers, and it didn't matter whether I played fair or not.

Slowly, I felt my aching heart return to its unfeeling state. In my bedroom, I took a deep breath and stared at the wall, letting the coldness seep back into my body.

She wouldn't make me weak. I wouldn't let her.

***

Ayla

I didn't know how long they kept me there, and I wasn't sure whether it was day or night. All I knew was that I wanted the pain to end. I couldn't take it anymore. My head pounded and my body felt weak.

My wrists were aching, and every time the rope pressed against my sensitive skin, I whimpered in pain. The skin was scratched raw and I'd been bleeding from my struggles.

"What information did you give the bastards?" Viktor asked again. Viktor, Nikolay, and Phoenix took turns interrogating me, and I was beginning to notice they were exasperated by my answers.

"I didn't do it," I said.

Why would I support monsters like Alberto and

my father? I loathed them. But Alessio and his men didn't know that, because I hadn't revealed the truth.

My life was already in jeopardy. Admitting I was the daughter of Alfredo and the fiancée of Alberto wouldn't help me.

The truth would put me in more danger. I was Italian and their enemy, so they would never believe me.

No matter how much I begged and sobbed, they wouldn't listen. They refused to let me go. "Ayla, damn it! Lying is not going to get you out of here!" Nikolay yelled as he paced the room.

Neither will the truth, I thought as I cried.

Sucking in a deep breath, I winced at my dry throat. "Please…Viktor, Nikolay. I didn't do it. Believe me. I don't know anything," I whispered, my voice scratchy from hours of crying. I could barely even talk from the constant throbbing pain in my throat.

Nikolay stopped pacing and stared at me, his eyes full of pity. I shifted my gaze to Viktor and saw that he was looking at me with the same sympathy.

I knew I was slowly weakening them. They wanted to believe me. They seemed almost convinced that I hadn't done it. I just didn't know how much longer I could stay strong. All I wanted was to go back to my bed and cuddle into my soft covers, forgetting about this nightmare.

We were still staring at each other in silence when suddenly the door opened. I blinked several times, trying to get rid of the fog in my eyes. I felt my heart stutter in panic when Alessio walked in.

He wore his regular three-piece black suit. His hands were bare—no black leather gloves. Alessio stared at me for a few seconds, his eyes blank.

He stayed at the door and crossed his arms over his chest. Looking at Viktor, he gave him a nod. My eyebrows furrowed in confusion when Viktor got up and came closer to me. Fear clawed its way inside me.

A few seconds later, I felt his hands on the rope. There were a few tugs and I winced at the discomfort and pain.

Then my hands were free.

They believe me? I didn't know what to do or how to act. Was I being released, or were they going to torture me some more?

"Get up," Alessio ordered in a gruff voice. I quickly did as I was told and cradled my wounded hands against my chest.

"Go to your bedroom. You are free," he said in the same emotionless voice. I sucked in a harsh breath, stumbling back against a hard chest. I didn't have to turn around. I knew it was Viktor.

He grasped my shoulders and held me up until my weak legs could support me. I shook so bad that if it hadn't been for Viktor, I would have been on the floor.

"Can you walk?" he asked, his voice strangely soft, as if he was talking to a wounded animal.

I nodded and he let me go. I stumbled forward and slowly walked toward Alessio, my legs heavy. My eyes stayed focused on him as I made my way to the door. He didn't move or say anything as he continued to stare at me.

When I walked through the door, Alessio's cold voice stopped me dead in my tracks.

"Don't even think of escaping."

I didn't look at him when I nodded. Escaping didn't even pass through my mind. I knew I couldn't escape. There was no point.

His men would just catch me, and in the end, I would have to pay for my defiance. I had no desire to come back to this basement or to feel Alessio's wrath.

I would live my life as a quiet maid and try to become as invisible as possible.

I heard Artur's voice. "Boss, why are you—"

Alessio lifted his palm, silencing him. My shoulders sagged and I wanted to cry in relief.

I followed Phoenix as he led the way. We climbed the stairs, bringing us to the main level. I couldn't see anyone and the house was completely silent.

"What time is it?" I asked nervously.

"Two-thirty in the morning," Phoenix replied.

My steps faltered. Almost seventeen hours. I had been in that basement for almost seventeen hours.

"Are you coming or not?" he asked when I stopped. Nodding, I followed him to the stairs as he led me to my room.

"Go take a shower and sleep," he said.

"Thank you," I whispered, looking down as I hid my tears from him.

I walked inside and he closed the door behind me. Blindly looking for the light switch, I turned it on and the room was instantly illuminated in light.

I was tired, weak, hungry, sleepy, and numb. All I wanted to do was sleep and never wake up.

Quickly shedding my clothes, I got into the shower. The warm water cascaded around me and I felt the warmth cover my cold body. My teeth chattered as I washed myself. Silent tears streamed down my cheeks. Tears of relief. I sank on the shower floor and cried while letting the warm water fall over my weak body. I didn't know how long I stayed in the shower, but when my body felt fully warmed and my tears had finally dried, I got up and walked out.

After putting my black pajamas on, I felt myself smile. I would sleep and forget everything. But that smile turned into a gasp of horror when I saw Alessio sitting on my bed. Staggering back, I curled into myself, fear spreading through my body.

He hastily got up from the bed when he saw me cowering behind the door. "Shhh, don't be scared. I'm not here to hurt you. I'm not going to hurt you."

My eyes widened in surprise at his tone, which was gentle and soft.

I have lost my mind. I must be dreaming.

I shook my head and sputtered. "You…you…I…"

My head grew dizzy when I saw him giving me a sweet smile. My legs gave out, but before I could fall on the floor, he rushed forward and grabbed onto my arms, pulling me into him. He cradled me to his chest, and I instinctively wrapped my arms around his neck and held on, scared he would let me go.

"It's okay. I got you," he whispered, walking to

my bed and gently placing me down.

He sat on the mattress, and that was when I noticed the first aid kit on the bed. Alessio pulled it onto his lap and removed some bandages and a bag of antiseptic wipes. He looked up and our gazes met. I froze when I saw his eyes glistening with emotion.

Leaning forward, Alessio gently grabbed my hands and placed them on his knees. He took the wipes out of the packet and gently rubbed my raw wrists. I hissed and he quickly mumbled, "Sorry."

Did he really say that?

Bending down, he blew on my wrists and continued cleaning the small wound. It stung, but with him gently blowing on the burning skin, the pain slowly started to diminish.

My eyes were closed when he wrapped the bandages around my wrists.

"There. All done," he whispered, slowly rubbing his finger on the bandage.

I opened my eyes and stared at him. Why was he doing this? My heart stuttered when he brought my wrists up and placed a single kiss on each of them. My mouth hung open. This wasn't actually happening, right? "I'm sorry, Ayla," Alessio said against my wrist. I stopped breathing for a second. He *apologized* to me. The Russian mafia boss, Alessio Ivanshov, a man who probably never uttered the word *sorry* to anyone, had just apologized to me.

I was in a state of shock. My heart was beating wildly in my chest and I fought to breathe. He looked up at me and my body started to warm up under his soft gaze.

This is not possible. Alessio couldn't be sitting in front of me right now and apologizing. He couldn't be this…gentle.

"I shouldn't have treated you like that. I can't apologize enough. But please know that I am so very sorry," he continued as he placed my hands on his knees again. Bringing his hand up to my face, he moved my hair behind my ears, letting his fingers linger on my cheek. "I believe you," Alessio added.

I gasped, then gulped hard, and continued to stare at him, my eyes wide. I didn't say anything. I couldn't.

"Please forgive me for my horrible actions. This won't happen again. You are safe here. Nobody will ever mistreat you again," he muttered, his voice a little rough but still gentle.

He stared at me for a few more seconds, his blue eyes twinkling with something I couldn't quite pinpoint. Alessio was always rude, arrogant, mean, vulgar, and menacing.

But this side of Alessio was strange, and against my own resolve, my heart did a flip. His kindness and softness was unnatural, but my heart grasped onto it and held it tight.

For a man like him to apologize, it meant something, right?

Suddenly, he drew away, but then his lips tilted upward in a small smile. "There's food here." He nodded toward my nightstand where a tray of food sat.

I looked back at him when he continued. "Please eat. You must be feeling weak. I will tell Lena that you are not going to work tomorrow. You need rest."

I nodded, still looking into his eyes, trying to find any sign of deception or trickery. But I only saw honest feelings. He really *did* feel guilty.

Still confused at the new turn of events, I stayed speechless. Alessio sighed when I didn't say anything. Moving away, he stood up and stared down at me.

"Goodnight," he said in the same smooth voice.

His expression was sad and dejected. Almost mournful.

My heart constricted and my eyebrows furrowed in confusion. Why was I feeling sad for him? He deserved to feel the guilt and sorrow over causing me unnecessary pain. But why did I feel bad for him?

As I tried to understand my own feelings over this whole ordeal, he gave me a final look and turned around. Without saying anything else, Alessio walked out of my bedroom and closed the door behind him.

I was left on my bed, speechless and confused.

Who was this new Alessio?

Chapter 13

I looked at the tray of food and my stomach growled.

But then I looked back at the closed door, my heart hammering as I expected Alessio to barge in and drag me back into the basement.

When none of that happened, I leaned against my headboard and looked down at my bandaged wrist.

He had bandaged my wrist, brought me food, and apologized. My feelings were all over the place. I was scared, but his kindness had warmed my heart. Was he being genuine?

Oh God, I hope so.

Rubbing my thumb over my wrist, I thought about how he kissed my wrists gently, almost like he was scared of hurting me. I never thought him capable of being gentle, but he proved me wrong.

His eyes had shown guilt and remorse. Looking back at the door, my heart constricted.

Either he really meant his apology or he was a really good actor.

There were so many uncertainties running

through my head and none of them were helpful. They all led to the same conclusion.

Alessio was unpredictable.

I couldn't trust him, not after the way he had treated me. Not when I knew the type of man he was. I felt vulnerable, and sometimes I could be gullible, but I wasn't *that* stupid.

But for now, I was still alive. And that was all that mattered.

Closing my eyes, I took in a deep breath and felt my muscles relaxing.

I was hungry, sore, and tired. My gaze went to the tray and my stomach growled again. I leaned over and brought the tray to my lap. My muscles protested with the movement and I groaned.

I ate until my stomach felt like it would burst. Eggs, rice, curry, fruits.

I sighed, feeling content. Sometimes this new life felt better than my old life—my life with Alberto. After placing the tray back in its original spot, I pulled the covers over me and snuggled deeper into the softness.

I stared at the door, blinking several times when my vision became hazy. Sleepiness took over my body and I had no desire to fight it. My body was languid and my eyes drifted shut.

When I couldn't hold them open any longer, I gave the door a final glance and then closed my eyes, slowly surrendering myself to exhaustion. Before I succumbed to the darkness, a strange thought ran through my head.

Don't fall for him.

But I never had a chance to analyze it. Sleep had

already taken over my body.

***

Alberto

"We haven't found her yet."

"Fuck!" I roared before throwing my phone across the room.

Pushing my chair away from my desk, I stood up and paced my office. That bitch. One week. One week since she fucking escaped.

One week since she tricked everyone and left. And all this time, I had been looking for her. I had dozens of men looking for her. Day and night. But no one found her yet.

Where the fuck could she be?

Punching the wall in rage, I felt my control slowly snapping. She would pay for leaving me.

She was *mine*, only mine.

She belonged to me. Her place was in my bed, with her legs spread, waiting for me.

Since she was seven, her fate had been entwined with mine. When I saw her for the first time, I knew I had to have her. She was meant for me.

But she left.

And I would make her bleed for leaving me. She would regret ever stepping a foot outside my estate.

When the door opened, I swiveled around to see Alfredo coming in.

"Have they found her yet?" he asked.

I shook my head, leaning back against the wall, watching him pace.

"Where could she be? How is it possible that none of our men have found her yet? They are the best trackers we have," he growled, raking his hand through his hair.

"I don't know," I said through gritted teeth. I was getting tired of the old man questioning me all the time.

Taking a step forward, Alfredo sent me a piercing glare.

"She was in your care! And I come back to find my daughter gone? I am rethinking your position as my second in command, Alberto. So you better fucking find her, and soon!" He stalked out of the room and closed the door behind him with a bang.

That fucking old man. I was done with his bullshit.

Second in command. I huffed at his words and let out a harsh laugh.

I was the motherfucking boss.

"Your time is done, Alfredo," I hissed, glaring at the closed door.

As I turned toward the window, I caught a glimpse of Ayla's photo on my desk. She was wearing a black gown and I had my arms wrapped around her waist. Her smile stiff as always. Her eyes empty and soulless.

You better hope that I don't find you. Because when I do, you will regret ever being born.

Chapter 14

Ayla

I awoke to the sound of continuous knocking. It vibrated through my ears and I groaned.

Pushing the comforter away from my face, I looked up, but quickly closed my eyes against the bright sunlight streaming into my room.

The day before was blurred and everything felt surreal. Blinking again, I stared at the door in confusion. Why was I in my room? Wasn't I in the basement?

But then my eyes widened when the rest of my memories came crashing back. Alessio had let me go and apologized for his behavior. He had bandaged my wrists and brought me food.

Letting my head fall back on the pillow, I let out a loud sigh. It must have been a dream. A beautiful dream. When I heard the rapping against the door again, I called out without thinking, "Come in." But as soon as the words left my mouth, I tensed.

Oh God. What if it's Alessio?

Quickly sitting up, I brought the covers up to my chin and stared at the door nervously. I saw the knob turning and then the door slowly opened.

I trembled slightly in fear, but when Maddie poked her head in, my muscles relaxed and I sagged against the pillows in relief.

Maddie was Lena's daughter. She was a few years older than me, but we instantly connected. Apart from Lena, Maddie was someone I had begun to trust.

"Ayla," she whispered, walking into my room and closing the door behind her. She ran to me and sat down on my bed, her expression filled with worry.

"Oh my God, we were so worried!" she exclaimed, taking my hand in hers. When she saw the bandages, a shocked gasp escaped her lips.

"Oh, Ayla," Maddie whispered. She bit her lips and her eyebrows furrowed.

"It's okay. I'm okay," I mumbled, withdrawing my hand, not wanting any more attention drawn to it.

"Ayla, it's not okay. How could he do that to you? When we heard you were brought to the basement, I think my mom almost had a heart attack!" She rose to her feet, putting her hands on her hips.

My chest ached at the thought of Lena being worried, and I looked down sadly. "He thought I was a traitor," I whispered as tears started building in my eyes. I sniffled, blinking the tears away.

Instead, I began to weep, but stopped myself, swiping away the tears.

"I know," Maddie replied, sitting back on the bed again.

"But I'm not!" Looking back up, I stared into her eyes with conviction and hoped that she believed me. But Maddie just smiled.

"We know, Ayla. It's clear as day you aren't. But Alessio is stubborn. If he suspects that you are a spy, he isn't going to let you go."

I nodded, turning my head to the side a little, looking at Maddie in confusion. "But he did let me go. And he apologized for treating me badly. So, I don't understand."

I saw her eyes widen in shock and then she smiled again. Placing her palm over my hand, she gave it a gentle squeeze. "Alessio is very unpredictable. But if he apologized, which he never does, and he let you go, then he probably really meant it. So, don't worry too much. You are safe now."

Her voice was soft, and I found myself relaxing, any doubts quickly evaporating.

"Are you sure?" I asked.

Maddie nodded and gave me a small smile. "Yes. I'm sure. Trust me, babe, Alessio never apologizes. I mean, it's weird that he did. That should pretty much erase all your doubts."

"He did look very remorseful."

Laughing, Maddie shook her head. "Then, there you go. You have your answer."

My heart did a flip and I felt my lips twitching into a small smile. With Maddie's reassurance, I felt light and my shoulders sagged in relief. "Thank you," I whispered, turning my palm over to hold her hand.

"It's okay. By the way, Mom is very worried about you. Alessio told her that you won't be working today. She sent me to check up on you," Maddie explained.

Pushing the comforter away, I struggled out of bed and stood up. "I want to see her."

I couldn't bear the thought of Lena being worried about me.

In a short time, she had become a second mother to me. I never had anyone hold me when I cried. Most importantly, no one had ever been worried about me.

But Lena had been, and all I wanted to do was hug her. I needed her comforting touch and soft smiles. I felt like a child desperate for her mother.

"Okay," Maddie said, her voice snapping back into the present. I looked back to see her standing up and fixing her black dress.

"I'll see you downstairs." She gave me a quick hug and then walked out of my bedroom, closing the door behind her.

I changed into my black dress. After brushing my teeth, and fixing my hair in a tight ponytail, I went downstairs. As soon as I walked into the kitchen, Lena gasped.

"Oh, my Lord. My sweet child. I was so worried!" She crushed my body to hers, holding me tight.

"Lena, I can't breathe," I managed to say. She instantly loosened her hold and took a step back.

"Let me look at you." Before I could say anything, Lena grasped my face in her hands and turned it left and then right, checking for bruises. When she didn't find any, she took a step back and inspected me from head to toe.

"Lena, I'm okay," I mumbled, the lump in my throat growing tighter. I thought my words would calm her, but when she saw my bandaged wrists, her eyes grew stormy.

"Stubborn man," she hissed. "I told him you were innocent. Took him long enough to realize his mistake." Her lips pulled down in a sad frown.

Taking a step closer, I wrapped her in my arms and gave her a hug. I took in a deep breath, her jasmine perfume filling my nose and instantly soothing me.

"As long as he believes that I'm not a traitor, then I don't have any problem," I said. Lena was silent, so I added with a reassuring tone, "I'm okay. Really." After a few seconds, she finally nodded and turned around.

"Sit down. Maddie and I are almost done with lunch," she said, pointing at the stools by the bar. As I settled myself in a stool, Maddie brought me a plate of toast, eggs, and potatoes.

"Thank you," I said, then ate in silence as I watched Maddie and Lena working in the kitchen.

I was slowly sipping my juice when Maddie spoke, and her words made my breath catch in my throat.

"Mom, why do the Ivanshovs and Abandonatos hate each other so much? I mean, I know it runs deeper than just two mob groups fighting. But I never asked *why*."

I almost choked on my juice.

Coughing, I placed the glass on the counter and brought a shaky hand to my mouth. Maddie and Lena turned toward me, looking concerned. I just brushed them off with a flick on my wrist, letting them know I was okay.

Actually, I wasn't okay. I could barely breathe.

"Oh dear, it's a long story," Lena said, sighing.

Straightening my shoulders, I instantly perked up. I knew our families hated each other with a fierce passion, but I didn't know why. A few times, I had heard Alberto talking about the Ivanshovs and how they would wipe out the Abandonato if they ever had a chance.

Clearing my throat, I said, "I was wondering about that too." When Lena gave me a strange look, I quickly made an excuse. "I mean, when Alessio thought that I was a spy for the Abandonatos, he was really furious. So, I was wondering why."

"He does truly hate them." Wiping her hand on her apron, she walked toward the bar and sat down on a stool. Maddie and I sat on either side of her.

"Maddie, you were still a baby. So, you won't remember anything. There was a big fight between the two families. I mean, they were always enemies, but after that night…" Lena paused and shook her head sadly. "Alfredo invaded the estate. Lyov, Alessio's father, wasn't home." A tear escaped Lena's eye. "It was a whole bloody mess. So many men died that night. And poor Maria, Alessio's mother. She was killed. Alfredo killed her and then left a note on her body. It said, 'Let that be a lesson for you.' She was pregnant." Lena broke off and started crying, her sobs filling the room.

My eyes widened and it felt like my heart would burst any moment. My stomach twisted so painfully that I thought I would puke. My body tingled. I felt as if I was being stuffed into a small box. Numbness swam through me.

Everything muted around me and the only words that kept ringing through my ears were, *Alfredo killed Alessio's mother.* My father had killed Alessio's pregnant mother.

It felt as if I had sunk deep underwater, and I suffocated as I tried desperately to take air into my lungs, but they burned with the pressure.

Placing my trembling hands over my thighs, I squeezed them hard, forcing myself to stay still and listen to the rest.

"She was five months pregnant. Lyov and Maria were so happy. They were having a girl. But everything ended that night. And poor Alessio," Lena continued with a hoarse voice, her words breaking my heart. "Alessio saw everything. He was hiding under the bed. Poor boy, he was only seven and saw his mother being murdered before his eyes. Nothing was the same afterwards. Darkness filled the house. Maria, our light, she was gone. She was our queen. It broke everyone's hearts. Eventually we all learned how to move on again. But Lyov and Alessio were never the same again."

My cheeks were wet with my silent tears. My heart constricted in pain and my chest swelled with the grief that consumed me.

How could my father be so heartless?

My mind fogged up and I felt my lips quivering

as I tried not to cry out loud. It was too much. Too much pain filled my chest.

I was truly the enemy.

I will never survive if they find out the truth.

"Alessio didn't talk for three years," Lena said. "Didn't show any emotions, and Lyov, he totally shut down. When Alessio finally spoke again, his first words were, 'I will avenge my mother.' Since then, that has been his goal. He vowed to kill every Abandonato. To make them all pay." She choked through the tears and buried her face in her hands, her chest heaving almost painfully with the force of her cries. "Maddie, your father died then, too. He died while trying to protect Maria. I didn't just lose my best friend, I also lost my husband that day."

The kitchen was silent for a few minutes, only our sniffles and cries filling the room. I closed my eyes and brought a hand to my mouth as I wept, my body trembling. Goosebumps rose on my skin and my breath hitched.

"I hope Alessio makes them all pay," Lena said, bringing her head up as she wiped at her tears. "They all deserve to die, every last one of them."

Her words were a slap to my face, and I froze for a moment, holding my breath. I let it out in a whoosh and stood from the stool. I brought my hand to my stomach, rubbing it gently, trying to get rid of the sick feeling. Lena and Maddie watched me, probably thinking I was crazy.

I felt crazy, and I'd begun to lose my mind.

Breathe, Ayla, breathe.

My chest felt tight, painfully tight. Clenching my fists tight, I gasped for air as I entered a full-blown panic attack.

My eyes were wide in terror as I stumbled back a few steps.

"Ayla?" Lena asked, her voice filled with concern as she stood up. My body felt cold.

Outside. Air. Breathe. Now.

I pressed my hand hard against my burning chest and quickly swiveled around, running out of the kitchen. But before I could make my escape, I hit a rock hard chest.

Bouncing back, I stumbled as a strong hand grasped my arm, pulling me straight up again. My vision blurred with dizziness and I felt my head rolling back slightly.

My head snapped up, and I met cold bluish-steel eyes. Only one person had these beautiful captivating eyes. *Alessio.*

As I stared into his eyes, Lena's words rang in my ears, causing me to whimper in fear and pain.

He vowed to kill every Abandonato.

And I was an Abandonato.

Chapter 15

Alessio

Viktor walked beside me as we headed for my office.

"Are we still on for the clubs' check-up tonight?" he asked.

I half-grunted in reply, nodding my head.

When we arrived, Artur, Phoenix, and Nikolay were already waiting. They stood up at the sight of me and nodded in greeting. They waited for me to sit down first and then took their respective seats.

"Alberto sent us another warning," I announced. "He's going after another club, and he doesn't care who he kills along the way. He wants the whorehouse as his. I want at least a dozen men there, protecting the place."

They said nothing, focused on me as I spoke, my voice ringing with authority.

Nikolay nodded. "I'll take care of it."

"The fucking Italians are not backing down. I think we have stayed silent for too long," Phoenix added through gritted teeth, his eyes crackling with anger.

I sat back in my chair and crossed my right ankle over my left knee. Leveling Phoenix with a glare, I spoke smoothly. My voice was slow and quiet, edged with threat. "The Italians can try as much as they want, but they aren't going to bring my empire down." I let out a harsh laugh. "They have been trying for years with no success."

Phoenix sighed and leaned back, raising his hands to his head in a gesture of surrender.

I shook my head. Funny prick, he was. All of us were silent for a moment.

"What's happening with the prostitution rings?" I asked Artur. Alberto had been running such establishments, which were different from mine in that he had a heartless approach to his *commodities*. "I will not have women being abused in those brothels," I added. "They are there because they have chosen to make a living that way, but I will not stand aside and watch them being abused."

"There's no way we can control that," Artur said. "We don't even own the brothels."

"Do I look like I give a fuck if I own them or not? I don't care how you do it, but it needs to be stopped. Understood?"

He immediately backed down. "Okay. I'll take care of it."

"Anything else?" I asked.

"We're good, Alessio," Viktor said. "We need to get this shit moving. Don't worry, I'll keep an eye on everyone and make sure nothing gets out of control. I've got your back."

Viktor was a man of few words, but his silence was not a weakness. When he said he had my back, I knew I could trust him.

If anyone could be more ruthless than me, it was Viktor. All my men were vicious—the five of us against the rest of the world.

"We're done then," I said, pushing my chair away and standing up. I fixed my suit and moved toward the doors, but Artur's voice stopped me in my tracks.

"Boss, there's something I don't understand. Why did you let Ayla go? We have no proof she isn't the spy."

"Shut up, Artur," Nikolay warned, but it was too late. I swiveled around and lunged for Artur, clutching at his throat and pushing him hard against the wall.

"You fucking dare question my decision?" I roared, squeezing on his windpipe until his face began to turn purple. His eyes rolled back in his head but I didn't let go. Viktor pulled me off before I could kill him.

However, that hadn't been my intention. Not yet. I wanted to warn him—for now.

Phoenix helped Artur stand, and the poor bastard was struggling to breathe, his gasps filling the room.

"S…S…Sorry…" Artur said, his hand clutching his throat.

"Ayla is no longer a suspect," I said, my fists tightening. Actually, she still was, but they didn't need to know that.

Torturing her wasn't the best way to get the truth out. There were other ways to find the truth, but I would explore that alone.

I gave them a final glare and left my office, shutting the door loudly.

I tried to calm my breathing. Artur had gotten me riled up, but his question wasn't the only source of my anger.

I was trying not to think about Ayla. But then he went and said her name. Fuck. I was losing it again. A fucking woman was making me lose my shit.

What was it about her?

When I let her go the night before, I couldn't stop thinking about her. Black shiny hair. Green eyes glistening with tears as she screamed her innocence. Oh, how badly I wanted to believe her.

She had me tied in knots and I fucking hated it.

My mind went back to the scene in her bedroom. She had been shocked at my change of character. Hell, I was shocked too.

Her vulnerability called to me, and surprisingly I had a desire to protect her. When I saw her in pain, my chest ached.

Lost in thought, I walked past the kitchen, but Lena's voice snapped me back the present and I stopped.

"I hope he makes them all pay. They deserve to die, every last one of them."

My eyebrows furrowed in confusion and I stepped closer, standing right outside the entrance of the kitchen. Ayla was there, sitting beside Lena at the bar.

I was about to take a step forward but stopped when she quickly jumped off the stool. Her tiny body shook violently and her face was red and puffy from crying.

She swiveled around and tried to run out of the kitchen, but I was in the way. She hit my chest and bounced back, then stumbled over her feet and I quickly reached out to catch her.

She was gasping for breath, her chest heaving.

Ayla trembled in my arms and brought her head up, her eyes meeting mine. Her breath hitched in surprise. She went still in my arms, and if I wasn't mistaken, she held her breath.

As I stared into her eyes, I could tell she was petrified. My hands tightened on her arms and she gasped, cowering in fear.

"I…" She sucked in a deep breath, but started coughing. Her hands went up to her neck and she rubbed furiously. "I…I can't…breathe…" She was having a panic attack, and struggled out of my arms. I let her go. She stumbled back and then ran past me.

I glanced in the kitchen, where Lena and Maddie were giving me worried looks. I didn't wait for an explanation. Turning around, I ran after the frightened kitten, and saw her running for the back door, which led to the garden. She rushed outside. I slowed to a walk and followed her.

Squinting at the bright sunlight, I found Ayla sitting on the top of the hill, huddling under a tree.

I gave her a few minutes by herself and then made my way toward her. She hugged her knees to her chest, her arms wrapped around them tightly, her face buried between them.

When I got closer, she tensed. Rolling my eyes with a sigh, I sat down on the grass beside her shaking body. She was slowly coming down from her attack.

I didn't know why I followed her, and I sure as hell didn't know why I sat down beside her. For some strange reasons, my heart ached at her pain. I wanted to offer comfort.

I rubbed my face tiredly. This girl. I closed my eyes tightly and pinched the tip of my nose in frustration. She was messing with my head.

I heard her sobbing quietly, but eventually she quieted down. "Why did you follow me?" she asked, her voice scratchy.

"You're crying." My voice came out hard, so I quickly cleared my throat and attempted to soften my tone. "Why are you crying?" I tried to sound gentle, but I sounded demanding instead.

Way to go, Alessio. Great way to get her to open up.

"That wasn't an answer," she replied, her voice barely audible. I was sure she didn't mean for me to hear it, but I did.

I bristled slightly at her tone but took a deep breath, not wanting to sound harsh. This wasn't the time to scare her.

"Well, that's the only answer you're getting," I said, turning to my side to face her. I didn't have any other answer for her.

Ayla lifted her head slightly and placed her chin on her arms, looking me straight in the eyes. "Lena told me about your mother."

I was taken aback—shocked. Ayla noticed, and bit on her lip nervously.

"I'm sorry," she mumbled, tears forming in her

eyes again.

Swallowing hard against the lump in my throat, I shrugged. "Why are you apologizing? It's not your fault."

"I know. But I'm sorry for your loss." A tear slipped from the corner of her eye.

I followed the single drop as it trailed down her rosy cheek. I felt my heart stutter at her admission. She was sorry for *me*. She was crying for *my* loss.

I stared at her, filled with confusion. Who was this girl? And what was she doing to me?

"Okay," I replied, my voice gruff. I couldn't say anything else because I didn't know what to say.

Ayla being nice to me was a big surprise. I never expected it. She always appeared scared of me, but now she was giving me her condolences for my mother's death.

She closed her eyes and sighed loudly, as if a big burden had been taken off her shoulders. I saw her trembling and she huddled tighter into herself.

Without thinking, I shrugged off my suit jacket and leaned forward, gently placing it around her.

She instantly stilled.

"It's a little cold today," I said, then shifted away from her.

Why the fuck was I explaining myself to her?

My body rigid, I stood up and brushed the grass from my clothes. I avoided looking at her. I felt annoyed at myself and the way I reacted to her.

Focus, Alessio. Focus on your task. Don't lose yourself in her beautiful eyes and gentle soul.

My hands tightened into fists, and without sparing her another glance, I turned around and walked back to the house.

Chapter 16

Ayla

When I told him I was sorry for his loss, I was afraid he would be angry.

He'd been right when he said it wasn't my fault. But my father had killed his mother. And if my father wasn't apologizing for his mistakes and wrongdoings, then I would. It had become my burden to carry.

I was living in Alessio's home, depending on him, but he had no idea I was his worst enemy. I might be personally innocent, but my blood wasn't.

I wished I could have told him the truth, but he wouldn't understand. Nobody would, not even Lena or Maddie. They saw my family as an enemy, but what they didn't know and wouldn't understand was that I had become a victim and I suffered too.

I didn't want to suffer anymore.

I wanted to be happy.

So, I couldn't tell them the truth—not ever.

I understood what it felt like to lose someone,

because I had lost my mother. I didn't remember her, but I still mourned.

Alessio confused me. One minute he was kind, and the next he was cold and angry. I pulled his suit jacket tighter around my body. It still felt warm from his body heat.

The smell of his cologne touched my nose and I let out a sigh.

I stayed on the hill that overlooked the large back garden, beginning to relax. From where I sat, the view was stunning. The garden bloomed with various colors, each flower part of a scene that reminded me of a painting.

A huge water fountain, bigger than the one out front, dominated the landscape. It looked so serene. As I stared at the majestic beauty, a sense of peacefulness encompassed my body and I felt light.

I waited for a few more minutes, basking in the blissful surroundings, and then I stood up, feeling stronger than before. Holding Alessio's jacket tight to my body, I made my way back to the house.

My steps were light and unhurried. I touched the soft petals of the flowers as I walked by, and smiled.

When I reached the kitchen, I walked in to find Lena and Maddie sitting by the bar, their expressions downcast. Lena looked up when I came in and quickly jumped off her stool.

I pulled her into my arms and gave her a tight hug, then stepped back and smiled nervously. "I'm sorry about your loss. And I am sorry for reacting the way I did. I had a panic attack, I…" I licked my suddenly dry lips and swallowed past the heavy lump in my throat. "I…I lost my mother too. It…makes me anxious. It was pretty emotional hearing about Alessio's mother, and I was mourning for his loss too."

Lena smiled sweetly, her eyes kind as she stroked my cheek. "It's okay, honey. You must be pretty emotional after everything that's happened. Why don't you have lunch and then go rest, all right?"

When I nodded, she stepped away and turned to Maddie, who gave me a pitiful look.

"Maddie, call in the other maids," Lena said. "It's time to serve lunch. Alessio and the others will be coming down soon."

Maddie took her phone out and quickly typed a message before putting it back in her pocket. She linked her arm through mine, pulling me toward the stool. "Are you okay?" she asked.

I nodded. "Yeah, I'm okay. Sorry about that sudden meltdown."

"No, it's okay. Totally understandable," she replied.

Soon, the other maids arrived in the kitchen, and each of them took something to serve on the dining room table.

It took them some time, but when they were done, the kitchen was quiet again. Lena had left, and Maddie and I were alone.

"Hungry?" she asked.

I shook my head and leaned against the stool. "Not really. Maybe I'll eat later."

"Okay," she said in an adorable, childish tone, before serving a plate of food for herself. She sat down across from me and dug in. I let out a laugh when I heard her moan at the first bite.

"So good," she said. "Damn, I didn't know I was this hungry."

Shaking my head, I snatched her towel from the table and threw it at her face. "Close your mouth when you eat."

She started to chew loudly with a teasing expression on her face, then gave me a wink and stuffed another spoonful in her mouth. And then she moaned out loud.

I crossed my arms over my chest and rolled my eyes. Behind me, someone cleared their throat. My back straightened and I turned toward the sound only to find Artur leaning against the doorway.

He didn't even spare me a look. He was only staring at Maddie, whose eyes widened when she saw him and her cheeks turned red.

She blushed and averted her eyes. I looked back at him and saw his lips tilt upward in a confident smirk.

When I saw him adjusting his pants, I looked away, embarrassed.

Artur cleared his throat and said, "Is Lena here? Alessio is looking for her."

Maddie shook her head and continued to stare down at her plate. Her hair fell over her face, hiding her from Artur's view, but I saw the tiny smile creeping up on her face.

"Okay then," he said, and he left the room. Maddie looked up, her expression softening, and I heard her sigh. A dreamy sigh.

"Maddie?" I asked, my tone filled with

questions. She turned toward me and bit down on her lips before letting out a small giggle. She stared at me for a few seconds before nodding, confirming my suspicions.

"You and Artur? Oh my God, Maddie. Since when?" I asked, leaning forward in anticipation.

"About six months now. I couldn't resist him any longer, Ayla. I mean, just look at him! He's so sexy. And God, so dreamy. He's perfect. I just...I don't know. I couldn't stop myself." She shrugged nervously. "I'm swooning, aren't I?"

"You are," I replied, laughing. She was so cute.

"He's so hot, Ayla!"

Well, I couldn't deny that. He was indeed good looking.

"And he's good in bed. Like *really* good," Maddie added, leaning closer so she could whisper. "He is a beast."

"Maddie! I didn't need to know that."

"I was just telling you," she mumbled.

We stared at each other, then smiled before bursting into a fit of giggles.

It felt good to laugh. I couldn't remember the last time I felt so free. Looking into Maddie's smiling eyes, my laughter died down and my nose started stinging. I could feel the tears at the backs of my eyes but I didn't let them fall.

I never realized that being happy would make me so emotional. Maybe it was because I never experienced friendship, laughter, or happiness. But Lena and Maddie showed me kindness that I never thought existed.

And I would forever be grateful for that.

Leaning forward, I touched her hand. "Thank you," I whispered, my voice a little hoarse.

She tilted her face to the side in confusion and then asked, "What for?"

"Just…thank you for being my friend," I said, not wanting to elaborate. I realized I had just made my first friend at the age of twenty-three.

How pathetic was my life?

Looking down, I tried to hide my tears. But when Maddie squeezed my hand, I looked up again. She smiled. "You don't have to thank me for that, Ayla."

I gave her hand a squeeze and then leaned back. That was how we spent the next few hours. We talked, laughed, and joked. When the house started to quiet down and all activities ceased, we realized it was close to sunset.

"Oh my God," Maddie gasped. "I'm so sorry, Ayla. You were supposed to rest and I lost track of time." She stood and wiped the counter clean.

"Hey, it's okay. I had fun. I enjoy talking to you."

"Still. You should go rest now or I'll never hear the end of it from Mom," she said, rolling her eyes in exaggeration.

"Well, you are right about that." Laughingly, I gave her a quick hug and she pushed me toward the door.

"Go. Go. Go."

When I got to my bedroom, I closed the door softly behind me. Without even removing my dress, I jumped in bed and cuddled under the warm, soft comforter.

Even though I had fun with Maddie, I was very tired. Now that I was in bed, my body felt heavy and languid. Sighing happily, I turned toward my window. The curtains were open and I had the perfect view of the sunset.

I watched the sun go down behind the back garden. I watched as the sky changed colors from red to orange and then with a mixture of light purple. The magnificent beauty took my breath away.

This could make such a beautiful painting. I could already imagine the large canvas smeared with alluring colors, creating a soft and peaceful landscape.

As the sky turned dark, my eyes started to get heavy. I yawned and blinked drowsily. Darkness surrounded me as I succumbed to my fatigue.

"Shhhh. Don't make any noise," he said harshly, clasping his hand over my mouth as I struggled against him. "Don't move. It'll be over quick. You won't even feel anything."

I tried to scream, but no sound came out. I fought against him but it was no use. He was unmovable.

No. No. Please no.

He brought his hand down my bare legs and slowly hitched my nightshirt up. He spread my legs open with his knees and settled between my thighs.

Sobbing, I continued to struggle but it had no effect on him. When he reached my underwear, he ripped it open without a second thought, baring me to him.

132

"You are mine! Mine! It's about time I take you," he hissed angrily. I heard his zipper open and I tried to move my legs together, but his knees stopped me.

His hand stayed on my mouth, stopping any sound from escaping. He moved over me and then I felt him near my entrance. I wanted to scream.

"It'll be over soon, love," he said into my neck, placing wet kisses along the length, biting hard and torturing the skin with his teeth.

I went numb and stopped struggling. When he noticed me going limp, he laughed in my ears. The fear that I felt was indescribable. I didn't just feel it. I could smell it. It was all around me. My heart beat hard against my chest. Hot tears spilled down my cheeks.

When I felt him push inside of me, my heart cracked into a million pieces. Pain. So much pain. I was blinded by pain. It felt like I was bleeding from the inside. My skin burned and my whole body spasmed violently. All I felt was deep agony. I cried out against his palm and to my horror I found myself paralyzed and unable to move.

Pushing deeper inside of me, he growled.

"Fuck. You are so tight. Made for me. I own you."

His loud pants filled my ears and that was all I could hear. It hurt so bad. Everything hurt. My body. My head. My heart. My soul.

When he stopped moving, I didn't feel anything. My body felt numb. Crippled with pain and fear. Pulling out of me, he removed his hand and placed his palms on the mattress on either side of my face.

He leaned over me and smiled.
"Happy sweet sixteen, love."
I would never forget that smile. It was forever etched in my memory.

I woke up trying to scream and shot up straight in bed, covered in sweat. I breathed heavily, my heart pounding hard against my ribcage. The veins in my neck throbbed and my head ached.

I felt hot. Too hot. I was burning and my body shook violently with silent tremors. I could barely breathe. Quickly scrambling off the bed, I stood and paced the room.

Unsteady with dizziness, everything around me blurred. My ears were making a strange stinging noise and then everything was muted.

"A nightmare. It was just a nightmare, Ayla. Just a nightmare," I told myself.

But it wasn't *just* a nightmare.

It was my reality. My truth. Images flashed through my head all at once and I fell to my knees. It was too much. I closed my eyes against the blast of agony that went through my body.

Burying my face in my hands, I sobbed. The pressure built in my chest and my stomach heaved. I felt empty inside.

My tears were never-ending and I began to gag. My whole body shook as I bent forward and dry-heaved. I laid down on the floor, curling into myself as I continued to weep.

I thought I ran away from my past, but it followed me. Even though I was no longer in Alberto's trap, he still held the strings.

I just wished for once that I could live without fear. Just once, I wanted to be absolutely free.

I wanted to scream. Rage at the unfairness bestowed upon me. But I couldn't.

I wanted to forget, but I was stupid to believe that I could be happy. My reality would always follow in the end.

My weeping turned to jerky breaths as exhaustion overcame me. Opening my burning eyes, the first thing that I saw was Alessio's suit jacket on my sofa chair.

Without thinking, I crawled toward the sofa and grabbed the jacket. I buried my face in the fabric and cried silently.

When my tears and hiccups finally died down, I slumped against the sofa and took a deep breath, and once again I could smell Alessio's cologne. I began to relax.

I didn't know why or how, but his smell calmed me. I breathed into Alessio's jacket. Other than his cologne, I could smell *him*. And that was enough to make me feel safe again.

All I wanted was peace and even if it was for a little while, I had found it. I didn't question it. I didn't want to. I just accepted it.

Lying down on the floor beside the sofa, I curled into a ball and pulled Alessio's jacket close to my chest and buried my face in it.

That was how I felt asleep again.

This time my sleep was free from nightmares and Alberto's evil grin.

All I felt was peace.

Chapter 17

Ayla

The sunlight shone on my face and I squeezed my eyes tightly against the glare. Turning around, I winced at the soreness in my back and felt my forehead crease in confusion. Why did my soft, cuddly bed feel so hard?

Groggily, I blinked my eyes open and came face to face with the bottom of the couch in my bedroom.

I rubbed my eyes in an effort to get rid of the sleepiness. A lazy yawn escaped from my mouth and I groaned, falling back on the floor again as I crossed my arms over my chest.

Turning my head to the side, I saw Alessio's jacket lying next to my face. I frowned in confusion and slowly brought my hand to the jacket, running my fingers softly over the fabric.

"Hmm," I hummed as I tried to think back to last night, feeling strangely disoriented.

Why am I holding his suit jacket?

As soon as the thought ran through my mind, I quickly sat up, dizziness rushing through me. My harsh breathing filled the room and last night flashed before my eyes.

I was worn out, tired of constantly thinking about the past. Tired of fighting my demons.

Feeling numb, I brought his jacket to my chest, holding it there as I closed my eyes. I hated my nightmares. When I escaped, the first few nights were horrible. I could barely get any sleep. But then for two nights, I didn't have any nightmares.

I felt hopeful.

Last night, all that hope came crashing down around me. I was so naïve to think that I could escape such a horrendous reality. Shaking my head at my own stupidity, I stood up and stumbled toward my bathroom.

I didn't even look at myself in the mirror. Instead, I walked straight to the shower and let the warm water cascade over me.

The warmth began to seep under my skin and my muscles relaxed. I stayed under the spray longer than usual, trying to gather myself again.

Closing the water, I stood still for a moment and closed my eyes. *Stay strong. Don't break. Don't show weakness.*

Taking a deep breath, I opened my eyes again and stepped out of the shower.

Stay strong. Don't break. Don't show weakness.

Quickly drying myself, I dressed in the same clothes I had been wearing for weeks now. My black maid dress.

When I was finished, I glanced in the mirror,

looking at my reflection in silence.

My eyes were red and puffy. Tiredness was clearly written all over my face. It didn't come as a shock to me. The face in the reflection…I had seen it a million times. Looking exactly like that.

Stay strong. Don't break. Don't show weakness.

I walked away without a second look. Alessio's suit jacket remained on the floor, where I had left it before.

I bent down and took the jacket in my hand.

I was trying so hard to avoid what I felt last night. There was no way to describe it. No words. I never felt that way before and I was still trying to wrap my head around it.

Peace. That was what I felt. In the middle of yet another panic attack, Alessio's jacket brought me peace.

He brought me peace.

How was that even possible?

My mind was a mess when I walked into the kitchen, where Maddie and Lena were waiting for me. When I walked in, both of them gifted me with genuine happy smiles.

"Good morning," Lena said, standing by the sink.

"Good morning," I mumbled, trying to act as chirpy.

"What are you doing with that?" Maddie asked, pointing at the jacket in my hand.

I ran my hand over the soft fabric before replying. "I forgot to return it yesterday. So, I'm going to return it now." I felt like I was in a daze.

Maddie took a big bite of her apple.

She stared at me with a strange expression and a smile on her face. Almost like she was having an inside joke with herself. She twisted her lips ruefully, trying very hard to hide that smile, but I still saw it.

I placed the jacket on the stool before turning to Lena. "I'll help you set the table for breakfast."

She nodded and handed me a tray of fruit. We were setting out the last plate when I saw Alessio and his men coming down the stairs.

They were all dressed in their black suits, as always. If it weren't for the guns attached to them, they would have looked like high class businessmen.

But the guns kind of took that away. It made them look deadly instead.

Everyone took their seats in silence as Maddie and I discreetly walked away. Instead of going into the kitchen, I stopped at the entrance. I didn't know what came over me, but I turned slightly and stared at Alessio from the corner of my eye.

I sucked in a shocked breath when I saw his focus already on me. Viktor was talking animatedly but Alessio wasn't listening. His eyes, his whole attention was on me. Biting on my lips unconsciously, a shiver went through my body and I quickly swiveled around, breaking the connection.

"Ayla, hurry. I wanna get this done," Maddie called from inside the kitchen.

"I'm coming," I said softly. I walked in to find Maddie eating her breakfast, with another full plate beside her. She nodded toward the plate. We quickly ate, and then cleaned while the men were still eating.

By the time the kitchen was spotless, they had finished their breakfast. Maddie and I walked out to see them getting up, and everyone scattered around the house, returning to what they'd been doing before breakfast.

***

I walked into the kitchen to see Maddie holding a tray. As soon as she saw me, her face lit up and she gave me a huge smile. "Oh my God, you're literally a life saver."

Giving her a confused look, I untied my apron from my waist. "What do you mean?"

Instead of answering, she pushed the tray into my hand. She placed a glass full of white stuff on it. "What is this?" I asked.

"Protein. For Alessio. I need you to give this to him," she said.

"What?" I didn't want to see him. And I sure didn't want to be in the same room as him. He was too intense. I had to stay away.

"Please. Do this for me," she begged.

I shook my head. "Maddie, why can't you go by yourself?"

"Because," she replied, biting on her lips nervously. "You know…"

"Maddie?" I asked, raising my eyebrows in question.

She was about to say something else, but then stopped. I turned to see what she was looking at, and saw Artur walking by.

"Ayla!" Maddie whined. When I didn't move, she glared at me and leaned forward to whisper in my ear. "He wants a quickie."

I gasped, but said nothing.

"See! Now you understand," she said. "C'mon, I can't deny him anything. And we couldn't do it for like two days. I'm sexually frustrated, Ayla."

I couldn't believe I was having this conversation.

"Close your mouth, Ayla."

I did so but then shook my head. "Maddie, I'm not going to Alessio. No way," I said.

"Why? You are supposed to see him anyway. You need to give him his jacket back, right?"

I was about to refuse again, but she folded her hands together and pressed them underneath her chin, looking at me with big, hopeful eyes. "Please?"

I couldn't say no. Not when she was making that face. "Fine."

Maddie jumped up with excitement and quickly blew me a kiss before running out of the kitchen. I sighed and looked down at the tray. God, I really didn't want to do this.

Balancing the tray in one hand, I took the suit jacket in the other and made my way out of the kitchen. Alessio's office was in the left wing and it looked the same as the rest of the house.

I walked down the long corridor toward his office and admired the large landscape paintings on the wall. They were beautiful. So serene. A big contrast to the people living in this house. As I neared the wooden double door, I saw Nikolay standing outside. His hands were behind his back, his feet shoulder apart with his back stiff as he stared straight ahead. His eyes were on me, watching my every step.

"I'm here to give Aless…I mean, Mr. Ivanshov his drink."

Without answering, he reached beside him and opened the door. Swallowing hard against the lump in my throat, I gave him a tight smile and walked in on shaky legs. Inside the office, huge windows overlooked the back garden.

The room was bright. The big desk sat in front of the windows, and Alessio sat behind the table, his chair pushed back as he faced the door. But then I saw a head of blonde hair on his lap.

Wait—what?

Oh my God.

My heart stuttered when I saw her head moving up and down. Alessio's hand was fisted in her hair, controlling her movements while he pushed his head against the back of his chair as he groaned.

And then I heard a loud moan.

I froze, and he glanced in my direction, his eyes making direct contact with mine. They flared with surprise but he didn't move. I saw his mouth tilted upward in a small smirk. I hated it.

He was by no means embarrassed. Instead, he held my gaze until he orgasmed. I was rendered completely speechless, and when I felt the tray shaking in my hands, I realized my entire body was shaking too.

"We're done here." His hard voice made me jump. He didn't sound or look affected by what had just happened.

Releasing the grip he had on the woman's hair, he pushed her upward. "Leave," he ordered as he zipped his pants and tucked his shirt back in.

She stepped away from him and grabbed her handbag, then sauntered past me, her steps confident. She didn't appear like she cared that someone else had seen her in such a position. The evil glare she gave me told me everything I needed to know. She was pissed they'd been interrupted.

The door closed behind me, but I stayed still. "What are you doing here?" Alessio asked.

My heart thumped in my chest and I was suddenly feeling light-headed. He was completely calm as his eyes raked over my body, while I was practically hyperventilating.

"Well?"

My body shivered at his voice and I licked my lips nervously. When I saw his eyes following the movement, I quickly sucked my tongue back in and pressed my lips tight together. "Maddie...I..." I stumbled over my words, then took a step forward and placed the tray on the coffee table. "Your protein." I kept my focus on the tray. I couldn't look at him, not after what I just saw.

I heard his chair squeak and from the corner of my eye, I saw him standing up. After fixing his suit, he walked around his desk and made his way toward me.

Panic filled my body and I scrambled backward.

Dropping his jacket on the couch, I kept my head down and mumbled in a rush, "And here's your jacket. I forgot to return it yesterday."

"It's—"

He'd started to speak, but without giving him a chance to reply, I sprinted out of his office.

Closing the door behind me, I leaned against it. Blood was roaring in my ears and my heart pounded.

"Sorry about that. I didn't know the boss had her inside," a deep voice said.

Letting out a squeak, I moved away in fright.

"Woah. It's just me," the man said.

I turned around to find Nikolay standing there with his hands up in mock surrender. There was no way he hadn't known what Alessio was doing in there.

"Look, I'm sorry. I seriously didn't know," he said, with a hint of sympathy.

I opened my mouth to tell him what I thought of him, but thought better of it. I didn't want to mess with the viper. Shaking my head, I walked away without sparing him or the door another glace.

I was done with infuriating men.

He's an absolute pig.

But a hot pig. The annoying voice had returned.

A disgusting pig.

I wanted to smack my head into a wall.

Chapter 18

I shouldn't have expected anything else. Alessio was a mob boss, a king. Ruthless. Cold. Heartless. Unlovable. He didn't care what people thought of him.

Men like him behaved exactly like that. I had the experience firsthand, and I should have known, but for stupid reasons I thought maybe he was *different*.

Clearly, he wasn't.

When I got downstairs, Maddie emerged from a closet beside the kitchen. Her hair was ruffled, her dress crooked, and she had a well-satisfied look on her face.

When she saw me, she winked and then walked into the kitchen. Artur came out after her, and stared at her ass as she walked away.

"Men," I muttered to myself.

I looked down as I walked past him, not wanting to see his lustful eyes.

"Hey, Ayla," he said.

I nodded but didn't turn around. "Good morning."

In the kitchen, Maddie leaned against the counter, a glass of orange juice in her hand. She sipped it, a small smirk playing across her lips.

"Why are you looking at me like that?" I asked.

"You look flushed. Out of breath." Maddie set her glass down.

I crossed my arms across my chest and shook my head. "I'm fine. What are you talking about?"

She laughed. Entwining our arms together, she led me out of the kitchen. "You aren't going to tell me, hmm?"

"I don't understand, Maddie."

"Stop playing with me! Did he kiss you? Did he do more than kiss you?"

My eyes widened in shock when I realized what she was talking about. Letting out a gasp, I pulled my arm away. "Why would you think that?"

She didn't answer but laughed instead at my expression. Maddie brought her hand up and pinched me on the cheek. "You're so cute."

I glared at her, but wasn't sure it came across the way I intended. I had been living separately from emotion. As the thought ran through my mind, I felt myself shutting down.

I felt happy here, but I was scared, because I had learned the hard way that happiness can be taken from you in a second.

I was waiting for whatever happiness I'd found here to be taken from me.

The moment when I would return to my cold room, chained to my bed, waiting for Alberto.

Someone squeezed my arm. "Where did you go?" Maddie asked.

146

"Nowhere," I replied, forcing a tight smile and linking our arms together again. She was leading me toward the maids' quarters. She pushed the door open and we walked inside the cozy living room. It smelled sweet, like roses. Only a select few of the maids actually lived in the mansion. It was big and beautifully modeled, the total opposite of how the maids' quarters looked in my father's estate. Maddie didn't live in the maids' quarters. She had her own room upstairs, same as Lena. But she enjoyed the large flat screen TV in the maids' quarters.

Maddie pulled me to the couch. She folded her legs beneath her and leaned against the couch sideways, facing me. "So? C'mon. I need all the juicy details," she demanded, her eyes twinkling merrily.

I shook my head. "Maddie, nothing happened. Seriously."

"Liar."

"Maddie—"

"Tell me!"

"Fine! Some woman was giving him a…a…"

Her eyes widened in shock. "What? What was she doing?"

"She was giving him a…you know." God, this was so embarrassing.

"Giving him what?" Her mouth twisted with amusement.

"You know…"

"Huh?" she said, feigning confusion.

Throwing my hands in the air in exasperation, I spoke through gritted. "A…a blowjob!"

147

As soon as the words crossed my lips, Maddie threw her head back and barked out a laugh. She held her stomach, laughing hysterically.

Sinking in the couch, I closed my eyes. I didn't find it funny.

"Oh my God, babe. You are so cute," she said through her laughter.

"And you are so mean."

"But you still love me." Her laughter had finally calmed down, but she still wore her gorgeous, sweet smile.

I shrugged. She was right. I still loved her. She was my only friend.

"So, that woman. What happened?" she asked. Maddie moved closer to me, her eyes wide as she stared at me expectantly.

"Nothing happened. I walked in and saw them. When he was done, he ordered her to leave. I left the protein on the coffee table and walked away without giving him a chance to say anything."

"You walked away? Why do I find that so hard to believe?"

"Okay, fine. I ran away," I mumbled.

"So he just finished right in front of you. No decency whatsoever to stop and apologize?"

I shook my head mutely. Did she really expect him to stop? He was the most infuriating and unpredictable man on the planet. No way was he going to stop his *extracurricular activities* and act decent. He didn't have time for decency, or privacy for that matter.

"Damn, he really is infuriating," Maddie said. "Who was she? I mean, how did she look?"

"I don't remember much. I was really embarrassed and shocked so didn't pay any attention to her. But she had blonde hair and she was tall. Lean. She was gorgeous."

"Ah. It's Nina. She's always coming for more. Doesn't matter that Alessio treats her like garbage after he's done. I wouldn't say it's his fault, though. He has his rules and he lets the women know before they get involved. No attachment, just fucking and then they leave. But they still want to get involved." She rolled her eyes.

Why would they let themselves be treated like that—by their own free will?

I never had a choice.

I was bound and beaten into submission. No matter how much I begged, I never had a choice, so I had to accept my reality. But other women could have better lives and a loving relationship.

Maddie's attention was on the TV.

"Maddie," I said.

"What is it?"

"Why do women accept such behavior…when they have a choice?"

She placed the remote control on her lap and turned to face me. "I don't know, Ayla. Maybe they want the same thing? Maybe they don't want a relationship. Maybe that's what works for them. It's their choice. But you know, even if you are the fuck buddy of a heartless mob boss, you are still under his protection. Which means money, a somewhat lavish life, and nobody messes with you."

"Hmmm." I was trying to understand, but still couldn't make sense of it.

"Forget that," Maddie said, then gave my knee a slap to bring my attention back to her.

"What?"

"Well, how did you feel when you saw him with that woman? Were you jealous?" She winked.

Her question surprised me. "Jealous? Why would I be jealous?"

I didn't even know what jealousy felt like because I never had a chance to be jealous. When emotions are the last thing in your life, you eventually forget what it means to *feel* something.

"C'mon, Ayla. I can see something between you and Alessio. The way he looks at you..." She fanned her face with her hands. "So hot! He literally eye-fucks you all the time!"

"Maddie!" I clapped my hand over her mouth. She had no control. I felt something wet on my palm and snatched my hand away when I realized she had licked me. "Eww."

"You are the one who placed your hand on my mouth while I was talking. Rude much?" She crossed her arms over her chest, a grin on her face. "So, do you feel something for him? Were you even a tiny little bit jealous?"

"I don't know, Maddie. How does jealousy feel?" As soon as the words were out, I bent my head down in shame. I sounded so pathetic.

You are pathetic, bitch. A pathetic whore. That's what you are. Useless. Alberto's voice rang through my head. I hated his voice. It never left me. No matter how much I tried to block him, he always came back.

I felt a comforting hand on my knee and knew it

was Maddie. She never questioned me when I asked something stupid.

She believed I had been living off the streets for some time, so she pitied me. I felt thankful that she didn't ask questions, because I had no answers.

"Well, I would describe jealousy as a wave. It comes crashing in your heart with so many mixed feelings. Anger and sadness. Most of the time, it's not the best feeling, but it hurts. You feel it right here," she said, placing her hand over her heart. "It hurts. Your chest grows tight and it feels like you can't breathe. Sometimes you might feel like crying. Or anger to the point of violence. Like punching someone in the face. I don't know how to describe it exactly, but it's pretty overwhelming."

Placing my hand over my heart, I looked down at my chest. "I don't know. I didn't feel anything like that. I was confused, shocked, and disgusted. I wasn't jealous."

"You weren't?" I heard disappointment in her voice, and I looked up.

"I don't think so. Why would I be jealous?"

"I don't know. I thought maybe you felt something for him. I mean, the air is practically crackling between the two of you."

I couldn't feel. That was an absolute *no*. I couldn't let myself get attached or feel love, especially not for a man like Alessio.

Getting emotionally attached meant heartbreak. I had learned not to trust men. I couldn't. Because Alberto's evil smile was forever etched in my memory, ruining me for any other man.

"There's so much sexual tension between you

two. Don't even think of lying. It's so there," she continued, not noticing that I had shut down. "Do you feel anything for him?" She sounded far away. "Ayla?"

I blinked a couple of times and realized she was shaking me. "I'm sorry," I said.

"Are you okay?"

I stood up on shaky legs. "I don't feel so well. I think I'll go rest for a little while and then come back when it's time to serve lunch."

When she gave me a slow nod, I forced a smile before walking away.

I felt confused. I didn't know what to feel or how I felt. With my heart racing slightly, I went to my room feeling completely drained.

But when I arrived there, my eyes widened and I froze.

"Ayla," he said.

Alessio was sitting on my sofa, his ankle crossed over the opposite knee. He leaned back against the seat with ease, looking like he belonged there.

"You know, one thing I totally despise is when I'm talking to someone and they don't pay attention. You turned your back to me while I was talking earlier. That's very rude, kitten," he drawled in a lazy manner.

When he called me that, it made my heart squeeze.

And I absolutely hated it.

My stupid treacherous heart.

I didn't know what it was about Alessio, but I was curious about him. I was still scared. But under all the layers of fear, he intrigued me.

He was angry one minute but gentle the next. So many mixed signals, and they were all tugging at my broken heart.

It made me mad that I didn't understand, and I hated him for that. For making me *feel*.

"Come here," he ordered, crooking his finger.

I didn't move.

He sighed loudly and shook his head, a small smirk playing across his lips. Alessio slowly stood, taking all his time by fixing his suit before he walked toward me. No, he *stalked*. His steps were long, powerful, and confident.

"You know, I hate repeating myself, but for you, I find that I don't mind," he said. He stopped right in front of me, crowding my space like he always did. But this time, I had a fair advantage.

I wasn't blocked from behind, so I quickly took a step back, putting some distance between us. But then he took a step forward.

He never gives up, does he?

I took another step back. And as expected, he took another forward.

"Are we going to keep doing this? It's boring, kitten. Let's find something more interesting to do. What do you think?" he asked, his eyes twinkling deviously.

I shook my head, my hair falling in front of my face as I took another step back but this time I froze when I came in contact with the door.

Alessio laughed and came closer again until his body was pressing mine into the door. "See what happens when you try to escape?" He made a *tsk* sound, shaking his head with fake pity.

He leaned forward until his face was next to my right ear. His breath tickled my ear and the tiny hairs on my neck stood up straight. A shudder went through my body and I brought my hand up to his chest to push him away but instead, Alessio held my hand there, trapping me to him.

"But I'm loving this chase," he said into my neck. His voice caused me to freeze and I gasped. Alessio pulled away just enough to look into my eyes.

"Did you like what you saw?" he asked, smirking.

My eyes widened at the question and my heart dropped to my stomach. What kind of question was that? He was horrible.

"Let me go," I tried to say, but it sounded more like I was gurgling.

"Do you really want me to, kitten?" Alessio asked gruffly.

I nodded mutely because I didn't want to embarrass myself more than I already had.

"Say it, then."

"Let me…" But I never had a chance to finish my sentence.

Before the words were even out, Alessio slammed his lips against mine. Taking them possessively, roughly. He pushed me harder against the door and wrapped his arms around my waist, pulling me upward so that he had better access to my lips.

His rough kisses sent my senses into a chaotic overdrive. My mind went numb and I hung limply in his arms. Without thinking, my lips moved hesitantly over his, while he continued to devour mine. I felt hot. Too hot. I was burning.

I felt his hand on my thigh and he slowly hitched my dress up. When his hand came in contact with my bare thigh, I tore my lips away from his.

What was I doing? How could I behave in such a vulgar manner? How could I let a man like him affect me this way?

Our loud breathing filled the room. My chest heaved with each breath. Staring at his blue eyes, I trembled at the smoldering look he gave me.

I swallowed hard. *Get yourself together, Ayla. Don't let him affect you.*

I grasped the hand that was still touching my thigh and pushed it away from me. His eyes widened slightly in shock at my bold action and he raised an eyebrow in surprise.

"Don't touch me. I'm not like...those women," I said through my heavy breathing as I gasped each word.

"Like who?" he asked, sounding amused. He knew very well what I meant but as always, he loved torturing the answer out of me.

"Like that woman. I'm not like her. Don't treat me...like one," I squeaked, pushing at his chest again, but he was unmoving.

"You mean, you are not a whore?" he asked, his voice hard.

I flinched at the word and closed my eyes tightly as painful memories assailed me.

Look at her. Broken down, lying on the floor, our come dripping from her. Exactly like a whore.

That's what you are, Ayla. Never forget it. You hear me?

I felt a hand on my cheek. My mind was reeling as I was brought back into the present. I hated that word. Alberto called me that more than he said my name.

"Ayla, I never said you were one," I heard Alessio saying. His voice was surprisingly soft. "If I thought you were a whore, then I would have sent you to one of my prostitution rings. But I didn't, did I?"

I never said you were one.

His words kept repeating over and over in my head. He didn't think I was a whore. He didn't call me such cruel words.

My heart stuttered when his thumb caressed my cheek. "Okay?"

I didn't answer.

He sighed and then slid his hand down until it rested at the base of my neck. "Fine, I won't touch you," he declared, moving his hand away from my neck.

I was shocked at his admission and stared at him suspiciously.

"I won't touch you. Not until you ask me to," he clarified, slightly bending his knees so that we were at eye level.

Well, that wouldn't happen. Ever. Which meant he would never touch me. My muscles relaxed in relief, but I was still filled with suspicion.

For now, I would take him at his word.

"Okay?"

I nodded and then swallowed hard against the lump in my throat. Were we done? I hoped we were, because if he kept playing with my mind like that, I would break down. And I couldn't let that happen.

I nodded again.

A small laugh rumbled from his chest. He moved against me, and that was when I realized his body was still plastered against mine.

I looked down and then back up at his face. He was staring at me amusingly. Clearing my throat, I tried to push him again and this time he slightly moved away. But he was still crowding my space, still trapping me against the door with his body.

"You...you said you wouldn't touch me," I stammered. Closing my mouth with a snap, I took a deep breath in and then continued. "But you are touching me right now."

"Am I?"

Was that even a question? His body was practically covering mine.

"You are," I said.

"Okay, then." Alessio stepped away from me and glided his fingers through his hair, ruffling it in the process.

He was about to say something but his phone rang. His forehead creased in frustration and he quickly pulled his phone from his pocket. With his eyes still on me, he answered the call.

"Yeah?" He was silent for a few seconds. "Okay. I'm coming," he said, his voice cold and deadly. Alessio put his phone away and walked toward me. I quickly stepped away from the door to give him access. I kept my head down, refusing to look at him.

I heard the door open but there was no sound of it closing. Confused, I was about to turn around when I felt a hot breath at the back of my neck. My body froze in panic. When I heard Alessio's voice, my muscles slightly relaxed.

"I won't touch you. Not until you *beg* me to."

His words made me tense. And my heartbeat quickened.

With that, I heard him walk away again and the door closed behind him.

Bringing a shaky hand to my chest, I breathed deeply.

Beg him?

Scoffing at his assumption, I walked over to my bed and laid down on my back. That was never going to happen.

Chapter 19

Alessio (seven years old)

My mommy sat on the big sofa chair with a book on her big round belly. She looked so comfortable and she had a small smile on her face. From where I was sitting on the floor, while arranging my puzzles, I saw her slowly rubbing circles over her stomach.

My baby sister was in there. Papa and Mommy called her a princess. Why didn't they call me a prince? I wanted to be a prince!

But Mommy called me her sweet boy, so that was okay.

"Mommy, can I feel the baby?" I asked softly. Mommy looked up with eyes the same color as mine. She smiled.

"Of course, baby. Come here." She motioned for me to get up as she placed the book on the small table beside her.

I quickly got up and ran to her. Mommy patted her lap and I climbed up and sat down on her lap, nestling into her chest. She took my hand and placed it on her round belly. As soon as my palm made contact with her stomach, I felt a hard kick. My eyes widened and I sucked in a shocked breath.

"She kicks hard," I whispered.

"You used to kick harder," Mommy replied, laughing.

"Really?" I looked up at her with wide eyes.

She nodded and made a humming sound. "You were a very strong baby."

"I like being strong!" The baby kicked again and I smiled. I couldn't wait to see my baby sister. "Mommy, I will always protect princess!" I said, looking at her stomach in awe. Papa always said that as her big brother, I had to protect her. And I vowed I would.

I won't ever let anything happen to princess, I thought as I rubbed my small hand over Mommy's round stomach.

Mommy placed a kiss on my temple and started humming some songs. She liked playing the piano and she was always humming. That would be our daily routine. Before going to sleep, she would play the piano for some time while humming. Most times, I would fall asleep on the sofa, listening to her play.

We sat there for a while and then I heard a knock on the door. Looking up quickly, I saw Papa leaning against the door, looking at Mommy and me with an amused smile on his face.

"Papa!" I exclaimed loudly, quickly jumping off Mommy's lap and running into his open arms. He pulled me up and hugged me tight to his body. I missed him so much. He had been gone for a few

days, but now he was back.

"Hey there, my boy. How are you?" he asked.

"I'm good. I was feeling princess moving."

"Oh, really? I want to feel too," he said with a small laugh, walking us back toward where Mommy was sitting. He stopped beside the couch and smiled down at her. Mommy had a big smile on her face, and she looked peaceful as she stared at Papa. He placed a hand on her stomach and asked, "How is our princess?"

"She is kicking a lot lately," Mommy said, placing her hand over his.

Papa let me down and then leaned forward, kissing Mommy on the lips. They kissed for some time, totally forgetting about me. I crossed my arms over my chest and huffed. They always did that.

Papa pulled away but then pressed his forehead against Mommy's. "I missed you, Angel," he whispered.

Angel. That was what Papa called Mommy. But I never understood why.

Moving forward, I stood on the other side of Mommy. "Papa, why do you call Mommy 'angel'?"

They pulled away and stared at me. Papa let out a small laugh while Mommy's cheeks turned red. He crouched down in front of me. "What is an angel?" he asked.

I felt my forehead crease in confusion and then shrugged. "Isn't an angel someone with wings? God's messenger. They are nice people. They are supposed to help others."

"Correct. But an angel is also someone who is sweet, kind, caring, and calm. The most beautiful

woman on the planet. Someone who is amazing in every way. An Angel is the girl who makes your heart beat faster when she walks into the room. The girl you need wherever you go. The girl who makes you want to be better. An angel is someone who is your rock. The person who you love with your entire heart. The person who you can't see yourself living without."

I stared at Papa in awe. He was a man of few words. I never expected him to give me such an explanation. And while he was talking, he stared at Mommy, his eyes shining with emotions that I couldn't understand.

"Oh," I mumbled quietly. I didn't know what to say. I heard him chuckle as I looked down. Mommy laughed softly too. I felt a hand on my arm and looked up to see Mommy pulling me toward her. I stood in front of her and she ran her fingers through my hair.

"And one day, you will find your angel," she whispered. My eyebrows furrowed in confusion and I quickly shook my head.

"But you are my angel, Mommy."

She gasped and then smiled. "My sweet boy." Shaking her head, she placed a kiss on my forehead. "No, baby, I'm not your angel. Your angel is waiting for you somewhere." She pulled back and palmed my cheek. "And when you do find her, don't ever let her go."

"Because if you lose her, then you will forever be incomplete," Papa added.

"Will she be like you, Mommy?" I asked, thinking about my angel. What would she look like?

Would she be as beautiful as Mommy and as sweet as her?

"Oh, baby, she might be better than me," she said, laughing.

"Impossible," Papa mumbled under his breath.

"Hush, Lyov," Mommy scolded, swatting his arm playfully.

He grumbled something that I couldn't understand and then stood up. He pulled Mommy off the couch and then sat down, pulling her onto his lap. He nuzzled her neck and I heard her giggle.

I stared at them, shaking my head with a sigh. I had been forgotten again.

I went back to my puzzles. Mommy and Papa were talking quietly while I played. I didn't know how long we stayed like that but the phone started ringing after some time. I looked up and saw Papa answering the call.

He looked frustrated and I heard him growl angrily. After a few seconds of listening to the other person from the line, he hung up.

"What's wrong?" Mommy asked, rubbing his chest soothingly.

"I have to take care of some stuff," he said, shaking his head.

"Oh, okay then," Mommy murmured, and then clumsily got off Papa's lap. They both stood up and Papa wrapped his arms around her, hugging her as best he could with her big stomach in the way. He leaned down and kissed her again. A long, deep kiss.

When he leaned back, I heard him whisper, "Love you, Angel."

"I love you too, Lyov," she whispered back, her voice a little hoarse. Was she crying?

My heart twisted a little. I didn't want her to cry. Papa placed a kiss on her forehead and then turned to me. "Alessio, come here."

I quickly got up and went to him. He crouched down and then stared into my eyes. "I have to go for a while," he said.

My eyebrows furrowed in confusion. "Again?"

"Yes. While I'm gone, I want you to be a good boy and take care of your mommy and princess, okay?"

I nodded my head. I was a big boy now. "Yes. I will."

"Good," he said, placing a kiss on my forehead and standing up. He nodded at Mommy and then walked away.

I heard her sigh. She sat back down and rubbed her eyes. "Mommy, why does Papa have to go away so much?"

"It's his work, baby. Your papa is a very busy man. He has a lot to do."

I went to Mommy and climbed on her lap again. Laying my head on her shoulder sleepily, I sighed. "I want to be like Papa. He is so strong. And everyone listens to him. I want to be tough like him."

Mommy shook her head. "No, Alessio. You aren't like your papa." She palmed both of my cheeks and then continued. "You are not ready to fight the world. You are my sweet boy. My sweet gentle boy. And I want you to stay just like this." Placing a kiss on my forehead, she whispered, "Let your papa do the fighting."

I didn't say anything else. Mommy always knew how to make me feel special. I would always be her sweet boy. That would never change.

Nodding my head, I closed my eyes. Mommy was rubbing my back soothingly, and in no time, I had fallen sleep. And my dream was riddled with a black-haired angel. She had green eyes.

I didn't know this would be the last time that I had a peaceful sleep. Our lives would change forever.

***

10 years old

I walked into the cold basement, closing the door behind me quietly so that nobody heard me. A man was strapped to the chair in the middle of the room. His face and clothes were bloody. He was sagging against the chair and from where I was standing, I could hear his whimpers of pain.

Looking at him, I felt red hot anger coursing through my body. Murderous anger.

Kill. Kill him. Spill his blood. Make him pay, my mind screamed as my body started to shake with the force of my fury.

He was one of them. An Abandonato. The Italians. I still remember his face from that night. His laughing face as he tortured my mother with the others.

Walking forward purposely, I came to stand in front of him. He looked up, and if possible, his swollen eyes widened.

He opened his mouth to say something but only a gurgling sound came out through the gag. My hands tightened in a fist and I punched him hard in the face, his nose making a crunching sound as my knuckles came in contact with his face.

He screamed and I laughed.

His pain made me feel good. My heart soared, but I needed more. I needed his blood. I needed to see him suffering.

I needed to kill him.

Only then would I be satisfied.

Walking to the table at the back of the room, I looked at all the weapons laid out. There were so many. Different style. Big and small. I had never been to the basement before, but I heard the rumors around the mansion.

Taking the big knife with the spiral blade, I walked back toward the man. The man I loathed with all my being.

He whimpered in fear and started to shake his head and tried to move away, but he couldn't. He was strapped to the chair at my mercy.

Actually, I wasn't going to show him mercy. Mercy was no longer in my vocabulary.

Holding the knife tightly in my hand, I pressed it hard against his cheek. Pulling it down, I made a big gash. He tried to scream again.

I stared at the blood and my heart pumped faster. Adrenaline filled me and my mind begged me. More. More. More.

I made another gash on his other cheek. And then on his arms. Big, long, deep cuts. Blood was *everywhere. Then on his chest. So deep that I could see his bones.*

He couldn't move anymore. His head was hanging down as he bled. I could see that he was quickly losing consciousness.

But I wasn't done yet.

He was still alive.

His heart was still beating while my mother's was not.

He needed to die. He needed to feel the pain.

Roaring with anger, I pulled the knife back and then plunged it deep into his heart, twisting it painfully. Mercilessly.

His head snapped back and he thrashed against the chair. His painful eyes started to go dull, slowly losing all signs of life.

A few seconds later, he was no longer breathing. His dead eyes were opened, staring at me.

I pulled the knife back from his chest and looked down. My hands were covered in blood. There was not even an inch of my skin that was clean. Blood. It was everywhere. On me. On my clothes. It blinded me.

I gasped as I realized what I had just done. But I didn't feel any remorse. I felt alleviated and satisfied.

But not full satisfaction. The others still needed to pay.

And I was going to find all of them, one by one, and I was going to kill them all.

I heard the door open behind me with a bang. I swiveled around to see my father running in with a few of his men. Their eyes went wide at the sight of me and I heard my father's shocked gasp.

"Alessio!" he screamed, running toward me. He stopped in front of me and snatched the knife away, throwing it on the floor next to the bloody dead man.

"What have you done? Oh, Alessio, what have you done?"

I stared into his eyes. "I will avenge my mother," I said, my voice scratchy.

My father's eyes widened in surprise and he stared at me in complete shock. I understood why he was in shock. That was the first time I had uttered any words in three years. Since that night when everything changed. The night that I lost everything.

"I vow to kill all of them. Every single Abandonato," I said. I couldn't recognize my voice. It sounded so foreign even to my ears. My father didn't say anything at first. After a few seconds, he stood up tall and his expression changed.

"Okay," he replied, his voice hard and deadly cold. Emotionless.

With that, I walked away. I didn't look at his men, but I kept my eyes forward, my shoulders squared with purpose and my chin held high.

This was my life now.

My mother had been wrong.

I was no longer her sweet, gentle, quiet boy.

I was a monster.

As I walked out of the room and into the dark corridor, I quickly pushed the thought of "my angel" from my mind.

Angels didn't exist.

I didn't have an angel, for a monster could never

have an angel.

***

Present Day

I woke up with a start, the memories still flashing in my head. They were painful and I quickly buried them deep inside me. I didn't have time for weakness. I couldn't think about the past.

I didn't know why I had that dream—why the past came crashing back, but it made me want to rage.

Closing my eyes, I calmed down. I locked away my feelings and the memories.

No weakness.

Chapter 20

Ayla

I was almost half asleep when I heard a knock on my door. My eyes snapped open and I sat up with a start, my heart racing.

"Ayla?" I heard Maddie's voice on the other side of the door.

I closed my eyes in relief and brought my hand up to my chest, trying to calm my rapidly beating heart.

"Yeah. I'm coming," I called out, my voice heavy with sleep.

"Okay. Hurry. It's almost time for lunch."

I bounced out of bed and quickly fixed my dress and hair.

Opening the door of my bedroom wide, I saw Maddie leaning against the door. She smiled when she saw me. "Hey there, sleepyhead."

I smiled and shut the door.

"Let's go. Mom is waiting for us," Maddie said as she grabbed my arm and started pulling me down the hall.

As we headed for the stairs, I didn't see Alessio or his men anywhere.

Viktor, Nikolay, Phoenix, and Artur were always with him wherever he went. They were his most trusted associates.

Artur was the only one who seemed friendly. Maybe I thought so because Maddie was with him.

Nikolay always glared at everyone. I didn't think he even knew how to smile. The only time I heard him talk nicely was with Lena, probably because she is the mother of house. Nobody talked harshly to her or even tried to be rude. Even Alessio.

As Maddie and I stepped off the last stair, I saw Alessio coming in, followed by his men.

They were whispering quietly. When Alessio made eye contact with me, his mouth froze. He stared at me, his eyes unflinching as he took me in.

And then, his lips twitched in that smirk that I hated.

Looking away, I followed Maddie to the kitchen. *Time to work.*

Food was served and I was about to retreat back into the kitchen when someone stopped us.

"You and Maddie stay back this time," said one of the other maids, a girl named Lila. For every meal, two of us had to stay back and serve if the men needed any help. For the last two days, Maddie and I had escaped that duty.

"Okay," I said.

Maddie scowled. She hated it, and I hated it too. Only because I had to be where Alessio was.

"Ayla, pass me the garlic bread." Alessio's

demanding voice penetrated my mind. My head snapped up and I looked at him, confused.

"Huh?"

"I said pass me the bread," he repeated, sounding annoyed. Maddie was standing closer to it.

I looked back at Alessio, but he was staring at me expectantly. He raised an eyebrow when I didn't move. Turning my head, I swallowed and then nodded at Maddie. Her eyes widened in amusement.

"Maddie, can you please give Alessio the bread? You are closer," I said as softly as I could, my voice quiet.

Her mouth fell open in shock, and from the corner of my eyes I saw all the men staring at me with amused expressions. I couldn't believe it either. I had just gone against Alessio and did it in front of his men.

As soon as the words were out of my mouth, I regretted it.

Maddie's mouth snapped shut and she chuckled under her breath. Before I could change my mind, she grabbed the basket and walked over to Alessio at the other end of the table. Placing it in front of him, she said, sounding almost sarcastic, "There you go, Alessio. Your hot, crispy, buttery garlic bread. Enjoy."

Alessio took his eyes off me and glared at Maddie. She smiled wide and then sashayed away.

She was playing with fire but she knew that Alessio wouldn't do or say anything to her. Alessio, Viktor, and Maddie were close when they were little. They grew up together, sisters and brothers from another mother.

172

Maddie told me stories about how they would always play together and how she would always follow them around and get in trouble together.

I snapped out of my thoughts when I felt someone poking me. Turning my head to the side, I saw Maddie standing next to me. "You are playing with fire, babe. Don't poke the beast or you won't be able to deal with it," she whispered in my ear before walking away and standing behind Artur.

I sighed, my shoulders slumping in defeat. She was right. I didn't know what came over me.

Standing there, I shifted on my feet a couple of times, suddenly growing nervous when I noticed their attention on me. I saw Viktor smirking, and then he went back to eating. When Alessio cleared his throat, everyone looked away.

I kept my focus away from Alessio, but I still felt his gaze on me. As each minute passed, my hands grew colder and my insides shook with tension.

"Ayla, can you bring me the rice?" he asked.

I knew it. I just knew it. I knew he was going to do this.

I looked up and saw that his eyes were twinkling with mirth and his right eyebrow was raised in challenge. I looked down and saw that the bowl was right next to me.

Releasing a long breath, I took the bowl of rice in my hand and slowly walked toward him. His eyes were on me the whole time and his smirk was back. He licked his lips.

When I stopped next to him, I placed the bowl down but he didn't move. Alessio looked up at me expectantly and then nodded toward the rice.

Sighing, I grabbed the spoon and put some rice on his plate. Something touched my leg, and I jumped in fright and then looked down.

Alessio had moved his leg closer and now his thigh was touching mine.

I gripped the spoon harder before putting it back in the bowl and quickly stepping away.

"Thank you, Ayla," he said, his voice smooth.

Feeling slightly flustered, I nodded and then walked away. The rest of lunch went smoothly. Alessio didn't call me again and he didn't look at me.

When everyone dispersed, I could finally breathe normally.

"Woah, babe. That was…" Maddie began. "Intense."

I didn't disagree.

***

I was balancing the last tray in my hand, as I quickly swiped the dining table with the other.

I straightened up and walked away from the table. I glanced down at my dress and noticed the little dirty spot.

I was still looking down when I crashed into a hard wall of muscles. My eyes widened when I felt myself falling backward.

I yelled out, trying to gain my footing again, but I was quickly going down. Closing my eyes tightly, I waited for my body to come in contact with the ground. But it never did.

Instead, an arm wrapped around my waist,

holding me still. With my heart in my throat, I opened my eyes.

Alessio.

My body was dipped backward but he was holding me firmly to his chest.

"Careful there. You need to watch where you are going," he said.

My heart stuttered and a shiver went through my body at his voice. Biting on my lips nervously, I nodded my head. My brain was a mess whenever he was near and no matter how hard I tried to understand why, I couldn't.

I looked at his arm around me and then remembered what he said in my room. My forehead creased in confusion. "You aren't supposed to touch me," I said.

He just saved me from falling flat on my butt and I didn't even thank him.

Alessio's chest rumbled with laughter and I saw his eyes twinkling mischievously. Oh no. I didn't like that look.

"Oops," he said.

And then I was on the floor. The tray fell out of my hand and crashed.

"Ow," I said when my hips hit the tiles painfully.

Holding the aching part, I looked up at Alessio in shock.

"My bad. I forgot," he said, his lips pulling up into a smirk.

He brought his hands up to his shoulders in mock surrender, as if showing me that he wasn't touching me anymore.

Jerk. An absolute jerk.

He gave me a nod and then walked away, leaving me baffled on the floor. He could have at least pulled me up straight, instead of just dropping me.

But that wasn't the case.

Grabbing the tray in my hand, I got up but then winced at the soreness in my hips. I was pretty sure it was going to bruise tomorrow. I glanced at Alessio's retreating back and huffed in frustration.

When I walked into the kitchen, I saw Maddie filling the dishwasher. She turned around and frowned at my sour look. "What's wrong?"

"Is Alessio always this frustrating?" I asked, placing the tray on the counter.

"You just realized that now?" She let out a laugh. "Yes, he is."

I was still rubbing my hips and Maddie noticed. She pointed at my hand and asked, "So what happened?"

Releasing a heavy and tired sigh, I sank down on the stool. "It's…a long story."

"Does it involve Alessio?"

I nodded and her lips stretched in a wide, excited smile. Running toward me, she pulled another stool and sat down in front of me. "Okay. We have plenty of time. Hurry. Tell me."

Starting from the beginning was the best option. Only then would it make sense. "It started on the first day that I came here."

I told about how Alessio threatened to shoot me if I didn't tell him who I was. I told her about Alessio's options. I also told her about the kiss and the orgasm he gave me. And then I told her about

176

this morning.

Maddie had interrupted me a lot and freaked out tons of times. "Damn…just damn…what? I don't…you…how….How could you not tell me this before?" Grabbing my shoulders, she shook me. "Ayla, this is big. Like big. You can't keep something like that from me! Oh my God, he kissed you? Gave you an orgasm? Oh my God!"

"Maddie, calm down," I said, pushing her away. She sat back down on her stool but her knees were bouncing.

"Okay, I'm calm," she said and then paused. A few seconds passed and then she shook her head. "No. I'm not."

"Maddie, it was nothing. He was rude. I can't believe he would do that, but he promised he won't touch me again. So that's good, right?"

Maddie stared at me blankly and then burst out laughing. "You are funny. You really think he is not going to touch you? Babe, he might not touch you, but he will find other ways. And he will most definitely find ways to make you beg for him. What can I say? He is very resourceful."

"This does not make me feel any better," I said, closing my eyes and rubbing my forehead in slight agitation. This man would drive me crazy.

"Sorry, babe. It's the truth. He is interested in you and he isn't giving up. When he wants something, he takes it. Doesn't matter how hard it is to get or if something is in his way. In his book, nothing is impossible."

At her words, my heart stumbled and I felt panic coursing through my body. "So, you are saying he isn't giving up?"

"Nope."

"Maddie, I don't want him. Why can't he understand that? I hate it." I felt tears at the backs of my eyes and my nose started to tingle. Why was I crying?

"Ayla, sorry for making it worse."

"No. I would rather hear the truth. But I just don't know." Swiping my tears away, I closed my eyes tightly. Taking a deep breath, I counted to ten before opening my eyes again. "Sorry. I have been getting emotional on you a lot."

"It's okay. I got this, babe."

"Thank you."

"No problem. Okay. Get your ass up. We got some cleaning to do before dinner."

Chapter 21

Night had fallen and almost everyone had gone to bed. The house was silent and peaceful.

I lazily climbed on the bed and as soon as my head hit the pillow, my eyes closed and I was already half asleep.

Burrowing deeper under my cover, I sighed in contentment as my muscles started relax and sleep took over my body and mind.

I was bent over his desk, my dress pulled up to my hips so that my ass was completely bare to him. I was never allowed to wear panties. He said it was for easy access.

He said he wanted to be able to take me whenever or wherever he wanted. And if I disobeyed, I would be severely punished. I had learned in the most painful way that I shouldn't go against him.

I felt his rough, cold hand running over my bare cheeks. And then a hard slap fell on one side, so hard that I flinched and tears quickly built up in my

179

eyes.

A second slap fell on the other side. Just as hard.

"I love your ass like this. All red from my palm. So beautiful," he murmured huskily in my ears.

I didn't say anything. I didn't move. I wasn't allowed to do either.

I heard him unzipping his slacks from behind me. I sucked in a deep breath as fear coursed through my body. I knew what was coming next.

He nestled himself between my thighs and when I felt his tip at my entrance, I shuddered in disgust. In panic. Pain. In absolute crippling fear.

I closed my eyes, my tears silently flowing down my cheeks. I bit down on the inside of my cheek to keep myself from crying out in pain when he slammed into me, burying himself to the hilt.

My inside was burning. It felt like I was being cut open from the inside.

His groans of pleasure filled my ears as I was stripped of my purity and dignity. Over and over again. Every single day.

He fucked me. Mercilessly. Painfully. Ruthlessly.

And all the while, two of his men were watching.

I heard their groans of pleasure too. Opening my eyes, I saw that they were rubbing themselves, their eyes filled with lust as they stared at me.

I couldn't take it anymore. Humiliated in the worst way possible, I closed my eyes again and sank deeper into the darkness.

Alberto came with a groan and he slipped out of my body. I felt his come run down my thighs but stayed still as I waited for his next order.

"My fiancée is so beautiful, isn't she?" Alberto

said.

"Fuck yeah, boss. Sexiest woman I have ever seen," one of the men replied.

"Yeah, boss. I gotta agree. You got yourself one pretty lady," the other man added.

"Hmm." Alberto hummed while running his palm over my ass. His fingers dug into my skin and I winced. "I share, you know," he said.

My eyes snapped open and my heart dropped to the bottom of my stomach.

No. No. Please God. No.

"Do you want to fuck her?" he asked, his voice cold as always.

No. No. Please. Say no. Please.

"Yeah, but only if you allow us," one of the men said.

"Well, what are you waiting for? Come here, then." I felt Alberto move away and I saw the two men standing up, walking toward me, their eyes filled with lust and hunger.

They walked around the table and out of my vision. I felt them standing behind me and Alberto came to stand in front of me. He grabbed my chin and pulled my head upward so that I was looking into his eyes.

"You will keep your eyes on me as they fuck you. And you will take it like a good girl," he hissed in my face. His nails bit into my chin and I winced.

Leaving my chin, he grabbed both of my arms and pulled them forward, holding me still. My heart cracked open in a million pieces when I felt one of them at my entrance.

My whole body was shaking violently and I

quickly went numb. The first man slammed into me. Over and over again. He came with a roar. And then the second man took his turn.

With each thrust, I lost a piece of myself. With each groan, I lost the pieces of my shattered heart. With each moan, I lost a piece of my soul.

I no longer felt anything. I was just an empty shell. It felt like there was a big hole in my chest and my stomach twisted painfully when the man finished inside of me. My throat closed up and before I could stop myself, I vomited on the table.

Alberto laughed and then pulled out his gun and pointed it behind me. Closing my eyes, I let my head fall on the table, my body broken, ravaged and limp. I silently begged for mercy.

I heard two gunshots.

My eyes snapped open and I saw blood.

They were dead.

I screamed.

My screams filled my ears as I sobbed. My cries were filled with pain and fear.

Please. No more. I can't take it. No more. Please.

I woke up crying and shaking. My ears were still ringing from the screams in my nightmare. I couldn't breathe. The pressure in my heart was painful. I gasped and then sucked in a deep breath, but choked instead.

My body shook violently and I gagged several times. My night dress was soaked with my sweat. My skin was itching. It felt like thousands of ants were moving underneath them. I scratched and scratched.

But I saw blood. I was covered in blood.

No. No. No.

Grabbing my head, I pulled at my hair. My scalp hurt and burned. My vision blurred with tears and dizziness filled me.

I was burning.

I was dying.

My heart was beating so hard in my chest that my rib cage was hurting. My stomach churned as my legs spasmed.

Pushing the comforter away with shaky hands, I stumbled out of bed and fell on the ground. My legs couldn't hold me. I looked at my hands and saw they were clean. No blood.

Gasping, I shook my head and closed my eyes. I gritted my teeth as a searing pain went through my skull.

My breathing was coming out in hard pants and my chest was squeezed so tightly I couldn't take in a breath. Opening my eyes, I looked down at my hands to see blood again.

Blood. *Their* blood.

I rubbed my hands over my dress, trying to get rid of it. I dry heaved, my body bending forward painfully. Snot ran down my face and tears were streaming down my cheeks as I cried, falling down on the floor.

I wanted to die. I couldn't take it anymore.

The pain.

I couldn't live with it anymore.

I wanted peace.

I needed peace.

Please, I begged. To whoever was listening. I begged. *Please.*

I didn't know what came over me, but I started crawling toward my door. My harsh gasps filled the room, and through blurry vision, I made it to the door. I pulled myself upward and opened it. Swallowing hard, I stumbled outside and fell down. My legs wouldn't hold me up.

I dragged myself to the bedroom down the hall. My sniffles filled the hallway and tears continuously ran down my cheeks.

Peace.

Just for one moment.

I needed it.

I needed to breathe.

When I reached the door that I wanted, I slumped against it. My heart clenched tight. I wheezed, my lungs fighting against the air I was taking. I choked on my breath as I tried to stand up. Holding onto the door, I dragged myself up and collapsed against it.

"*Alessio*," I whispered, my eyes rolling back in my head as I started to lose consciousness.

Peace.

Alessio brought peace.

And I needed it.

My hand slapped against the door. I could barely move my hands but I tried.

Just when I was about to give up and fall down, letting my impending death take over my body, the door opened and I fell forward. Right into his arms.

Peace.

Clenching his shirt in my fist, I cried.

"Make…it…stop. *Please*. I can't…take…it."
I sobbed.
"Make it stop."

Chapter 22

Alessio

I was just about to the turn off the lights when I heard a light knock on the door. My forehead creased in confusion as I stood up straight and stared at the door. I heard the tap again.

It was late. Who could it be?

I waited for the knock again, but it didn't come. Instead, I heard something rustling against the door. Quickly walking toward it, I grabbed the knob and opened the door wide.

Before I could blink or see who it was, someone tumbled forward into my arms. My eyes widened. Ayla.

She was trembling from head to toe, her whole body shaking so violently that she could barely keep herself up. I wrapped my arms around her waist and held her to my body.

Her fingers grasped my shirt in a death grip, her nails digging into my skin. She was crying. Her body shook with her sobs and she buried her face in chest.

My mind was filled with confusion and unanswered questions as I held her limp body in my arms. She gasped and choked on her cries.

"Make…it…stop. Please. I can't take it," she cried into my chest.

I froze and my heart stuttered.

"Make it stop."

"Ayla?" When I started to push away so I could see her face, she cried harder and gripped my shirt tighter, refusing to budge.

"Please. Please. Make it stop. I can't…I can't…breathe. I can't…take…it…anymore."

"Ayla, what are you talking about?" She wasn't making any sense and I didn't know how to react to this.

What was she talking about? I never would've expected her to come to me this way.

She released her hold on my shirt and went completely limp in my arms. Her legs gave out, and if it hadn't been for my arms around her, she would have fallen on the floor.

"Shit." I lifted her into my arms, cradling her to my chest. I carried her to my bed and placed her on the mattress. Kneeling in front of her, I took her chin in my hand and made her look at me. Ayla refused to open her eyes. She whimpered and brought her hands to her chest, curling into herself. She was panting for air and covered in sweat. Her hair was sticking to her forehead and her cheeks were wet with tears.

She trembled, and when my fingers tightened on her chin, she cowered backward and let out a sharp cry.

My eyes widened in shock and I quickly released her. "Fuck. I'm not going to hurt you."

She whimpered in response.

"Ayla, talk to me. What's going on?" I coaxed. She brought her hands up to her head and twisted her fingers around her hair, then shook her head multiple times and started crying again.

"It hurts. It hurts so much. Please."

She kept repeating over and over again.

Did she have a nightmare?

"Ayla—"

Her eyes snapped open, wide with panic and fright, and she heaved forward.

So much pain. Her eyes were filled with so much pain. My heart constricted at the sight.

Ayla looked down at her arms and her face scrunched up in panic. "No. No. No," she mumbled under her breath.

She started rocking back and forth and her fingers were scratching at her arms, turning the skin bright red with her nails. They left long red lines, and if she continued that way, she would draw blood.

"Look. Look," she cried, pushing her arms into my face. "Blood. I'm covered in blood…"

What the fuck?

"Ayla, you aren't covered in blood," I soothed, taking her arm in my hand and gently rubbing my thumb over the skin.

"No!" she wailed, snatching her arms away. "Look! Blood. Make it stop," Ayla whispered, looking up at me with tearful eyes. The look she gave me broke my heart. I felt a searing pain pass through my chest at her agony. "You can…make…it…stop. Please," she gasped between shallow breaths, staring at me expectantly. She was *begging* me with her eyes.

But she wasn't making any sense and I couldn't understand the pain filling my chest.

When I didn't answer, I saw her eyes turn empty. I had seen a lot of stares like that. Every time I killed, I stared into lifeless eyes, and hers looked just like that.

Even though Ayla was breathing, alive, her eyes were dead.

Her shoulders sagged and she slowly slid off the bed until her knees hit the floor in front of me. She closed her eyes and pulled her legs up to her chest, wrapping her arms around them.

Sitting there, she looked like a lost child. She looked like someone who was utterly broken with no hope.

"Ayla." I swallowed hard against the heavy lump in my throat.

She rocked back and forth and I heard her mumbling something under her breath.

Leaning closer with my heart hammering wildly against my ribcage, I tried to listen to what she was saying. And what I heard took my breath away.

"Make it stop. Make it go away. No more blood. Make it go away."

"Ayla, shit!" I swore loudly, pulling away as I ran my fingers through my hair in frustration.

She cowered in fear from my outburst and pulled her legs closer to her body, as if she was protecting herself from me. When I moved closer, she flinched and her eyes went wide as she waited for my next movement.

She was having a mental breakdown. I had witnessed men go through the same thing after their first kill.

I placed my hands out, palms facing her. "I'm not going to hurt you," I said, moving slowly closer so that I wouldn't scare her.

She watched my every movement but never responded, her eyes just as bleak and spiritless as before. When both our knees touched, she glanced down and I saw her swallowing hard.

"Ayla," I whispered, trying to bring her attention back to my face. "Ayla," I said a second time.

She slowly shifted and stared at me apprehensively.

"Is there still blood on you?" I asked, nodding toward her arms. She looked down and I saw a single tear escape from the corner of her left eye. She continued to stare at her arms and nodded slowly.

"Please," she whispered.

"Ayla, look at me, "I said. She did as she was told. When her eyes met mine, I continued, "We are going to get rid of the blood, okay? We will wash you up and then there won't be any more blood, okay?"

Her eyebrows furrowed in confusion and she looked back down at her arms. She moved her hands up and down the length of her arms. She looked lost in her thoughts.

"Ayla," I said again. She didn't look up but she

did stop rubbing her arms, so I knew she heard me. "I'm going to touch you. Are you okay with that?" I asked, bending my head down so that I was peering into her green eyes.

She didn't answer. No words were spoken. I placed my hand on my knee and waited for a few seconds.

When she didn't flinch or move away, I moved closer and wrapped an arm behind her back and the other under her knees. I quickly stood up with her cradled to my chest and I heard her shocked gasp.

"Shhh. It's okay. I've got you," I whispered against her hair, walking to my bathroom. Ayla slowly brought a hand up and placed it on my chest. Against my own accord, my arms tightened around her.

Walking over to the tub, I placed her down on the edge. I came to stand in front of her. She was looking up at me, her eyes filled with confusion and wonder.

Half of her face was covered with her hair and she was shivering. Her arms were placed on her lap but I noticed her fingers scratching at the skin. She was doing it mindlessly.

Leaning forward, I pried her fingers away from her arms. "Don't do that," I said softly, my voice coming out a little gruffly.

She kept her eyes on me when I moved back. Her arms were limp on her lap and she sat there frozen. I gave her a small nod before walking toward the sink. Grabbing the small white towel in my hand, I wet it with hot water and then squeezed the excess water out.

She watched my every movement silently but attentively. Stopping in front of her, I knelt down and took her right hand in mine. I looked up and our eyes met. My heart stumbled at the torment I saw there. But that wasn't all.

I saw trust in the depths of her vivid forest-green eyes. Ayla was waiting for me to take her pain away.

Keeping my eyes on hers, I gently moved the towel over her arm. She frowned but didn't look down. I saw her wince a little as I rubbed the towel over her skin.

I continued to *clean* her arm, and with every rub of the towel, Ayla's tense shoulders started to relax. Not once did she look away from me, not even when I began to clean her other arm.

Our eyes stayed fixated on each other as I brought her peace. Her lifeless eyes, which were staring at me with fright before, now watched me with wonder.

When I was done, I swallowed against the emotions that choked me. My lips parted but no words came out. After clearing my throat several times, I said, "Look. There's no blood now."

Ayla's head snapped down and she gasped, her eyes widening with shock. She brought her arms up and I saw tears building in her eyes, making her eyes glassy.

"No blood," she whispered hoarsely. Her voice was scratchy from crying. "There's no blood." She rubbed her thumb over the length of her arms.

She blinked and the tears that had built up in her eyes fell down her rosy and already tear-streaked cheeks.

Before I could stop myself, I brought my hand up and brushed my thumb over her soft cheeks, gently swiping her tears away.

She tore her gaze away from her arm and looked at me again. Ayla swallowed hard multiples times and I realized that she was struggling to find words, so she just stared at me speechlessly.

My hand was still cupping her cheeks, so I moved it slightly upward and brushed her hair out of her face. I brought the towel up and rubbed it over her forehead and cheeks. Her shoulders sagged in relief and she closed her eyes, a sigh of contentment escaping her lips.

Fuck. What the hell is wrong with me? I'm acting like a fucking pussy. I quickly took my hands away when I realized what I was doing.

Shaking my head, I stood up and Ayla blinked in surprise. She cocked her head to the side in question but didn't say anything.

"You look better," I said.

She licked her dry lips but still looked slightly confused. She was still coming down from her panic attack, so she wouldn't completely understand what was going on.

I sighed and took her hands in mine, pulling her upward. She stumbled forward and I pulled her up to my chest again before walking out of my bathroom. Ayla laid her head on my shoulder with a sigh.

Stopping in front of my bed, I placed her down and pulled the covers away. She moved under the black comforter and laid down. I tugged it around her body and her eyes started to close sleepily.

Standing up straight, I looked down at Ayla. She looked so innocent lying there. So fragile and vulnerable.

I couldn't wrap my head around what just happened. Did she have a nightmare? Or was it a memory haunting her?

I didn't know anything about Ayla. Her identity. Her truth. Her past. Nothing. And I was intrigued. It made me want to uncover her hidden truth.

She sighed sleepily, and when I looked down, she blinked up at me, a small sleepy smile playing across her lips.

I started to walk away but a sudden cry of panic stopped me dead in my tracks.

Quickly swiveling around with my heart in my throat, I saw her sitting up on my bed. Her eyes were wide with terror and indescribable panic.

"No. Please don't leave me...alone," she stuttered.

"Ayla," I started to say, but she shook her head. Moving the comforter away with a rush, she stumbled out of my bed.

"Shit," I muttered. Quickly moving toward her shaking body, I pulled her up in my arms and placed her on the bed again. She gripped my arm tightly and stared at me with dread.

"Please. Don't leave me," she begged, tears streaming down her cheeks.

When I wanted Ayla to beg me to touch her, this wasn't how I envisioned it happening.

What a fucking mess.

"Hey, hey, hey," I soothed, sitting down on the

bed in front of her. Pushing the strands of her hair behind her ears, so that her face was fully visible to me, I cupped her cheeks reassuringly. "It's okay. I'm right here. I'm not leaving."

She hiccupped a sob and her fingers tightened on my arm. "It's okay," I said again. Gently grabbing her shoulders, I pushed her down on the bed. After pulling the comforter over her, I patted her knee. "I'm right here."

I kept my eyes on her as I stood up. She followed my movement with her unflinching but tearful eyes. When I climbed on the other side, Ayla turned and faced me.

We stared at each other, our gazes unmoving as we settled under the comforter.

I didn't know how long we stayed like that, but eventually her eyes started to droop sleepily, her long dark lashes fluttering against her pale skin. Tiredness took over her body and she went limp. An almost inaudible sigh escaped her lips as she fell asleep, her body cocooned warmly and safely under my comforter and my watchful gaze.

What happened tonight changed everything. It made me want to know more about her. I could make assumptions about what happened to her, but I wanted to hear it from her.

A few minutes later, I closed my eyes as the darkness enveloped me.

The last thing I saw was Ayla's sleeping and peaceful face.

Chapter 23

Ayla

I felt disoriented and my head was pounding. I blinked my eyes open but then closed them again because of the bright sunlight.

Wait, what?

My eyes snapped open in alarm and I quickly sat up in bed. I wasn't in my room. I looked down at the soft black comforter. Panic filled my chest; I looked around the strange room. It was familiar to me.

Turning my head to the left, I shrieked in surprise. Alessio was sitting beside me, his back propped against the headboard as he mutely stared at me panicking.

I was in *his* room.

The last thing I remembered was falling down on my bed tiredly as sleep took over my body and mind. But after that, everything was blank.

"How did I get here?" I asked, bringing the comforter up to my shoulder. Alessio raised an eyebrow at me in surprise.

"You don't remember?" he asked, his voice gruff from sleep.

I shook my head. He stared at me for a few seconds, the air crackling with tension between us. There was an awkward pause before he continued.

"You came to me last night," he said.

That didn't make any sense.

"What do you...you mean?"

He sighed in annoyance. "You had a panic attack. Came to my room, knocked at my door, and *begged* me to make it go away. I did, and then you fell asleep on my bed," Alessio explained. When he was done, he stared at me expectantly.

Bringing my hand up to my head, I rubbed my forehead, trying to ease the horrendous headache. When I closed my eyes, sudden clipped images of last night crashed behind my close lids.

My nightmare. The hallucinations. Crying. Begging Alessio to make it stop. I remembered him cleaning my arms, telling me there was no blood on them.

My eyes snapped open and I stared at Alessio in shock. He raised an eyebrow in amusement and made a *tsking* sound. "Ah, so you remember now." Embarrassment and shame filled me as I tore my eyes away from Alessio's penetrating gaze. My throat went dry and my body grew cold.

Silence filled the room. Neither of us moved.

After a few minutes filled with tension, I licked my lips nervously and started to move toward the end of the bed. When Alessio didn't say anything, I kept my eyes down and pushed the comforter away before getting off the bed.

Just walk away, Ayla. Walk away. Get your thoughts together. Make up an excuse.

I locked my knees together and continued toward my escape.

When I reached the door, Alessio's voice filled the room. I tensed and my hand froze.

"Are you seriously going to leave without saying anything?" he asked, chuckling under his breath.

That was the plan. I thought he wouldn't say anything, but clearly I was wrong. How naïve of me that I kept thinking of him as the good guy.

He is the good guy, though, I argued with myself.

"Ayla, turn around," Alessio ordered in a hard, cold voice.

I stiffened at his tone and swiveled around. My head stayed down, and I refused to look at his judging, questioning gaze.

The bed squeaked, and from the corner of my eyes, I saw him getting up. For the first time I noticed that he was in different attire than usual. He wore grey sweatpants and a long black shirt that was tight over his chest.

He moved toward me, his steps fluid and confident.

When he stopped in front of me, my heart stuttered with anxiety and my stomach twisted with tension.

I knew what he was going ask and I didn't have the answers to his prying questions. They weren't answers he would want.

He gripped my chin between his fingers, tilting

my head up so I was staring at him. His eyes were cold and I saw anger in them.

A shiver went through me and I tightened my hands into fists, my nails biting into the skin of my palm. The slight pain kept me grounded.

"Explain," he demanded, his eyes turning into slits.

I couldn't.

"There is nothing to…explain," I stammered. At my words, his fingers tightened on my chin and anger coursed through his eyes.

"Ayla, I know when you are lying. And I fucking hate it when people lie to me. It will be better for you if you tell me the truth. Explain what happened last night."

Angry Alessio was scary. His body tensed and his eyes were deadly cold, showing his true character as the heartless mafia boss.

"I'm telling the truth. It was…just a nightmare."

That was the partial truth. He wouldn't understand the whole truth. He would only see me as the daughter of his worst enemy, *not* a victim.

"Damn it," he growled as he released my chin. "You are lying, Ayla." When he sent me an intense glare, I cowered back a little and quickly looked down.

But lying was keeping me alive. For now.

"No, I'm telling the truth," I whispered and unknowingly took a step back. He noticed and took a step forward.

"You had a panic attack. You were having hallucinations about blood on you. You were crying. Totally losing it. That. Was. Not. A.

Nightmare," he said, punctuating each word with fury.

"No." I shook my head. "It was. I have very vivid nightmares." I quickly made an excuse, desperately hoping he would believe me. And even if he didn't, I hoped he would let it go.

But being Alessio, he didn't let it go.

"Did you witness a murder?" he asked, his tone a little gentler than before, but still hard.

At his question, I just wanted to crumple down and cry. My heart ached at the thought. Yes. Yes, I had witnessed a murder. Not one. Not two. But several murders.

Alberto killed them mercilessly in front of me. He never cared about my screams of terror.

Looking Alessio in the eyes, I shook my head. "No," I whispered. The lie left a bitter taste in my mouth.

His rigid blue eyes narrowed. The burning hard stare caused me tremble with uneasiness and fear.

"Fuck, did you kill someone? Are you running away? Is that it?" His loud, harsh voice boomed around us.

My eyes widened and I flinched at his assumption. Did he really think that I could kill someone?

"No. No." I shook my head wildly. "I didn't kill anyone."

"Ayla, you were hallucinating about blood on you. So, either you killed someone or you witnessed a murder. Which is the truth?" He was losing patience.

"I didn't kill anyone, and I didn't witness any

murder. I'm telling the truth. It was just a nightmare. A bad one and I lost it. That's all." I stared into Alessio's eyes and saw the disbelief in them.

So, I tried one last time.

"Please. Believe me. Please." This time I begged, hoping it would have an effect on him.

He glared at me and ran his fingers through his hair in frustration. "You may seem innocent, Ayla, but you are so fucking stubborn."

He took a step closer to me until our bodies were only a breath away.

"I can protect you. If you tell me the truth, I can protect you. So, tell me," he said.

Oh, how I wanted to believe him. My heart stumbled at his words and my eyes burned with tears. I wished it was true. I wished I really did have someone to protect me.

But Alessio wouldn't protect me if he knew the truth. He would kill me instead. It was as simple as that.

I couldn't look into his eyes any longer. Shame and guilt filled my body. Shame for what I had been through. I wasn't who he thought I was.

I wasn't innocent.

And then guilt. Guilt because I lied to his face and was living in his house, living off his generosity when I didn't deserve it.

I also felt confused because I couldn't understand why I went to him last night. Why did I go to him at my lowest point?

Why was he my *peace*? Alessio made a frustrated sound and then took a step away from me.

My forehead creased in confusion and I slowly brought my head up to look at him.

He stared at me blankly, completely devoid of any emotions.

"Fine," he said, his voice strangely calm.

What?

This man loved playing with my mind. I could never truly read him.

"You believe me?" I asked in astonishment.

He let out a harsh laugh. "Believe you? No, kitten. I don't believe you. But I will accept what you are saying for now." He stepped forward and leaned down so that his lips were next to my ears. "You will eventually tell me the truth. It is only a matter of time."

His words felt like lashes against my body. I reared back in shock and Alessio stepped away. He gave me a nod and turned around, walking toward his bathroom.

"I will see you at breakfast," he said, dismissing me without a second glance.

I stared at his back with wide eyes. He closed the bathroom door behind him, hiding his view from me and I let out a sigh of relief. My tensed muscles relaxed but his words kept playing in my head.

It is only a matter of time.

Turning around, I walked out of his bedroom and into my room in a daze.

He was right. It was only a matter of time. How long could I keep hiding the truth?

Chapter 24

Alberto

I walked down to the cold basement, my muscles relaxing at the familiar feeling and smell. When I reached the bottom, I paused and my lips slowly stretched into a smirk.

"Hello, Alfredo," I said calmly, my voice loud, vibrating around the silent room.

Alfredo's head snapped up and he sent me a fierce glare.

"You fucking bastard. What is the meaning of this? Let me go," he roared in fury, as he struggled against the chains around his ankles and wrists.

I chuckled at his failed attempt and leaned against the wall. He'd been chained against the wall, his ankles bound as well as his wrists, bloodied from his struggles. His head was bleeding from where I'd hit him with the back of my gun.

His face was covered with sweat and grime. A few strands of his hair were sticking to his forehead and he was breathing hard from exhaustion. I knew he'd been struggling for hours.

He looked like a poor bastard, a helpless man. I laughed at the thought. He was never fit to be the fucking king. He was too weak. And now it was time for his end and the start of my reign.

I had to get him out of the picture, permanently.

And maybe I'd enjoy it.

"Now, now. Calm down," I said.

His face turned bright red and he spat at my feet. "Alberto, I'm warning you..." he started, his voice laced with anger. He never got a chance to finish his sentence.

I knelt down in front of him and grabbed his face, my fingers digging deeply into his cheek. I leaned in close and hissed through gritted teeth. "Or what? What are you going to do? Shoot me? Alfredo, let me remind you. You are the one chained to the wall."

He winced at the pressure I was putting on his cheek and his pain pushed me on. I dug my nails deeper and then moved my hands downward and wrapped them around his neck. His eyes widened when I pressed my hands harder around his neck, choking him.

He struggled, his face turning almost purple, and he gasped for breath. When I saw him starting to lose consciousness, I let him go.

"Now, where were we?" I asked, moving to the chair in the corner. I sat down and leaned back, crossing my left ankle and my right knee and waiting for him.

"Wh...why?" he asked through his coughing fit. After the words were out, he looked up and leveled me with a glare, his eyes showing me exactly how much he hated me.

Shaking my head at his attitude, I shrugged. "It's simple. I want to be the boss."

"You fucking shit," Alfredo roared and tried to stand up, but fell to his knees instead. "After everything I have done for you, this is how you repay me?"

"Aren't you the one who taught me there's no gratitude? Gratitude is a show of weakness, isn't it? After all, we do what benefits us the most."

"I gave you everything, Alberto. I made you my second in command. I gave you power. I gave you my daughter!"

His begging didn't faze me. Instead it made me feel powerful.

His life was in my hands. I controlled everything.

Power and dominance coursed through my body as I stared at him struggling against his chains. I couldn't help but laugh again. It sounded harsh against the walls of the cold cellar.

"I wanted more, Alfredo. And it's simple, I'll take it," I said in response before standing up and slowly walking toward him. He stopped fighting against the shackles and looked at me straight in the eyes.

I saw disgust and hatred there. But none of it mattered. He couldn't do anything. He was helpless. And he knew it. In the depth of his eyes, I saw resignation and fear.

Moving my hand to my back, I took out my gun and pointed it straight at Alfredo, the barrel in front his forehead, placed in the middle of his eyes. I saw him swallowing hard, his prominent Adam's apple bobbing almost painfully in his throat.

"I handed my daughter to a monster," he bristled, as the gun was pressed against his forehead. My eyes widened when he mentioned Ayla and sudden intense fury coursed through my body.

Pulling my gun away, I brought it forward with force and smacked the back of it against Alfredo's cheek. His head snapped to the side and his eyes closed tightly with pain but he never made a sound.

"You are not any better," I hissed, kneeling down in front of him. Grabbing his chin, I made him look at me before continuing. "Did you forget about Leila, your wife? The same wife you murdered in cold blood because she was fucking a Russian?"

Alfredo's eyes widened in shock and I laughed at his reaction. "Or what about Lyov's wife? Ah, that one was the best. Attack their mansion, kill half of his men and then kill the unprotected Maria. She was pregnant, wasn't she?"

Shaking my head at him, I released his chin and pushed his head back with force. It banged against the wall and this time he winced.

"So you see, you aren't any better than me. I learned from the best, after all," I paused and sent him a wink. "But I surpassed the master. You should be proud."

I saw his fingers tightening into fists and he growled at me. "You fucking bastard," he bellowed. I had enough. Getting bored of the back and forth, I aimed the gun at his forehead again.

Time for him to meet his maker.

"Any last wishes?" I asked, the corner of my lips slightly lifting upward into a smirk. Alfredo struggled and tried lurch forward, but his chains stopped him.

"Fuck y—"

I pulled the trigger and a loud *pop* was heard. There was gasp of breath and then silence.

Utter and complete silence.

I stared at Alfredo, his pitch black eyes open, but glazed over and lifeless. Empty. Hollow. Opened wide in his final death throes.

He was limp against the wall. And in the middle of his forehead was a tiny hole where my bullet had gone. Thick blood ran down his face and my smile widened at the sight.

Finally.

The Italians were mine, and soon enough, the Russians would belong to me too.

I would be the motherfucking king.

Chapter 25

Alessio

"I tracked every single phone. And still nothing," Viktor growled as his ran his fingers through his hair in frustration.

I was sitting behind my table, my arms across my chest. Viktor was pacing the room like a caged animal, his anger clearly evident. Phoenix was sitting on the couch, his head back with his eyes closed. He looked completely worn out.

"I can't fucking believe this. How is it possible that we haven't found the fucker yet?" Viktor continued.

Phoenix mumbled, "He is good. He is very good. The fucking bastard knows how to stay hidden."

I had to agree with that. My men had been looking for the traitor for a few days now. I had the best trackers and yet, nothing.

Moving my head left and right, I tried to ease the tense muscles there. I rubbed my forehead in frustration and leaned forward, placing my elbows on the table.

"You are right. He is definitely good. But he can't stay hidden forever," I said.

"But the longer we take to find him, the more damage he is causing!" Viktor retorted.

"We will find him." Even though I appeared calm, I was anything *but* calm. The anger coursing inside was indescribable. I was going to make him pay. Severely. Bloodily. He was lucky that I hadn't found him yet. He got an extra few days to live.

Phoenix opened his eyes and stared at me. His lips parted and he was about to say something but the door banged open and Nikolay came rushing in.

He was panting, his eyes wide with shock and his face twisted angrily. Everyone stared at him in surprise, including me.

Pushing my chair away, I stood up. That was the first time I ever saw Nikolay so tense. His chest heaved with each breath he took. Sweat formed on his red face, veins bulging in his forehead and neck.

"He is dead. The motherfucker is dead," he snarled through his gasps of breath.

My forehead creased in confusion and I cocked my head to the side in question. Nikolay swallowed hard before answering my unvoiced questions.

And his answer was like a gunshot right through my heart.

"Alfredo is dead."

"What did you say?" I asked, punctuating each word carefully.

"Alfredo is dead."

"Fuck," Viktor growled.

Rage built like deep water currents inside of me.

It came out faster than magma but just as destructive. My body was vibrating with it.

Alfredo was dead.

He was dead and it was not me who had killed him.

I didn't get my vengeance.

I felt empty as the rage consumed me. My skin was scorching and I grew hotter until it felt like I was suffocating. My vision blurred with my fury and all I saw was my mother's lifeless eyes.

Muscles tensing, neck stiffening and back stretching, I roared, "Damn it!"

I leaned forward and pushed everything off the table, shards of glass flying everywhere. I kicked my chair against the wall and paced.

I was supposed to take his life! His blood should've been on my hands! I had to avenge my mother.

But now…

Every muscle in my body was twitching, itching, and on fire.

My hands tightened in fists, so hard, so tight that my knuckles started to hurt and my hands slowly went numb. I gripped my hair and pulled.

"He was mine to kill!" I roared before punching the wall, creating a deep hole. The drywall bent with the force and the paint came off as I pulled my bleeding fist back.

I felt a hand on my back and I swiveled around, wrapping my hand around the person's neck. Viktor stared at me blankly, waiting for me to calm down. My fingers tightened slightly but his expression still didn't change.

I released his neck with a snarl and pushed him away. He stumbled back, but quickly gained his footing again.

"Don't fucking touch me. I won't be held responsible for my actions," I growled before taking a menacing step toward him.

Viktor straightened his back before turning toward Phoenix and Nikolay and nodding at the door. They left without a backward glance. When the door closed with a bang, I sagged against the table.

There was too much fury coursing inside of me. I had to release it before I completely lost it.

Shrugging off my suit jacket, I removed my tie and pulled at my collar to loosen it. I ran a shaky hand over my face.

Looking down at my hands, I slowly clenched them into fists, my knuckles cracking. With a frustrated sigh, I walked to the door and opened it wide.

The hallway was empty and my hard steps echoed as I walked downstairs to the gym. My sight was on the punching bags. Without a second thought, I landed a punch on the bag, my bare knuckles hitting it with a crack.

I didn't know how long I kept at it. Punching. Kicking. Roaring in anger with each punch and kick. My knuckles were bleeding, the skin torn apart. My fingers were hurting and a crippling pain went through my hands and arms, but I kept going.

The pain. It felt good. I needed it.

I heard the door open and stopped in mid-swing. Placing my hand on the punching bag, I stopped it from knocking me down. Hissing through gritted teeth, I turned around to look at the intruder.

Viktor walked forward, his steps slow. I stared at him closely, following his movement with unflinching eyes.

When he stopped a few feet away, my eyebrows furrowed in confusion. Viktor took his suit jacket off and threw it on the ground before rolling the sleeves of his shirt up, showing the tattoos that covered the length of his arms.

He kept his eyes on me the whole time, and when he was done rolling his sleeves, he reached up and unbuttoned the first two buttons of his white shirt. Rolling his neck around, he took two steps forward and then stopped.

Viktor pushed his legs apart, shoulder wide. He cracked his knuckles before pointing at me and then moving his finger to his chest. "Come at me," he ordered, his voice cold and hard.

My eyes widened slightly and fury surged through me. With a deafening roar, my feet lurched forward. A red mist of anger clouded my vision as I made the first strike.

We fought. Punched. Kicked. Scrambling around like animals. Viktor didn't go easy on me. He retaliated. We both fought for power, each of us letting our anger out.

I saw his fist moving toward my face and I quickly dodged it before punching him in the gut. Viktor groaned in pain and went down to his knees, holding his stomach. I didn't let him go. Pushing him down, I continued my assault. He still fought back.

When I noticed him growing weaker, I pushed him away from me. Viktor laid on his back on the ground, his hands over his chest as he gasped for breath.

Sinking down on my ass, I sat beside him. Licking my lips, I tasted my blood.

"Better?" Viktor gasped, turning his face toward me. He stared at me through swollen eyes and I shook my head.

"Not even close." My whole body was sensitive and aching, but still, I couldn't get rid of the rage.

"Shit. I don't think I can move," he groaned and then winced in pain. Viktor pulled his head back and bellowed at the top of his lungs.

"Nikolay!"

The door opened and he came in.

"It's your turn," Viktor said, his lips turning up in a small smirk.

Nikolay nodded and then took his suit jacket off. After rolling his sleeves the same way Viktor had, he braced himself and gave me a nod. I didn't wait for another signal. Letting the rage take hold, I rushed forward.

Before I could punch him, Nikolay moved out of the way and landed a punch on my shoulder instead.

It pissed me off more.

Shifting to my side, I kicked him in the leg. He stumbled back but quickly gained his footing and then he was rushing toward me again. We kept going like that, back and forth, teeth clashing together in anger as we reveled in our fury. When Nikolay was done, Phoenix took his place. Adrenaline kept me going. Artur was next.

My body eventually started to weaken and I could barely land a punch. After Artur fell to the ground beside Viktor, Phoenix, and Nikolay, I sank to the ground too and laid there, staring at the ceiling.

These men had my back. They were my brothers, not by blood but by choice.

"Alessio," Viktor started, but I quickly cut him off.

"Don't. Just don't say anything." I struggled to sit up, then sighed before running my aching hand through my sweaty hair.

Rolling my neck around, I winced at the pain and then stood up on shaky legs. I nodded at them and I walked out of the gym.

The fury inside of me, the beast, the monster inside me was finally calm. But for how long? How long before I lost it again?

I went straight upstairs. But instead of going into my bedroom, I walked to the room beside it, the one between my room and Ayla's. Pushing the door open, I turned on the lights.

My gaze went to the large piano in the corner of the room. My heart stuttered in pain at the sight of it and my stomach twisted painfully.

I made my way to the piano. As I neared it, my heart ached and my eyes started to burn. I stopped in front of the piano and slowly brought my fingers up, pressing softly over the keys.

I couldn't stop the memories that came crashing around me.

A loud bang jostled me awake and my eyes went

214

wide with fear. "Mommy?" I called. I felt her hands on me and she pulled me out of the bed. The lights were on and as I blinked the sleepiness away, I heard another bang. I flinched when I heard screams.

"Mommy, what's happening?" I asked, my voice filled with fright.

She knelt down in front of me and my eyes widened at the sight of terror on my mommy's face. My stomach dropped and my lungs squeezed together.

"Mommy," I whispered.

"Alessio, listen to me carefully. I want you to hide under the bed. Okay?" she started, her voice small and shaky. "No matter what happens or what you see or hear, you don't come out. Do you understand?" Mommy grabbed my shoulders and shook me gently. I nodded but didn't understand what was going on.

The fear on her face made me scared. My mommy was never scared. She was always laughing and smiling. I had never seen my mommy like that. Her small body was shaking and I saw tears in her eyes. She ran her hands up and down my body and pulled me to her chest.

She peppered my face with kisses and then pulled back. "Mommy, what about you? Why am I hiding under the bed?" I asked.

"Alessio. Don't ask me questions, okay? Please, baby, just listen to Mommy. Hide under the bed and don't come out. Not until Papa, Lena, or Isaak come looking for you," Mommy said urgently.

But why?

I was about to ask again, but she shook her head and a tear escaped the corner of her eye. "Please, my baby. Promise Mommy that you won't come out," she begged.

I quickly promised and she cried. Pulling me to her chest again, she whispered in my ear, "I love you. I love you so much, my sweet boy. Never forget that."

We pulled apart when another bang was heard from outside the room. The sounds were nearer. I shivered in fear and Mommy's eyes went wide with horror.

She pushed me toward the bed and stood up. "Go, my baby. Don't come out. Don't make any noise. No matter what? Do you hear me?" Mommy whispered, her voice filled with tears as she pushed me under the high bed.

I felt sick and my throat started to close up. So I just nodded. She gave me a final look before pulling the sheet down and separating us.

My heart thumped wildly in my chest and I sucked in a deep breath a couple of times but I couldn't. My heart was hurting. I was confused. And I was scared.

I heard the door open and it crashed against the wall with a loud noise. I jumped slightly and brought my knees closer to my chest as I lay under the bed. I tried to peek under the comforter and saw my mommy's feet.

When I heard a strange and unfamiliar voice, my hands grew cold and my heart twisted.

"Maria. How lovely to see you again."

"Alfredo," Mommy replied, her voice hard.

"I'm surprised Lyov left you unprotected."

"Why are you here?" Mommy asked in the same scary tone. That was the first time I ever heard my mommy talk that way.

"You know exactly why I am here, sweet Maria."

Mommy screamed and I flinched. No. He was hurting her. The bad man was hurting my mommy. My eyes widened when I saw my mommy falling to the ground. Her face hit the ground and her big round belly was pushed hard against it. Mommy grabbed her stomach as she yelled in pain.

Holding her stomach, she cried out.

No. Princess! My mind screamed.

The bad man was hurting princess too. I couldn't take it. I promised I would protect both Mommy and princess. I was about to move from under the bed when Mommy opened her eyes and made direct contact with mine. Tears were falling down her cheeks and she slightly shook her head. It was so small that I almost missed it but it was there.

And her eyes were begging me not to come out.

My nose tingled and my cheeks were wet. I realized that I was crying.

Mommy gave me a final look and then turned around while she still held her stomach. "Please, don't do this. I beg you. Have mercy."

A laugh boomed around the room and the man knelt down. I tried to see his face. It was hard but I got a tiny glimpse of it.

I hated him at first sight. How dare he? He hurt my mommy and princess.

"I can show you mercy if you agree to come with me. Be my whore and then maybe I could show you

mercy."

I didn't understand what he meant but I felt relief. He said he wasn't going to hurt my mommy. Oh, thank God.

Mommy's eyes widened and she scrunched up her face in disgust. "Never," she spat. "I will never allow another man to touch my body. I only belong to Lyov. I would rather die than have you touch me."

No! I wanted to scream. Don't say that, Mommy. Please, Mommy, do what he says. He won't hurt you. I wanted to beg.

The man grunted. "Is that your final decision?"

Mommy didn't answer but she kept her cold, unflinching eyes on the man.

"Well, okay then," he said.

And then he was pointing a gun at my mommy's forehead.

Oh, no! No! Please no!

"Why are you doing this?" Mommy whispered, her voice breaking.

"Don't you know, Maria? The best way to bring a man down is by his weakness. And you, my sweet, are Lyov's weakness."

And with that, a loud bang filled the room.

I closed my eyes tightly and my heart rammed against my ribcage. Pulling my knees closer to my chest, I wrapped my arms around them. Burying my face in between my knees, I tried to hold in my cry. I promised. I promised I wouldn't make a sound.

I couldn't break the promise I made to Mommy.

My heart was hurting so bad and my body slowly started to go numb. I couldn't feel anything. After *counting to ten, I lifted my head up and slowly opened my eyes.*

What I saw took my breath away. I felt dizzy and my eyes blurred with tears as they fell down my cheeks in a never ending flow.

My mommy's head had rolled toward me and her face was covered in blood. Her eyes were open and staring directly at me. But instead of seeing the warm, sweet, and loving gaze that she always gave me, her bluish-steel colored eyes were lifeless.

My heart pounded. No. No. No. No.

My mommy. This couldn't be happening.

Mommy.

Mommy.

I wanted to scream. But nothing came out.

My lips parted and a silent scream came out. I gasped and shook violently. Holding my knees close together, I buried my face in them again, crying silently.

As I cried, I thought about how I never got a chance to say 'I love you' back.

I fell down on my knees. The memories played over and over again in my head. I was suffocating and I brought my hands up to my throat, rubbing up and down forcefully.

My stomach cramped as I gasped for air. The pressure in my heart was painful. My lungs squeezed tightly together and I pressed a hand to my burning chest, trying hard to alleviate the pain. But nothing worked.

It never worked.

My pain was constant.

I had lived with it for twenty-two years. I should have been accustomed to it by now, but every time, it was worse. The pain never ceased. I was chained to my past.

Holding the side of the piano, I laid my head on it as the tears fell down my cheeks. I couldn't stop them. They fell freely and I squeezed my burning eyes tightly.

"I'm sorry. I'm so sorry. So sorry," I whispered through a broken voice.

Chapter 26

Ayla

Maddie squealed beside me. "Oh my God! This is hilarious!" She turned toward me, still chuckling. "You have to admit, this one was pretty funny."

I shrugged and turned back toward the movie. We were watching *Hangover 2*. It was too vulgar for my taste.

Although I did find my stomach cramping from laughter when a man found out he had sex with another man whom he thought was a woman. I shivered when the truth was revealed. Too much nudity.

Maddie eventually paused the movie and turned toward me.

"Okay. What do you want to watch? You clearly aren't enjoying this. C'mon, pick something funny and we will watch it," she suggested.

Since my nightmare last night and my encounter with Alessio this morning, I had been a little down and quiet. I was constantly living in fear.

Maddie noticed and she made it her job to make my day brighter. She succeeded a couple of times. It was hard not to laugh at her enthusiasms and failed attempts. She embarrassed herself to make me laugh. And I was thankful for that.

"It's pretty late," I started and then smiled. "I think we should go to bed. I'm worn out."

Maddie pouted and leaned against the arm of the couch. "But I barely even got you to laugh."

"And that's where you are wrong. You made me laugh at least five times and that's amazing in my book. You made my day better, Maddie," I said softly. Placing my hand on her knee, I gave it a squeeze.

"Are you going to talk to me?" she replied, her tone just as soft and inviting.

I wanted to. I wanted to tell her. It was tempting, but the fear instilled in me, it stopped me from taking a step toward that direction.

So, I shook my head sadly before looking down. "It's okay," Maddie murmured before wrapping her arms around me. "You can tell me when you are ready."

Hugging her back, I nodded and then leaned back. She smiled and I felt my lips stretch into another smile.

We got up and made our way to the kitchen. Turning on the lights, she rummaged through the refrigerator and took out the poutine that Lena made for dessert.

"You want some?" Maddie asked as she closed the refrigerator.

I shook my head and she shrugged. Putting a

spoonful in her mouth, she mumbled, "Let's go."

Maddie and I were about to say goodnight when we heard a door open. We both swiveled around and saw Alessio coming out of the gym.

My eyes widened and my body froze when he approached into the light.

Alessio wasn't wearing his full suit. Instead he had his black linen shirt on, which was halfway unbuttoned and his sleeves were rolled up to his elbows. But that wasn't what surprised me.

He was a mess. A bloody mess. There were cuts on his face and his cheeks were swollen. His left eye was slightly swollen too and his lips were bleeding. He was limping, his body sagging forward.

"Oh my God," Maddie gasped.

He looked lost, deep in thoughts. He held on to the banister and slowly made his way upstairs, his legs dragging. Pain was evident on his face and in his posture.

My forehead creased in confusion and I turned to Maddie. Her eyes were no longer on Alessio but she was staring at the gym door.

"I don't want know how the other guys look," she whispered, her eyes wide. As soon as the words were out of her mouth, the door opened and they stepped out.

This time I was the one who gasped. They looked even worse. Maddie rushed forward and I quickly followed.

"What happened?" she asked, horrified.

"Fuck," Viktor said, rubbing his hand over his face tiredly but he winced when his hand made contact with his face.

"Alfredo is dead," Nikolay replied, his voice as deadly as ever.

At his words, my breath came out in a whoosh. It felt like someone had punched me in the stomach.

My mind twirled, my vision going slightly blurry. I blinked and gasped, my hand going to my neck as I started to rub up and down.

"What?" I whispered, my voice so little that it was barely audible.

"Alfredo is dead," Nikolay repeated before closing his eyes with a tired sigh.

My father was dead.

I brought a shaky hand to my mouth as I tried to keep the tears at bay. I didn't know why I was crying. Tears blinded my vision and I closed my eyes, trying to make them go away.

"Alessio isn't taking it so well. Hell, I'm not taking it well! This was supposed to be our revenge," Viktor hissed.

"Oh, dear," Maddie whispered beside me. "He is doing badly, then?"

"Pretty bad," Phoenix said.

They were leaning against the wall, all of them deep in thought. But the anger on their faces couldn't be mistaken.

"You should go clean up. Alessio can't have you losing it too," Maddie suggested.

"I should go," I whispered. My heart was thumping fast against my chest and I had to get out of there. They couldn't see me break down.

I nodded at Maddie and quickly walked away before they could reply. Closing my door, I leaned against it and sank down to my butt. Pulling my knees together, I placed my head on them and tried to breathe.

My eyes burned with unshed tears and my quiet gasps filled the silent dark room. There should have not been any tears. Not for my father, a man who gave me to a monster and turned a blind eye to my pain. But still, I couldn't stop the tears.

My chest squeezed tight with pain and the tears fell freely down my cheeks. I cried for him and for the pain he caused me.

I cried for the love I could have had but never experienced because of him. In the end, I cried for me.

He took my peace, my freedom, my everything. Even though I should have hated him, I didn't.

I just felt sad. I felt empty. Hollow. Weak.

Eventually, I found myself in bed. I stared into the distance, only the lamp on my nightstand was on, casting a soft glow around the room.

I didn't know how long I stayed like that, but I couldn't bring myself to close my eyes. I thought of my father and Alberto. I was scared of the nightmares.

I turned around in bed and tried to find another comfortable position, but to no avail. Nothing worked.

Blowing out a tired breath, I rubbed my face in frustration and sat up in bed. My thoughts went to Alessio, and my body instantly grew tense. I could understand his anger and pain. After what my father had done, this was Alessio's revenge.

He was going through a harder time than me.

When I saw him, his pain was obvious and my heart ached.

To see a man like Alessio crumble, it hurt. It was painful.

And strangely, I wanted to offer comfort.

Maybe because I understood. Was it sympathy, or guilt?

I didn't know, but through my pain, I felt his. And my heart was breaking for this man, who was my enemy.

The irony of it. An Abandonato wanting to comfort an Ivanshov.

My mind was a jumbled mess and I just wanted silence for a moment.

I closed my eyes and the first thing that flashed behind my closed lids was my grand piano. My eyes instantly snapped opened.

That was it.

The piano.

I knew we weren't allowed in the room, but everyone was sleeping. Maybe I could just sneak in. Quickly getting off the bed, I padded to my door and quietly opened it. Looking left and right, I made sure that no one was in the hall before stepping out.

I softly tiptoed to the next room but immediately stopped when I saw the lights on. The door was slightly opened and I leaned forward, peeking inside.

My heart stuttered at the sight.

Alessio was sitting on the couch, facing the piano in the corner. There was a glass in his hand and he was staring intensely at the piano. He slowly brought the glass to his lips and chugged the rest of the drink in a gulp.

He looked horrible.

With my heart heavy and thumping fast in my chest, I started to quietly move away from the door but his voice stopped me.

"I know you are there."

I froze and my eyes widened.

Placing my hand over my chest, I bit on my lips nervously.

Should I just leave? My mind and heart were in a constant battle.

In the end, I slowly opened the door wider and walked inside, but stopped at the entrance. Alessio didn't look toward me but kept his eyes on the piano.

I shuffled on my feet nervously. After a few minutes of silence, he spoke up.

"Do you come in here often?" he asked, his voice rough and hard. I shivered and shook my head quickly. When I realized he couldn't see me, I whispered, "*No.*"

Then it was silence again.

I looked away from him and stared at the grand piano. It was beautiful and I instantly felt peaceful.

Wrapping my arms around myself, I took a few steps in the room and stood in the middle. My eyes were still on the piano and my fingers were itching to play. I wanted to feel the soft keys.

My shoulders sagged in defeat. I looked away from the piano and turned toward Alessio. He was already staring at me, his eyes intense but unreadable.

We stared at each other, our gazes never

wavering.

After a few seconds, I swallowed hard and looked away. Moving my gaze to his chest, I followed the path down and almost gasped out loud.

His hands were bleeding, his knuckles bruised so bad. There were gashes all over, the skin torn off from his knuckles. He hadn't cleaned up at all.

My heart squeezed at the sight.

I looked back up and saw his eyes still on me. Licking my lips nervously, I squeezed my cold hands in fists. Alessio gave me a blank look and then looked at the piano.

Silence again. There was no movement and it felt like we weren't even breathing. "Do you play?" he asked gruffly.

My mouth fell open at his words. I never expected him to ask me that question. With my heart racing, I swallowed against the lump forming in my throat.

"Yes," I responded.

Silence. I waited for him to say something but he didn't. It was like I wasn't even there anymore. But I still waited. I didn't know exactly for what but my feet stayed grounded.

I tugged on the hem of my dress. What was I even waiting for?

I slowly backed away. Alessio needed time by himself.

Without looking up at him, I turned around and made my way out. But before I could a step out of the room, his voice stopped me. My steps faltered and at his words, my heart stuttered.

"Do you want to play?"

"I can play?" I asked, taking a step forward and away from the door.

He turned toward me. "Do you want to?"

I nodded, my body shaking with excitement. I couldn't hold the smile the spread across my lips. I felt giddy.

He stared at me with the same dead eyes, but he slightly nodded toward the piano. That was the only indication I needed.

I walked toward the piano and stopped in front of it. With my heart light, I placed my fingers on the keys and closed my eyes.

When I looked at Alessio, he was staring at me intently, waiting.

With our gazes still connected, I let my fingers move. Softly. Gently. And a sweet melody came through. The music washed around us like a slow, gentle wave, and I smiled.

Alessio's eyes widened. He brought his hand over his chest and pressed hard, as if he was having trouble breathing.

I closed my eyes and continued to play. My heart full of peace, I felt content. Happiness enveloped my body as my fingers moved swiftly over the keys of the piano.

This. This was what I needed.

Peace.

Chapter 27

Alessio

No one had touched the piano, not since my mother's death. This was *her* piano.

My soul was in pain, my heart aching.

So, the words tumbled out of my mouth before I could stop them. For some reason, Ayla's presence brought me comfort.

When the first melody came through, searing pain went through my heart and I brought my hand up, pressing it hard against my chest.

Twenty-two years since I'd heard someone play the piano. Twenty-two years since I heard this exact melody.

Ayla opened her eyes and looked directly at me. She was still smiling and then she closed them again. She continued to play, oblivious to the world around her. Her face was serene and she was lost into the music. A tiny smile remained on her lips.

She looked happy and at peace.

And as I listened, the pain in my heart started to

diminish. It was still there, but I could breathe again. My tense muscles started to relax. My heart stuttered and I brought a shaky hand to my face.

I closed my eyes and felt something wet on my aching cheek. I was crying. A single tear. The music flowed and I swiped the tear away.

"Mommy, play for me, please!" I begged.

She laughed and pulled me to the piano. "Okay, my baby." She sat down and placed me on her lap. "There you go," she said, giving me a kiss on the cheek before moving her attention to the piano. Mommy ran her fingers over the keys softly at first and then started to play. As soon as the music came through, I relaxed against her and sighed in contentment.

In no time, I was slowly falling asleep, as always.

This was my favorite part of the day. Just Mommy and me, and the piano.

I closed my eyes at the memory. It hurt, but my heart wasn't squeezing in pain as it was before.

I could breathe without it feeling like I was being cut with a hundred sharp knives.

With my eyes still closed, I listened to Ayla playing. After a song, she played another. And then she started humming.

My eyes opened and I stared at her. Her eyes were closed, her body moving slowly with the music. My stomach twisted and my heart ached at the sight.

With her black hair falling down in waves

around her shoulders, her cheeks flushed red and her white dress, only one thought came to mind.

Something that my father told me about, so many years ago. I shook my head and squeezed my hands in fists. A throbbing pain went through my fingers, but that wasn't enough to snap me out of my thoughts.

I couldn't take my eyes off Ayla.

As the soft, gentle and beautiful music continued to flow around us, enveloping us in a peaceful melody, I could only think of one thing.

Ayla.

She looked like an angel.

***

Lena

I was awake, my mind racing. In was one of those nights when I couldn't stop thinking about Maria.

My eyes were closed, but when I heard a beautiful music, I opened them again, my forehead creasing in confusion. I quickly sat up. I looked at my ceiling and gasped. It was coming from the sitting room. The piano.

But how was it possible? Nobody was allowed in the room. No one except Alessio himself.

Who could be playing? I walked toward the music. As I drew closer, it sounded so beautiful, haunting yet peaceful.

No one had played the piano since Maria's death. Lyov and Alessio had forbid it.

The door was open. Leaning against the wall, I peeked inside. Alessio was sitting on the couch. His eyes were focused intently on the piano, but it was his expression that took my breath away.

He looked completely mesmerized.

I leaned forward, and this time I had to press my hand over my mouth to stop the gasp that threatened to escape.

Ayla was playing the piano, her eyes closed as she hummed, a soft smile on her face.

I looked back and forth between them. They were both enthralled.

Ayla was lost in playing the piano while Alessio was lost in her.

I sniffed as the tears fell down my cheeks. What a beautiful sight.

Slowly stepping away from the door, I smiled. This was it, the moment I had been waiting for.

He is going to be okay, I thought.

Looking up at the ceiling, I softly whispered, "He is going to be okay. He found her, Maria." Tears blinded my vision. "You can rest in peace now. Your sweet boy has found his angel."

Chapter 28

Ayla

After playing the first song, I couldn't help myself, so I didn't stop. Instead, I played another. One of my favorite songs, called *I Won't Give Up*. I used to play that every day.

As the song flowed around me, I felt myself singing to the melody. My voice was a quiet whisper, soft even to my ears. My racing heart slowed to a soothing beat.

After so long, I felt at peace and strangely hopeful.

The piano had always been my escape. When life failed me, my piano never did. It always gave me the sanctuary I needed. It always brought me the peace I was desperate for. And I was grateful I could feel that way again.

The second song ended and I played another one, hoping Alessio wouldn't tell me to stop. But when I didn't hear him, I continued to play. This time I played *A Thousand Years*.

As my fingers flowed on the keys and the third song came to an end, I slowly opened my eyes, instantly meeting Alessio's gaze. His stare was intense, unflinching, and he looked deep in thought, and maybe a little lost.

My hands were still resting on the piano as we stared at each other. The smile on my face dissipated as nervousness filled my body.

As long as I was playing, I didn't care what happened around me. Nothing mattered. But now, looking at Alessio, his eyes as intense as always, I grew anxious.

But though his stares were intense, they were warm. Something I never saw in him before.

When he didn't move or say anything, I cleared my throat. At the sudden sound, his eyes widened and he looked away. He raked his bloody fingers through his hair.

I winced at the sight and got up and stood in front of the piano. From that position, Alessio wasn't far from me, only a few feet away.

I could see his bruised face clearly and winced again. His cheeks were red and quickly turning into a slight purple shade. There was a cut on his eyebrow and dried blood covered his lips.

"You can leave," Alessio said in a hard voice. Flinching at his sudden change of tone, I took a step back and hit the piano. My hands played with the hem of my dress in nervousness.

He was doing it again. From warm to cold in seconds.

"You should clean your wounds so they don't get infected," I said. Keeping my eyes on him, I watched for his reaction.

He didn't give me any. Instead he glared at the wall to his side, his jaw locked tight together.

My heart started to gallop again as worry filled me. Maybe I had overstepped my limits. I shouldn't have played the piano. I shouldn't have even been there.

As I continued to fidget with my dress, I bit on my lips as my hands grew colder.

"I said leave!" Alessio growled.

My eyes widened and I scurried away from the piano. At the door, my steps faltered and I slowly looked over my shoulder. He had the brown glass bottle in his hand and he was staring at it, his other fist clenched tight. Shoulders heavy in defeat, I walked out of the room.

I knew he wasn't going to clean his wounds. Alessio was too lost in his pain, and I understood his feelings. His pain made my heart ache because I knew what it felt like to be hopeless.

Making my way to my room, I got inside and turned on the lights. I quickly rummaged through my drawer and found the first aid kit. Holding it close my chest, I let out another sigh.

I was a little apprehensive to go back there. But maybe if the first aid kit was in front of him, he would clean his wounds. Without a second thought, I closed the drawer and quickly walked out of my room and made my way back.

The door was partially closed, exactly how I left it. I found myself chewing on my nails, but forced myself to put my hand down. After a few seconds of standing outside, shuffling from one foot to the other, I pushed the door open.

Peeking inside, I saw Alessio still sitting in the same spot. This time his head was resting on the back on the plush couch and his eyes were closed. He was still holding the bottle on his thigh, but it was empty. It had been half-full when I left.

My heart twisted at the thought of him drinking himself to oblivion.

I walked in and his eyes snapped open, annoyance and frustration clearly written on his face as he stared at the ceiling, refusing to look at me.

With shaky hands, I placed the first aid kit on the coffee table and then buried my hands in my skirt to hide the nervousness brewing inside of me.

His gaze moved toward the coffee table and then he closed them, silently dismissing my presence.

Time for me to leave, I thought, staring at Alessio's emotionless face. Even though he was in pain, he didn't show it.

To a man like him, feelings meant weakness. And there was no weakness in this life. Our weaknesses would only get us killed.

"Please clean your wounds," I begged softly. After sparing him another glance, I walked away.

Closing the door behind me, I leaned against it and closed my eyes. After the moments I had with Alessio, no matter how awkward and weird it was, I didn't want to go back to my room alone.

I also was scared of the nightmares. I was scared of the memories that would come to haunt me as soon as I would close my eyes. Alberto's face haunted me.

I had just a few moments filled with serenity and now I was petrified of feeling the all-encompassing pain that blinded me.

Dread filled me as I approached my room.

I closed my eyes and willed myself to open the door. I just wished that I could sleep peacefully without memories haunting me.

Just as the thought went through my head, my eyes snapped open as I remembered the scene in my room a few nights ago.

I did have a peaceful sleep.

Alessio's jacket.

It kept the nightmares away.

With wide eyes, my head swiveled to the left in the direction of Alessio's room. The one right next to the piano room. Maybe, just maybe, if I had his jacket with me, I could sleep again.

It seemed pathetic, but I just wanted to sleep. Without fear, without pain twisting my heart.

Quickly making up my mind, I stepped away from my room and walked toward Alessio's. My steps were slow, yet determined.

When I saw no one, I opened the door and slid inside. The room was dark and I searched for a light switch.

As soon as I found it, I turned on the lights and the room was instantly illuminated. Without wasting time, I made my way to his closet, filled with tailored suits and dress shirts. Most of his suits were dark colors, a representation of him. I couldn't imagine Alessio wearing anything but dark colors.

With my heart beating wildly, I took a black suit jacket off the hanger and held it to my chest. I placed the empty hanger at the back of the closet so he wouldn't find it.

Bringing the jacket up, I buried my face in the soft fabric and inhaled. The same scent of cologne filled my nose. My tense muscles started to relax and I sighed.

I couldn't explain it. How could Alessio bring me peace? Even though fear was a constant factor, he calmed my heart in a strange way.

I hurried out of his room and into mine.

With my gaze still fixated on what I was holding, I mindlessly made my way to my bed and slid under the soft comforter.

I brought the jacket next to my face on the pillow, holding it tight, as if scared someone would take it away from me.

My eyes started to close. A tired yawn escaped me and I settled deeper under the comforter.

The last thing I saw before falling asleep was Alessio's suit jacket. As sleep took over my body and mind, I prayed that the painful memories wouldn't come back.

***

The sun peeked in my bedroom window, lighting the room like a fiery halo. I lifted my head from the pillow, my black hair tumbling down my back like a waterfall.

It was morning already.

Alberto hadn't visited my dreams. I closed my eyes yet again, the sun's waking rays warming my body. I felt warm inside too. Full. Relieved. Maybe a little content.

Memories of the night before ran through my sleepy mind and I couldn't help but smile.

Alessio had let me play the piano. My heart quickened at the thought and my smile widened. Alessio, even though he was cold and hard. Sometimes rude and mean. He could be sweet.

I turned around and saw his black suit jacket lying next to my face on my soft pillow. Bringing it close, I placed my head on it.

Because of this, I had a good sleep, a sleep without any of my past memories haunting me.

Maybe this was my key to stopping my nightmares. I looked at this jacket, my heart racing against my chest.

After giving it a final stare, I sat up in bed and folded the jacket and carefully placed it under my pillow.

"You are my secret," I whispered, getting out of bed.

I quickly went through my morning routine. After taking a hot shower, I twisted my hair in a bun and then slid into my black dress. Tying the white apron around my waist, I looked at my reflection.

I looked different somehow. My cheeks were rosy and fuller. There weren't any black circles under my eyes but instead, my green eyes were shining brightly. A small smile was playing across my lips.

It was weird. My father had died last night, yet I felt content.

Placing both my hands on the counter, I exhaled. Who knew? Living in the enemy's house, I had found friends and a mother figure. I was happy here.

On my way toward the stairs, I passed the piano room. My steps faltered in front of it and I stared at the closed door.

Was Alessio still in there?

Curious, I stepped toward the door and slowly turned the knob. The door opened and I tensed.

I peeked inside and sucked in a shocked breath at the sight. Alessio was still sitting in the same spot, bloody and in the same dirty clothes. The first aid kit sat on the coffee table, untouched.

My heart twisted as I stepped inside, and my nose started to tingle. My vision blurred slightly with unshed tears. His head was resting against the back on the couch with his eyes closed.

His breathing was even, his chest moving slowly up and down. Alessio was asleep. I gazed at him as he slept.

I walked forward and stopped right in front of him. A few strands of his hair fell on his forehead, and before I could stop myself, I bent forward and softly brushed them away. Lines of tension creased on his forehead, showing that even in his sleep, he was riddled with pain.

But as I continued to stare at his sleepy face, I couldn't help but think that he looked kinder. My gaze raked the length of his body. His black shirt was unbuttoned at the top, revealing a little of his muscled chest. The sleeves were rolled up to his elbows and I stopped at his hands.

They looked worse than the night before. Dried blood covered his swollen knuckles and fingers. I winced at the sight. I had a feeling he wouldn't listen to me, but I still hoped.

I was tempted to clean his wounds for him, but I didn't want to overstep my boundaries.

I didn't want to anger him more, not when he was already going through so much.

I bit on my lips as I continued to step back, but with each step away from Alessio, my stomach sank deeper.

I stopped and stared at the broken man in front of me.

I couldn't be this heartless, could I? I couldn't leave him in this state when I could help instead.

Placing my hand over my beating heart, I chewed on my lips. I moved closer to him, slowly.

Keeping my eyes fixated on his sleeping form, I knelt down in front of him. Moving my eyes from his face, I stared at his bruised hands. I opened the first aid kit and removed the antiseptic wipes and some bandages. There was also a small hand towel folded under the bandages, so I took it out too. After placing them on the coffee table, I turned back to Alessio.

With my heart racing in my chest, I placed my shaking hand on his to see if he was awake.

He didn't move.

I sighed in relief and then took his hand in mine.

I waited again.

He didn't move.

I picked up an antiseptic wipe and gently cleaned his hands. I made sure my movements were soft and careful so I wouldn't hurt him.

As the blood came off, I saw his knuckles were

bruised, but not much. The blood made it look worse. His fingers were slightly swollen, but thankfully not broken.

After cleaning his left hand, I gently wrapped the bandage around his hand, making sure that it wasn't too tight. After I was done, I leaned back and placed his hand on his thigh again.

I glanced up at Alessio, expecting him to still be asleep, but that wasn't the case.

I sucked in a surprised breath when I saw his intense blue eyes focused on me.

I had been so lost in cleaning his injuries that I didn't realize he was awake.

"Alessio," I whispered.

His gaze raked over my face and then moved to his bandaged hand.

Both of us stared at it. Sweat formed at the back of my neck as nervousness filled me.

"I...I saw that you didn't clean your hands," I stuttered. Taking a deep breath, I quickly continued. "I thought that maybe I could clean them for you."

I waited for him to answer but he didn't.

"It could get infected. That's why I cleaned it," I said.

He still didn't answer.

Oh no. I messed up. I really messed up.

I started fidgeting with the hem of my dress again. Looking at his other hand, I swallowed at the sight. It still needed to be cleaned.

Slowly shifting away, I said, "You should clean your other hand."

His expression showed confusion as he kept staring at his bandaged hand. Letting out a sigh, I started to get up but his arms snaked out so fast it was a blur. His fingers wrapped around my wrist, and with a tug, he pulled me back down so that I was kneeling in front of him again. But this time, between his spread thighs.

He held my wrist with his bandaged hand. I tipped my head back to look in his eyes as he gazed down at me with indescribable emotions.

I saw him swallow hard and then he looked down. My eyebrows furrowed in confusion and I stared down too, only to find him pushing his other, still bloody hand toward me.

My eyes widened in realization and my heart flipped as my stomach twisted in knots. I looked back up, my eyes filled with questions, but Alessio didn't answer. He just continued to stare at me silently. Expectantly.

He let my wrist go and I released a shaky breath. With my heart pounding vigorously against my ribcage, I took his hand in mine.

His head was cocked to the side as he stared at me. I forgot how dark he was, how sinister and how huge he was. As I kneeled between his thighs, I felt his forceful and dangerous energy around me.

Looking down at his hand again, I got to work.

No words were spoken.

There was only silence between us.

But even through the silence, it felt comforting.

I cleaned his wounds just as carefully and gently as before, and then bandaged his right hand too. All the time, I was aware of his eyes on me. I could feel his gaze on my skin. And I grew warmer from it.

When I was done, my eyes stayed on his hand

which was still in mine. Alessio didn't pull away either.

Unconsciously, I found that I was rubbing my thumb over his knuckles. When I realized what I was doing, I quickly let his hand go. It fell back onto his lap.

I looked up and our eyes met again.

Blue to green. Both unflinching.

We stared.

We breathed. Together.

When I couldn't hold his eyes any longer, I looked down.

A few seconds later, before I could move, I felt a tug behind my head and then my hair was falling down my shoulders in waves.

And I saw my hair band in Alessio's hand.

I looked up at him in surprise, and his piercing eyes stared back.

Then he spoke. And his words went straight to my heart. My breathing stuttered.

"You look more beautiful with your hair down," he said, his voice gruff from sleep.

Chapter 29

Alessio

When Ayla brought the first aid kit, I didn't want her to see me like this—broken and in pain—so I ignored her. She saw enough already.

Emotions I never wanted to experience were coursing through my body and self-loathing took its place. Feelings were a sign of weakness. And I showed Ayla my weakness.

Whenever she was near, I couldn't think straight. No matter how hard I tried to be indifferent, she always knew how to break through the walls.

When she played the piano, I saw my mother sitting there.

The pain in my body reminded me of why I was in this position.

Alfredo. Whatever death he experienced, it wasn't enough. He shouldn't have died so easily.

The image of my mother's lifeless, bloodied body flashed behind my closed eyes and the ache in my heart was almost unbearable.

All these years, I kept it in. I locked it inside of me, refusing to feel.

"What am I supposed to do now?" I whispered to myself.

I had lived with one goal. To kill Alfredo, to end his family and his empire.

My revenge was on him. But the only thing left of him now was his family. By the time I was done, nothing would be left.

Every single Abandonato would be wiped off the Earth. His allies. Everything would be mine.

That was my last thought before closing my burning eyes. My restless sleep was haunted by images of a black-haired, green-eyed angel, laughing and happy. But far from my reach. No matter how hard I tried to catch up, she always slipped right through my fingers. Always leaving me feeling empty as she faded away.

At some point, I heard the door open.

As the footsteps grew closer, my body instantly warmed. I didn't have to open my eyes to know that Ayla stood in front of me. Keeping my eyes closed, I feigned sleep as I waited for her next move. I needed her far away from me. Her sweet smell. Her melodious voice.

She came so close that I could smell her vanilla shampoo. Then she knelt down in front me and I found it hard to keep my eyes closed. I wanted to see her. The total contradiction of what I wanted a few seconds ago.

My heart wanted her near while my brain told me to push her far away.

Feeling conflicted, I kept my eyes closed instead.

And then her small hands were holding mine. I resisted the urge to quickly pull away. She was so near. Touching me.

Control. Keep in control, I admonished myself as Ayla rubbed her fingers over my bruised knuckles. And then I felt something wet rubbing over the backs of my fingers. It stung and I bit down my lips to keep from hissing in pain.

When realization crashed through me, my eyes snapped open. I looked down at Ayla and saw her bent over my hand as she cleaned my wounds with an antiseptic wipe.

She took her time, slowly and gently cleaning each knuckle, then the rest of my hand. She applied the bandage, then sighed and leaned away.

I couldn't take my eyes off her. She was so damn beautiful.

At the thought, my heart stuttered and I swallowed hard.

Get a grip on yourself, Alessio.

And then she looked up, her eyes widened, and her lips fell open in shock. "Alessio." My name was a whisper on her lips.

Her cheeks were slightly flushed and it made her even more beautiful. Moving my gaze away from her face, I looked at my bandaged hand.

"I…saw that you didn't clean your hands," she stuttered. "I thought that maybe I could clean them for you."

She had no idea what that did to me. She cleaned my wounds. She still cared for me when I was harsh to her.

"It could get infected. That's why I cleaned it,"

she continued.

When was the last time someone took care of me? My heart raced wildly.

"You should clean your other hand," she said. She sighed and then started to get up.

Panic filled my chest and before I could think, my hand snaked out and I wrapped my fingers around her wrist and tugged until she was kneeling down again. She fell back on her knees in front of me.

I needed her closer. I wasn't ready to let her leave yet. Ayla tipped her head back and stared at me in shock.

I needed a reason to keep her there, so I held out my other hand.

As she worked, the silence brought me comfort. But what was more comforting was Ayla sharing the silence with me. Her presence brought me comfort even as I tried to deny it.

When Ayla was done, she didn't let go of my hand immediately, but instead gently rubbed her thumb over my bandaged knuckles.

Then she let go and stared at me again, our gazes meeting, both unflinching. Both of us lost in each other.

And then she broke the connection. My focus was drawn to her black hair, twisted in a tight bun.

She was a beautiful woman, but I wanted to see her with her hair down again. Before she could move, I leaned forward and pulled off her hair band.

When I told her how beautiful she was, I knew those were the most honest words I'd spoken in a long time.

With her twinkling green eyes, her red lips, her cheeks flushed, and her long black hair falling down her back, she was an image impossible to forget. The look she gave me made my heart race.

So fucking beautiful.

She had sunk deep under my skin and I had to get her out as soon as possible.

Only one way to do that.

One fuck and then I would move on.

Ayla would be no different to me. I had to make sure of it.

Chapter 30

Ayla

At his words, my heart flipped and my stomach twisted. He called me *beautiful*. I quickly ducked my head.

He coughed and then cleared his throat. "Thank you for cleaning my wounds."

I nodded and then looked up. "I want to thank you too. For taking care of me the night before." Nervously playing with the hem of my dress, I continued, "I should have thanked you earlier, but didn't get the chance."

"Is that why you bandaged my hand?" Alessio asked.

I shook my head quickly and whispered, "No."

"Was it pity then? I don't need your pity, Ayla," he growled.

"It was not pity. I just wanted to help." And it was true. I didn't pity him. I felt for him instead. I felt his pain and my heart begged me to offer him comfort. So I did what I could.

251

"Why is it so bad that I bandaged your hand?" I asked.

Alessio glared down at me and he released a frustrated breath.

"I wanted to help, Alessio. It wasn't pity. And even if you didn't take care of me that night, I would have still cleaned your wounds." He stared at me through hazy eyes and clenched his jaw.

I pinned my hair behind my ears and smoothed it. "I can't say that I totally understand what you are going through—"

"Don't," he hissed.

"But I know what it feels like to have so much pain that you feel like you're going to die." I *needed* him to understand, to see that I was broken too. "So, maybe a little, I do understand your pain. Because I felt it too. Not for the same reasons, but I know what it feels like." I stared at his bandaged hands. "When I did that, it was me showing you that I understood. I was trying to give comfort in return." I choked on the last few words.

"I don't need your comfort, Ayla," he said through gritted teeth.

My head snapped up at his words and I shook my head. "Everyone needs comforting sometimes."

"Why the fuck do you make everything so hard?" Alessio growled, standing up. At his sudden action, I fell back on my butt, but quickly scrambled up to my feet. He moved away from me and turned to the wall, giving me his rigid back instead.

"I'm sorry." Tears blinded my vision and my nose started to tingle. Why was he being so hard? Why couldn't he just accept it?

"You need to stay in your limits, Ayla," he warned. At his words, my body froze and fear took place. He was right. I did overstep my boundaries. I was lost in the moment, so lost in his sweet words and gentle gaze that I forgot who he was and who I was.

"I'm sorry," I whispered again, my voice shaking.

"Leave!" Alessio ordered.

It felt like a slap in my face and I quickly shuffled backward. When I didn't move fast enough, he yelled, "Did you not hear what I said? Fucking leave!"

I choked back a sob and quickly swiveled around, then ran out, but stumbled into a hard chest on my way out.

I looked up and saw Nikolay's angry face. His eyes roamed over my face and then glanced behind me.

"What were you doing in there?" he snapped.

"I—"

"Stay away from that room." He glared at me. "And stay the fuck away from the boss. He doesn't have time to deal with you. Understood?"

I nodded without saying anything as the tears fell down my cheeks. Nikolay was indifferent as he walked past me and into the piano room. The door closed behind him.

My heart ached at the thought of Alessio suffering alone. He desperately needed solace, yet refused to accept it even when it was being given to him freely.

Why couldn't he see my pain? Why couldn't he

see that I was the same as him?

He was too blinded by his own past.

Chapter 31

Ayla

I swiped away my tears as I walked down the stairs in a daze. I couldn't understand Alessio. He was unpredictable and short-tempered, and he hid his feelings well.

I just wished he let his guard down and let me in. I wanted to know what he was thinking.

As strange as it sounded, I wanted to help him.

But he shut me out every time, first gentle and then rude and heartless.

Every time I was with him, I felt a pull. His touch was fire, his voice silk. And his eyes penetrated my soul.

I should fear him. I *did* fear him, but under the layers of fear, I cared. He made me feel even when I didn't want to.

Neither of us wanted to feel. We both tried to hide it.

I walked into the kitchen and found Maddie and Lena there. "Hey," Maddie chirped from her spot

255

behind the counter.

Lena turned to face me and wiped her hands in her apron. "Good morning, Ayla," she said with a sweet smile.

Smiling back, I gave her a hug. "Good morning," I said as I stepped out of her warm embrace. I helped them in the kitchen, trying not to think about that morning.

"I'll message the others to set the table," Maddie muttered as she took out her phone. She was still typing the message when I saw Viktor walking into the kitchen, his face hard and cold.

"Boss wants his breakfast in his office," he said briskly before leaving. We didn't even have a chance to reply.

Was Alessio going to eat alone? I thought back to our earlier encounter, his fury as he told me to leave the room, and the flash of pain I saw in his eyes before he shut me out.

I felt someone nudge me, snapping out of my thoughts. Maddie stared at me in confusion.

"What's wrong? You've been quiet this morning," she asked, leaning her elbows on the counter as she waited for an answer.

I shrugged.

Maddie leaned forward. "Is it about Alessio?"

I chuckled. "You are a mind reader, Maddie."

Her eyes twinkled and she winked. "I know. So, what happened?"

"Well, last night, I went to the piano room and Alessio caught me there. But when I was about to leave, he let me play—"

"What?" she squealed. "You played the piano?

Alessio let you play the piano?" Her mouth hung open in shock.

I nodded.

"Wait. You played the piano in front of Alessio?"

Before I could answer, she continued, "Ayla, this is big! He never lets anyone play the piano. It's forbidden. It's his mother's, and since her death, nobody was allowed to play it."

The news took my breath away and I stared at her in shock.

If that's why he was angry at me, why did he let me play in the first place?

I bit down on my lips in frustration. Alessio was a confusing man.

"Mom! Did you hear that? Alessio let Ayla play the piano!" Maddie exclaimed loudly next to my ear. Wincing, I took a step away.

"Yes. I heard," Lena replied, her voice soft. I turned toward her and saw that she was smiling at me, her eyes shining merrily.

Turning back to Maddie, I continued, "But it didn't end well. He ordered me to leave afterwards. He was really angry. And this morning too."

"This morning?"

"I went back to check on him to make sure he cleaned his wounds. But he didn't. So, I cleaned them for him. He was nice about it, but then got angry again," I muttered.

"Wait. You cleaned his wounds and he got angry at you?" Maddie bristled slightly. When I nodded, she placed her hands on her hips and tapped her foot on the ground in annoyance. "God, he is so damn annoying. What exactly did he say?"

At her question, I grew somber. "I kind of told him that we all need comforting sometimes and he shouldn't have to deal with it alone. But he got really angry and told me to stay in my limits. And he yelled at me to leave."

"What. An. Ungrateful. Bastard," Maddie growled.

"Maddie! Watch your language," Lena scolded.

"I'm serious, Mom. How dare he? Ayla helped him, and this is how he treats her?"

"We all know how he is. Alessio doesn't like the attention. Or comfort. He doesn't do well with emotions." Lena placed a comforting hand on my back.

"I know," I whispered.

Maddie still looked angry. "Maybe you should have just left his hands bloody so they would get infected. He sure as hell deserves it. Asshole."

"Maddie! Enough!" Lena reprimanded her loudly.

"Fine!" She crossed her arms against her chest. Lena gave her a glare, but it didn't look threatening at all. I didn't think she could ever look angry, even she tried hard.

After giving Maddie another serious look, she turned to me and palmed my cheek. "Don't take Alessio too seriously. He is like that to everyone. Give him some time," she said softly, before smiling and then walking out of the kitchen.

As soon as Lena was out of sight, Maddie started swearing. "That little fucker. He is lucky I wasn't there. I would have sucker punched him for talking like that to you. Asshole. Jerk."

She kept going, moving around the kitchen almost furiously. She slammed a plate full of breakfast on a tray and then made a glass of protein while I stood there watching her rage. When Maddie was done, she pushed the tray in my hand.

"Go give that him," she ordered.

Was she crazy? Why would she send me back to the lion's den?

"What? No." I pushed the tray back.

"Nuh-uh, girl. You are going up there and giving him his breakfast. And you are going to act like nothing happened."

When I didn't move, she sighed and her shoulders dropped. "Considering how long I have known him, I'm pretty sure he is feeling guilty right now. So you are going to go up there and make him feel guiltier and shitty about himself. Yeah?"

"Maddie—"

"Trust me. He will probably even apologize. But you are going to act nonchalant and walk away. Understood? Make. Him. Feel. Guilty," she huffed.

I tried to shake my head but she was already talking over me. "Ayla, you are too sweet for your own good. Which makes it much worse. You didn't deserve how he treated you. So, humor me, okay? Please."

"No," I snapped.

Maddie threw her hands in the air in frustration.

"Maddie, I don't want to hurt him. He is angry and doesn't want to see me," I replied.

"And that's where you are wrong. Alessio wants to see you. He let you play the piano, for God's sake. It means something. It means a lot. He is just frustrated at himself and that's why he took it out on you," Maddie explained in a rush. "I know him, Ayla. Just do as I tell you and everything will be good."

"But—"

Maddie shook her head. "No. You are getting late. Go give Alessio his breakfast." When I didn't move, she gently pushed me toward the door. "Go. And good luck! You can do this."

As I slowly walked out of the kitchen, I heard Maddie call out behind me, "I'll be waiting here for you."

"Okay," I muttered, my voice trembling.

I passed by Nikolay and Viktor as I made my way upstairs. The tiny hairs on the back of my neck prickled as I felt their stares on my back, but I kept my gaze down, purposely avoiding them.

With each step I took toward Alessio's office, my heart hammered almost painfully in my chest. My hands grew cold and a trickle of sweat ran down my neck and between my shoulder blades.

Stopping in front of the door, I took a deep breath and then brought my hand up. As soon as my fist knocked against the door, Alessio's voice came through.

"Come in."

I walked inside to find him facing away from me. He was only wearing his black shirt and black slacks. I cleared my throat and he quickly turned around, his eyes widening at the sight of me.

I sighed in relief when I noticed he had showered. He was wearing a clean dress shirt, and his hair appeared wet. His face was cleaned from the blood too.

I also noticed that he was struggling to wrap his bandages again.

"I brought your breakfast," I said, surprisingly without stuttering. He stared at me silently, his face impassive, and then he nodded toward the coffee table.

I placed the tray down before straightening and turning to look at Alessio. We stared at each other for a second before I stared at his hands.

Taking a step closer, I cleared my throat again before nervously asking, "Do you want me to bandage them again?"

He had made it clear that he didn't want my help before, but there was nothing wrong in offering to help again. Right? It was his choice to accept it or not.

Alessio looked down at his hands and then shook his head. "No. It's okay. I'll do it."

"Are you sure?"

"Yes," he responded briskly. He tried to wrap the bandages around his hands and I stayed still as I watched him struggle with it.

It was a mess. Without thinking of the consequences, I walked to him and took his hands in mine. Alessio went rigid and I felt his breath on my forehead. With my head bent, I started to wrap the bandages around his hands.

He stood perfectly still, his muscles barely moving. His breathing was slightly erratic. My heart thumped in my chest and my stomach twisted nervously at being this close to him.

When I was done, I stepped back and gave him a wan smile. "Done," I whispered as our eyes met.

Alessio didn't answer. I didn't expect him to. Giving him another smile, I turned around and started to walk away. Just as I neared the door, his voice stopped me.

"Wait," he demanded.

I stopped. When I heard him sigh, I decided to face him. Turning around, I saw him running his hand through his hair. He looked down and then leaned against his desk, crossing his ankles.

"About this morning," Alessio started as he looked back up. "I shouldn't have yelled. That was a mistake."

He looked a little uncomfortable. Even though his words were meant to be nice, his face was still hard and cold. But I didn't care. It was the words that mattered. It wasn't an apology but it was enough for me.

That was all I needed to hear.

My heart fluttered at what he said and I smiled again. "Okay," I replied.

Alessio nodded and if I wasn't mistaken, he looked relieved.

Maddie had been right. He had been feeling guilty. But I was glad that my acceptance took this burden away from him.

When the room filled with silence again, I took it as my cue to leave. But Alessio spoke again. His words took my breath away, my hand going to my chest.

"You can keep playing the piano if you want."

I stared at him in confusion as my heart went

wild. I had to lock my knees together to keep from falling on the floor.

Hope blossomed in me at his words and all I wanted to do was cry.

"I can?"

Alessio nodded and his expression changed to slight embarrassment. "That's my way of making it up to you," he replied.

How could he be sweet and gentle yet heartless and cruel at the same time?

His words meant one thing, while his actions spoke something else entirely.

I was scared to hope…only because he could change his mind in the blink of an eye and it would crush me. But I couldn't help the feeling of happiness coursing through my body.

"Thank you," I said, my voice filled with emotions and gratefulness as tears blinded my vision.

He nodded again without saying anything. He appeared to swallow almost nervously.

After a few seconds of him avoiding eye contact with me while I stared at him through tear-filled eyes, I decided it was time for me to leave.

Turning around, I reached for the knob, but didn't open the door. Instead I paused and wiped my tears away before whispering again, "Thank you."

I didn't know if he heard it or not, but I didn't give him a chance to answer. Opening the door, I walked out, my body light with contentment.

I skipped downstairs, barely containing the smile on my face.

As soon as I got to the kitchen, I ran to Maddie and hugged her tightly. She laughed.

"I take it things went well. I would say *very well* from that expression on your face," Maddie said lightly as she hugged me back.

I nodded and then laughed with merriment. "He told me I can keep playing the piano!"

Maddie's eyes softened even further and she smiled brightly. "There you go. See, I told you."

"Maddie. I think I am…happy."

"I know. I'm happy too."

I nodded and smiled back. My cheeks were hurting from smiling too much and too hard.

When was the last time I smiled and laughed like this?

I didn't know. I didn't care.

All that mattered was what I felt now.

Chapter 32

2 weeks later

"Maddie, stop!" I giggled as she continued to tickle my sides. "Ouch. It hurts. Stop!"

"That's what you get for throwing whipped cream in my face." She laughed.

"You did it first," I argued back through my giggling.

"Ahh, stop…too much…I can't breathe…"

"Do you accept defeat?" she growled, trying to mimic Alessio's voice. That made me laugh even harder.

"Yes. Yes. Oh my God." I breathed out as she slowly stopped her attack on my sides.

But as soon as she let me go, I twisted around and caught her by the legs. Giving her a challenging look, I trapped her legs underneath mine and started to tickle her.

It was my turn to laugh.

"Got you!"

She was struggling and gasping for air through

her laughter.

"Maddie! Ayla!"

I quickly stopped tickling her when I heard Lena's voice from behind me.

"Busted," Maddie whispered.

Rolling off her, I stood up and straightened my dress while she did the same.

"What did you do to my kitchen?" she gasped. The horrified look on her face was funny. Bringing my hand up, I coughed into my palm to mask my laughter. Maddie didn't even try to hide it.

"There is whipped cream everywhere! You guys were suppose to make dessert, not turn the kitchen into dessert!" Lena said almost angrily, with her hands on her hips as she leveled us both with a glare.

"Sorry, Lena. We will clean it up. Promise," I said with a smile and blinked innocently at her.

"Don't try to act innocent with me, young lady. Maddie is rubbing off you," she remarked.

Maddie laughed again and linked her arms through mine. "Definitely," she said with a wink. Lena shook her head but I saw the smile peeking on the corner of her lips.

"Don't worry, Mom. Ayla and I will clean it up in no time."

"You better. C'mon. Hurry to work now," Lena replied before turning around and walking out of the kitchen.

"Lena is right. We did make a mess of the kitchen," I said with a sigh as I looked around.

It had been two weeks and I felt like I had been given a new life. Two weeks and I'd had no nightmares, my sleep filled with peacefulness. Two weeks of only laughter and smiles.

I felt happiness that I had never felt before. At first, I was scared that maybe all of this was a dream. I was scared that all of it would be taken away from me. But when I woke up each day and was still living this life, I started to hope that maybe this was it.

This was my new beginning.

"Done?" Maddie asked. Her voice snapped me out of my thoughts and I smiled. Looking at the cleaned counters, I nodded.

"Done," I replied.

"C'mon, let's go. There is still about two hours before dinner. We can fit a movie in," she said cheerfully as she pulled me out of the kitchen.

As we made our way upstairs to my room, Maddie chatted about her day with Artur. She was definitely lost in him. I asked her if she loved him, but her response was that she didn't know.

I didn't believe her.

I was sure she loved him but was scared to admit it. She had nothing to be scared of. From what I had witnessed, Artur really did care about Maddie.

When we reached the top of the stairs, I stopped dead in my tracks. In the process of doing so, Maddie had to stop too.

"Huh? What's wrong?" she asked.

All I could do was stare in front of me in shock.

Not again.

Then I heard Maddie mutter angrily. "Seriously?"

There he was. Alessio. But he wasn't alone. He

was with Nina, the same blonde I had seen in his office.

Alessio had her pressed against the wall, with her legs wrapped around his waist. They were kissing and didn't appear to realize we were standing there.

"Seriously, dude. You wanna fuck, then get a room. That's what rooms are for," Maddie hissed loudly.

Alessio's head snapped back and he stared at us, his gaze laced with lust. I shifted my eyes away.

"Well, you can leave if you don't want to see anything," Nina fired back.

"This is a hallway. Anyone can pass through and nobody wants to see your saggy boobs hanging loose, so get a room," Maddie said, her voice calm yet filled with venom.

"You know…" Nina started to say, but she didn't finish. Alessio had opened his door and was about to go inside, with Nina still wrapped around him like a vise.

She turned her head toward us and gave us a smirk before burying her face in his neck. That was the last thing I saw as the door closed.

"That little bitch. I swear to God, I will rip those fake hair extensions off her head one day. She makes me so violent. And I swear, I'm *not* a violent person," Maddie fumed beside me.

"Why do you hate her so much?" I asked as we entered my room.

"Is that even a question, Ayla? She is freaking annoying. Nina thinks that just because Alessio fucks her, she is special. Like, bitch, *please*, he fucks anyone with boobs and a pussy."

I watched her jump on my bed and lay down.

"Nina probably thinks that he will marry her one day. So delusional. Alessio doesn't even care for her. She is just so easy and always comes for more. If she never comes back, Alessio wouldn't even bat an eye or go looking for her. He has plenty of other women lining up for him."

"Hmm," I said, stretching out beside her.

"But I hate her because she is ruining my ship."

My forehead creased in confusion at her words. "What do you mean?"

Maddie's eyes went wide for a second and then she shook her head. Biting down on her lips, she shrugged. "Nothing."

"What ship? What are you talking about?"

"It's nothing," Maddie said as she sat up. She leaned over me and took the remote control. "What do you want to watch?"

I stared at her for a second before turning toward the TV that Artur installed for me a few days ago. Maddie was definitely changing the topic and I was curious by what she meant.

But I decided to let it go. I would get it out of her later.

***

"Goodnight," I called, waving at Maddie. Smiling, I made my way upstairs.

Dinner was over a long time ago and after cleaning the dining room and kitchen, we decided that it was time to call it a night.

I stopped at the piano room but didn't knock. This was my routine. Well, *our* routine. Alessio and I would avoid each other during the day, but at night, I would play for him before going back to our bedrooms. It was our unspoken agreement.

Gentle and sweet Alessio was only at night. During the day, he was cold Alessio. And a teaser too. I was back to being called "kitten."

If there was a time we crossed paths by accident, he would give me the same heated look. He would tease me with his slight touch and then walk away as if nothing happened.

But today, after what I saw in the hallway, I felt a little apprehensive. My stomach was twisted in knots. I was embarrassed for both me and him. I knew he didn't care, but I did. It felt weird to catch him in such a compromising position.

But I also wanted to play the piano. It had become my obsession. But it wasn't *just* the piano.

I treasured the small, gentle, and silent moment that Alessio and I shared every night. We barely talked. I played and he listened. And then we would go to sleep. But still, it was important to me.

So, I raised my hand and knocked on the door.

When I heard him call me in, I opened the door and walked inside before closing it behind me. Tonight Alessio was sitting on the couch as always, but this time he had his laptop. He was typing furiously, but when I got closer, he looked up and stopped.

I smiled but he didn't. As always.

Alessio closed his laptop and placed it on the coffee table before leaning back against the couch and stretching his legs in front of him.

That meant one thing. He was ready for me to play. Giving him another smile, I walked to the piano and sat down behind it. My eyes closed and my fingers moved.

The sweet melody came through and my muscles relaxed. I played that song every night, while quietly singing the lyrics.

With each song, my chest grew fuller with contentment. It felt like I was flying. I was *free*.

After two songs, I opened my eyes and stared at Alessio. And as every night, his warm blue eyes were fixated intensely on mine as he watched me play.

I played the third song, our gazes still locked. We stared. We breathed. I played. I sang. He watched. And it was the most beautiful thing I had ever experienced.

After the third song, I stopped. Alessio kept his eyes on me as I stood up. Walking slowly toward him, I stopped a few feet away.

"Goodnight," I whispered.

"Goodnight," he said.

And every single night, those were the only words spoken by us.

Giving him a soft smile, I walked out of the piano room. I closed the door behind me and leaned against it. My heart continued the same pitter-patter dance.

I walked to my bedroom with the same constant smile on my face. When I got inside, I quickly shrugged off my black dress and put on the light pink night dress that Lena bought for me. I crawled

271

into bed and closed my eyes. Moving my hand under my pillow, I searched for Alessio's jacket.

But my hand only made contact with the mattress. My eyes snapped opened and I quickly sat up. Pushing my pillows away, I looked for the jacket.

I couldn't find it.

No. No. No.

Jumping out of my bed, I went around my bedroom, desperately looking for his jacket. My peace.

I couldn't sleep without it.

I needed it!

But it was nowhere to be found.

I was breathing hard, my hair a wild mess. Bringing my hand up, I pressed it against my chest as panic coursed through my body.

Milena had cleaned my room this morning. She must have found it and taken it away. I was so stupid. I should have known. But I had completely forgot.

Sinking down on my bed, tears blinded my vision and they fell freely down my cheeks.

I couldn't sleep without it. The nightmares would come back.

I laid down and hugged my legs to my chest, sobbing into my pillow.

"Did you want him? Huh? Answer me!" Alberto *hissed as he continued to rain the whip down my bare back.*

"No!" I cried out as pain blinded my vision. My back and my legs were on fire. I was naked and tied

in a spread-eagle position. The chains from the ceiling were wrapped around my wrists, holding me up. My toes were barely touching the ground.

"I saw the look you were giving him! You wanted to fuck him, didn't you? You wanted his cock inside you, huh?"

I shook my head violently and cried out when the whip made contact with my back again. "No," I gasped. "I didn't do anything. I don't want him."

It was true. The man was giving me weird looks all night. He even tried to touch me, and I had tried my best to stay away from him. I barely even looked at him. He made my skin crawl.

But Alberto being Alberto, he only believed what he wanted.

If a man wanted me, it was my fault. I tempted him. It was my body. Me. It was all my fault.

And I had to pay for it.

Because I betrayed him. My body betrayed him.

"Alberto, please."

But he was relentless. He showed me no mercy.

Fisting my hair around his fingers, he pulled my head back sharply. I winced at the pain that shot through my neck. He slapped me hard against the face and I tasted blood where his ring cut my lips.

"Liar," he spat in my face.

"Please. Believe me," I begged.

"You are mine! Mine! Your body is mine. Your lips are mine. Your pussy is mine. Your ass is mine. Do you understand! All mine!" Alberto hissed through gritted teeth. His fingers bit into my cheeks as he grasped my chin, making me look him straight in the eye.

I quickly nodded and agreed, hoping that he would stop his torture on my body. "Yes. Yes. I'm yours, Alberto. I belong to you. Only you! My body is yours. Please. I'm sorry. I didn't want him," I sobbed.

My body was burning. My cheeks were aching. My heart was pounding. And my heart was breaking.

"You need to be taught a lesson. Then you will understand," he said, letting my chin go. Raising the whip high in his hands, I flinched before it made contact with my body. And when it did, I screamed in agony.

When he was done abusing my body, he dropped the whip and started to unzip his pants. His cock was already hard.

Closing my eyes, I waited for what would come next.

But no matter how much I tried to prepare myself, the pain was always the same. It always felt like I was being cut from the inside. I cried out as he slammed into me, my toes completely leaving the ground.

He painfully rammed inside of me a few times and then he was roaring his release. Pulling out of me, he grabbed my chin again. "Look at me!" he ordered harshly.

My eyes snapped opened and I stared at his furious black eyes. His lips slammed down on mine and I winced. It hurt. Pulling back, he pressed his nails into my cheeks.

"You are mine, Ayla. Never forget that."

My eyes shot open. Sitting up in bed, I felt sick and my skin was burning. It felt like I had just been whipped. My stomach twisted violently and I struggled out of my bed. I limped to the bathroom and fell down in front of the toilet before retching.

I gagged. Vomited. And cried.

I was shaking uncontrollably and dizziness clouded my vision as I continued to sob. The pain. Oh, God. It was pressing down on my chest and I couldn't breathe.

Everything was going too perfectly.

This was supposed to be my new beginning.

I had hope. I really thought I had moved on.

But how false it was.

There was no hope, no peace.

It was all a dream. A fantasy. False hope. Jaded hope.

I was living a constant nightmare.

What was the point of living? What the point of continuing on when all I felt was pain, indescribable pain?

Looking up, I noticed the shaving razor Maddie had given me. It was on the counter. Right next to me, as if it had been placed there for me to use at this moment. Moving to my knees, I reached for it. I held it in my shaky hands as my harsh breathing continued to fill the bathroom.

My hands were trembling so hard that the razor almost fell out of them, but I grasped it hard. Moving back, I sat against the tub and pulled my knees up to my chest as I stared at the razor.

I wanted silence.

I didn't want to hurt anymore.

The tears continued to run freely down my cheeks, the evidence of my past and pain.

I didn't know what I was doing. I couldn't think straight.

All I wanted was peace. Alberto's voice in my head was driving insane.

Placing my wrist out, I held the razor to it. Closing my eyes, I let my head fall back against the tub. I didn't feel anything when I pressed it hard on my skin and dragged it upward. I opened my eyes and saw a long red line. Blood.

It was seeping from the cut I had made. But I still didn't feel anything.

Why didn't I feel the burn?

Why didn't it hurt?

Growing frustrated, I placed the razor on my other wrist and pressed it down hard, twisting it in my skin. I made a similar cut as the other wrist.

Dropping the razor, I stared at the mess I made. My skin was cut open and there was blood everywhere. It covered my arms. My dress. The floor.

The bathroom swam in front of me and my vision blurred so terribly that I barely saw anything. My head rolled back and my body started to sink down on the floor. I fell sideways, my head hitting the floor hard.

Black dots appeared in front of my vision and I started to go numb. I felt *nothing*.

And for a brief moment, it was beautiful.

As my eyes started to close and I sank deeper in the darkness, I *smiled*.

Silence. There was only silence.

And that was all I needed.

***

Maddie

"Hmmm…" I murmured against Artur's lips.

"I miss you," he replied before giving me a quick peck.

Giggling, I pushed my fingers in his hair and pulled his lips back to mine, kissing him deeply. "You saw me last night."

"I missed you the moment you left."

"Stop being so sweet," I replied, biting on his lips.

"Only for you, baby."

He was so sweet sometimes. Ayla was right. I did love him. But I was scared. Was this the right thing? Was he truly the one?

I always wanted epic love. Is this my epic love?

He was sweet, caring, and gentle. But he never said that he loved me. I was waiting for him to confess first. And I was growing desperate as each day passed and there was no confession.

I felt his hands on my ass and he pulled me closer. I was sitting on the kitchen counter with my legs wrapped around his waist. I could feel him against my core.

"Not here," I whispered. "Mom is going to kill us."

"I know," Artur growled. He slightly pulled away and pouted. "Fuck, baby, I need you."

"After breakfast?"

277

"Torture," he shot back. I jokingly slapped his chest and pushed him away from me. I was just about to unwrap my legs from his hips when I saw my mom behind Artur's back.

Oh shit.

Busted.

"Oh God! Not on the counter. Please not on the kitchen counter!" Mom gasped.

I quickly pushed Artur away and jumped off the counter. "I swear, we were just hugging. We weren't going to take it that far."

Artur's cheeks were slightly red and I felt myself blushing too.

"Maddie," Mom warned.

"I know. I know. It won't happen again," I sighed.

"Well, I have to go. See you at breakfast," Artur said before leaving. Before he walked out of the kitchen, he sent me a wink.

Coward. I couldn't believe he left me alone to deal with this.

Mom was glaring at me and I pouted, giving her my best puppy eyes.

"Mom. I swear we weren't going to do anything on the counter. It's clean," I said.

"Maddie, are you using protection? Please tell me you are protected."

Here we go again.

"I think I got that covered."

"Okay. I was just checking." She shrugged before moving to the oven. "Where is Ayla?"

That was a good question. She was late.

"I don't know. I haven't seen her," I said,

growing slightly worried.

Mom stopped what she was doing and gave me a worried look too. "Do you want to check on her?"

"Yeah, I should," I agreed before making my way out of the kitchen. I quickly went upstairs and stopped in front of her bedroom. But she didn't answer when I knocked.

Growing more worried and with panic going through my body, I opened the door and walked inside. "Ayla?" I called. There was no response. She wasn't in her bedroom.

Was she with Alessio?

These two were so adorable. If they didn't get together any time soon, I would have to take care of it myself. Both of them were too stubborn.

They definitely needed a helping hand.

I was about to turn back around when I saw the bathroom light on. My eyebrows pulled up in confusion and I walked toward it.

She probably left it on.

I pushed the door open, but the sight that beheld me took my breath away, causing my heart to drop in my stomach.

Letting out a scream, I ran into the bathroom and fell down beside an unconscious Ayla. She was covered in blood.

"No. No. No," I whispered in panic and fear.

Pulling her body to mine, I held her close and noticed the long gash on her arms.

"Oh God!" I cried. "Ayla! Why?" I gasped as tears ran down my cheeks.

My stomach cramped and I felt sick. My heart was heavy like an invisible pressure was pressing down hard.

"No!" Pulling her tighter to me, her blood covered my dress.

I screamed.

"Mom!"

Patting Ayla's hair, I continued to cry.

"Alessio!"

Chapter 33

Alessio

"He is threatening the people. They are scared," Phoenix said as we walked out of my office. I tried to keep my anger in check but it was coursing through my body with such ferocity that I was shaking with it.

Ever since the news went out that Alberto had killed Alfredo, my people were scared. Considering he killed a Boss and took over, they knew he was serious with his threats.

"What's your plan?" Viktor asked beside me.

"He won't be getting to my people. I will make sure of it. Artur, I want you to keep an eye on everyone. Make sure the Watchers are on task and reporting everything back," I replied in a calm voice, even though I was feeling anything but.

"Yes, Boss," he replied quickly before giving us a nod and walking away.

Turning to Phoenix, I nodded at him. "Let the main families know that we will be visiting. I want to talk to them personally."

He nodded in response and quickly fished his phone from his pocket. After typing furiously for a few seconds, he placed it back into his pocket. "Done," Phoenix said.

If Alberto really thought he could overpower me and take my Empire, then he was highly mistaken. I had built this empire with my bare fucking hands for almost ten years. Half of my life dedicated to make it the strongest mafia family. I wasn't giving up now and I sure as hell wasn't losing to that fucker.

We were walking down the stairs when a sudden scream stopped us in our tracks.

Nikolay already had his gun out and I saw Phoenix and Viktor reaching for theirs.

My eyes widened when I heard my name. Reaching behind my back, I took out my gun too.

"That's Maddie's voice," Phoenix hissed, but I was already running back up, taking two stairs at the time.

When I reached the top of the stairs, I paused, looking left and right as I tried to figure out where she was. I heard her scream again, and with my heart pounding hard in my chest, I turned toward her voice.

"Shit," I whispered. It was coming from Ayla's room.

The door was open. Pointing my gun forward, I pushed the door wider with my other hand. I glanced over my shoulder and saw that my men were in a similar position.

I gave them a sharp nod before moving inside.

They followed close behind. Walking further inside the room, I tensed when I didn't see anything.

The room was empty, except someone was sobbing.

Turning to the side, I saw the door of the washroom open and the lights were on. Before I could move, Phoenix walked over to the door and pushed it open.

"Oh, shit! Shit! Fuck!" He panicked and rushed inside.

My heart was wild and my stomach dropped at Maddie's cry. I followed Phoenix, but when I got closer, the smell of blood hit me. My eyes went wide in alarm and I ran inside.

The sight almost brought me to my knees.

Maddie looked up at me with tearful eyes and sobbed. "Ayla. She…"

Ayla was covered in blood. Her eyes were closed and she looked deathly pale. A look I never wanted to see on her. Rushing forward, I sank down to my knees beside Maddie.

"Here," I heard Viktor say beside me. I glanced up and saw that he was handing me some towels. "We need to put pressure on her wounds to stop the bleeding."

He was right. We had to stop the bleeding.

"Call Sam!" I ordered harshly, without tearing my eyes from Ayla's face. Taking the towels from Viktor, I placed them on the cuts and pressed down gently. She didn't move. Not even a flinch. Maddie was still crying silently, her chest heaving with each quiet sob.

Leaning forward, I took Ayla from her arms and

pulled her closer to my chest, not caring one bit that I was getting blood all over me.

I brought a hand up and palmed her cold, pale cheek. "Ayla?" I whispered, my voice sounding hoarse and strange even to my own ears.

She didn't respond. Instead she laid limp and still in my arms. But she was breathing. It was faint, but it was there. Ayla was alive and I forced my brain to accept that fact even though it felt like my heart was being split into two. The pressure building there was unbearable and my stomach cramped almost painfully.

The last time I felt that way was when I witnessed my mother's death.

I sucked a painful breath at the thought and shook my head. *No.* This wasn't happening again. *I won't let it.*

Wrapping my arms tightly around Ayla, I stood up. I kept my eyes on her as I walked out of the bathroom and made my way to her bed. Gently placing her on the mattress, I sat down beside her and pulled her arms forward so that I could continue putting pressure on the wounds.

With her eyes closed, her face so pale, and her black hair cascading on the pillow, she looked so fragile. Vulnerable. And so broken.

The sight made my heart ache, and I closed my eyes at the flash of pain.

I shouldn't have been feeling this way, but it hurt seeing Ayla in this state. And I couldn't understand why she would do something like that. She seemed happy.

Opening my eyes, I stared at her arms. Why

would she try to kill herself?

Even though I asked the question a hundred times in my head, I could guess the answer. But I wanted to know the *real* truth. I didn't want to assume anymore.

I leaned forward slightly and moved away the few strands of hair covering her face. I let my fingers linger there, hoping for a reaction from her. When I didn't get anything, I sighed and took my hand away.

Ayla's chest was moving slowly up and down, her breathing slightly labored. I felt powerless as I stared at her.

Shifting my eyes away from her, I looked at Viktor, who was standing behind me. His face was grim and worried. "Where is Sam?" I growled.

Sam was our personal doctor, who lived on the estate. The hospital wasn't always a good choice and we needed someone who would be quick on their feet without asking us questions. The best option was having someone in the same lifestyle.

And Sam fit the role perfectly.

"I'm here," Sam said as he rushed forward.

His gaze roamed over Ayla. "Damn it," he whispered. Sam leaned forward and I regretfully let go of Ayla and stood up, moving out of his way.

He sat down in my place and took the towel off from Ayla's hand, slightly hissing at the sight.

"Is it bad? How bad is it?" I asked as pins and needles crept up my legs. I grew more panicked when I saw Sam's pensive face.

He shook his head and whispered while he continued to inspect Ayla's cut. "I need to clean the

285

blood away to see how bad it is. Her breathing is shallow, but it is okay. Her heart rate isn't that bad either."

That was good. That should be good. I kept repeating the words over and over again in my head as I tried to calm down.

Sam cleaned some of the blood from Ayla's arm and we saw a long cut going vertically up her arms. I wanted to roar. I couldn't imagine the pain that she must have been through. The thought of her going through this felt like a serrated edge over my thumping heart.

"Thank God," I heard Sam breathe out.

"What?" I asked, leaning forward.

"The cut is not that deep. Cutting vertically could be deadly, but she didn't put much pressure in the cut, so no major artery or veins were damaged," he explained. "She is lucky she is still alive. It's obvious she's lost some blood, but not a lot. She was found fairly quickly. I wish I could use the skin glue. It would be less painful, but the best option is stitches." He looked up at me, waiting for my response.

Why the fuck was he waiting?

"Just do it then. Stop wasting time!"

He nodded and got to work.

It took him a few hours to clean up the wound, stitch the cuts, and bandage it carefully. The whole time, I paced the room, growing impatient. I couldn't shake off the uneasy feeling. As the minutes and hours passed, no matter how hard I tried to hide it, I couldn't.

I was worried. Scared. And helpless.

Maddie was still silently crying. Phoenix had his arms wrapped around her, trying to calm her down. Nikolay and Viktor were both leaning against the wall, trying to look disinterested, but they were clearly worried by the look on their face.

Nikolay's cold face was ashen and he kept his eyes on Ayla, while Viktor was fidgeting around, clearly showing his nervousness.

And Lena. She almost fainted when she came into the room. Viktor had to take her away as she cried.

"Done." Sam sighed from his spot next to Ayla.

I stopped pacing and shifted my gaze to her.

"Is she going to be okay?" Maddie asked, her voice soft and croaky from the tears.

"If you are talking about her wound, yes. I stopped the bleeding. She is breathing fine. But emotionally and mentally, I don't know. This could have been a suicide attempt, but if it was, she would have cut deeper. As long as she stays unconscious, we won't get our answers. But what's more important is figuring out why so we can help her."

"But there was nothing wrong with her," Maddie argued as she stepped out of Phoenix's protective embrace.

"Did she try this before?" Sam asked.

"Not that I know of," Maddie replied. She walked closer and sat down beside Ayla.

"There could be a lot of factors in play. The biggest of them all is depression. Something obviously led her to do this. Does she have nightmares?"

My eyes widened. "Ayla has nightmares. She

was even hallucinating that she had blood on her."

"Nightmares, hallucinations, and a suicide attempt," Sam said, his gaze still on Ayla. "My best guess is post-traumatic stress disorder."

"Fuck," I swore, running my fingers through my hair in frustration. It was right there in front of me. It was so fucking obvious and yet I didn't see it.

Or maybe I didn't *want* to see it. I had refused to acknowledge her pain.

I saw Nikolay moving away from the wall and he took a protective step forward. He crossed his arms over his chest as he stared at Sam expectantly.

"PTSD?" Maddie questioned. "You mean that something happened to her?"

"It's the only thing that makes sense. It could be anything. Rape, abuse, or she witnessed something," Sam explained. "Something happened that affected her to the point where she has nightmares, hallucinations, and she was so far gone that she even attempted suicide."

"She never said anything," Maddie whispered.

"A lot of PTSD patients don't say anything. Ayla doesn't know us well enough. There needs to be a lot of trust between the patient and the person he or she shares her experience with."

"How do we deal with this? How do we help her? We can't let her live like this." Maddie started to panic again, her voice rising an octave.

"We are going to help her," Nikolay said from behind me. Those were the first words he'd spoken since we found Ayla bleeding on the floor.

"But how?" she cried, fear in her voice.

"First of all, be patient and understanding with

her. Don't push if she doesn't say anything. You could coax her, but not too much. The best way to deal with a PTSD patient is be as loving as you can. Show that you care and support her. Don't let her feel alone. Joke. Lighten up the mood. Make sure she is happy," Sam suggested.

There had to have been a trigger. Rubbing the back of my neck in frustration, I tried to relieve the tension there but it was useless. My muscles were corded and tensed. My head was pounding. My stomach felt sick and my heart hurt.

I was so lost gazing at Ayla's still form that I almost missed what Sam was saying.

"I'm going to prescribe her an anti-depressant. It won't treat her PTSD, but for now, it could calm her and make her feel less sad, worried, or on edge. I'm also going to give her sleeping pills. It might keep the nightmares at bay. Just make sure she doesn't take too many at a time," Sam said. "I would suggest keeping the pills away from her so that she doesn't have access to them. One of you should be responsible for giving her the pills at the prescribed time."

"I'll do it," Maddie said.

"Good. She needs to be taken care of. Be gentle."

Gentle. That wasn't in our vocabulary. We didn't know what gentle was.

"Boss. Can I take my leave?" Sam asked after a few minutes of silence.

I nodded without looking away from Ayla.

"Maddie, you should get cleaned up," I heard Phoenix say behind me.

"Let me change Ayla's clothing first. She is covered in blood. I will change the bedding too and then I'll go," Maddie said.

***

After Maddie demanded we leave the room, we waited outside the door. None of us spoke.

I paced. Each passing minute without Ayla was pure agony. I didn't like being away from her when she was in this state. The thought made me cringe. All the emotions coursing through my body felt foreign. Ayla was making me lose control.

Fuck, I *had* already lost control and didn't even realize it yet. She was deep under my skin. Ayla made my cold, unfeeling heart…feel. I felt pain. I felt sadness. All for her.

Leaning against the wall, I banged my head in defeat and closed my eyes with a sigh.

When I heard the door open, my eyes snapped open and I moved away from the wall. "Did she wake up?" I asked. Maddie shook her head dejectedly.

"I will keep an eye on her," I said, my voice ringing with finality as I walked inside the room. Closing the door behind me, I moved the wooden chair next to Ayla's bed and sat down heavily on it.

I had to touch her, to feel her. To make sure that she was really alive, breathing and real. Leaning forward in my chair, I gently rubbed my thumb over her fingers and then moved up to the inside of her wrist that wasn't covered with the bandages. I stroked the tender skin there and ran my thumb over her steady pulse.

I had learned how to mask my emotions and feelings, yet this woman knew how to change it all. In the short time that I had known her, she made me feel more than I had in twenty-two years.

Pulling my hand away, I ran them through my hair. There was no time for weaknesses. And emotions were definitely a weakness. It would only get me killed.

Sitting down beside Ayla, while waiting for her to wake up, I tried to drill that thought into my brain.

And when she did finally wake up, I had my emotions in check. Schooling my features to be impassive, I straightened in my chair when I saw her shifting in the bed.

Her eyes fluttered open and she stared at the ceiling, confused. I saw her wince and she slowly turned to face me. Her eyes widened and she let out a shocked gasp.

"Good morning," I said.

"Good…morning…"

"How are you feeling?"

Her forehead creased and she looked deep in thought. "I don't know. Weird. My head hurts."

Ayla brought her hand up but she winced again. Her eyes widened at the sight of the bandages wrapped around her arms. She froze, her hand still in the air over her face.

"Do you remember?" I asked, leaning forward.

She was silent for a few seconds and then nodded, slowly and cautiously.

"Ayla, why did you do it?" I tried to keep my

voice soft, making sure that I didn't spook her with my questions.

But she didn't answer.

She sighed and her hand fell back down on the mattress. Her gaze moved to the ceiling again and she purposely avoided eye contact with me.

"If you don't talk to us, we can't help you, Ayla. And we want to help," I whispered. "Say something," I begged when she didn't answer.

It was like I wasn't even there anymore.

I moved my hand so that it laid next to hers, our fingers resting mere inches apart.

"Ayla." Sucking a deep breath in, I tried to calm my rapid beating heart. "I can assume what happened. I can guess. But I don't want to assume. I want to hear the real truth from you. Say something. Anything."

No words were uttered from her.

Nothing.

She stayed stubbornly silent.

I rubbed my other hand tiredly over my face and pinched the bridge of my nose before blowing out a frustrated breath.

This was harder than I thought.

After a few minutes of utter silence between us, I leaned closer. "You are worth more than you think," I whispered softly, hoping that the words would have some effect on her. "You bring happiness to others. You bring light, Ayla. You have people who care about you. People who want to help. Let us help."

But she didn't react. Her body stayed rigid as she continued to stare at the ceiling, almost unflinching.

I hated the unfairness that Ayla had to go through. I wanted to know the truth. No, I was desperate for the truth. I needed to know who she was and who the fuck hurt her.

I looked down at our hands. They were next to each other but not touching. I inched my fingers closer to hers, feeling the heavy tension and anguish rolling off her in waves.

"Can I touch you?" I asked.

I shifted my gaze up just in time to see her eyes widening in shock at my question. "Can I hold your hand?" I murmured, wanting another reaction from her.

But Ayla stayed silent. Her green eyes lost focus again. If it was possible, she grew even more tense and I started to worry if I had pushed too hard, too fast.

Rather than answering, Ayla slowly moved her hand. But she didn't move toward me. Instead, she took her hand away and placed it over her stomach.

That was all the answer I got. But it spoke volumes.

She was shutting down and refusing any comfort.

I blew out a sharp breath and then sighed as I stood up. "I just want you to know that you are loved. You matter. To Maddie. To Lena." I paused and swallowed hard. *And to me*. But I didn't say it out loud.

Silence.

Ayla closed her eyes, effectively shutting me out. She was reclusive. Unresponsive.

I stared at her one last time before turning around

and walking away. Each step I took away from her was painful but I forced myself to take them.

She needed time alone. To think and to come to terms with what happened. But I just hoped that she heard the words I said.

Because they were the truth.

Chapter 34

Ayla

The night before felt like a blur. I was ashamed that Alessio and the others had found me this way. They had to see me in my moment of weakness.

Alessio continued to ask me questions. He coaxed me to reveal the truth. His words felt like they were coming under water and my body felt like it was floating.

He begged. He cajoled. He sounded desperate. He told me I was worth more than I thought, yet I couldn't bring myself to respond.

He was wrong. I was worth nothing. I was a whore. Dirty. Used. I was just an empty vessel.

His words hurt because he was lying.

I wanted to scream. I hated him. *Stop lying, please.* My heart was aching. It hurt so much. I didn't bring happiness. I was not light. I was darkness. Nobody cared. I was on my own.

Alessio bent closer and I felt his warmth next to my hand that laid on the bed. His hand was close to mine. So close yet not touching.

"Can I touch you?"

I went rigid. *No*. He couldn't touch me. I didn't think I could bear a man's touch at that moment. Or anyone's touch.

It felt like I would crumble and fade away in the air.

Please leave. Please go. Leave me.

I heard him blow out a sharp breath and he stood up, pushing the chair away. He was leaving.

"I just want you to know that you are loved…you matter. To Maddie. To Lena," Alessio murmured gently.

His words felt like sharp knife against my heart.

Closing my eyes, I gave him only silence. I didn't say anything. I couldn't.

His words hurt. I wished they didn't, but his lies broke my already fractured heart. I trusted him, yet he fed me lies.

As he walked away, his footsteps faded away until I didn't hear him anymore. When I heard the door close, I sighed and kept my eyes shut.

I rubbed my fingers over the bumpy bandages and my nose tingled as the tears started to form behind my close eyelids. I never thought I would take such a step. I didn't even remember it happening. I was so lost, so far gone that I didn't realize what I was doing.

But I remember the silence that I felt when I lost consciousness. It felt nice. Empowering. It felt like I was in charge of my emotions for once. However, I knew it was wrong.

As a single tear slipped down the side of my

face, I pulled the covers up under my chin. Turning to my left side, I faced the window but still kept my eyes closed. Swiping the trail of tears away, I sighed and let the tiredness take over my body.

A few minutes later, I was asleep again. And Alessio's voice never left me.

"You are worth more than you think."

***

My eyes snapped open and I quickly blinked the sleepiness away when I heard my door open. My body stiffened.

A few seconds later, I felt my bed shift beside me and the scent of rose perfume teased my nose.

Maddie.

I looked up and saw her staring down at me, her face sad. Her eyes were red and puffy and she looked haggard.

"Hey," she whispered.

"Hey," I replied softly.

She stared at me silently for a few seconds and then she sniffled. My eyes widened when I saw hers filled with unshed tears.

"Don't ever do that again," she said, quickly swiping away the tears that fell down her cheeks.

"Maddie." My chest felt impossibly tight at the sight of her crying.

"You…know…how hard that was…seeing you like that. Finding you in that state?" She wept.

I closed my eyes as guilt encompassed my heart and body.

"You can't ever do that again, Ayla. You can't."

"I'm sorry."

Maddie pushed her hair from her face and wiped away the fallen tears.

"Ayla, we can help. You just have to say it. Talk to me. Please. I can't see you like this. You don't deserve this. Let us help," she whispered, her hand slowly moving up so that it was resting on my head. She absently patted my hair, her eyes still on mine. "I'm sorry."

Sorry? Why was she sorry? I blinked up at her, confused, and she looked away sadly.

"I should have known. I should have noticed, but instead I had let myself believe that you were happy. I should have been there for you."

"You are wrong." When I had finally pulled myself in a sitting position, I took Maddie's hand in mine. "I was happy," I admitted. "The happiest I had ever been. And you gave me that. You. Lena. Alessio."

She looked at me, confused, her eyes showing suspicion. She seemed to be trying to find any hints that I was lying. But I wasn't. They were the truest words I had ever spoken.

Swallowing hard, I grasped at the small bit of determination inside me. "I had a nightmare last night."

Maybe I could tell her. Not the whole truth. But parts of it. Maybe then she would understand.

"I don't remember much, but it was horrible. It was bad. It hurt so much," I whispered. "Even when I woke up, it wouldn't leave me. I just wanted it to go away. I just wanted silence."

Her eyes were wide and her mouth was opened

in surprise. "Do you have a lot of these nightmares?" she asked gently, her face softening as she regarded me with sorrowful eyes.

I was looking at her, but looking right past her as the images of my nightmares flashed in front of me. "Yes. Most of the time," I whispered, my voice sounding a little lost. And that was exactly how I felt. Lost. I didn't know where I belonged anymore. I didn't know what to feel or want. "I didn't have them for some time. But last night it came back," I admitted. The only reason I didn't get the nightmares was because of Alessio. Because of his jacket. But my peace was snatched away from me."

"Is there a reason why it stays away and comes back again?" Maddie asked, her tone cautious. Her fingers were wrapped around mine and she was rubbing them soothingly.

Shrugging, I looked away, avoiding eye contact with her. This was my secret. I couldn't tell her. It sounded pathetic even in my head. I could only imagine how bad it would sound to Maddie.

"Okay," she said. I was thankful that she didn't push. "Thank you for telling me." She squeezed my hand in a comforting manner.

I nodded mutely.

"Ayla, you can always talk to me. I'm here for you. So, whenever you are ready, I will be waiting. I'm not going to push. This is your choice. But know that I am here for you. Not only me, but Mom and Alessio too. And everyone else." Maddie leaned forward and placed a kiss on my forehead. "There is always light at the end of the dark tunnel," she whispered before pulling back. Her words took my breath away and the tears stung the back of my eyes again.

"Maddie." I sniffled.

"Shhh, I'm here," she said, wrapping her arms around me. I buried my head in her shoulders and cried. I cried for the years of pain that were bestowed upon me. I cried for the painful life that I had to live. I cried at my hopelessness.

And I cried for the kindness that was being shown to me. They were supposed to be my enemies but instead they had showed me more goodness than I had ever seen in my entire life.

"Thank you," I choked as Maddie rubbed my back soothingly.

"It's okay. It's going to be okay. You are going to be okay," she whispered, her voice soft and filled with compassion.

I didn't know how much time passed. But by the time my tears had dried, I felt completely drained. But lighter. My heart didn't hurt as bad and I could breathe better. More calm.

Pulling away from Maddie, I wiped away my tears as she gave me a small encouraging smile.

"You must be hungry," she said, changing the topic. I was grateful for her understanding. I nodded and placed my palm over my stomach.

"A little," I replied.

"Okay. Sit tight. I will bring you your breakfast."

"Wait," I called when she was near the door. Maddie stopped and faced me again.

Biting on my lips nervously, I push the few strands of hair away from my face. "Where is Lena?" I asked, finally voicing the question that I had been dreading to ask.

Maddie lost her smile. "Mom is downstairs. When I go down, I will let her know you are awake. She will come up so fast that you will not have time to blink."

"Is she angry?" I knew I disappointed and hurt them with my actions. But I didn't want Lena to be angry at me.

Maddie quickly shook her head, her eyes going wide at my question. "No," she gasped. "Never. Ayla, Mom was so worried. She will be happy that you are awake. She can never be mad at you."

"Okay," I replied, my heart settling in a steady pace again.

Maddie gave me another smile and then winked. "I will be right back."

"Okay."

Chapter 35

I avoided looking near the tub as I turned off the light and walked out of the bathroom. It was spotless clean but I didn't want the memories to come back.

Walking over to my bed, I sat down on the edge. The sun was setting and it cast a light orange glow into the room, filling it with serenity.

Even though I had spent most of the day sleeping, I still felt tired. After Maddie had brought me breakfast, Lena had come up. The look on her face had broken my heart. She scolded me. She cried. We cried together.

And afterwards, she pulled me down on the bed and her sweet singing voice had lulled me to sleep. Her hands were patting my hair comfortingly and as I fell asleep, a small smile had stretched across my lips.

Maybe Alessio was right.

Maybe I was loved. I desperately wanted to believe it.

A knock at the door snapped me out of my

thoughts. "Yes?" I called out, glancing toward it.

The door slowly opened and I gaped when I saw Nikolay walking in.

"How are you feeling?" he asked, his tone impassive as always.

"Okay…"

What was he doing here?

"Are you really?" He cocked his head to the side in question as he stared at me expectantly. I placed my hands on the bed and absently traced patterns on it. His presence made the room look smaller and his dark intense stare caused a shiver to run down my spine.

"I'm…feeling better," I corrected myself. He nodded and kept his eyes on me. Nikolay looked thoughtful for a second before he walked forward and came to a stop in front of me.

Droplets of sweat trickled down my back as my nervousness grew. Why was he here? Did he come to taunt me? The thought made me cringe.

We stared at each other in silence and then he moved. Keeping his eyes on me, he took off his suit jacket and laid it on the chair beside him. My eyes widened when I saw him starting to unbutton his white dress shirt.

"What…are…"

"Do you know how I got this scar?" he asked, bringing a hand up to point at his face. I tore my eyes away from his chest and looked up. His eyes were blank, but his lips had thinned into a hard line.

Most of the time, I didn't even pay attention to the scar on his face. It was likely because I had always avoided looking at his cold and angry face.

But now that he pointed at his scar, I stared at it. The scar ran from his right eyebrow and down to his chin. It was deep and looked like a puckered slash.

It must have hurt a lot. I winced at the thought, but I wondered how he got it.

When I finally shook my head at his question, he nodded and continued to unbutton his shirt. Nikolay turned away from me, giving me his back as he faced the opposite wall. In a flash, he had his shirt removed.

Bringing my hand up, I covered my mouth as I gasped at the sight.

"Oh my God," I breathed.

His back was covered with scars. They looked old, but none of them had faded away. Some were long and deep. The agony he must have gone through.

I saw his back muscles bunch as his body tensed at my gasp. Nikolay turned back toward me and I let out a whimper, this time tears blinding my vision.

His chest and stomach were covered in scars too.

"How?" I croaked.

"Six years ago, I was taken by Italians. They held me captive for almost four weeks, torturing me day and night. They wanted information."

My heart stumbled at his words and I tried to calm my breathing. The Italians? Oh God. No. Not another one.

How many people did my family destroy?

"Did you? I mean, did you say anything?" I whispered, keeping my gaze on his scarred chest.

When I heard him scoff, my eyes snapped up. He

looked at me like I had lost my mind. Shaking his head, he sighed. "No, Ayla. I didn't spill anything. I would take a bullet for Alessio. Do you really think I would betray him?"

No, I didn't think he would betray him. Nikolay was cold and hard. He appeared unfeeling, but from what I had seen during my short time here, he was loyal. And protective of Alessio.

When he said he would take a bullet for Alessio, I believed him. He looked proud when he uttered the words.

"I was barely alive when Alessio and the others found me. Because of severe blood loss, nerve damage, and brain swelling, I was in a coma for three weeks." Nikolay paused and took a deep breath. "When I woke up, I had to learn how to walk again. And two days after, I was diagnosed with PTSD."

My heart broke at his confession. I never expected this. Even though his expression had hardened, I saw a flash of pain in his eyes. And the tears that had built up in mine fell freely down my cheeks. Nikolay's eyes widened at the sight of my tears and I saw his throat move almost painfully when he swallowed hard.

"Nightmares, hallucinations, deep anger, depression, and self-loathing. They became a constant in my life," he continued, his eyes shifting away from mine.

His pain spoke to me. Because I knew what it felt like.

"I remember pointing a gun at my temple, wanting to end it all," he said.

No.

"But Alessio talked me out of it. Viktor. Phoenix. Artur. Lena. They were all there. They cared. I'm alive today because of them," he said.

When his expression softened, the cold look disappearing from his face, I sucked in a deep breath.

"You must be wondering why I'm telling you this?" He let out a harsh laugh before shaking his head. "I'm telling you this because I want you to know that I understand. Whatever you are going through, I understand. *We* understand. Nobody is perfect in this mansion. Some of us have painful pasts while other have less painful pasts. But we know. We understand. And we want to help."

Nikolay was man of few words and for him to say this to me, it took my breath away.

Maybe they would understand, but I was still the enemy's daughter.

Maybe if I was someone else, maybe if I wasn't an Abandonato, it wouldn't have mattered. But would they still feel the same way if they knew that I was Alfredo's daughter? An Italian? The same family that they hated so much.

"I don't know what you have been through. But if you've come this far, then you are a fighter. You are not weak," he continued in a surprisingly soft voice.

Nikolay slowly moved toward me and stopped only inches away. He was so close that his legs were almost touching mine. I swallowed nervously, and from my sitting position, I had to bend my head backward to look up at him. He was so tall that the top of my head only came up to his stomach. Nikolay towered over me as I blinked up at him with tearful eyes.

His pitch black eyes were intense and piercing, impossible to read, and they gleamed in the glow of the sunset.

My eyes widened when I felt something warm on my arm. I looked down quickly to his hand placed gently over my bandages. He rubbed his thumb back and forth, causing my stomach to flip.

"You are worth more than this," he whispered.

At his words, I remembered what Alessio said this morning. His voice rang through my mind. *"You are worth more than you think."* I brought a hand up and covered my mouth as a sob broke through.

"You are a fighter, Ayla. So keep fighting. Don't give up now." He gently caressed my arm one last time before pulling his hand away and stepping back.

He walked away silently, and I continued to cry, my eyes still fixated on my bandaged arm.

I never thought of myself as a fighter. I was weak. Broken.

But he had called me a fighter. He was right, I had come this far. I endured years of torture, so why was I giving up now?

I laid down on the bed and stared at the ceiling as the tears continued to run down my cheeks.

"You are worth more than you think."

Alessio's voice kept repeating over and over again my head. I had Maddie, Lena, Alessio…and Nikolay. They understood me. They didn't question. They just accepted.

Maybe I do matter, I thought.

I didn't know how much time had passed, but I was still lost in my thoughts when I heard another knock on the door. Sitting up on the bed, I called out, "Come in."

The door opened and Maddie walked in with a big smile on her face. And in her hands was a large bouquet of pink flowers.

"How are you feeling?" she asked cheerfully.

"Good," I responded, my eyes on the flowers. They were so beautiful. Pointing at them, I looked up at Maddie curiously, "What are you doing with these?"

Her hazel eyes twinkled and she gave me another smile. "They are for you, silly."

"For me?" I asked, astonished.

"Uh-huh. They are pink calla lilies," she replied, walking over to my nightstand. Maddie took out the other flowers there to put these ones.

"They are so beautiful." I couldn't take my eyes off them.

Maddie paused in what she was doing and turned toward me. "Alessio got them for you," she said slowly. "He said to get well soon."

My back straightened at her words. I looked up at her in shock, my eyes filled with questions. She smiled and nodded.

Placing my hands out, I whispered, "Can I hold them?"

She gave me the flowers. As soon as my fingers wrapped around the stems, I brought them closer to me and inhaled the sweet scent. It smelled refreshing. Sweet.

But that was not what made my heart race.

Nobody had ever given me flowers before. No one.

But Alessio bought me flowers. He was the first person to give me flowers. The most beautiful flowers ever.

My heart did a flip and I couldn't help the tiny smile that stretched across my lips. It was small and faint, but a smile nonetheless.

"They are so beautiful," I whispered again, holding the bouquet close to my chest.

"I know," Maddie whispered back.

I looked up at her and she smiled, staring right into my eyes, "For once, I agree with his *choice*." She mumbled something under her breath that I didn't comprehend, but I didn't pay attention to it.

All I cared about was the bouquet of flowers I was holding in my hand. Bringing them close to my face again, I inhaled its sweet scent.

You are loved. You matter.

Alessio's voice rang through my head as I closed my eyes.

When he first said those words to me, I hated them. I hated him. They had cut deep into my heart, hurting me. Yet at this very moment, those same words brought me peace.

Chapter 36

Alessio

I paced the length of my office, my mind filled with Ayla. She was all I could think about the whole damn day. I couldn't get rid of her face. Her frail body as I held her in my arms, her blood surrounding us.

I had locked myself in the office so I wouldn't be tempted to go to Ayla. She needed time, I told myself. But it was a struggle being away from her when all I wanted was to offer comfort.

I just wanted her to open up, yet she stayed stubborn.

When a knock sounded at the door, I growled at the person to enter. The door opened and I turned around to see Nikolay walking in.

"So?" I demanded when he closed the door. "Did she say anything?"

Nikolay's face was blank, his eyebrows drawn together as he regarded me impassively. He shook his head at my question and then sighed.

When Ayla had closed down on me, refusing to listen to a word I said, I thought that maybe she would connect with Nikolay if he told her what he'd been through. He was a man of few words. He loathed talking about what happened, but I knew he wouldn't refuse me. As soon as I had laid my thought on the table, Nikolay had nodded and left without saying anything.

I had hopes that maybe Ayla would open up. If not to me or Maddie, maybe to Nikolay. But she clearly didn't.

"Nothing at all?" Taking a step back, I leaned against the table and crossed my arms across my chest.

"No, boss. I tried, but she isn't ready. I don't think she will be ready any time soon," Nikolay responded.

I sensed a hint of understanding from his tone. It took him years to finally overcome his PTSD and even now, he was not fully recovered.

"We just need to give her time," he continued, his voice softening slightly. If there was someone who understood Ayla to the core, then it was Nikolay.

I swore under my breath, running my hand through my hair in frustration.

"We can't push her too hard."

"I know that," I said, glaring at him.

"What are you going to do now?" he asked curiously.

And that was a question that I didn't have an answer for. I was lost at what to do or how to deal with Ayla. She was so fragile that I was scared of taking a step that would end up hurting her. Or worse, have her shutting down further.

"I don't know," I answered truthfully. He grew silent at my response. The room was filled with tension and I turned my back to Nikolay, facing the large window that overlooked the back garden.

"But I will figure it out," I said with conviction.

"Do you need me for anything else?" Nikolay asked

Shaking my head, I dismissed him. "No. You can leave."

I placed both of my hands on the table and leaned forward. "What am I going to do with you, Ayla?" I whispered, my eyes fixated on the window.

After a few minutes of staring into the distance, I straightened up and shrugged on my suit jacket before leaving the room. My plan was to go downstairs for dinner, but instead, as I got closer to the stairs, my steps faltered.

Looking to my right, I stared at the hallway that led to Ayla's room. It was tempting. I spent the whole day away from her and now I was standing just a few steps away.

But what if she didn't want to see me?

Feeling frustrated at the uncertainty, I tightened my fingers into fists and took a step down the stairs, but then stopped.

"Fuck it!" I hissed before moving back and walking toward Ayla's room. Stopping in front of her door, I took a deep breath and released it quickly before knocking at the door. My heart started to beat a little faster as I waited for her response.

Damn it! Was I nervous?

Swallowing hard at the realization, I started to think that this was a bad idea. I took a step away from the door and was about to leave when I heard her sweet voice.

"Come in."

That did it. Those two words and her soft voice was enough to stop me from leaving. Placing my hand over the handle, I slowly opened the door and walked inside.

I found Ayla sitting on the bed, the comforter covering her legs as she stared at the walls thoughtfully. Her head snapped toward me when I entered the room.

"Alessio," she whispered, her lips barely moving.

"Ayla." We stared at each other, both of us lost for words.

Instinctively, I took a step forward and walked closer, stopping beside her bed. Her green eyes blinked up at me surprisingly and she licked her lips nervously.

Clearing my throat, I asked softly, "How are you feeling?"

"Better," she replied quickly. I was surprised she even answered. I didn't think she would. Cocking my head to the side, I stared at her questioningly. She shifted her eyes away from mine and looked down at her lap, her fingers twisting in the comforter.

"Did you eat yet?" I questioned when I felt the air growing awkward around us. I wanted to see

313

her, yet I didn't know what to say. Nothing about this woman made any sense to me and my reactions toward her made no sense either. She confused me. And my conflicting feelings only made it more confusing.

Ayla nodded. "I ate lunch a little late. So I am not hungry."

"Okay."

Ayla grew silent again and this time, I didn't know what to say. So I cleared my throat one more time and started to back away from her bed. Her head snapped up and I saw her body slightly move forward. Her mouth opened to say something but then she closed it.

"I just wanted to see how you are doing," I said gently, keeping my eyes on her. "I should go. You need to rest."

Ayla's shoulders sagged and she nodded, her eyes growing sadder.

My brows drew together at her expression. Did she not want me to leave? But when she didn't say anything, I sighed and turned around.

As soon as I took a step away, her voice stopped me. "Wait," she called softly. Swiveling around, I faced her again.

"Yes?" Perplexed by her abrupt call, I merely nodded in her direction, curious as to what she would say to me.

Her hand fluttered to her throat and then she pushed a few strands of her hair behind her eyes, her hands slightly trembling with nervousness. I saw her swallow a few times with visible effort, trying to find her voice again. I waited, surprisingly patiently.

"I…want to thank…I mean…" She stumbled over her words, stuttering badly over each one. Ayla quickly snapped her mouth shut, her lips forming a hard line. Her eyebrows furrowed together and she looked somewhat frustrated.

Ayla closed her eyes and took a few deep breaths. She sighed and then opened her eyes again. "Thank you for the flowers," she said so quickly that I almost missed it.

Her cheeks colored in a beautiful shade of red and her gaze fell. She wiped her hands on the comforter over and over as she waited.

But I was completely lost.

Flowers?

What the fuck is she talking about?

"Flowers?" I echoed, not at all sure what she'd just said. Why was she thanking me for flowers?

"Yes," she said, nodding toward her nightstand. I followed her eyes and saw some pink flowers in a vase. They were beautiful.

But they weren't from me.

"Maddie told me you got them for me. They are so beautiful," Ayla murmured softly, making me turn toward her again.

Maddie? Fuck. This girl. What the hell was she thinking? My jaw twitched in anger. She had overstepped her boundaries this time.

"Thank you so much," Ayla whispered again, gazing up at me. Her expression took my breath away. Her green eyes were twinkling and her face had softened, her cheeks flushed.

At her sweet words and soft expression, I

couldn't bring myself to tell her the truth.

"Right. Flowers. I'm glad you like them," I said.

"I do," she breathed, looking back at the flowers again, a small smile appearing at the corners of her lips.

Ayla gazed at the flowers, and when she didn't turn back around, I slowly started to step away. "I should go."

"Okay," she whispered.

"Okay." After giving her a final look, I tore my gaze away. I swiftly walked out of her room, and as soon as the door was closed behind me, I let the anger take place.

"Maddie," I hissed.

Quickly walking away from Ayla's room, I made my way downstairs and straight into the kitchen, where I knew I would find Maddie.

With each step I took, I grew angrier at the lies she fed Ayla. Stepping into the kitchen, I snapped loudly, my voice resonating with my annoyance and fury.

"Maddie!"

She jumped and swiveled around with a gasp, her hand going to her chest in shock. Her eyes went wide, but when she saw me, her shoulders sagged in relief. "You scared the crap out of me."

"Alessio, what's wrong?" Lena asked, coming to stand beside her daughter.

"I have to speak with Maddie," I growled.

Lena's forehead creased in confusion and she faced Maddie. "What did you do now?"

"Me? I didn't do anything," she replied, her voice squeaking as she feigned innocence.

Taking a step forward, I grabbed her arm and started pulling her out of the kitchen. I heard Lena sigh behind me and she grumbled, "Here we go again."

I pushed Maddie into the wall, my fingers still wrapped tightly around her arm. "You are hurting me, Alessio."

I let go of her and she rubbed her arms, glaring at me. "This is going to bruise tomorrow."

And I didn't give a fuck.

"Don't test me now, Maddie. Why did you lie to Ayla?" I snapped in her face.

"Ahh, that." She rolled her eyes.

Smiling wide, she placed her hand over my chest and gave me a pat. "I got this. Just leave it to me. I have everything planned out. The wedding. The babies."

I gaped at her in shock. "Maddie," I warned.

"Alessio."

"Enough! I am done with your shit." Pointing a finger at her, I glared as my body vibrated with the force of my anger.

"No. You stop!" she rebuked, glaring just as fiercely. If she was one of my men, my fingers would already be wrapped around her neck. She was lucky I considered her a sister and not someone who worked for me. Maddie knew she could get away with anything, so she used it as her advantage. Every. Single. Time.

"Why are you so stubborn? What are you trying to hide, huh? Your feelings?" she hissed angrily. "Guess what? It's too late. You should have thought about that before you let Ayla touch the piano. As soon as she played for you, you gave yourself to her."

Each word was like a knife to my heart. And it made me furious. I started to interrupt, but she continued, her voice trembling with her anger.

"You think I don't know? She plays the piano every single night. For you. You care, Alessio, yet you try to hide it. Stop it. Just stop and fucking admit it for once, that you care. Why is that so hard? Stop hiding behind your anger."

I scowled harder and snapped, "Maddie!" My voice came out louder than I expected and her eyes widened. She crossed her arms across her chest, her mouth snapping shut. "You don't tell me what to do. This is none of your business. And I want you to stay out of it."

She stayed quiet, her mouth hardening in a thin line. I stepped away from her and pinched the bridge of my nose in frustration before letting out my breath in a long puff.

Her words only made me angrier because they were true.

It was a truth I didn't want to acknowledge but Maddie had said it out loud, giving me no choice but to face it.

I did care. I hated to admit it, but I did care. Ayla had successfully made her way into my heart, making me feel after so many years.

"You should have seen her face when I told Ayla you gave her the flowers," Maddie whispered. "The way her face lit up, her eyes twinkling, and she smiled."

At her words, I felt my fury slowly leave my

body. I sighed and sagged against the opposite wall. "You are giving her false hope, Maddie. She will only get hurt in the end. I'm not the man for her."

"But—"

"No. Stop whatever you are thinking or planning. Wedding? Babies? Are you crazy, Maddie? Don't be delusional. There's none of that in this life."

"But if you let it happen, then maybe…"

I scoffed and then laughed, because what else was there to do? Did she forget what happened twenty-two years ago?

"My father let it happen and see where that got us," I said, my tone chilling.

She flinched and cowered back into the wall, her gaze falling. "That doesn't mean it will always end up that way. Maybe you just need to see the light and accept it."

"No. That's where you are wrong. Whatever I feel is a weakness. A weakness that will only hurt Ayla in the end. This is not about me. It's about *her.*"

And with that, I spun on my heels and stalked away from her, but not before I saw Maddie's shoulders sagging in defeat.

***

Dinner was the most painful. There was only silence. None of us spoke. Only the noise of our utensils scraping the plates filled the room. Everyone was lost in their own thoughts. But it was obvious we were all thinking about the same thing.

Ayla.

After my conversation with Maddie, my chest felt tight, my heart heavy and aching. I wanted badly to let my guard down but I couldn't. It was agony keeping it inside, when all I wanted was to go up and hold Ayla in my arms.

When dinner was over, I silently pushed my chair away and stood up. Nodding at my men, I walked away without a word and went upstairs. I was about to go into my room when I saw the door of the piano room open.

My eyebrows went up and I found myself frowning as I made my way to the room. Stopping in front of the door, I pushed the door open wider and took a step forward. My heart stuttered when I saw Ayla sitting at the piano.

When she didn't move, I cleared my throat, alerting her of my presence. Her head snapped up, her eyes flashing with alarm. Her stance was immediately defensive, but when she saw me, I saw her shoulders falling with relief, the panic in her eyes disappearing.

"What are you doing here?" I asked, my voice soft so that I didn't scare her.

Ayla blinked up at me and then moved her gaze to the piano. "I wanted to play."

That made sense, but why wasn't she playing?

Her next words took my breath away, and I had to close my eyes as the wave of emotions went through me.

"I was waiting for you."

Opening my eyes again, I made contact with hers. "Okay," I responded, walking further inside the room. I didn't think I could deny her anything.

Taking my place on the couch, I leaned back and spread my legs in front of me, waiting for her to play.

And she did. But this time she didn't close her eyes. Instead, Ayla kept her gaze on me. She played a different song, one that I didn't recognize, but it was just as beautiful.

And the person playing it with her sweet beauty, her gentle gaze, and her soft eyes…she made my unfeeling heart feel. My cold heart accelerated with every second in her presence. She was so fucking beautiful. Just like an angel.

The thought didn't make me cringe or get angry. I was just too lost in her.

And when the third song ended, Ayla stayed seated, as if she didn't want to leave. Shockingly, I didn't want to leave either.

"Aren't you tired?" I asked.

She shook her head.

"What do you want to do?" My voice was just above a whisper, our eyes focused on each other.

Ayla shrugged and looked down to her lap.

I shifted my eyes away too and looked around the room. My gaze fell on the shelves that were filled with my mother's books.

Taking a deep breath, I asked, "Do you like to read?"

"Yes," she replied.

I pointed at the shelves. "There're plenty of books here."

It was hard saying the words. She was getting deeper and deeper into my world. The piano. And now the books. I didn't know why I asked her about the books. The words had just tumbled out of my mouth before I could think clearly.

I heard Ayla move and from the corner of my eyes, I saw her standing up. "I can use these books?"

When I nodded, she quickly made her way to the shelves. Ayla took her time choosing a book and when she finally got one, she turned back around to face me. "Can I borrow this one?"

"You can read whatever you want, Ayla."

"Thank you," she said. Ayla sat down on the couch beside me, and curled her legs beneath her. She laid her head on the arm of the couch and opened the book.

The room was filled with silence. But it felt peaceful. After a few minutes, I looked away and pulled my laptop that was sitting on the coffee table to my lap.

She read while I worked, trying to keep myself busy. But I was barely concentrating on my emails.

My gaze kept moving back to Ayla.

And I started to see her slowly fall asleep. Her green eyes closed, her breathing even and soft as she succumbed to her tiredness and sleep.

Placing my laptop back on the coffee table, I pushed myself up and stepped toward Ayla's sleeping form. I took the book out of her grasp and placed it beside my laptop. Leaning down, I carefully wrapped an arm behind her back and the other behind her knees. I gently pulled Ayla up and cradled her to my chest, making sure that she didn't wake up.

She moaned sleepily, but then laid her head on my shoulder. Her eyes were still closed and I was sure she was still asleep.

I walked into her room and placed her down on the bed. Ayla immediately curled into herself as I pulled the covers over her body. I stepped away and stared at her sleeping face.

She looked so fragile. Small. A sense of protectiveness coursed through my body.

Taking a deep breath, I tried to calm my racing heart. I gave Ayla a final glance, and walked away, softly closing the door behind me.

I should have been more careful with her since the beginning. I shouldn't have let myself get in so deep. And now it was too late.

Chapter 37

Ayla

"I still remember it clearly. He was acting all bad-ass but then the next minute, he was on the ground." Maddie laughed. She was sprawled next to me on my bed, while I was on my side facing her.

"Yeah?" I smiled at her story.

It'd been three days since I broke down and cut myself. And I had been trying to understand myself during these last three days.

I was barely left alone. Maddie was with me most of the time. If she wasn't, then it was Lena. And I spent most of my evenings with Alessio.

That was the best time of my day. Every night, I eagerly waited for the time when I would go to the piano room. After dinner, I would go in and wait for Alessio. I would play the piano while he silently gazed at me from afar. And then I would read while he worked on his laptop.

These moments were filled with peacefulness. I was thankful for they kept me grounded.

"Yup. And Alessio was just standing there laughing his ass off too. But Viktor being Viktor, stood up and acted like nothing happened," Maddie's voice broke through my thoughts.

"Hmm," I hummed with a smile. She was always telling me stories about her childhood, the time she spent with Viktor and Alessio. And they always made me laugh. They were such a mischievous and funny trio.

Maddie opened her mouth to continue but a knock on the door stopped her. She glanced at it and called out, "Come in."

The door opened and Milena came in. "Hey."

She had brought me breakfast before. Taking the empty tray in her hand, she gave me a small smile. "Tell Mom I will be down soon," Maddie told her. She nodded and started to walk away, but then stopped a few feet from my bed.

She turned back around and stared at me questioningly. "I wanted to ask you this for some time now but never got a chance," Milena started.

At her words, my eyes widened and I started to panic.

"Why was Alessio's suit jacket under your pillow?"

Even though I knew what she was going to ask, it still took my breath away and I swallowed hard as dread filled my frozen body.

"What?" Maddie asked incredulously beside me.

"I found Alessio's jacket under Ayla's pillow when I was cleaning her room a few days ago," Milena explained, her intense gaze still on mine as she waited for my answer.

I didn't have to turn to Maddie to know that she was staring at me in shock. I felt her stares burning holes into my skin. My panic grew with each passing second.

My fingers tightened around the comforter. Turning my head to the side, I stared at Maddie in alarm, begging her with my eyes to save me from this.

She must have seen the desperation in there because her face turned hard and she glared at Milena.

"That's none of your business. Leave," she ordered harshly. Milena glared back and then huffed in annoyance before walking away and closing the door harder than usual.

Maddie turned her head toward me again, her eyes softening as she stared at me expectantly. "Ayla, what were you doing with Alessio's jacket?" she asked.

"Maddie…" I looked away. I couldn't bring myself to lie to her. Not after everything she had done for me.

Swallowing hard, I looked back up into Maddie's understanding eyes. She understood me. And she had been there for me when I needed her the most. Maybe she would understand this time too.

"You don't have to—"

"I sleep with it," I said.

Maddie's mouth hung open in shock as she stared at me with wide eyes. "What?" she sputtered.

"I sleep with it." My fingers were entwined tightly together, my knuckles almost white. "It

326

keeps the nightmares away." My voice was small, as shame and embarrassment took over my body.

Maddie must think that I am pathetic, I thought as tears blurred my vision.

"Alessio's jacket keeps your nightmares away?"

I nodded, and then felt her hand on my shoulder.

"Ayla, look at me," she urged.

I stared into her compassionate, hazel eyes. They were free of judgement, instead glowing with understanding.

"Ayla, is that why you got the nightmare three nights ago? Was that the trigger? Because you didn't have the jacket?"

I felt the color drain from my face as my body went numb, my muscles coiling tightly at her words. "Yes." It was hard to say the word and I sucked in deep breaths, trying to calm my racing heart.

"Oh, Ayla. Come here." Before I could move, she had pulled me closer, her arms wrapped tightly around my shoulders. She moved her hand up and down on my back, soothingly, as I choked back a sob. "Let it out. I'm here."

It felt good to be finally be understood. To have a shoulder to cry on.

I didn't cry this time, though. Blinking the tears away, I just let Maddie hold me and offer me comfort.

Palming my cheeks, she made me look straight into her eyes. "I'm going to ask you something. Answer me honestly, please," she started. I swallowed hard at her confession, but nodded. "Is it his jacket that keeps the nightmares away, or is it *him*?"

My heart stumbled at her words and I closed my eyes. The truth was evident. I didn't want to believe it. I didn't want to acknowledge it, but it was right there and I couldn't hide from it anymore.

"*Him*," I whispered, my voice hoarse from my tears.

It was the truth. Alessio brought me peace. He was the one who made it all go away. He gave me life. He was the one who made me...*feel*.

Alessio was my peace.

Opening my eyes, I stared at Maddie, only to see her giving me a wobbly smile. "That's all I wanted to know. Why don't you tell him?"

"No!" I said, my voice cracking. Shaking my head, I grabbed her arms. "No. You can't tell him. Please, promise me. Don't tell him. You can't."

I was panic-stricken, fear building inside my body.

Alessio couldn't find out. He couldn't. I didn't want him to think differently of me. I didn't want him to think that I was stupid or pitiful.

Even though I was all of the above, I didn't want him to think that. Maybe he already did, but this truth would only make it worse.

Maddie soothed me gently. "I won't say anything. It's okay. Calm down. It's okay."

"Promise," I whispered, my breathing harsh.

"I promise."

Maddie rubbed my hands and then nodded toward the bathroom. "Why don't you go take a hot bath? I have to go help Mom with lunch, and then I will come right back up."

"Okay," I agreed, realizing I needed that. She nodded and waited for me to get off the bed first before doing the same.

"I'll see you later," she said with a smile.

Nodding, I went into the bathroom. I closed the door behind me and opened the tap, letting the tub fill with water. I shrugged off my nightgown and twisted my hair up in a tight bun.

After the tub filled, I climbed in and let the water surround my cold body. I made sure my arms were on the edge and not submerged in the water. The doctor said I shouldn't get my stitches soaked or they might get infected.

The warmth started to penetrate my pores and I relaxed and closed my eyes. It felt so good. I didn't know how long I stayed like that, but when the water started to get cold, I washed up and stepped out, quickly wrapping the towel around my body, and keeping the cold air away.

I quickly got dressed and walked out of the bathroom. As I made my way toward my bed, something on it caught my eye. My steps faltered and I let out a gasp.

Alessio's jacket. Running toward it, I stopped in front of my bed and grabbed the jacket, pulling it to my chest. My fingers were wrapped tightly around the fabric, my breathing hard as I tried to wrap my head around this.

I looked down at it, my mind, breathing, and body instinctively calming.

Maddie.

It must have been her. That was the only option. Happy tears blinded my vision, and I sent a silent thank you to her.

Thank you. Oh, thank you so much.

I couldn't wait to see her so I could thank her in person. It felt like she had given me my life back. My peace. This was all I needed.

I was holding the jacket tightly to my chest when I heard a knock on the door. My body stiffened at the sound and I lurched forward, pulling my pillow up so that I could hide the jacket underneath. Straightening back up, I called out softly, "Come in."

The door opened to reveal Alessio. My heart stuttered at the sight. He walked inside but didn't close to the door, instead staying in the doorway.

"Are you busy right now?" he asked.

I shook my head and he nodded, looking satisfied with my response.

"Come. I want to show you something," he ordered gently.

My eyebrows furrowed in confusion and I didn't move.

Alessio took a step forward. "Do you not trust me?"

I couldn't believe he asked me that question. Wasn't it obvious? Even though I shouldn't trust him, I did. He was my enemy, yet I trusted him more than I had ever trusted anyone.

I walked toward him, my heart doing the same pitter-patter dance it always did whenever he was near. Stopping in front of Alessio, I peered up at him through my thick eyelashes and noticed a slight twist to his mouth and the faint indentation of the dimple on his cheek.

"I trust you," I whispered.

"Good." He nodded, the corner of his lips slowly turning up in a slight smile. It was barely there. So faint that I would have missed it if I wasn't paying attention. "Let's go," Alessio said, turning around. He didn't look back to see if I was following, but he knew I would. And so I did. Without any questions asked, I followed him.

We walked down the stairs silently, and when he led me outside to the back garden, my steps faltered. "Where are we going?" I asked.

"Just wait and see. I don't want to ruin the surprise," he muttered. A resigned sigh brushed across my lips and I nodded in agreement.

But I was curious. And a little giddy with excitement.

My excitement quickly evaporated when he led us into the woods behind the estate. As we walked further, I started to grow nervous. Leaves and twigs crushed under my feet as I followed Alessio silently. He appeared determined in his lead.

This wasn't good. Not good at all.

My eyes went wide and I stopped walking. Alessio must have felt it because he turned around and stared at me expectantly.

"What's wrong?" he asked, cocking his head to the side in question.

"Why…where…are we…going?" I stuttered in fear and panic.

"I told you, it's a surprise. C'mon. We are almost there." When I didn't move, he sighed. "Ayla, trust me. Okay? I'm not going to hurt you."

At his words, the fear slowly settled, but it was

still there.

Stupidly, I followed him.

And when I finally found out what he wanted to show me, I was glad I followed him.

When the forest started to grow less dense, my eyes finally settled on an opening where light cascaded around the woodland, bringing life and beauty to trees that it touched. And faintly I could hear the sound of rushing water. It felt refreshing and I quickened my pace so that I was right behind Alessio.

Finally breaking free from the trees, Alessio came to a stop. I almost stumbled into his back, but quickly righted myself. "We are here," he murmured softly.

My eyebrows lifted in question and I walked to the side, so that I was standing next to him. And when I finally saw what he wanted me to see, I gasped out loud. My hands came up to cover my mouth in shock, as I took the magnificent beauty in front of me.

"Oh my God," I whispered in complete utter shock.

I took a hesitant step toward the stream that ran in the middle on the woods. The rocks glistened in multiple hues of brown, black, and red. The water running over them sparkled under the bright sunlight.

Beautiful and colorful wildflowers surrounded the edge of the stream. They were all different colors. Purples, yellow, red, white. They only intensified the breathtaking beauty in front of me. On the other side of the creek, there was a field filled with the same flowers.

The only sound I could hear was the water moving and the sweet singing of the birds. I was completely awestruck and speechless.

It was the most beautiful thing I had ever seen. I couldn't tear my eyes away.

My body felt light and free. My stomach twisted with butterflies and I smiled widely.

"This is so beautiful," I breathed. I felt Alessio moving closer. He was so close that I felt his heat penetrate my body.

"It is," he agreed softly.

We were silent for a few minutes, both of us basking in the beauty.

"I come here when I want to clear my mind," he said. Tearing my eyes away from the stream and the field, I turned toward him. He was already looking down at me, his eyes glistening in the sunlight.

Keeping his gaze on mine, he continued gently, "I thought that maybe you would want to see it. You need it more than I do."

"Thank you."

This made me deliriously happy.

"I thought this would help. I don't know how to make you feel better. I'm at a loss, but maybe this can give you the peace that you need. Even for just a little while," Alessio confessed, looking a little nervous.

He didn't know that he already brought me peace. What he just gave me was more than I could ever ask for. He didn't know, but *he* was my peace.

"Thank you," I said again, my throat closing around the words. "This is truly so beautiful."

Alessio nodded and stayed silent, his eyes never shifting from mine. But I was the one who broke the connection. Turning back around, I stared at the creek and field again, another smile stretching across my lips.

I turned my face up toward the sky and into the sunlight. Closing my eyes, I basked in the serenity and welcomed the warmth that brushed over my skin.

I was always trapped inside my father's mansion. Never allowed to leave. I was only allowed to walk around in the backyard but never further away. When I escaped, that was the first time I had been outside the gates and into the real world.

Keeping my eyes closed, I felt Alessio watching me. He made me feel warm and happy. I opened my eyes but didn't look at him. Instead, I stared straight ahead.

I didn't know how long we stayed like that. Me admiring the beauty while Alessio kept his gaze on me. But after some time, my feet started to hurt from standing and I felt Alessio shift beside me.

"We should go back. It's almost time for lunch," he said, softly.

I turned toward him, and blinked up, disappointed. "We can come back tomorrow," he suggested.

I nodded and then looked back at the stream. "C'mon," he urged. When I felt Alessio moving away, a sudden panic filled my chest. I turned around to see his back to me.

I didn't know what came over me, but I lurched forward and grabbed the back of his jacket, halting his movement.

Alessio glanced back toward me, his eyebrows furrowed in confusion and question. My hand was shaking and I didn't know why.

I wanted...*no*...I needed something, but I didn't know what it was. My fingers tightened on the fabric of his jacket and his eyes shifted to them. Alessio turned around and I had no choice but to let go. I felt empty.

Bringing my hand up, I placed it over my chest, trying to calm my wildly racing heart.

"Ayla?" he questioned.

His eyes were intense on mine as he waited for me to say something. Taking a deep breath, I stepped closer to him. His eyes widened slightly and he cocked his head to the side, waiting.

I stopped and then looked down.

"Can you please hold me?" I asked softly.

Alessio had given me this beauty but I needed something more.

I needed him, his warmth. His arms around me, holding me safely. I needed the peace that only he could give me.

I simply needed him.

When I felt Alessio moving closer, my heart stuttered. He stopped only an inch from me. I felt his finger on my chin and he slowly tilted my head up so that I was staring into his eyes. He seemed surprised.

"Are you sure?" he asked. I swallowed hard and then nodded. That was the only answer Alessio needed. He wrapped his arms around me, and gently pulled me into his body, holding me firmly in his embrace.

My head was right over his heart and I closed my eyes. His heart was beating just as loudly and fast as mine. Placing my hands on his chest, I curled into his body, sinking into his warm, gentle embrace.

My fingers tightened around the fabric of his jacket as I held on, never wanting to let go. His warmth surrounded me, until the only thing I could smell, feel, and think was him.

We stayed like that for what felt like eternity. And when he started to pull away, I didn't want to let go. So I didn't. My fingers stayed wrapped around the fabric as I tilted my head up to stare at Alessio.

He blinked down at me and I saw him bring his hands up. His fingers feathered over my cheeks and I sighed in contentment.

Alessio's gaze was soft and warm on mine, as he palmed my cheeks gently. He slightly bent down, his lips inches away from mine.

My heart did a flip at the thought of his lips on mine. My fingers tightened on his jacket and I instinctively moved even closer until our bodies were pressed together.

I didn't feel repulsed. Instead, all I felt was…peace.

Alessio stared into my eyes and then moved his gaze to my lips. I saw him swallow hard and he looked back into my eyes again. I knew what he wanted.

So, I gave him a small nod.

His eyes flared in surprise but then his lips pressed ever so gently on mine.

I gasped against the fullness of his mouth and relaxed into his hold. He held me so gently, as if I was made of glass and he was scared of breaking me. His lips were soft on mine.

Alessio was exceedingly tender as he explored my mouth. His lips moved over mine, almost feather-light, and then he created the slightest pressure.

It was intoxicating. I felt a rush I'd never felt before, and I never wanted it to end. As he continued to kiss me, his tongue brushing lightly over my tender lips, I felt his fingers caress my cheeks and then he deepened the kiss just a little bit.

When I let out another sigh, he slightly pulled away, his lips only an inch away from mine. He was breathing hard, his chest heaving under my palm. I felt the exact same way.

Looking up at him, I found him staring at me with wide eyes, filled with emotions I couldn't place.

When I brought a hand up and touched my tender lips, his eyes softened even further.

What he didn't realize was this kiss…

This kiss was my first real kiss.

Chapter 38

Alessio

Ayla's gaze was fixated at the beauty in front of her, while all I could see was her. The small yet sweet smile that stretched across her lips had lightened up her whole face. Her vivid green eyes were glistening with excitement and pure happiness. Her cheeks were slightly flushed and I couldn't take my eyes off her.

All I could think was how beautiful she looked in that moment.

She tilted her head up at the sky and closed her eyes. I took a step closer and then stopped. Swallowing hard against the ball of emotions in my throat, I turned my gaze away from her and stared straight ahead.

We were both silent for some time. For some reason, I felt nervous. This place was sacred. After my mother's death, I would come here almost every day, desperately trying to clear my mind.

It felt like I had given her everything that I had.

Everything that I held close to my heart, it was hers now. And I didn't know how to feel about that.

I was confused. The way my heart stuttered when I looked at her. And the way I always found myself lost in her. I didn't understand those emotions. I wish I knew how to deal with them. They only got me frustrated.

Taking a deep breath, I looked down and then cleared my throat.

"We should go back. It's almost lunch time," I said softly. I felt Ayla shift beside me and I looked up just in time to see her turning toward me.

She seemed disappointed, losing her smile. "We can come back tomorrow," I said.

And there it was. That beautiful smile again. She nodded and then looked back at the stream.

"C'mon," I urged, taking a step away from her and turning back around toward the path that led to the creek.

But I came to a sudden stop when I felt a tug on the back of my suit. Frowning, I glanced back to see Ayla looking at me with panic in her eyes.

Turning around so that I could face her, Ayla slowly let go of my jacket. She brought her hand up and placed it over her chest. I could see her breathing harder than before, her face filled with uncertainty and nervousness.

"Ayla?" I questioned, worried.

She took a deep breath and then stepped closer. My eyes widened at her bold movement and I sucked in a shocked breath.

Ayla looked down and I waited, my heart beating wildly in my chest.

Her next words were my undoing.

"Can you please hold me?" she asked softly, her voice barely a whisper.

I never expected her to utter those words. When I brought Ayla here, all I wanted was to give her this small peace. But I never expected anything in return.

I didn't realize how badly I actually wanted to hold her in my arms. Not until she said those words.

With my heart in my throat, I took a step toward Ayla, until we were only an inch apart. We were so close; I could feel her warmth. She was still looking down, purposely avoiding my gaze. But I wanted those beautiful green eyes on me.

Bringing my hand up, I placed a finger under her chin and tilted her head up until her warm eyes met mine. "Are you sure?" I asked, wanting her confirmation. I was scared. Scared that she would take it back, leaving me hopeless again.

But then she nodded. And that was all the answer I needed. Without wasting any time, I wrapped my arms around Ayla's tiny waist, gently pulling her into my body until I had her firmly enveloped in my arms.

She felt so small against me. So fragile. And I felt intensely protective. My arms slightly tightened around her as she rested her head on my chest, right over my racing heart. Ayla placed a hand over my chest and she curled into my body, making herself comfortable.

I closed my eyes, letting her warmth and sweet smell fill my senses. When was the last time I held someone in my arms?

340

Never.

When was the last time I felt like this? So peaceful. And lively.

It was as if Ayla had breathed life into me.

With her wrapped in my arms, I didn't want to move. I didn't want this moment to end.

I didn't know how long we stayed like that, lost in each other. Lost in this perfect moment. But I knew it had to end.

Slowly pulling away, I looked down at Ayla. Her fingers were still wrapped around my suit, refusing to let go. She tilted her head back, staring up at me. I blinked down, completely mesmerized by her.

Every time I tried to get myself under control, she made me lose it. Ayla didn't even have to do anything. One look and I was completely lost in her.

Without thinking, I brought a hand up and ran a finger down her soft cheek, my touch almost feather light. She sighed in contentment and a small smile played across her face, bringing my attention to her lips.

I could feel myself losing the small control I had left. Palming her cheeks gently, I bent my head toward hers until our lips were only inches apart. But I stopped.

Ayla moved closer to me, until our bodies were plastered together. My heart fluttered but still I didn't touch my lips to hers. I looked into her eyes and waited.

I had promised Ayla that I wouldn't touch her until she asked me. Until I had her permission. And this moment, I wanted it to be her choice.

I wanted her to choose. I wanted her acceptance.

Ayla's gaze softened and she gave me a small nod. I didn't give her a chance for second thoughts, instead as soon as I saw her nod, my head was already descending toward hers until my lips were pressed gently on hers.

I waited for Ayla to pull away, but when she sighed against my lips and melted in my arms, my heart stuttered at her reaction. I held her gently, as if she was a precious jewel. My lips explored hers at a slow pace. I kissed her as if we had all the time in the world.

My lips moved tenderly over hers, taking my sweet time. When I put the slightest pressure, deepening the kiss just a little bit, I felt her fingers tighten around the fabric of my suit.

I didn't push for more.

It was just a kiss. A small, sweet kiss.

That was it. Nothing more. Yet it felt more.

When Ayla let another sigh, I pulled away. We were both breathing hard. I could feel how fast her heart was beating. It matched the same rhythm as mine.

Ayla's cheeks were flushed, her lips a little swollen and red from my kiss. She blinked up at me, and the look in her eyes…it took my breath away.

Her eyes were warm and soft. But that wasn't it. It was the look of pure adoration there that took my breath away.

In that moment, I realized that was the first time I had given her a kiss.

We kissed before. Twice to be exact. But those kisses…I took them. Without considering her feelings. All I cared about was me. What I wanted.

But this kiss…I gave it to her, wholeheartedly. The look in her eyes, I gave this to her.

Her eyes were filled with awe as she brought her hand up and placed a finger on her lips. At her reaction, I felt myself softening even further.

For years, I had lived in the darkness with no emotions. I had remained unfeeling.

Yet, with one look from Ayla, I felt everything.

And that scared me.

Whenever I felt something for Ayla, Alfredo's voice resonated in my head. I would never forget the words he said to my mother.

The best way to bring a man down is by his weakness.

What I said to Maddie was the truth. This was not about me. It was about Ayla and what was right for her.

I let her go, and she blinked in surprise when I took a step back, forcing her to let go of me.

"We need to get back," I said, turning around, refusing to look at her confused expression.

"Okay," she whispered, her small voice hinting her sadness.

Both of us were silent on our way back to the mansion. As we got closer, the sound of the rushing water started to fade until we didn't hear it anymore. Breaking away from the forest, I took a deep breath as we walked into the back garden.

Ayla was right behind me, her steps so close she almost tripped herself over my feet. When we walked inside, I slowed down and turned toward her.

She stopped too and grabbed onto the hem of her dress nervously. "I'll see you later," I muttered. Ayla nodded and then walked away without saying anything.

I felt my eyebrows furrow in confusion when I saw her walking toward the kitchen. Quickly moving forward, I grabbed her elbow, halting her movement.

She gasped in shock and swiveled around, facing me with wide eyes. "Where are you going?" I demanded, letting go of her arm.

"To the kitchen," Ayla replied.

Crossing my arms across my chest, I leveled her with a stare. "Why?"

She cocked her head to the side, as if debating what to tell me. "To help Maddie and Lena."

"You are supposed to be resting, Ayla. No work for you."

"But I have been resting for three days now. I can work. I feel okay."

"No," I said.

"But it's boring. I want to help."

"No, Ayla. You are going upstairs to rest."

"But—"

"No. Stop arguing."

Her mouth snapped shut and she cowered. The beautiful smile disappeared.

I didn't like her sad expression.

Frustrated, I ran my fingers through my hair and looked away. Fuck.

"Fine. You can go. Just don't overwork yourself. You don't want to tear those stitches," I said.

But it was worth it when I turned around to see

her staring at me with twinkling green eyes, and then a breathtaking smile spread across her lips.

"Thank you," she said before turning around and quickly walking away. I stayed frozen, my eyes glued on her retreating back.

Fuck. I was losing it.

***

The rest of the day was spent avoiding Ayla. I stayed locked in my office and then went to the gym to vent my frustration on the punching bag.

Leaning against the wall, I tried to catch my breath.

"You are going to kill us one day," Viktor said.

"You are too stubborn to die," I told him, breathless.

"Well, I have to agree on that." He shrugged.

I pushed away from the wall and walked to the bench, grabbing a towel. "Are Artur and Phoenix coming back tomorrow?" I asked, rubbing the towel over my face.

"They are supposed to report back. We are going to Mark's tomorrow," Nikolay replied from his position at the door.

"Any news about the clubs?" I asked.

Nikolay shook his head. "No. Mark said he will give us the details when we meet."

Since Alberto took over, he'd made it his mission to take over my clubs. So far, he had been unsuccessful, but everyone was taking extra precautions. Mark was one of my top managers, handling over ten clubs, brothels, and underground

345

rings.

Nodding toward Nikolay and Viktor, I left the gym. It was late at night, and most of the lights were off.

After Ayla had played the piano and gone to her room, I couldn't go to sleep. I stayed seated for some time, staring at nothingness and feeling frustrated at myself. When I couldn't take it anymore, I went downstairs and spent more time in the gym.

When I went back up again, I stopped in front of my bedroom. Instead of going in, I turned to the left and stared at Ayla's door.

I knew it was late and that she'd be sleeping, but I still couldn't stop myself. I took several steps forward, walking past the piano room, until I was in front of her room. Placing my hand over the knob, I slowly twisted it and opened the door.

The room was dark. Only the small lamp beside her bed was on, barely illuminating the room. Walking deeper inside, I came to a stop beside Ayla. She was on her side, curled into a ball with the comforter up to her waist. Her eyes were closed, her breathing even as she slept soundly.

The lamp cast a soft glow on her face, making her look so peaceful.

Leaning forward, I lightly brushed a finger over her soft cheek, moving the few strands of hair away. At my touch, she moaned sleepily and shifted a little. I froze, waiting for her to wake up, but instead she kept sleeping.

Sighing in relief, I felt my lips twitch in a small smile as I stared at her sleeping form. My eyes moved from her face, down to her shoulders, and then her chest.

She was holding my suit jacket against her chest, her fingers wrapped tightly around the fabric.

I couldn't help but smile at the sight. So, it *was* true.

Walking out of the room, I made my way to Ayla's, deciding to check on her. But when I saw Milena coming out, looking affronted, I stopped in my tracks. She seemed surprised to see me, but then bent her head down in respect before walking past me without saying a word.

"What the fuck was that?" I muttered to myself, before resuming my walk to Ayla's room. Stopping by her door, I was about to open it when I heard Maddie's voice.

"Ayla, what were you doing with Alessio's jacket?"

At her words, I froze, my eyes widening in shock. What the fuck?

Leaning forward, I placed my ear against the door, hoping nobody was roaming the hallway.

I waited for an answer but instead all I heard was silence.

"You don't have to…" Maddie said.

"I sleep with it."

"What?" Maddie sputtered. I had the same reaction.

"I sleep with it," Ayla repeated, making my heart flip again.

And then her next words were enough to bring me to my knees. My hands tightened in fists against the door and I closed my eyes.

"It keeps the nightmares away," she admitted, her voice so soft that I barely even heard it. But I did. I heard it as if she'd whispered it in my ear.

Rubbing a hand over my face, I paced the hall outside of her door, trying to come to grips with what I had just heard.

My eyes widened when I heard Maddie at the door, telling Ayla that she would come back soon.

I quickly rushed into the piano room and closed the door behind me. Leaning against the door, I closed my eyes and leaned my head back, feeling uncertain about whether I should act on this new revelation.

When I felt Ayla shift under my hand, I snapped out of my thoughts. I knew one thing for certain.

If my jacket kept Ayla's nightmares away, that was all that mattered.

I rubbed my thumb over her cheek one last time before stepping away. Ayla sighed in her sleep, a small smile playing across her lips.

"Sweet dreams," I whispered.

Giving her a final glance, I turned around and walked out of her room, closing the door softly behind me.

***

I stared at the beige walls. Mark's house was *homey*. Toys were spread out over the carpet.

"So far, Alberto's made no move toward the clubs I'm taking care of," Mark said. My attention returned to him as he leaned back against his sofa. "I'm surprised. They are the most popular places. If he wanted to go big, those would have been his first targets."

Alberto had some kind of plan, but every lead my men followed brought them to a dead end.

Every time we made a move, he was ready for them. Whoever the insider was, he'd been getting the information back to Alberto quickly, barely giving us time to put our plans in actions.

"What are you going to do?" Mark asked.

I scoffed. "The question should be, what am I *not* going to do?"

He raised an eyebrow and then chuckled. "Well, you definitely have something planned."

"Always. I want you to keep a close eye on all the clubs. Every single one of them. If you can't do it alone, I will send one of my man to help," I said, my voice hard.

"I can handle it. I have been doing this for years, boss. But I think it would be better if you send another man. This way, we can keep a better watch."

Nodding, I sat back against the couch. Just then, a small girl came running in the living room, a bright smile on her face.

She was wearing a purple dress, her short black hair hanging loose on her neck. She smiled up at us.

"Sophia," Mark admonished softly. "You aren't supposed to come in here."

But the little girl paid no attention to her father. She was only two years old. All her attention was fixated on Nikolay, who stood stoically beside me.

349

Sophia took a step closer toward him and stopped right in front of him. I looked up to see his jaw twitch at how hard he was grinding his teeth.

He moved his eyes down to the small girl in front of him and I saw him swallow hard. Sophia raised her arms and said, "Up."

When Nikolay didn't move, Sophia lost her smile and she demanded again, "Up. Up."

Mark rose to his feet. "I'm sorry, Boss." He looked embarrassed. But just when he was about to move toward Sophia, Nikolay bent down and pulled the girl into his arms.

"What the fuck?" Viktor muttered beside me, voicing what I'd been thinking.

Sophia giggled. "Hi," she said.

Nikolay didn't answer, instead he glowered at the girl in his arms. But Sophia didn't seem affected by his glare.

Instead she turned her attention to his scars, and her hand moved to cup his cheek, her tiny palm right over his scars.

"Shit," Mark muttered.

But instead of Nikolay erupting in anger at the girl's touch, he stayed still, tense, and completely silent.

"Boo…hurts?" Sophia asked.

I heard a gasp and turned to see Bree, Mark's wife, standing at the doorway, her eyes wide.

But I quickly turned my attention back to Nikolay and Sophia.

When he didn't answer, Sophia repeated her question again.

"She is asking if it hurts," Bree translated.

350

Nikolay swallowed hard and then he shook his head.

"No. Not anymore," he said.

"Good. No hurt," she replied with a smile, and then started to twist around in his arms, clearly wanting to be let down.

Nikolay set her down and then she was running to her mother, who gave us a sheepish look. "I'm sorry. I was busy and she ran before I could stop."

"It's okay," I said. I got up and Viktor followed. "I will see you next month," I told Mark.

"Sure, Boss. I will keep you updated."

Nikolay was still visibly shaken by what had just happened. Fuck, even I was. That took us all by surprise.

We were almost out of the door when something caught my attention. Stopping, I glanced at it. Flowers. They were different from what Maddie had given Ayla but they still reminded me of her.

"Nice flowers," I said dryly, trying to appear disinterested.

Bree smiled. "Thank you. Mark gave them to me for our anniversary."

Nodding, I looked away from the flowers and walked out, followed by Viktor and Nikolay.

As Viktor drove us back to the estate, all I could think about was the flowers. And the beautiful smile on Ayla's face when she was looking at them.

Flowers. Ayla's smile. And Maddie's words.

Sighing, I asked out loud, "Where do you get flowers?"

"What?" Viktor asked, confused.

"Where do you buy flowers?" I asked again.

"Flowers? What the fuck do you want to do with flowers?" He glanced back at me in the rear view mirror before moving his gaze back to the road.

"Nikolay," I said, my voice hard.

"Yes, Boss." He nodded and took out his phone. I saw him typing something and after a few minutes, he passed me the phone.

"I already dialed the number," he said.

Placing the phone to my ear, I waited for someone to pick up.

"Hello, Starbright Floral Design. How can I help you?" a woman said.

"I want flowers," I said abruptly. I heard Viktor chuckle from the front seat and I glared at the back of his head.

"Okay?" I waited, but she didn't say anything else.

"I said, I want flowers."

"Yes. I heard you, sir. But what type of flowers?"

"Any flowers," I muttered impatiently.

"Any flowers? But, sir—"

"Just give me the best flowers you have," I snapped.

"Okay. How many?"

Pinching the bridge of my nose in frustration, I leaned my head against the back of the seat. Why the fuck was ordering flowers so damn complicated?

"Twenty, thirty…" I growled into the phone.

"I need an exact number, sir." The woman sounded impatient. That was an understatement of what I was feeling.

"Damn it, just give me thirty."

"Okay. When do you want them del—"

"In an hour."

"An hour? Sir, we can't do it in an hour—"

"I said, I want it in an hour."

"Just give me a minute." I heard her talking in the background and then she was back. "Okay, sir. Give me your address." I quickly rattled off the address and then hung up, throwing the phone on the seat next to me.

"So, flowers?" Viktor asked.

"Not now!" I growled in warning before closing my eyes.

When the car lurched to a complete stop, there was a van outside the gate. The words **Starbright Floral Design** were written boldly across the side of the van.

"Nice timing," I said when the driver stepped out of the van. He had a large bouquet of pink and white flowers in his hands.

Walking toward him, he nodded in greetings. "Sir, were you the one who ordered the flowers?"

"Yes," I replied sharply.

"Here you go. You need to sign here." He pushed a paper in my hand. After signing, he handed me the bouquet. The *very* big bouquet.

I looked down at it curiously. "Did I really order this much?"

I heard Viktor cough beside me. "If I remember correctly, you ordered thirty. That looks like thirty to me." Glaring at him, I realized that I asked that question out loud.

I flipped him the finger and nodded at the guard

to open the gates.

I didn't care if it was five or thirty, as long as Ayla loved them. That was all that mattered.

Chapter 39

Ayla

I was lying in bed completely lost in the book that I was reading, when my door opened without a knock. Sitting up with a start, I dropped the book. It fell on my mattress soundlessly while my heart was beating loudly against my rib-cage.

Maddie walked inside, her face bright and in her hands was a large bouquet of pink and white flowers. "Alessio got you flowers!"

Again?

My eyes went wide as she got closer and I was able to take a better look at the flowers. Holding my hand out, my heart danced with excitement. Maddie gave me the flowers and I gasped.

They were so beautiful. Even more beautiful than the flowers he gave me before. And it was such a large bouquet.

Pulling it to my chest, I smiled up at Maddie. "What are they called?"

"Peonies. They are beautiful, aren't they?"

I nodded, completely speechless. They were breathtaking. And the mixture of colors made the bouquet even more gorgeous.

I couldn't help it. I was smiling hard and then a small giggle escaped my lips. "I can't believe he got me flowers again," I whispered.

My heart was going wild in my chest and my stomach was filled with butterflies. Holding the flowers close to my chest, I sighed in contentment.

As I held the flowers, all I wanted was to see Alessio. I wished he was the one who gave them to me. I wished he was here, so I could thank him.

I wished he was here, so that he could see how happy he made me.

Looking up at Maddie, I saw her smiling down at me. "He can be a romantic sometimes," she teased with a wink.

I heard myself giggle again. I was giggling. *Unbelievable*. Placing my hand over my mouth, I looked down at the flowers and then nodded.

"He kissed me," I admitted, my smile so wide that my cheeks were hurting.

Maddie gasped. "What?" she squealed.

I ducked my head shyly and bit down on my lips as Maddie went crazy beside me.

"He kissed you? Alessio kissed you? When? How?"

Closing my eyes, I inhaled the sweet scent of the flowers. "Yesterday. When he brought me to the creek."

I could still feel his lips on mine, moving gently as he held me in his arms. The kiss and our sweet moment at the creek, that was all I could think

356

about since it happened.

And I would never forget the way he held me or kissed me. As if I meant something to him. As if I was precious. I would cherish it forever in my heart.

"Oh, Ayla," Maddie breathed beside me. "I can't believe this. You have no idea how happy I am."

"I am happy too. Deliriously happy," I whispered, my eyes still closed. "He makes me so happy, Maddie."

Opening my eyes, I glanced up at her. "I should go thank him for the flowers!"

"Now?" Maddie asked. I nodded enthusiastically. She laughed and then stepped back.

"Go ahead, babe. He was downstairs the last time I saw him."

"Thank you," I replied, quickly putting on my flats, still holding the bouquet in my hands. I ran out of the room, feeling giddy. My heart was doing several flips.

I slowed down when I walked down the stairs and saw Viktor and Nikolay engaged in a heated conversation.

They stopped mid-sentence when I approached them. "Ayla," Nikolay said in greeting. Viktor nodded and then looked at the flowers in my hands, his eyebrows going up in surprise.

"Do you know where Alessio is?" I asked softly.

I saw Nikolay's eyebrows furrowed before he replied. "He is in his office."

"Oh. Okay, thank you," I gave them both a smile before walking back up.

"Wait," Viktor called out.

Stopping in my tracks, I turned back around.

"Yes?"

"Where are you going?" Nikolay asked.

"To Alessio's office. I want to thank him for the flowers."

Their eyes widened and they looked at each other. "No," Nikolay quickly snapped.

"Huh?" I flinched at his tone. His expression softened at my reaction and he looked sheepish.

"That won't be good idea," Viktor swallowed nervously. What are they talking about?

"I won't disturb him, promise. I will just say thank you and then leave. That's it." I really wanted to see him. I felt...desperate. And strangely, I had missed him.

"Maybe you can go later. He is busy right now," Nikolay argued. Viktor nodded quickly in agreement, his expression almost pained.

My shoulders sagged in defeat and I looked down at the flowers. "Okay," I whispered. Looking back up, I saw Nikolay and Viktor sighing in relief. Why did they look so tense?

Shrugging it off, I smiled at them again. "I will go later."

"Yeah. Later," Viktor agreed. Turning around, I walked back upstairs, feeling wistful. I wished I could see him right now.

Bringing the flowers to my chest again, I shook my head. "Oh, well. I will see him later," I muttered, before burying my face in the bouquet. The feeling of defeat left me and I felt myself smiling again.

When I reached the top landing, I turned to my left toward my room, but something caught my eye to my right.

Alessio.

Swiveling around, I was about to call him when I saw someone else. Not just anyone. But Nina.

My smile was lost in an instant.

His back was turned to me so he didn't see me. But Nina saw me and she smiled. It was devilish. It was one that was filled with triumph. She brought a hand up and laid it on Alessio's arm and moved closer.

"Alessio," she crooned enough for me to hear.

He was saying something in return, but I didn't hear him. All I saw was how close Nina was. She was practically plastered to Alessio's body.

My stomach twisted almost painfully and I took a step back. My arms fell limply beside me as my nose stung.

All the happiness, everything that I felt just seconds ago evaporated, leaving me empty.

But then I felt something I never felt before boiling inside of me, like waves crashing around me. My chest grew tight, squeezing as I continued to take steps backward.

Why did he do this?

He let me play the piano. I played for him every night. He shared the creek with me. He kissed me. He held me in his arms. And he gave me flowers. I thought we had something special.

I thought it meant something. I thought *I* meant something to him.

I realized I was crying. I swiped the tears away.

My heart was hurting.

Placing a hand over my mouth, I muffled any

sounds that might emerge.

"I would describe it as a wave. It comes crashing in your heart with so many mixed feelings...it hurts."

Maddie's voice rang through my mind as I stared at Nina and Alessio. When I saw them walking into his office, I quickly turned around and blinked away the tears in frustration. I placed my hand over my chest, where my heart was raging.

I couldn't understand. Could Maddie be right?

Was I...jealous?

Chapter 40

Under the layer of hurt and disappointment, I was angry at Alessio and at myself.

Why did I care?

It was a foreign and weird feeling coursing through my body. Anger. I didn't remember the last time I let myself feel such emotion. I had learned how to turn off all my emotions, becoming numb to everything and everyone around me. Yet I felt hurt, disappointed, angry, and jealous.

Alessio gave me laughter, smiles, and peace. And now, in my heart, it hurt. It felt like he had taken all of that away.

I wasn't supposed to care, but no matter how hard I tried to keep myself from getting emotionally involved, I had failed.

Looking away from the door, I stared down at the bouquet in my hand.

A sigh filled with dejection escaped past my lips, and I turned away from his office, slowly making my way to my room. Walking inside, I found Maddie sitting on my bed, with my book on her lap.

Her head snapped up when she heard me.

"Ayla?" Maddie questioned, her eyebrows furrowed in confusion. Placing the book on the bed, she motioned me to come forward. "What's wrong? I thought you were going to see Alessio."

Swallowing hard against the ball of sadness, I shook my head and brought the flowers close to my chest. "He was with Nina."

There was silence at first and then she erupted. "What?" she said, getting up angrily from the bed. "That little—"

"I didn't get a chance to talk to him. He didn't see me." The image of them flashed before my eyes, causing a sudden wave of anger inside of me. I looked at the flowers and then without thinking, I threw them on the bed.

"Aww, baby…" I heard Maddie whisper beside me, her voice almost soothing. Swiveling around, I faced her, placing my hand over my chest.

"What is this feeling? I hate it. Is this what it feels like? Jealousy? If it does, then I don't like it."

Maddie's eyes reflected sympathy and understanding. She walked closer and placed both hands on my shoulders. "Was does it feel like?"

"It hurts. I feel hopeless. Sad. And then angry. Maybe at myself, because I hate feeling like this."

Looking back at the flowers that I had carelessly thrown away, I felt guilty. Another confusing feeling. Bending forward, I grabbed the flowers again and pulled the bouquet close to my chest. Burying my face in the soft petals, I closed my eyes with a sigh.

A tear escaped the corner of my eye, falling onto

the petals. "I thought what we shared together meant something to him."

"It did. I know it did. He is just too stubborn to admit it," Maddie argued.

But I shook my head in response.

She released a tired sigh from behind me and then I felt her hand on my shoulders.

"Tell me something," she whispered. "Why do you think you feel this way?"

I shrugged.

Maddie smiled at my response. "You feel something for him," she stated confidently.

I sucked in a sharp breath, my heart fluttering at her words, while my stomach twisted in knots. Her words were shocking yet so true.

Maddie was right. I did feel something for Alessio. Whenever he was near, my mind and body felt like they weren't my own anymore. When he was close, I felt light and liberated. And when he was far, my heart called out to him, wishing he was close again.

I didn't want to admit it but Alessio had become the reason for my happiness. He had given happiness that I had never felt before. He made me smile, without even trying. My heart was at peace when I was with him.

I refused to admit that Maddie was right. She let out a small laugh, her eyes twinkling with mischief.

"Do you trust me?" she asked.

Taken aback by the sudden question, I nodded slowly. "Yes. Of course."

"Will you do whatever I tell you?"

Staring at her in confusion, I asked a question of

my own. "What do you mean?"

"Just trust me, okay? I got this. Just go with the flow and do whatever I tell you."

I shook my head and gave her a serious look.

"Maddie, what are you talking about?"

"I'm really sorry. Like really sorry. I will apologize more later." She bit on her lips nervously, and looked extremely guilty. I saw her wince and then I felt a sharp pain in my ankle. Did she just kick me?

"Ow!" I yelled, bending forward.

"Sorry." Maddie took the bouquet from my hand and pushed me down on the bed, so that I was sitting.

I flinched at the pain and bent forward, rubbing a hand over my aching ankle.

I glanced up at Maddie and she pouted.

"What was that for?" I asked, completely stunned.

"Trust me, okay? Just bear with the pain. I'll be right back," she said, walking backward. Before I could answer, she ran out of the room.

Maddie was absolutely crazy. What was she doing now?

***

Alessio

Sitting back on my sofa chair, I watched Nina place her handbag on the coffee table as she took the seat in front of me.

"So?" I asked, feeling impatient. Just when I had

been about to go see Ayla, Nina made her appearance. She was supposed to report back to me, but I had completely forgotten about it. I had only been thinking about Ayla.

And even now, all I wanted to know was whether she'd liked the flowers.

"Nothing much happened," Nina said. "Alberto and his men are still treating the women badly. It's still the same. Nothing changed. He has more power now, so it's going to be harder to stop the abuse in the brothels and clubs."

I'd sent her to keep watch on the clubs, acting as a whore so she could report back to me with internal information. So far, nothing had changed.

Sighing in frustration, I raked my hand through my hair. "Fuck."

"I'm sorry. I wish I could help more, but…"

"You've done more than enough. But I want you out of there now. It's getting too dangerous, and every time you go there, you are putting yourself at risk. Your services won't be needed anymore," I told her.

She looked confused for a moment, and then nodded. "What do I do now?"

"You are free to do whatever you want. I don't want you anywhere near the clubs, understood?" I replied, my tone firm.

Nina nodded, keeping her gaze down in respect.

Leaning back against the sofa, I crossed my arms over my chest.

"You can leave," I ordered.

"Oh." Nina's mouth fell open in shock. I knew what she was expecting, but she wasn't getting it.

Not today. Not anymore.

Her eyes widened for a second, and then she smiled, her expression turning seductive and sultry. She licked her lips and then scooted forward, her short skirt rising higher in the process until her thighs were barely covered.

"Alessio," she whispered, getting up from the couch and walking around the coffee table toward me. I gritted my teeth in annoyance at her desperate attempt to seduce me.

A few days ago, I would have accepted her advances, and bent her over my desk, my cock inside her in a matter of seconds.

But right now, all I could think about was Ayla. Her sweet smile, her flushed cheeks, and swollen lips after my kiss. She had taken over my mind and senses, making everything and everyone else appear bleak in comparison to her.

I raised a hand to stop Nina's advances when she leaned forward, showing me her barely covered cleavage.

"Nina—" Before I could finish, the door crashed opened, startling both of us. Turning my head, I saw a breathless Maddie running inside.

"Ayla," she gasped. "She's hurt."

My eyes widened and I quickly stood up, causing Nina to lose her balance and stumble.

"What happened?" I demanded, my voice filled with panic.

Maddie took a deep breath and glanced at Nina before answering. "She twisted her ankle really bad and she can't walk. She's in her room."

I swore, rushing out of my office. I made my

way to Ayla's room and found the door already open.

"Ayla?" I walked inside. She was lying on her bed but quickly sat up at the sound of my voice.

"Alessio," she said, and then I saw her wince, her forehead creasing in discomfort.

Rushing forward, I stopped in front of her. "Are you okay?"

"I'm all right," she said.

I looked down at her reddened ankle, then knelt in front of her, but didn't touch her, afraid I might hurt her more.

When she moved her feet closer to the bed and away from me, I placed a hand on her knee, stopping her. "Don't move." Gently taking her foot in my hand, I inspected it. "Does it hurt when you move?"

"A little."

I looked up at Ayla. She was staring down at me, seemingly confused.

Standing up, I bent forward and wrapped an arm behind her back and one under her knees, pulling her up so that I was cradling her to my chest.

"What are you doing?" she asked.

"I'm taking you to Sam. He will know whether you are okay or not," I replied, walking her out of her room and downstairs to Sam's bedroom.

Ayla was silent in my arms. When we got closer, I heard her sigh. "How did you know I was hurt?" she asked.

"Maddie told me you twisted your ankle. She said you couldn't walk," I replied.

"Oh." A small smile appeared on her lips. It was

faint and quick, but definitely there.

I stopped in front of Sam's room and Ayla leaned forward to knock at the door. It opened within a few seconds and Sam stood in the doorway. His eyes widened at the sight of Ayla in my arms and he quickly moved back, motioning for me to enter.

"What happened?" he asked.

I placed Ayla on his bed, and stood beside her. "She twisted her ankle."

Sam knelt down in front of Ayla and inspected her ankle. His lips twisted thoughtfully and he asked Ayla several questions while I hovered over her, anxious and worried. The thought of her being in pain didn't sit well with me.

The sense of protectiveness I felt toward her was a first. The need to keep her safe and happy was a primal feeling inside of me. Every day it grew stronger, until only she mattered to me.

"It's not bad. Nothing to be worried about. Just a very tiny sprain that won't even hurt after two days," Sam said.

He looked up and smiled kindly at Ayla, his brown eyes crinkling at the corners. "I'll give you some pain relieving cream. Just rub it over your ankle twice a day until it doesn't hurt anymore," he said.

Ayla nodded and looked up shyly at me as a faint color tinged her cheeks. When she saw me staring, she quickly looked down nervously.

Sam came back with a small tube in his hand. "Here. This should help with the pain. Rub it gently over the aching area and it should do the work."

"Thank you," she said.

Maddie stepped into the room. "So?" she asked, walking straight to Ayla.

Ayla gave her strange look and shook her head. "I'm fine," she replied before mumbling something under her breath.

She stood up and wobbled a little, and I instinctively wrapped an arm around her waist, pulling her close to me.

She placed a hand on my chest and tried to step out of my embrace, but my arms tightened around her, stopping her movement.

"I can walk," she said, her voice coming out a little breathy.

"You shouldn't put too much pressure on your ankle."

Ayla glanced at Maddie. "She can help me. I'm sure you have other things to take care of."

"Right. I'll help her. Don't want to disturb you from your work and all," Maddie added, glaring at me.

Before I could answer, Maddie was already pulling Ayla away from me and I had no choice but to let her go. As she stepped out of my embrace, I suddenly felt empty and already missed having her small body against mine.

When they were out of sight, I nodded to Sam and then made my way upstairs. I saw Nina at the top of the steps. She smiled brightly, her eyes shining.

"Alessio," she whispered.

"You need to leave," I ordered, my voice harsh and unyielding.

"What?" she sputtered, her eyes widening.

"Exactly what I said. Leave. I don't want you here anymore." Nina was good at her job. She was an asset but I didn't need her anymore, *except* for her work in the field.

"But Alessio—"

"I told you, your services won't be needed anymore," I said through gritted teeth, punctuating each words so she understood the meaning.

Her mouth opened shock. "You mean…?"

"You heard him. He doesn't want to fuck you anymore. So get lost."

At Maddie's voice, I closed my eyes in frustration and pinched the bridge of my nose. Taking a few deep breaths, I opened my eyes to see her glaring at both of us.

Nina's face turned stormy and she twisted her lips angrily, then looked back at me, waiting.

I gave her a cold stare and crossed my arms over my chest, raising an eyebrow in question.

"I'm going," she snapped. Her expression was cold as she walked around me. Nina was a cold-hearted bitch and she loved it that way. And Maddie had to tread carefully before she got herself into trouble.

"Bye, Felicia," Maddie called as she rolled her eyes.

When I reached the top landing, Maddie stepped in front of me, blocking my way.

"I swear to God…if you are playing Ayla…" she warned, anger glittering in her eyes.

"Why the fuck would you think that?" I growled, taking a step forward, completely outraged by her question.

She indicated where Nina had been standing moments ago. When realization sunk in, anger deserted me and I winced at the thought.

"Nothing was going to happen," I said.

Maddie looked suspicious. "Ayla saw you going into the office with Nina. She thought…she was completely heartbroken, Alessio."

Guilt coursed through my body and I swore under my breath.

"Imagine how you would feel if you saw Ayla with another man," Maddie added.

The thought made me see red. My hands tightened into fists until my knuckles hurt. I gritted my teeth.

She raised an eyebrow. "Exactly," she muttered before heading back toward Ayla's room.

I stared at her back and then leaned against the banister, my mind filled with dangerous thoughts.

When I first saw Ayla and proposed that she work for me, this wasn't what I had in mind.

She was supposed to work for me and I kept her close because I wanted to fuck her. That was my intention. But it wasn't about lust anymore. It wasn't about fucking her and being done with her.

It was more, something I couldn't wrap my head around. A feeling that I didn't understand.

But I wasn't against it anymore. I let myself bask in this foreign emotion, waiting to see where it would lead me, hoping it wouldn't destroy either of us in the process.

Sighing, I raked my hand through my hair. I thought I was the only one feeling what was

371

between us. But Ayla felt it too, and I had hurt her.

A connection so deep, so irrevocably beautiful yet haunting and dangerous. It brought us peace, even through the pain.

Chapter 41

She was waiting for me, sitting at the piano, her gaze on the wall before her, looking completely lost in her thoughts.

At the sight of me, she smiled, and I sat on the sofa in front of the piano, keeping my focus on her the whole time.

I hadn't had a chance to talk to her since this morning. If I wasn't mistaken, she was avoiding me.

As soon as she saw me, she would walk the other way or act like she didn't see me. If her eyes caught mine, her expression was impassive, her lips thinned in a hard line.

As I continued to stare at her, the piano the only thing between us, she gave me a strange look and then her expression was blank again before she looked down at the keys.

As I listened to the hauntingly beautiful music, I felt completely transfixed by her beauty and the peaceful look on her face.

All she had to do was sit there silently and she

already had my complete attention.

After three songs, she stopped and then opened her eyes, making direct eye contact with me. I smiled, trying to look as gentle as possible, but she ignored it, then went to the book shelf.

She took her time choosing a book, making me nervous with each passing second.

Grabbing a book in her hand, she walked back and sat down on the sofa beside me. All the time, she did it silently while keeping her eyes away from mine.

I waited for her to say something.

I didn't know how long we stayed like that. I tried to get some work done but I was too lost in Ayla to think.

My gaze kept moving to her, and a few times I noticed her peeking at me, but she would quickly move her gaze away when she noticed me looking. I even saw her scowl at the book and then she twisted her lips in annoyance.

When I couldn't bear the long, frustrating silence anymore, I cleared my throat and shifted a couple of times in my seat, trying to bring Ayla's attention to me.

But she was stubborn. Clearing my throat again, I opened my mouth to say something but quickly snapped it shut when I realized I didn't know what to say.

I stared at the wall in frustration but the painting caught my attention. It was a beautiful landscape painting of a field of vibrant, colorful flowers.

That's it, I thought.

"Did you like the flowers?" I asked, breaking the

painful silence between us.

"They were okay," she replied stiffly before looking down at the book again.

What kind of answer was that?

"So you liked them?"

Ayla shrugged. "They weren't bad."

"Oh," I murmured, my shoulders dropping in disappointment.

She didn't like them.

Swallowing hard, I leaned back against the sofa. Ayla was so happy with the flowers that Maddie had given her that I thought she would love them.

I rubbed a hand over my face and closed my eyes tiredly. In my attempt to make her feel better, I messed up.

After a few minutes, I realized she was looking at me. She stiffened and her gaze quickly snapped down. I saw a defiant scowl on her face.

Suddenly, she stood up and started to leave.

"Where are you going?" I asked, standing up too. Her steps faltered and she turned around, facing me again. Her shoulders were pushed back boldly and she looked straight at me, her green eyes vibrant and filled with unreadable emotions.

"I'm going to sleep," she said. "It's late."

That's it? I cleared my throat and then nodded. "Okay. Goodnight."

We stared at each other silently for a few seconds. Nodding at me mutely, she swiveled around and walked out of the room.

I stared at her retreating back, speechless. What the fuck just happened?

I stepped back until I hit the sofa.

Ayla hadn't even said goodnight.

***

It had been three days. I growled in frustration and pushed the papers away. Three days of Ayla barely speaking a word to me.

I sat down against my chair and rolled my neck left and right, trying to release the tension.

I didn't understand what I did wrong. I tried everything, yet she stayed completely closed off. I knew she wasn't like that with the others. I saw her talking animatedly to Maddie, a smile always present on her face, her eyes shining brightly.

But with me, she either scowled or frowned in my direction. Or sometimes, her expression was completely impassive.

And I was growing desperate. Just once, I wanted her to smile at me. I wanted to see her eyes sparkle with happiness while she looked at me. Just like at the creek or when she played the piano the first time.

Closing my eyes tightly, I rubbed my forehead, a weary sigh escaping my lips. When I heard the door open, my eyes snapped open and I leaned forward to see Maddie walking into my office.

She closed the door and then leaned against it silently.

"What is it?" I asked, placing both elbows on my desk as I waited for the answer.

"What is Ayla to you?" Maddie asked, stepping closer.

I was completely taken aback by her question.

Pushing my chair away from the desk, I stood up and walked around it. "What type of question is that?"

"It's an important one."

I wasn't in the mood to discuss it. I sent her a chilling look. "Listen—"

"Ayla is not someone to play around with. So if you just want to fuck her, then don't. Don't hurt her, Alessio. She doesn't deserve it and she's not like those whores you fuck around with," Maddie spat.

"What are you talking about?" I growled. "I would never treat Ayla like that!" When I took a step forward, she only pushed her shoulders back in defiance.

"How do you feel about her?" Maddie was going to drive me crazy.

"None of your business," I hissed.

"Yes, it is! Because if you hurt her—"

"I'm not going to hurt her!"

Her shoulders dropped and she sighed. "Ayla was really hurt when she saw you with Nina."

"I know," I murmured.

"She likes you, Alessio. A lot. She's already emotionally involved."

My heart accelerated and my stomach felt weird. A ball of emotions sat at the base of my throat as my chest felt unbearably tight. The thought of Ayla feeling even a little bit of what I felt made my heart go wild.

Fear was always a constant. I didn't want to mess this up, but I never knew how to deal with my feelings. Whenever they became too much, I closed down. And I didn't want Ayla to feel the impact of it. I wanted to protect her from pain.

"If you don't feel the same way, let her go. Don't hurt her," Maddie added.

I swallowed and then shifted my gaze away. "What I feel for Ayla…I don't understand it. But I can't bear to see her hurt or sad. When I'm with her, I'm completely lost in her. She is all I can think about."

Her eyes widened in shock.

"I'm not going to hurt her, Maddie. Hurting her is the last thing I ever want to do."

She beamed. Shaking my head at her, I smiled.

"Is that why you came here? To know how I feel about Ayla?"

Maddie nodded. "I'm just worried. She's not someone to play around with. She is innocent and fragile. You need to woo her gently and with patience."

"I know."

Maddie clapped her hands together and bounced on her toes. "Okay," she said.

"Is that it?"

"Yup. You can go back to work now."

Maddie sent me another smile and then turned to leave. "Wait," I said.

"Yeah?"

How the fuck was I supposed to phrase this without looking like a complete idiot?

I swallowed hard.

"What type of flowers do women like?"

As soon as the words were out of my mouth, I wanted to punch myself.

Maddie stared at me for a few seconds in complete silence. And then she burst out laughing.

I sent her a fierce glare and she quickly covered her laugh with a cough. "Sorry!"

Crossing my arms over my chest, I waited impatiently for her answer.

Maddie shook her head. "You are so silly," she said.

"I don't think Ayla liked the flowers I gave her," I fired back in my defense.

Instead of answering me, she turned around and opened the door.

"She loved the flowers, Alessio."

Then she winked and left, closing the door behind her.

I stood speechless, astonished.

Ayla loved the flowers?

When realization dawned, I leaned against the desk and let out a chuckle.

Ah, so the kitten is playing, I thought with a smirk.

Chapter 42

Ayla

"How long am I supposed to keep this up?" I asked.

Maddie lay down beside me and stared at the ceiling. "You have to make him work for it."

"I don't think I can keep this façade on any longer."

"Just a little longer."

After the Nina drama, Maddie lectured me for an hour, telling me how I should and shouldn't act with Alessio. Every single day, I struggled to be nonchalant around him.

Every time he smiled and I didn't, I felt guilty. I could see he was losing hope and growing frustrated each day. I hoped Maddie's plan worked and all this drama wasn't for nothing.

Sitting up, I brought my knees up and laid my chin on top of them. "Maddie, I don't understand. How is this going to work? I...like...him..." I stuttered the last words. It was hard to admit, but it

380

was the truth.

"What do you mean? If you want him and he feels the same way about you too, then what's there to think about?"

I sighed and got up from the bed, standing in front of the window.

"How does a relationship work?" What I had with Alberto wasn't a relationship. I didn't know how to be in one.

The relationships I had read about or saw on TV, I could only dream about them. They were never my reality.

"You've never been in a relationship before?" Maddie asked.

I closed my eyes tightly against the wave of pain. Placing my hand over the glass, I steadied myself and tried to calm my racing heart.

"I have been in one," I whispered.

Maddie's forehead was creased in confusion and she stared at me patiently, waiting for me to elaborate.

"But it wasn't the same as the one in there," I said, pointing at the book in her hand. "I don't think you could call it a relationship. He hurt me a lot."

Tears blinded my vision. I never thought I would admit such a thing. When I was still living with Alberto, I thought that was how a relationship should be. Even though I knew it was wrong, I accepted it.

What I had with Alberto was dysfunctional.

He destroyed me. Heart, body, and soul.

But in the short time I had been living with Alessio, I began to think maybe I could be fixed. I could be happy.

Maybe I could be happy with Alessio.

"Ayla." Maddie got up and walked over to me. I was about to swipe my tears away but she did it for me.

Leaning forward, she placed a kiss on my forehead and then wrapped her arms around me.

She pulled away from me and then gave me a wan smile, trying to lighten the mood. "A relationship...hmmm..." Her eyes twinkled. "I would say a relationship is when both partners support each other, comfort each other, bring happiness and laughter to each other. It's a connection filled with love, acceptance, and understanding. You don't have to love someone to be in a relationship. Sometimes love comes later. Alessio is a stubborn man, but he is crazy about you. I can see it in his eyes. It is so obvious. He has feelings but he just needs a little push. I don't know how a relationship will be with Alessio, but he loves deeply. He loves with his heart. Something he's scared of. But you can change that. You can be his strength."

"He is mine," I whispered. "He is my strength."

"Alessio will realize it soon. And when he does, he won't be able to stay away from you. Fuck, he can't even stay away from you now. Do you see him? He always follows you like a little puppy. Oh my God, that was such a bad comparison. Alessio is nowhere close to a little puppy."

I laughed.

"We wait for him to make a move," Maddie said.

"He has been making a move for the past three

days." He had made several attempts to talk to me.

"Well, he needs to make a better move then. If you know what I mean." She wiggled her eyebrows mischievously.

"Maddie!"

She shrugged. "No, seriously. Maybe he should bring you flowers again. Or maybe just another kiss. This man is driving me crazy."

I didn't know what I was going to do without Maddie. She always knew how to make me feel better.

"We wait then," I said with a smile.

She winked and I laughed.

I would wait…because I needed him.

***

I walked inside the piano room to wait for Alessio. He was the never late. He was always there at exactly ten.

I could play the piano even if Alessio wasn't here, but I didn't.

I wanted to play for him. I wanted to bask in the warmth of him watching me as I played.

Sighing, I looked down at the phone for the time. *Any minute now.*

Something caught my eye. My gaze shifted to the sofa chair I usually sat on and I let out an audible gasp.

Bringing my hand up, I covered my mouth in shock. But I couldn't stop the smile that played across my lips.

A single white peony was lying on the seat.

Slightly bending down, I took the peony in my hand and brought it close to my chest. Straightening up, I held it there.

Alessio.

He was so sweet.

I couldn't believe he put the peony there for me. This wasn't a big bouquet. It was just a single peony, but it held the same value and meaning. It still made my heart flip, and my cheeks were hurting from my wide smile.

"I can safely assume that you love the peony."

My eyes widened and I quickly swiveled around to see Alessio leaning against the door, his arms crossed over his chest. His head was cocked to the side, a small smirk on his face.

I wanted to say that I hated that smirk…but truly, I didn't.

I tried to hide my smile. "I…" I paused and then sighed. I couldn't lie. "It's beautiful. I love it."

He slowly walked toward me, his eyes intense as he kept his gaze on me. As he got closer, my heart went wild and my stomach twisted with butterflies, a feeling that I always got when he was close.

Alessio stopped in front of me. I could feel his warmth on my bare skin. I looked up into his eyes. He was so tall.

His gaze, filled with need, shifted to my lips and I instinctively licked them. Alessio took a step closer until we were barely an inch apart. I sucked in a deep breath and my chest brushed against his.

He brought his hand up, trailing a finger down the length of my bare arm. I shivered and my fingers tightened around the flowers.

"Alessio…"

"Ayla," he whispered, leaning his head down.

We stared at each other, and then he leaned closer until his lips were only an inch from mine. "I'm going to kiss you," he said.

"Okay…"

I saw a little smirk on his face and then he lowered his lips to capture mine. My breath caught. His lips brushed gently against mine and I sighed.

Alessio slowly moved his tongue on my lips, waiting patiently for me to open my mouth. He coaxed me gently, unhurriedly. He put the slightest pressure on my lips, and I gasped. He took the opportunity to slide his tongue in. Softly brushing against mine, he kissed me slowly, as if to savor the kiss.

This time I boldly returned his kiss. I had grabbed hold of my courage and put it all on the line. I didn't think that kissing Alessio was something I'd ever grow tired of. It felt like I had been starving for his kiss.

His hand slid up my neck, to just beneath my ears, and his fingers splayed out, his hand cupping my jaw. His other hand glided through my hair, tilting my hair slightly upward for better access to my lips.

I placed both hands on his chest and leaned closer into his body, letting his warmth envelop me. In his embrace, I felt safe. I felt wanted.

Alessio didn't rush and he let me direct the kiss. He licked the seams of my lips and I let out a small sigh. So soft, so warm, so sweet.

I was drunk on his kisses.

He gently bit down on my bottom lips and then he claimed my lips again. This time his kiss was a little harder, a little more demanding.

And I gave it to him.

We were both breathing hard when he pulled away. Alessio laid his forehead against mine as he fought to catch his breath.

"I don't think I'll ever get tired of kissing you," he said, his voice gruff.

I blinked up at him to see his gaze already on mine. His eyes were soft and filled with adoration, a look that stole my breath. In the depth of his gaze, I saw his need there. His want for me.

I was completely transfixed by his eyes. His hand moved from my face, down to my hips. Wrapping his arms around my waist, he pulled me close into him, anchoring my body into his. My heart was pumping wildly and my knees grew weaker at the fervor in his gaze.

He held me as if I was precious. He looked at me as if I was the only thing he could see.

I felt beautiful.

"Alessio," I said. I didn't know what else to say.

He leaned down and gave me a quick peck on the lips before stepping away. He nodded toward the piano with a smile. "Go," he urged.

My lips stretched in a wide smile and I nodded, quickly hurrying toward the piano with the flower still in my hand.

Our gazes stayed connected, both of us completely captivated by each other as I ran my fingers over the keys.

I didn't close my eyes even once. I didn't look

away from Alessio.

When I was done, I let my hand rest on the piano key and swallowed hard, suddenly feeling nervous and shy under his penetrating gaze.

"Are you not going to read tonight?" he asked.

"Oh." I smiled and then got up.

I walked over toward him and stopped in front of the coffee table, picking up my book. "I will. I'm in the middle of this one. I can't wait to finish it."

He chuckled. "You sound excited about it."

"I am," I replied, taking my seat on the sofa chair next to his. "It's a really good book."

"I'm glad you like it."

I opened it, and felt Alessio's eyes on me the whole time I was reading. It was so hard to stop myself from peeking up at him.

And I lost that battle many times.

Whenever our eyes met, Alessio would smile and I would send him a smile of my own.

My heart was doing flips. My stomach was filled with butterflies. I felt light with euphoria. And a sense of peacefulness overcame me.

I wanted to stay just like this. But then I yawned.

"You should go to sleep," Alessio said, sounding wistful.

"Hmm." I closed my book. Alessio leaned forward and brushed the few hair strands out of my face, letting his fingers linger on my cheeks longer than needed.

He brushed his thumb over my jaw and then suddenly leaned forward. I let out a soft whimper when he pressed his lips on mine. He gave me a quick peck and then leaned back, letting me go.

I missed his touch almost immediately.

Placing my book on the coffee table, I got up and stood in front of Alessio. Smiling down at him, I whispered, "Goodnight."

"Goodnight," he replied.

Biting on my lips, my shoulder dropped at the thought of being away from him after spending such an exquisite time with him.

Giving him a final glance, I started to walk away but I felt an arm wrap around my waist, pulling me back. I yelped when I fell on Alessio's lap. My eyes widened in shock and I looked up at him.

He gave me quick peck on the lips and then pulled back with a smirk. I couldn't help but giggle.

He sucked in a sharp breath. Placing a finger at the corner of my lips, he whispered in complete amazement, "This is the first time I've heard you laugh."

I ducked my head shyly and pressed a hand on his chest.

Alessio placed a finger under my chin and tilted my head up again. "You should do it more often." He brushed his thumb over my lips. "You have a beautiful laugh."

Before I could say anything, his lips claimed mine again, this time almost possessively. He pulled at my bottom lip, demanding entrance. His arm was like a band of steel around my waist and his other hand came up to cup my jaw.

He kissed with such intensity that my heart stuttered and I melted into him.

His kiss eventually slowed and I sighed against his lips. His eyes were intense with need. His touch was fire, and his kisses were intoxicating.

He was all I could think about.

I closed my eyes and lost myself in his kisses and sweet, gentle caresses.

Chapter 43

"They are leaving!" Maddie pouted as she walked into my room. "Artur said they will be gone for a few days."

I straightened and looked at Maddie with wide eyes. "Alessio is going too?"

She nodded and pouted. "Yeah."

He didn't say anything. I saw him last night, yet he never said a word. The thought of being without him made my heart ache.

It had been a week since the first time he kissed me in the piano room. Sometimes during the day, he would take me to the creek. And then we spent most of the night together.

He always bent down and kissed me soundly on the lips. He would steal kisses while I read. Sometimes, he would pull me on his lap. I would lay my head on his shoulder and read while he played with my hair. He never pushed for more.

These days had been the most beautiful. Each day, my heart grew fuller. Alessio had weaved his way into my heart and I didn't want to let him go.

Instead, I embraced it.

And now, I felt distressed at the mere thought of spending even one day without him.

"How long will he be gone?" I asked.

"I don't know. Artur said a few days."

"Oh," I muttered, looking down at my hands, which were twined tightly together.

She stood up. "C'mon, let's go."

"Where?" I asked.

"They are probably about to leave now. Let's go say goodbye to our men."

When I quickly stood up at her words, she smiled. I followed her out of my room, my heart thumping hard as we made our way down the hall.

As we made our way down the stairs, we saw the men at the bottom. Nikolay and Viktor were talking, while Artur leaned against the wall. Alessio was looking at his phone.

When he heard us, he looked up and I saw his gaze soften at the sight of me.

Maddie ran down the rest of the stairs and jumped into Artur's arms. I continued to slowly make my way down, keeping my eyes on Alessio. He gave me a small smile when I stopped on the last stair, feeling nervous.

I ducked my head shyly and played with the hem of my dress. I felt him coming nearer and he stopped in front of me. Alessio placed a finger under my chin and tilted my head upward until I was staring into his soft blue eyes.

"I was just about to come up and say goodbye," he said.

"Oh."

"Something came up and I have to take care of it. I'll be gone for a few days."

I nodded. "I understand."

Walking down the final step, I stood beside him. I saw Artur dip Maddie low and she laughed. He kissed her soundly on the lips.

I peeked up at Alessio and saw that he was staring at me. He brought a hand up, and gently trailed a finger down my cheek. He brushed his thumb over my lips and then whispered, "I'll see you later."

"Bye," I whispered.

"Bye."

Alessio took a step away from and after giving me final look, he turned around, walking away. The other men followed closely behind him and Maddie came to stand beside me.

Letting out a dejected sigh, I brought a hand up and placed it over my chest.

As I watched his retreating back, my shoulder dropped and my chest felt tight.

I already missed him.

As the days went by, I realized how much I needed Alessio. His presence had become addicting. His touch. His kisses. His blue eyes. His gentle caresses. His smiles. Everything about him was deep ingrained in me.

***

Alessio

It had been three long, torturous days without

Ayla. Every night, I wished I was with her.

As I walked into the mansion, my chest grew lighter at the thought of being close to her again.

She was constantly on my thoughts.

And I was fucking happy to finally be back.

I looked down at my watch and saw it was almost two in the morning. She would be sleeping right now. My heart sunk in disappointment as I made my way upstairs.

"Tomorrow," I whispered.

But when I stepped on the second floor, I felt the need to see her. Being this close to her and not seeing her—the thought itself was painful.

I had to see her, even if she was sleeping. Just a peek at her beautiful face and I would be happy.

As I made my way to her room, I stopped dead in my tracks when I saw the door of the piano room open. Was Ayla still awake?

My heart flipped at the thought and I quickly walked inside. My steps faltered when I saw her curled up on the sofa chair, sleeping.

But that wasn't what took my breath away and made me smile.

She wasn't sleeping on her chair; instead she was curled up in *mine*.

Walking closer, I stopped in front of the sleeping beauty.

There was a small smile on her lips, her face looking peaceful as she slept. Bending down, I gently took the book from her hand and placed it on the coffee table.

I turned back around and wrapped an arm under her back and one under her knees, carefully and gently lifting her up from the couch, making sure that I didn't wake her up. She moaned sleepily, instinctively laying her head on my shoulders.

I smiled and carried her out of the piano room. Pushing her door open, I walked inside and laid her down in the middle of her bed. But when I was about to step back, I felt something tighten around my lapel, stopping me from stepping away.

Ayla's fingers were wrapped around my shirt. She was still sleeping.

I placed my hand on hers and gently unwrapped her fingers. They tightened slightly but I was able to get them off, keeping my eyes on her face the whole time. When I saw her eyebrows furrow, I sighed and sat down on the bed beside her.

I couldn't bring myself to leave. Instead, I surprised myself by lying down beside Ayla. I wrapped an arm around her waist and brought her closer. She burrowed further into my chest, as if seeking the warmth and comfort I offered. Her fingers wrapped around my jacket again as she clung to me tightly.

And I was just as content to hold her just as tightly in return.

I placed a kiss on her temple and looked down at her sleeping face. For the longest time, I laid there with her in my arms, her head tucked underneath my chin.

Just for moment, I told myself. Just for a few more minutes.

Chapter 44

Ayla

I could feel the warm sunlight but I refused to open my eyes. Instead, I snuggled closer against the warmth beside me. I was too comfortable and languid to even move.

So warm, I thought to myself, wrapping my arms tighter around the warmth. I sighed in utter contentment and buried my face in the chest next to me.

But as I cuddled closer, a strange thought registered in my mind.

My eyes snapped opened and I quickly blinked the sleepiness away, only to find myself staring at a wide, hard chest.

Panic filled me and I quickly looked up as my heart continued to hammer. Then I let out a tiny gasp.

Alessio.

He looked so calm in his sleep, the total opposite of what he represented when he was awake. His face was soft and his lips were slightly open. I couldn't help but smile at the sight in front of me.

I tried to move but I felt something tighten around my hips. My eyes traveled down to see his arm wrapped around me. I also saw that I had a leg thrown over his, tangling us together.

Feeling completely mortified, I slowly moved my leg away and tried to scoot out of his embrace, but his hold was relentless. So, I gave up with a sigh and looked up at his sleeping face again.

I brought my hand up to his face, letting it hover there, right over his cheek.

The thought of my hand making contact with his skin, touching him freely without fear, was tempting. It was an alluring image floating in my mind, and as I continued to stare at Alessio's face, I found that I couldn't stop myself any longer.

I gently placed my hand on his cheek, watching for any indication that he might be waking up. When he didn't move, I rubbed my thumb over his cheek, feeling the slight rough stubble under my fingertips.

I traced his forehead, down his nose, and then over his full lips. I felt my cheeks heat as I thumbed his lower lip and then I traced the curve of his jaw and over his cheeks.

A smile tugged on my lips as I continued to run my fingers up until they met the few strands of hair that laid limply over his forehead.

My touch was light and soft, while my heart was wild in my chest. What I was doing felt forbidden. But at the same time, it excited me. To have this small power over Alessio. To be able to touch him so freely.

But most of all, I was happy that I was able to touch a man without feeling disgusted and my body vibrating with fear.

I laid my hand over his cheek with a sigh of contentment and my eyes closed, letting myself feel his warmth as it surrounded me.

But the next time I opened my eyes, his eyes were open and he was looking at me.

"Good morning," he whispered gruffly, his voice laced with sleep.

I opened my mouth to say something but quickly snapped it shut. Glancing at my palm that was still resting on his cheek, my teeth grazed my lips nervously.

Oh no, I got caught.

My fingers flexed on his cheek and I was about to move my hand away when suddenly his hand was over mine, trapping my palm against his cheek. I gasped and stared into his mesmerizing eyes.

When Alessio's lips tilted up in a small smirk, I ducked my head shyly as my cheeks heated in embarrassment. As I hid my face in his chest, I felt it rumble with a small chuckle.

He was such an aggravating man. I couldn't believe he was laughing at me.

I tried to move my hand away again but he held on tightly, entwining our fingers together.

"You didn't say *good morning* back. That's rude, kitten," Alessio murmured in my ear.

So, I was back to being *kitten*.

"Good morning," I mumbled. He laughed and released my hand. I tried to move away from his comforting embrace, but his arm tightened around my waist, refusing to let me move even an inch.

Instead, he pulled me closer until my breasts were pressed against his chest. I could feel everything. Even his hard-on pressing into my stomach.

I was completely mortified. Pressing my eyes closed tightly, I took a deep breath through my nose.

"Ayla, look up at me," Alessio demanded.

I shook my head and pressed it harder into his chest.

"You know I'm not letting you go until you give me what I want," he teased.

When I didn't answer, he pressed his fingers gently into my hips. "Hmm…or maybe you just want me to keep holding you."

At his words, my eyes snapped open and I looked up quickly, staring widely into his eyes. Another chuckle bubbled deep from his chest at my reaction. His eyes twinkled mischievously and he gave me a wink.

"There you are." He whispered so softly that it made my heart ache. "Don't look away from me again."

I nodded. I didn't think I would ever be able to look away even if I tried. Alessio had completely captured my full attention.

With our eyes still locked together, I felt his arm start to loosen around my waist until he wasn't holding me any longer. I took a deep breath and slightly moved around, testing my freedom.

But as I moved away, I realized that I didn't like

it.

I liked it better when he was holding me. When his arms were wrapped safely and gently around me. Such conflicting feelings.

Giving Alessio a final glance, I sat up, pulling the covers to my chin and looked away.

"You are looking away from me again," he mumbled.

He was so frustrating.

Releasing my breath in huff, I turned toward Alessio and looked at him straight in the eyes. "There," I said.

"Better."

"Why are you in my room?" I asked, bringing my knees up to my chest.

I saw Alessio's eyes widen in surprise as if he just figured out that he was here. He quickly sat up and cleared his throat. "You fell asleep in the piano room and I brought you back to your room."

I was silent, waiting for him to continue. I saw him swallow nervously and he got off the bed.

"I was putting you to bed but you wouldn't let go of my jacket. And I didn't want to wake you up," Alessio grumbled. He looked away and then cleared his throat again. "I'll see you at breakfast."

"Okay."

Alessio sent me a look from the corner of his eyes and then he walked away without saying anything else. I fell back on the bed as soon as the door closed behind him.

Alessio had kept me safe in his embrace, pushing away all the bad memories. I had been cocooned in his warmth and as I laid back on the bed, I felt strangely empty. I faced the side where Alessio had been sleeping.

I placed my palm over the mattress and slid it up and down, right where he'd been just moments ago.

My heart was doing the same pitter-patter dance as whenever Alessio was near, while my body felt light. Placing my other hand over my chest, I closed my eyes.

What is this feeling?

***

After all the men were seated at the table, Maddie and I stayed behind, ready to offer help if needed. My fingers were playing with the hem of my black dress as my feet shifted beneath me.

I didn't think it would be this nerve-wracking. Being this close to Alessio but avoiding eye contact with him. We were a few feet away, yet it felt like he was right beside me. I could feel him staring. His gaze burned into my skin, marking me.

"Ayla."

Alessio's voice broke through my thoughts. He gave me a teasing smile and then nodded to the basket in the middle of the table.

"Can you bring this for me?"

I looked at Maddie and saw her hiding a smile behind her hand. With an annoyed sigh, I got the basket and brought it to Alessio.

After he took the toast, I was about to walk away but his next words stopped me.

"Thank you, kitten."

My mouth fell open. I couldn't believe he called

me that in front of everyone. His words were spoken low, but still. I hoped they hadn't heard. When it seemed they weren't paying attention, I sighed in relief.

I said nothing, and placed the bowl back in the middle of the table.

The rest of breakfast was uneventful. Alessio's eyes were on me most of the time, but I avoided him.

When all the men stood up and left, my shoulders dropped in relief and I finally relaxed. "Why is he so..." I started to ask Maddie, but couldn't find a word to describe Alessio.

"Infuriating? Annoying? Frustrating? Hot? Sexy as sin?" Maddie said.

I glared at her. "The first three."

"He likes to tease you, but I think it's payback."

"Payback?"

Maddie nodded. "For ignoring him before."

"He is so infuriating," I grumbled, as I helped Maddie clean the table.

"I know."

***

Maddie was talking animatedly when we heard a knock on the door. Both of us turned toward it with a confused expression. "Come in," I said.

The door opened and Alessio stood in the doorway. My eyes widened and I quickly sat up while Maddie tried to look busy with the book in her hand.

"Do you want to go to the creek?" he asked, his

gaze slightly shifting to Maddie.

My heart soared and I nodded with a smile. "Yes."

"I'll wait for you downstairs," he said, stepping out and shutting the door behind him.

Placing a hand over my mouth, I tried to hide the giggle that threatened to slip out. "You are too cute for your own good, Ayla." Maddie laughed.

I quickly jumped off the bed and was almost at the door when Maddie's voice stopped me. "Wait."

"What?"

"Why don't you change? Instead of wearing your uniform?" she suggested, sitting up on my bed.

"I don't really have any other outfit," I said. "Except the pair of jeans and white shirt that Lena got me."

"Not a problem. Give me minute." Maddie got off the bed, and ran past me and out the door.

As I waited, I grew nervous and more impatient.

After a few minutes, she ran back into the room holding a dress. She gasped for breath and shoved it into my hands. "Hurry. Go change."

Staring at the dress, I took a step back. "What—"

"Don't ask questions. You are wasting time. Hurry," Maddie snapped.

I went into the bathroom and changed, then stared at my reflection. "Wow," I said.

The white lace dress was simple yet elegant. It came down to my mid-thigh and there was a brown belt around my waist. It had been a long time since I wore a light color but this dress was absolutely beautiful. I ran a hand down my ponytail.

"You look more beautiful with your hair down."

402

Alessio's voice rang through my head and I bit down on my lips nervously as a feeling of giddiness overcame me.

Without a second thought, I pulled the hairband off, letting my hair fall down my back in waves. Alessio was slowly taking over my mind and there was no way to stop it.

Instead of fighting against it, I was letting it happen. I didn't have the strength to fight my feelings any longer.

I walked out of the bathroom and Maddie clapped her hands.

"You definitely look prettier in the dress than me," she said with a wink. "Alessio won't be able to take his eyes off you."

"Hush," I muttered, looking down shyly.

"Okay. Go now. Alessio is an impatient man. He doesn't like to wait."

I laughed as she rolled her eyes in exasperation. "I know."

I quickly ran out of my room and down the stairs. He was outside.

As I walked out, I closed my eyes and took a deep breath in. The sweet smelling flowers and fresh air filled my nose, instantly relaxing me. I turned to the side and saw Alessio leaning against the wall.

His eyes widened at the sight of me. His gaze traveled down my body, resting a little longer on my legs before moving back to my face.

Under his penetrating gaze, I felt flushed and a slight shiver went through my body. He stepped away from the wall and took a step toward me before stopping.

Alessio cleared his throat and nodded toward the forest. "Let's go," he said. I nodded and he started to walk away, leading us down the path to the beautiful creek.

A wave of disappointment crashed through me when he didn't say anything else. I followed silently behind him, leaves and twigs crunching under our feet.

We walked deeper into the woods and out of sight, next to each other.

My breathing stuttered when he took my hand. My gaze snapped back up, staring at his face.

A small smile tugged at my lips. Alessio's touch was soft and gentle. His fingers moved over the back of my hand, almost feather-light. And then they slowly entwined with mine, holding my hand firmly in his as we made our way toward the creek.

My heart fluttered in my chest. Instinctively, my fingers tightened around his and he gently squeezed my hand back, letting me know he felt the same way.

I locked the image in my mind and heart, for I would always treasure it. My small pale hand was wrapped protectively in Alessio's rough and much bigger hand. The image represented more than just two hands holding each other.

It was a bond we shared in our darkest and weakest point.

"We're almost here," Alessio said.

I hummed in contentment.

We finally broke free from the trees.

I let go of his hand, then stopped in front of the

stream and knelt down on the grass. Leaning forward, my hands hovered over the running water for a few seconds before I dipped my fingers into the stream.

The water was cold but soothing. I drew circles and some weird patterns into the water, completely lost in the moment.

"Isn't the water cold?" he asked, stepping up behind me.

"It's not that bad." Cupping some water in my hands, I stood up. "Here," I said, moving toward him.

His looked down at the water cupped in my hands. "Not bad," he whispered back, feeling the temperature. I let the water slide through my fingers.

When I looked up, Alessio was fixated on me.

I was about to take a step back, trying to put some distance between us, but Alessio wrapped his hand around my waist, pulling me tightly against his hard body.

My shocked breath resonated around us and small smile appeared on his lips, showing the indent of his dimple on his cheek. I melted into his embrace, my knees going weak as he continued to stare at me with the same intense blue eyes.

Alessio brought a hand up and took a lock of my long black hair, wrapping it loosely around his index finger. "I like your hair like this. When it's down."

His voice was soft. At his words, I struggled to suppress the smile forming on my lips.

His words were sweet and simple, but they

tugged at the strings of my heart. They brought life to my broken heart. Such a simple truth…it was enough to piece back a shattered fragment.

With each day, Alessio slowly put back the broken pieces of my heart. With only soft gentle caresses and sweet words, he was breathing life back into me.

"You should let it down more often," he continued, his fingers softly brushing over my jaw.

"Okay." In that moment, I was ready to do anything he'd asked.

Alessio slowly bent his head down until his forehead was resting against mine, his lips just an inch away from mine. All I had to do was slightly move forward and our lips would touch.

But I didn't.

"Alessio," I whispered.

"Yes?"

"What is this?" I asked, finally pulling the courage from within me.

Alessio's eyebrows furrowed in confusion and he pulled his forehead away but kept his arms wound tightly around me. "What?"

"This, between us. What is this? How is this going to work?"

While he was gone, those same questions haunted me day and night. Alessio plagued my thoughts and heart. He was all I could think about but I was also scared. The uncertainty was slowly making me lose control.

I needed to know what he truly wanted.

Alessio stared into my eyes, his face impassive for a second. My stomach dropped, caving into an empty pit at the expression on his face.

My heart stuttered. I felt the tears at the back of my eyes but then his eyes softened and his lips stretched into a smile, showing me his dimple again.

"I don't know," he whispered. My eyes widened, but he kept talking. "I don't know what this is. I can't put a name to it because there's no name to describe this. All I know is that I want you and I can't let you go. Even when I tried, I couldn't."

I sucked in a sharp breath at his confession, feeling my heart melt at his words. I never expected these words from Alessio when I asked him the question. But he had given me more than I needed.

He had given me *hope*.

"I want to see where this goes. I want to try." Alessio placed his forehead back on mine, his fingers tangling in my hair.

My eyes fluttered closed and I took a deep break before opening them again, staring deeply into his eyes. "I want to try too," I whispered.

I was playing with fire. I would burn in the end, but sometimes when the fire is raging within, you can't let go. And I couldn't. I was desperately holding on, even when I knew the fire was going to burn us both in the end.

Alessio's eyes lit up, as if I had given him the only one thing he wanted.

I expected him to kiss me but he didn't move. Instead his arms stayed around my waists like band of steel, his forehead rested on mine while his lips were only an inch away from mine.

I looked into his eyes for any indication that he would kiss me. And I saw the need there, but when he didn't, I grew confused.

His eyes flickered to my lips again and his hands stiffened around my waist. When realization dawned, I grasped his jacket for support and grew nervous. My fingers tightened around the fabric and I felt myself swallow hard.

Moving forward until our bodies were molded together, I tilted my head up and then stood on my toes. Our gazes stayed connected as I gently pressed my lips to his, and my eyes fluttered shut.

I heard a growl rumble from his chest and he pressed his lips harder against mine, demanding access. I gasped and he took the opportunity to slip his tongue inside. He explored my mouth slowly. I was hesitant at first, but when he bit down on my lips and then sucked at my tongue, I grew bold.

Letting go of his jacket, I moved my hands upward until my fingers were wrapped in his hair. When I sucked at his tongue, his fingers tightened around my scalp, a groan vibrating from his chest. I moaned in return.

Alessio licked my lips and I shuddered against him, my fingers pulling at his hair. He slightly pulled away and swore. "Fuck." We were both breathing hard. Seeing a man like him undone was shocking to me.

Before I could say anything, his lips crashed into mine again. This time he took my lips possessively, as if he was starving for me. And I returned his kisses with the same fervor.

Alessio pressed me against a tree, holding me tightly against him. He never broke the kiss. Instead, he claimed my lips, marking me as his.

Releasing my waist, his hand started to move lower until it was at the edge of my dress. He pulled back and then licked my swollen lips. I was in haze, his kisses driving me crazy.

"Did I tell you how beautiful and sexy you look in this dress?"

His words sounded like they were under water but I understood them. So, I shook my head. Alessio leaned closer until his lips were right next to my ear.

He bit down on my earlobe. "You look so fucking beautiful in this dress," he whispered gruffly, his voice sounding husky and laced with desire.

His movement was slow, but I shivered when I felt him move my dress upward. Alessio took my lips again.

Too much. It was happening too fast. My head was spinning. My skin burned. My body felt light and heated…too warm. I felt my knees shaking and I clung to his shoulders, my fingers biting into them. Alessio hissed into my lips.

When he didn't move, I wrapped my fingers in his hair again, and pulled. Alessio groaned unhappily but tore his lips away from mine. Our harsh breathing filled the silent forest and I fought for air.

"Too fast?" Alessio asked.

"A little," I replied, my chest heaving.

"Okay." He placed his forehead against mine again and I opened my eyes, making eye contact with his. He gave me a small smile before bending down to place a sweet gentle kiss on my swollen lips.

Alessio let go of me and stepped away. I missed his warmth almost immediately. The look in his eyes told me he felt the same way.

He brought a hand up and rubbed his thumb over my lips. "I like your lips like this…swollen and red from my kisses."

"Alessio…"

He smirked and then bent down to kiss me again before pulling away. "I'll just have to kiss you often then, to keep them looking like that."

This man was impossible.

I couldn't help but giggle at the look on his face and his words. Ducking my head shyly, I smiled. But Alessio wasn't having any of that. He placed a finger under my chin and tilted my head up.

"What did I tell you?" he asked, his eyes fierce and intense.

My mouth formed an 'o' and I cocked my head to the side. "You told me to never look away from you."

Alessio moved the few strands of hair that fell over my face behind my ear, before cupping my jaw, rubbing his thumb softly yet possessively over the curve. "Good. Remember that, kitten."

"Hmm." I smiled up at him.

"C'mon. Let's go back," he said.

This time, he didn't walk ahead of me. Instead, he took my hand in his, entwining our fingers tightly together before walking away from the creek. Our steps were slow and unhurried, almost as if we lost in our thoughts.

But truthfully, we were lost in each other. Both

of us never wanting this perfect beautiful moment to end.

Happiness couldn't be a word to describe what I was feeling. Inside, my feeling was joyful. I felt giddy. Warm and completely euphoric. My cheeks were hurting from my wide smiles but most of all, my heart…it was whole.

It fluttered every time Alessio's fingers tightened around mine. It danced with happiness every time I thought about our kiss. And it sang with the intensity of Alessio's eyes on mine.

As we walked back toward the mansion, I just prayed that this happiness, and whatever was between us, wouldn't burn out before it could bloom.

***

"Goodnight," I whispered to Alessio, my head lying on his shoulder as I sat on his lap.

"Goodnight," he murmured back.

But still we refused to let each other go.

"I should go."

"You should."

"I'm tired," I said.

"I know. Me too," he replied, his words soft.

"I really should go." My voice was barely a whisper as I pulled my head up and stared into Alessio's eyes. He nodded and the sighed, releasing his hold on me.

Was that a pout? It was so small, but it was definitely there. But then it was gone. I thought it was just my imagination, but I had seen it.

"You were pouting," I said.

Alessio glared at me and then grumbled something under his breath. "You are delirious from lack of sleep, kitten. Go to sleep. You need it."

"I'm not."

He sent me glare again. "Ayla."

With a sigh, I got off his lap and stood in front of him. "Goodnight."

He gazed up at me and then smiled. "Goodnight, kitten."

As I walked out and closed the door, I mumbled under my breath, "He was definitely pouting."

After quickly washing my teeth and face, I closed the tap and dried my face. When I had changed into my light pink nightgown, I opened the door of my bathroom and walked out.

But I stopped when I saw Alessio sitting on my bed.

"Alessio?" I took a step closer but then stopped again.

He was holding his jacket, the one I kept under my pillow.

I started to panic, my stomach twisting painfully in knots as my heart raced wildly in my chest.

I took several deep breaths, trying to control myself.

"I can explain," I whispered, desperately hoping he would understand.

Alessio stood up, still holding his jacket. Our eyes met.

His gaze was intense while mine was filled with fear.

Alessio took a step closer and then threw the

jacket on my sofa.

Keeping his eyes on me, he whispered his next words.

And they took my breath away. This time my heart accelerated, but for a different reason.

"You won't be needing this anymore."

Chapter 45

I stared at Alessio in complete shock, my lips parted in astonishment. My gaze moved from his and to the sofa chair where the jacket sat.

"How?" Looking back at Alessio, he stared at me with knowing eyes.

Realization sank in and my stomach dropped. I brought a hand up to my neck and rubbed it nervously. His eyes tracked my movement and then he cleared his throat.

"You were the one who kept the jacket there?" I questioned, my voice barely audible. I had asked the question but the answer was already clearly written on his face. Alessio's face softened at my question and he gave me a sharp nod.

Shaking my head, I tried to get rid of the web of confusion. "But how?"

Alessio let out a tiny sigh and raked his fingers through his hair, a sign of either nervousness, frustration, or anger. But in this moment, I didn't know what he was feeling.

"I heard you and Maddie talking. When she

asked you about my jacket." His eyebrows furrowed when I took a step back.

"Ayla—"

He cared.

And that wasn't something I expected from Alessio. Not from a man who was supposed to be ruthless, heartless, and a killer.

Tears blinded my vision and I swallowed past the heavy lump forming in my throat. This moment felt surreal. A fragment of my imagination.

But it was real.

I opened my mouth to say something. Anything. I just didn't want this moment to vanish. I didn't want to lose this feeling that was blooming in my heart.

But when I finally spoke, my words came out as an accusation. "You were spying?" I asked.

I flinched at my own tone and I saw Alessio's eyes widen before his back straightened in a rigid posture.

"I was not," he replied, looking very much affronted. "I heard you and Maddie when I was walking down the hallway." He paused and then rubbed his jaw, giving me a sheepish look. "Well, I did stop when I heard Maddie ask about the jacket. I was curious."

He shrugged and walked toward me, stopping right in front of me. Alessio brought a hand up and trailed a finger down my cheek, swiping my tears away. "Can't blame me. Anyone would be curious."

Cupping my cheeks in his hands, Alessio tilted my head up. "Why are you crying, Ayla?"

"You gave me your jacket," I whispered

415

brokenly and then closed my eyes. I sounded so pathetic.

"I did," he agreed. I felt his thumb right under my eyes and he rubbed the spot gently. Instinctively, my hand came up and I grabbed hold of his jacket in a death grip, holding him close to me. Alessio was my anchor.

"Open your eyes," he muttered. My fingers tightened around him and my eyes fluttered open with his soft command.

"But you won't need it anymore," Alessio said. His words rang with finality and I shivered in his arms.

"What do you mean?" I murmured. He smiled at my question and bent down, brushing his lips gently over mine.

"I'd rather show you," he whispered against my lips before claiming them in a hard kiss. He let go of my face and brought his hands down, wrapping them around my tiny waist as he pulled me closer into his body.

My body molded to his. Hard against soft. His hold was unyielding as I returned his kiss with just the same intensity. I was lost in him when he pulled away and I moaned in protest. "Shhh. I've got you," he muttered through the hazy fog that clouded my thoughts.

Alessio bent down, sliding an arm behind my back and my knees before lifting me up in his arms, cradling me to his chest.

"What?" I said.

He chuckled low in my ear and placed a kiss there. "Relax, Ayla," he soothed, his voice deep and rough.

At his words, I instantly relaxed in his arms and wrapped my hands around his neck. "Where are you taking me?"

"You ask too many questions," he said. Alessio looked down at me, his lips tilted up in a small smirk, his eyes gleaming with intensity—the same intensity that made me weak in the knees and my heart flutter every time.

"But…"

His arms tightened around me in warning. As Alessio walked us down the hall and stopped in front of his bedroom, I didn't have to ask any questions. He didn't look down at me when he opened the door, but I saw a ghost of a smile on his lips.

He walked inside and kicked the door shut. As soon as we were in the middle of the room, he lowered me down until my feet hit the floor. Alessio turned me around so that I was facing him.

"You won't be needing my jacket anymore because you will be sleeping with me."

I knew it was coming. I knew what he would say but the words still took me by surprise. "Alessio," I whispered, taking a step closer to him. He cupped my jaw and rubbed his thumb over the curve. I pressed my cheek into his palm and a sigh of contentment whispered past my lips.

"But why?" I asked, wanting to understand him further.

Alessio smiled wide and rested his forehead against mine. "I had the best sleep last night," he said.

I moved closer. He was the same as me. I melted into his body, his sweet words, soft eyes and gentle touch taking over my senses.

"It's simple. You need me, and in some ways, I need you too," Alessio continued, his gaze intense. I swallowed hard and brought my hand up, placing it over his. "You...calm me."

Just like he was my peace...I had the same effect on him.

Bringing my other hand up, I placed it over his cheek. "You bring me peace. I don't know how. But you do. You make it all go away. The pain. The darkness. The hurt. I feel peace when I'm with you."

I saw Alessio smile and he slowly brought his lips down to mine. "I know," he whispered back before taking my lips. He moved his hand to the back of my head, holding me firmly. His kiss was soft and sweet.

"We should go to sleep," he said, pulling back. His voice was husky and rough. The way his eyes glinted dangerously in the light, I knew that was the last thing he wanted to do.

But I was grateful he stopped there. I wasn't ready for more. Whatever was between us at the moment...it was already too much.

Alessio let go of me and I stepped back. "I need to change. Get yourself comfortable." He nodded toward the bed.

I watched him go into the bathroom and close the door behind him. As soon as he was out of sight, I moved back to his bed.

I still remembered the first time we met, his eyes

filled with fury and his gun pointed at me.

All I could see now was affection in his soft gaze. All I felt were gentle caresses. He was no longer the killer I met the first time.

He might be a monster out there, but to me he was my savior. My anchor.

Moments later, he returned wearing only grey sweatpants, his chest bare

"Oh." My mouth fell open as I took him in, my gaze drawn to his muscular body. Lean, big, and hard. He was sculpted, beautifully rugged. Intense, dark, dangerous.

There were still some droplets of water on his perfectly tanned body. But what got most of my attention were the tattoos weaved around the length of his arms, ending just above his elbows. The most prominent looked Celtic and almost tribal in design but I couldn't make out the other design.

It was dark, intense, and fierce…just like him.

Alessio walked toward me and my gaze roamed over broad shoulders and chest. He stopped in front of me and I had to tilt my head up. He was so big and powerful like this.

"Do you mind if I sleep like this?" he asked. "I usually sleep naked, but I thought you wouldn't be comfortable with that. I can accommodate with the sweatpants, but I hate sleeping with shirts."

"Umm…right.". Shaking my head, I tried to find my voice. "I mean, yes. I'm okay with this."

Alessio brought his hand up and trailed a finger up from my jaw to my ear, moving my hair to the side. "Good."

He leaned forward until his lips were right next

to my ear. "Let's sleep," he said, placing a kiss there before stepping away. He had a smirk on his face and he wasn't even trying to hide it. His blue eyes gleamed with a devilish glint as he nodded toward the bed.

Instead of standing up, I pushed myself back on the bed and crawled backward until I was on the right side, close to the window. Alessio followed my each and every movement, his eyes burning brighter with intensity.

My fingers tightened around the comforter and I swallowed hard, my body trembling slightly under his fierce gaze. He must have seen my nervousness because he cleared his throat and looked away.

I turned toward the window, purposely facing away from him.

I heard him shuffling around the room and then the lights were off, casting darkness around the room, with only a tiny glow coming from behind me.

Thank goodness. I hated sleeping in the dark.

The bed moved under his weight as he got in. The comforter shifted and then I felt his heat next to me. We both stayed silent, unmoving. Only our slow breathing filled the room. I placed a hand over my chest, trying to calm my pounding heart, hoping he didn't hear it.

Then he moved closer. My heart stuttered as I waited for his next move. I bit on my lips when I felt his arm around me.

Alessio pulled me into his body until my back was against his front, tangling his heavy legs with mine as his arm curved almost fully around my body.

"Alessio," I whispered, my heart going wild in my chest.

He brought his face next to mine and I felt his lips at my temple. When he said nothing and his breath evened out, I placed my hand over his, which was wrapped around my stomach.

"Alessio?"

His arm tightened around me and he gave me a powerful squeeze. "Sleep," he ordered, his voice soft even with his demanding tone. My hand pressed hard against his as I contemplated what just happened.

"Ayla, stop thinking so hard. Sleep."

At his words, I sighed and relaxed, settling into his body.

And that was how I fell asleep. With Alessio wrapped around me like a vine, his lips on my temple, and our hands entwined together.

***

A week later

It had been three weeks since I cut myself and my last nightmare. I was supposed to remove my stitches a few days ago but Sam said it was better to keep them in for a little longer to make sure the cut was sealed properly.

So much happened in those weeks.

My relationship with Alessio was growing stronger each day. His patience and gentleness sang to my heart. He was considerate and never pushed for more.

My feelings for him was indescribable, and Maddie was on cloud nine.

I finally understood what she meant when she said her ship was sailing. Shaking my head, I smiled. She was so silly but the greatest friend and sister anyone could ever ask for. If it wasn't for her, I wouldn't be here, *happy*.

Looking up at the clock, I said, "Almost time. He told me to see him before lunch."

"Want me to come with you?"

"Of course. I'm expecting you to," I replied, putting the cut vegetables in the bowl next to me.

"What about Alessio?" she asked.

"He said he is busy," I muttered.

I heard her sigh beside me, making me look up.

"Artur has been pretty busy lately too. Something is wrong with the clubs, from what I've heard."

I nodded and wiped my hand in my apron. "Alessio has been a little stressed out. Always lost in his thoughts. I tried to get him to talk to me but he said he didn't want to worry me about his problems."

Maddie shook her head with an exasperated sigh. "Artur said the same thing. Men." She washed her hands. "Let's go."

Sam was already waiting for us in his office. He gave us a small smile as we settled in.

"How are you feeling?" he asked.

"I'm great," I said.

"Any nightmares?"

Shaking my head, I presented him my arm as he

got his stuff ready. "No. No more nightmares."

He nodded and took my arm in his hand. "Good. Are you taking your medicines on time?" This time, he looked at Maddie.

She nodded and placed a hand on my shoulders. "I give her the medicines on time. It's all good."

"If you feel a little uneasy with my removing the stitches, just avert your gaze. I'll be done in no time," Sam suggested.

"Okay," I said, looking away.

While Sam worked on getting my stitches out, Maddie talked. Sam even joined sometimes, making some random jokes. I didn't even realize when he was done until he said so.

"Done," Sam said, leaning back and pushing his chair away. I looked down at my arms.

They were free of the stitches but not from the scars. From where the stitches used to be, there was a faint pink line.

Sam noticed me looking. "It's going to take some time for the scars to fade away."

The words made my heart ache. He might have been talking about the scars on my arms but the words meant more to me.

It would take some time for my scars to fade. My physical scars and my emotional scars. I didn't know how long it was going to take for me to be rid of them.

I was finally living a life but the scars ran too deep. Sometimes, I wondered, would I ever forget and move on fully?

"Cocoa butter is a great way to help. I would suggest you apply it on your scars every day or two.

Depends on you. I will prescribe you a tube of scar-fading cream. That might help," Sam said.

I nodded. "Okay. Thank you."

"But it will take some time. Even years," he added.

"I know," I replied, finally looking up. Sending him a smile, I continued, "At least they will fade, right? Even if it takes years."

Maddie's hand tightened on my shoulder.

"That's the spirit," Sam said.

"Your scars are your strength," Maddie added and I looked up at her. "They show what you have been through and that you are still here, fighting. They are a part of you."

"You're going to make me cry," I joked lightly even though her words meant everything.

But then another voice was added to the mix. This time I did cry.

"And it shows that you are stronger now."

I looked up through tear-filled eyes to see Alessio standing in the doorway.

He sent me one of his beautiful smiles and he walked into the room. "I'm sorry I'm late. I was held back at the last minute."

"It's okay," I said as he stopped in front of me. He leaned down and gave me a quick peck on the lips before straightening up.

"Everything good?" he asked.

"Perfect," I replied.

"Well. We are done here." Sam cleared his throat. Maddie gave me another squeeze and then let go of me.

"I'll see you later," she said with a wink before

leaving.

Alessio wrapped an arm around my waist, pulling me into his body. He placed a kiss on my forehead before turning to Sam. "Thank you," he said. Sam nodded and Alessio led me out of the room.

"How are you feeling?" he asked.

"Good. I'm glad the stitches are out. They were very annoying and itched a lot."

Alessio laughed and kissed me as I pouted. "I know. You have been complaining about them for days."

When he pulled away, I didn't like it. Leaning on my toes, I brought my lips to his and kissed him. It was quick and then I pulled away. "You are such a tease," Alessio growled, his arm tightening around me in almost a bruising grip.

A small giggle escaped past my lips at his words and I shrugged. Placing a hand on his chest, I looked up at his shining blue eyes. "You were gone before I woke up this morning," I said.

Alessio nodded solemnly. "I had to take care of some things. You looked too peaceful while sleeping, I didn't want to wake you up."

"I missed you."

My admission was a surprise to both of us. His eyes flared dangerously and I trembled in his embrace. "Well, fuck," he whispered harshly before slamming his lips on mine.

He pushed me against the wall, his lips devouring mine. I absorbed his kisses hungrily, like I was starving for him. His hands delved into my hair and he grasped it tight in his fist, tilting my head back.

My fingers dug in his shoulders and I moaned when he sucked at my tongue, kissing me deeper. His kisses were rough and hard, as if he was claiming me.

And then suddenly, he wasn't in my arms anymore.

He pulled away harshly and took several steps away, his breathing hard, his eyes glittering with need. "If we don't stop now, I won't be able to stop later. And we are in the hallway," he said.

"Okay," I replied.

"I'll see you for lunch," Alessio said, his eyes showing his desperate hunger for me yet he held himself back. For me. All for me. Everything he had done so far…was for me.

I nodded speechlessly and he quickly swiveled around, walking away. When he was out of sight, I sank against the wall and wrapped my arms around my middle, holding myself together.

I knew what Alessio wanted. It was clear in his eyes and every time he looked at me. He held himself back, waiting for me to make the next move. His need for me grew stronger each day. I saw it every time he lost control.

But I wasn't sure if I was ready.

Chapter 46

When I heard the shower turn off, I let out a sigh of relief and closed my book, turning toward the door as I waited for him to come out.

It had been almost half an hour and he was still inside.

He stopped in his tracks when he saw me on the couch. "You aren't in bed yet," he mumbled, drying his hair with the towel. "Are you not sleepy?"

I shook my head and looked down at the book on my lap. "I wanted to finish the book before going to sleep. And I'm not that sleepy."

"Hmm." Alessio threw the towel on the plush bench in front of the bed, before sitting down on the bed, facing me.

"How many pages do you have left?" he asked.

Opening the book, I checked and then shrugged before looking back at him. "Thirty-two pages. I have two chapters left."

"Go ahead then. Read it and then we'll go to sleep."

"Are you going to stare at me like that while I

427

read?" I teased with a small laugh.

"Is that a problem, kitten?"

"It's a little creepy."

"I like looking at you. I find that I can't take my eyes off you when we are in the same room."

I smiled, looking down at my book. I had to read every paragraph twice, because I didn't understand what I was reading.

My mind…my body was hyper-aware of Alessio's stares. With each minute, my body heated under his penetrating gaze.

When I finally finished the book, I snapped it shut, leaning against the sofa.

"Done?" Alessio questioned. I nodded and closed my eyes.

But I felt him moving closer and closer, until I felt him right in front of me. His heat made my heart flip and I licked my lips nervously as my eyes fluttered open.

"You are so beautiful, do you know that?" he whispered, leaning forward to touch my lips. He rubbed his thumb over it and then moved to my cheeks, trailing his finger upward. My eyes opened to stare into his.

"Stand up," he ordered softly. My body trembled as I did to his bidding. So many feelings…foreign feelings coursed through my body as I stood up in front of him.

"These lips, I will never grow tired of kissing them," he continued, his lips just inches away from mine.

"Please." I didn't know what I begged for. All I knew was that I needed him. And he understood.

Alessio brought his lips to mine and kissed me gently, sweetly. He wrapped his arms around my waist and pulled me close to his body and my hands instinctively went to his chest, making contact with his skin.

He kissed me while I explored every inch of his naked skin, my hands moving up his chest to his shoulders and then down his biceps and the length of his arms.

The more I touched him, the harder and deeper his kisses became. Our tongues danced together, in perfect harmony. We kissed each other like we had been kissing those same lips for years. We touched like our bodies were accustomed to each other.

His hold on me tightened and he pulled me deeper into his body until I was completely plastered against him. Our bodies molded together. We fit as if we were meant to be.

I could feel his heart beating hard, and I smiled against his kisses. Our hearts danced as if they had recognized their mate.

With that thought in my mind, I melted in Alessio's embrace and welcomed his kisses. I was nervous but I wasn't scared. Not of Alessio.

He continued to kiss me with the same fervor. He bit, sucked, nibbled, and kissed my lips.

He was claiming me.

His hands moved down my body until they were at the end of my nightgown and he slowly pulled the hem upward, stopping mid-thigh. Alessio slightly pulled away and I moaned at the loss of him.

"Ayla, this is the time to say *no*. If we continue

now, I don't think I will be able to stop. I need you too much," he whispered.

I stared at him through hazy eyes and brought a hand up to his cheek. He rubbed against my palm and I saw a small smile appear on his lips, his dimple popping, making its appearance. My fingers caressed the indent in his cheek.

Finding the courage inside of me, I looked into his eyes and whispered back, voicing my own need. "I don't want you to stop."

Alessio's eyes widened in surprise and then he smiled. His hands continued to move upward with my nightgown but he didn't remove it. Instead he stared into my eyes, asking for permission.

I found it endearing that he was being so sweet, gentle, and considerate. When I gave him a nod, he didn't waste any time. In a blink of an eye, my nightgown was off and he dropped it to the floor beside us.

The cold air kissed my bare skin and I trembled under Alessio's intense gaze. "So fucking beautiful," he muttered, taking a step closer. He brought his hand to my back and I felt his fingers on the latch of my bra. His hands trembled against me. It was shocking to see Alessio just as nervous.

When he unlatched my bra, he slowly removed the cups from my breasts, pulling it away from my body and letting it fall on the ground at our feet. As soon as I was bare, I tried to hide myself.

"No. Don't hide yourself from me," he chastised gently. Alessio brought his hands up and carefully pulled my arms away. My heart clutched and I swallowed hard against the ball of nervousness.

When I saw his eyes flare in satisfaction as he took in my naked body, my courage was back. I felt powerful. I felt desired and beautiful under his gaze.

Alessio leaned down and kissed me again. His kisses were a mixture of possessiveness and gentleness. Without breaking our kiss, he walked me toward the bed until the back of my legs hit the mattress.

He pulled back, his fingers tightening around my hips. "Lay down," he ordered gruffly, his voice laced with desire. I did as I was told and laid in the middle of the bed in nothing but just my black panties.

Alessio stared down at me, his gaze filled with lust.

I was no stranger to lust for I had looked into lustful eyes for seven years. Alberto had looked at me like a man determined to own me, to rip me of my identity until I was only his whore. He wanted to possess me...mind, body, and soul.

But the way Alessio looked at me, it was different. I could see the lust there but I also saw the gentleness. His gaze was soft as he took me in. He looked at me as if I was his everything.

He looked at me as if I was the only one he could see.

His stares told me everything I needed to know.

He cared. I wasn't just a toy or someone to be owned. I wasn't a whore in his eyes. Alessio looked at me like I was a precious jewel, someone to cherish and love.

And I soaked it up, holding this moment close to my heart, savoring every look, every touch, every beautiful whisper. My heart ached in a good way.

His eyes still on me, he quickly pulled his sweatpants and boxers down, standing completely naked before me.

He was already hard.

I ducked my head shyly, feeling my cheeks flame at the sight. Alessio chuckled and then I felt the bed dip as he joined me. He cupped my jaw.

"So sweet," he whispered before taking my lips again. Alessio tugged me onto my side so I was facing him.

As he continued to kiss me, I felt his hands moving over my body until they stopped on my breasts. My nipples hardened as though begging for his touch. I wanted him. My need for him just as powerful and overwhelming as his for me.

My body was hypersensitive of his every touch as he trailed a finger over the swell of my breast and then circled my puckered nipple.

I hummed against his lips. He nibbled his way down my jaw to my ear, all the while playing with my nipples. He masterfully toyed with them, driving me crazy as my moans filled the room.

I fidgeted restlessly under his hands, my head falling backward, giving him better access to my neck. He grazed his teeth over the curve of my neck, finding my sweet sensitive spot that elicited another moan from me.

I shivered against his lips, my hands going up as I delved my fingers into his hair.

His lips continued downward, leaving a hot damp trail over my skin. He kissed over my collarbone, and then he stopped right over a rigid nipple.

Alessio blew over the tip and my fingers tightened around his hair in anticipation. He licked the puckered tip of my nipple and I gasped, arching my back as I pushed my breast into him, demanding more.

He wrapped his lips around my nipple and sucked hard. I moaned loud, my nails dragging over his scalp. He licked, sucked, and teased, driving me crazy with each movement of his tongue over my nipple.

"Alessio…"

And then he moved to the other nipple, giving it the same attention. I was already wet and I quivered against him, pressing my thighs together.

Releasing my nipple with a pop, he gave it a last lick before shifting himself on his elbows. Alessio rolled on top of me, balancing himself on his elbows so that his weight wouldn't crush me.

He brought a hand up to my throat and slowly dragged a finger down to my stomach. He drew small circles around my belly button and I shivered and moaned against his touch.

"You have the softest skin. So beautiful," he whispered. And then his lips were following the same path as his fingers. In no time he had my panties off and I was completely bare to him.

Alessio used his hands to spread my thighs, positioning himself between them as he continued to trail kisses down my breasts and then my stomach. When he didn't stop and continued down there, my eyes flared in surprise and my head snapped up.

433

"Alessio. No. What are you doing?"

He chuckled low and pressed a hand on my stomach. "Lay down, Ayla. Let me show you how it's done."

I started to argue but he nipped at my stomach.

"Shhh…I'll make sure you love it," he whispered before continuing.

When I felt Alessio's fingers over my pussy, an unashamed moan escaped past my lips and my head fell back on the pillow.

He spread my wetness over my folds and I moaned at the new sensation.

"You're dripping," he groaned huskily.

His fingers latched on my clit and I jerked, letting out a sharp cry. "Oh God…"

My fingers tightened around the comforter as indescribable pleasure filled my body. When he lowered his head down there, I gasped, my fingers instantly going to his hair.

He filled my senses. He overwhelmed me. His touches, his lips were driving me crazy with pleasure. I used to be vessel for the pleasure of others yet Alessio made it his mission to give me this new feeling.

I felt his tongue over my entrance and I arched my back, my hips leaving the mattress as I pressed harder against his lips.

"So fucking responsive," he groaned, running his tongue over my entrance and then upward as he licked at the wetness gathered there.

I shook uncontrollably, my fingers tightening in his hair. He pushed my legs upward, until the soles of my feet were on the bed and I was wide open to him and his masterful mouth. Alessio slowly pushed a finger inside my opening as he continued to lick at the tiny nub.

I moaned as he pumped a finger inside of me and his tongue played. And then he eased another finger inside of me, this time plunging deeper and faster.

My hips rocked against his mouth and fingers as I twitched uncontrollably. I sighed and moaned as his groan mixed with mine.

When he latched on top of my clit and sucked hard, the same time pushing a third finger inside of me, my hips bucked upward with a cry.

This sensation inside of me was building, hard and fast. I clenched around his fingers, my hips moving against him, increasing the sweet torturous friction.

"Alessio…" I moaned, as he stretched my wall, pumping harder and faster.

I closed my eyes as my body arched upward and I let out another moan.

"Alessio," I cried out. I was taut as a bowstring as a mixture of pain and intense pleasure filled my body and mind.

"Oh…please…" I was dangling over the edge of ecstasy and my body trembled violently against his.

"I've got you, Ayla," he said quietly as he removed his fingers, replacing them with his tongue. My walls clenched around him, wanting more.

He swirled the tip around my opening and then slid inside.

My eyes went wide and I gasped and then moaned loud. Letting out a cry, I clamped my thighs tightly around his head. I twitched beneath him but I never had a chance to think, because he pressed his fingers hard against my nub at the same time.

"Ahhhh…" I cried, my hips leaving the mattress as my orgasm crashed through me, my body twitching as I came hard.

I heard him moan and I whimpered.

He brought his head up, looking at me with heated blue eyes. His chin was wet with my juices and my body trembled at the sight.

Never had I felt such pleasure. He had given me an orgasm before but this one had sent me over the edge.

Alessio wiped his chin with the back of his hand and he smirked. "You are so fucking beautiful when you come. Your face all flushed, your eyes hazy with pleasure…so beautiful."

Parting my thighs wider, he positioned himself between them and settled himself in place on top of me. "But I'm not done yet," he whispered huskily.

My eyes went wide and I grabbed his shoulder. I felt him at my entrance and I moaned. His hand grasped my thigh, spreading me just a little wider. Alessio's eyes had turned darker, the hunger there clearly written. He ran his cock up and down my wetness, coating his tip with my cream.

My body trembled underneath his…in desire, anticipation, and slight fear.

Grasping my hip with one hand, he wrapped his other around my thigh as he thrust slowly inside, filling me completely.

But as soon as he was inside me, I gasped, my

eyes widening as a darkness fell upon me.

No. No. No, I screamed in my head. *Not now. Please not now.*

But it was too late.

Instead of Alessio…

I saw *Alberto*.

All I felt was pain as my body and heart shattered in a million pieces.

Tears blinded my vision as my body froze. Alberto's words invaded my mind. His evil smiles, his face as he took me repeatedly against my will…they all crashed around me.

Such a perfect moment it was, and now I was back to the nightmare that blinded me.

Alessio thrust again inside of me, oblivious to what was happening deep inside my soul.

Alessio's groans were replaced by Alberto's groans and grunts of pleasure.

My body ached, my heart squeezed so tight in my chest that I gasped for air…for mercy.

I felt myself going numb, my body and mind slowly closing down. It hurt so much. I was bleeding from the inside. The pain was like thousands of sharp knives against my skin.

All I saw and felt was Alberto. He was the one moving inside of me, thrusting, pounding relentlessly inside of me.

Please, I begged. *Make it go away.*

As the numbness took over my body, I left this world. I was no longer here. I was gone. My spirit vanished, broken in a thousand pieces.

Chapter 47

Alessio

Thrusting a second time inside Ayla, I groaned. Fuck, she was so tight. I didn't think I could hold on much longer and I was barely inside of her for a few seconds.

She was so responsive when I ate her pussy. When she came, I thought I was going to lose it right there like a fucking horny teen.

I was about to push back inside when I noticed her eyes. They were filled with tears and I saw the change right in front of me. Her beautiful green eyes slowly went blank…numb.

And that was when I realized that she was frozen underneath me.

"Ayla?" I whispered, my voice hoarse.

But she didn't answer.

My heart stuttered almost painfully in my chest at the sight beneath me. She stared up at me like she wasn't seeing me. Like I wasn't even there.

Oh no, no, no, I chanted in my head, quickly

438

pulling my cock from her wet heat.

"Ayla?" I tried again, my hands shaking as I brought it up to her face, softly caressing her cheeks.

She flinched away from me and a single tear slipped from her eye, falling down her cheeks, leaving a single wet trail. And that sight broke my heart. It exploded until my body went numb with pain and anger.

Ayla rolled on her side, bringing her knees up to her chest as she curled into herself. She sobbed quietly.

Rubbing a hand over my face, I felt something wet on my cheeks. Fuck, I sat on my ass as my tears unashamedly ran down my cheeks.

This wasn't happening. It couldn't be true. Not to my Ayla. Not my sweet beautiful Ayla.

Not my angel.

"Ayla," I whispered, moving closer to her, desperately trying to bring her back to me but she whimpered in fear and pain. She made a wounded sound and curled tighter into her body. I stopped any movement, my heart splintering open at her pain.

Bringing a trembling hand up, I placed it over my mouth as I choked back my tears.

The darkness settled around us, throwing us back into the pit of pain.

Closing my eyes, I sank my head in my hands.

I didn't want to believe it.

I didn't want to believe that my Ayla had to go through this pain.

But as much as I hated to admit it, as much as I

wished it wasn't true…
My guess was right all along.
Ayla had been raped.

Chapter 48

I wanted to pound that bastard's face. Whoever he was, he would pay in the worst way possible.

The signs were right there in front of my eyes. I saw them. All of us saw them but we didn't want to think the worst. We didn't want to believe that Ayla had gone through this.

But I knew what she had been through. My cold, unfeeling, fucking heart felt it. Her pain.

Ayla's small body was shaking violently with her cries. And as she curled herself tighter and buried her face in the pillow, my chest grew tighter. My heart ached at the sight of her looking so broken.

But apart from the searing pain filling my chest, I felt immense fury. Deep anger and resentment at the bastard who has brought tears to her eyes.

He was a dead man walking. I was going to get my hands on him soon. But not before torturing him until he would beg me for his own death. And then I would gladly send him to hell.

But at that moment, what mattered most was

Ayla.

I would let my anger out later. I would spill blood later.

I couldn't let the monster out yet. I had to rein in the need to kill.

Inching closer to her, I brought my hand forward to touch her but she flinched away and sobbed harder. She pressed herself harder into the mattress and I heard her mumbling something incoherent. Her words were lost in her cries.

"Ayla," I whispered gently, trying to coax her.

But my next words were cut abruptly when I saw her hands moving blindly under the pillows. Her eyes were closed tightly as she searched for something, her movements frantic and almost desperate.

"No, no, no, no…please no…" she mumbled between her sobs, her chest heaving with loud hiccups as she continued to cry.

When realization dawned at what she was looking for, I quickly jumped off the bed.

The jacket. The fucking jacket.

Quickly striding toward the sofa chair, I pulled on my sweatpants and went back to bed, getting in beside Ayla. Lying down, I moved a little closer.

She didn't open her eyes, but she went completely still as I moved closer, her muscles visibly coiling tighter in fright and tension.

"Shhh…" I soothed in a soft voice. "I'm not going to hurt you."

"Jacket. I need my jacket. Please…I can't…I need it…" She gasped through her tears.

She wasn't getting it. Instead, she was going to

442

have *me.*

This time, *I* was going to take away her nightmares and her pain. *I* was going to bring her back. And *I* would be the one to wipe away her tears.

Not my jacket. But *me.*

The blank eyes and the numb expression, I was going to change that.

I would bring *my* Ayla back.

Moving just a little closer, I whispered, "Ayla, open your eyes."

At my words, she tensed. Her hands fisted and she recoiled backward, but I quickly wrapped my arms around her waist, pulling her into my body. Ayla let out a sharp cry. One that was filled with fear and panic. But as soon as her body made contact with mine, she froze, her hands landing flat on my chest.

"I'm here. I'm right here, Ayla. I won't let anything happen to you. I'm right here," I said into her hair, my voice soft and scratchy as I fought back my tears. Placing a kiss on her temple, I let my lips linger there. "Please look at me."

But she refused to open her eyes. Instead, she moved closer against my body and curled herself into my embrace, as if she was hiding in me. Her hands trembled on my chest and I brought a hand up, grasping hers and holding them tight against my skin.

"It's me. Alessio. I'm here. I'm with you, Ayla, and I'm not leaving. We are going to get through this together. I'm here," I continued in a soothing voice. "Can you feel that?" I asked, holding her hands over my wildly racing heart.

It took me some time to bring her back from the black pit and painful memories she was thrown back in again. I coaxed for hours. Ayla continued to cry, each tear breaking my heart further. I filled her ears with gentle, soft words, hoping that it would make a difference. Desperately hoping it would bring Ayla back to me again.

I didn't know how long it had been, but then I saw a change. A slight change that made my heart leap with pure elation and intense relief.

Her sobs slowly diminished into quiet hiccups and she buried her face into my chest, resting her cheek right over our entwined hands.

Ayla let out a barely audible soft sigh and I felt her tense muscles start to loosen. She completely relaxed into my arms, letting her rigid shoulders drop with another sigh.

My arm tightened around her waist and I placed another kiss on her forehead. "You're safe. I won't ever let anything happen to you."

Those words were a vow that came from within me and my cold, broken heart.

And they were a vow I would never break.

Ayla was mine. My sweet, innocent Ayla.

And I protect what's mine, I thought, looking down at her in my arms.

Her eyes were closed and she settled against my chest. I could feel that Ayla was quickly letting go, surrendering herself to sleep, fatigue, and mental stress. Her cheeks were red and tear-streaked.

Removing my hand from her hips, I quickly swiped away her tears before wrapping her in my arms again. She mumbled something quietly and then sighed sleepily.

"Alessio." My name was a whisper against her lips.

And then to my utter surprise a small, barely visible smile appeared on her beautiful red lush lips. It was as if she was dreaming, her mind elsewhere.

At her peaceful and sleepy expression, the unbearable tightness in my chest slowly started to loosen until I could breathe normally again.

Placing another kiss on her temple, I left my lips there as I closed my eyes, letting myself relax against her too.

"Sleep, angel. I will watch over you," I whispered against her skin.

In a matter of seconds, her breathing evened out, her chest moving softly and slowly up and down as she let herself go and succumb to her sleepiness.

But I didn't sleep.

I couldn't.

Because every time I closed my eyes, all I saw was Ayla's eyes becoming blank and her face twisting in pain. It was all I could see, and the thought of her being in this much agony drove me mad.

The rage fueled deep inside of me.

And I couldn't wait to unleash it on the fucker who had hurt *my* Ayla.

***

Ayla

My head was pounding and all my muscles were aching. I felt languid as I blinked my eyes open and pressed my face harder into the pillow, trying to wrap my head around what happened yesterday.

Everything was a blur and it felt like I was missing pieces of puzzles. Rubbing my eyes, I turned around in bed to find myself alone. Alessio was already gone.

I realized I was completely naked, cold air on my bare chest, and the memories started to come back.

I couldn't remember much after we'd started. Did Alessio notice? Had he kept going?

The thought almost choked me and a single tear fell down my cheek.

All I remembered was suddenly feeling peace as I fell asleep. Only a peaceful feeling had surrounded me.

I looked around the bed and didn't see the jacket anywhere.

Falling back against the pillows, I cried softly when realization sank in.

Alessio…

It was him.

He had calmed me last night. He brought me back from the darkness.

I was still lost in my thoughts when the bathroom door open. My eyes widened and I sat forward in shock when Alessio came out, wearing a white unbuttoned dress shirt and black slacks.

His eyes met mine, and I saw him whisper my name. When he took a step forward, I grabbed the comforter up, hiding myself from him.

Alessio visibly swallowed hard and looked down, pinching the bridge of his nose as he did so. He took several deep breaths in and then stared up at me again. I ducked my head nervously, feeling ashamed that he had to see me in such a position last night.

I felt him coming closer and then the bed shifted under his weight. Closing my eyes tightly, my fingers tightened around the comforter.

"Here. Wear this," Alessio said.

My nightgown was lying in front of me. I swallowed hard and trembled slightly when he knelt down, and with one hand, he pulled the comforter away, his movement gentle as he watched all my reactions carefully.

I had to stare up into his face and he quickly pulled the nightgown over my head and waited for me to put my arms through. Not once did he look away from my face. He didn't even look down at my naked body.

Instead, he kept his eyes away, giving me respect.

Respect...something I never had in my life before. Yet Alessio was here, being gentle, sweet, and so considerate that it made my heart ache.

Keeping my eyes on his, I placed my arms through it and Alessio pulled the nightgown down the rest of my body, eventually covering my naked self from his eyes.

He slowly brought a hand up and gently moved my hair away from my face, pushing the strands behind my ears so that my face was fully visible to him. Alessio cupped my jaw and rubbed his thumb over my cheek and then under my eyes.

"Ayla," he murmured, his eyes showing me raw emotions. I couldn't look into his bluish eyes anymore.

I saw pain there. Anger. Desperation. Sadness. Grief. Heartbreak.

So I glanced away from his mesmerizing eyes. I looked away before I could see the disgust.

Because it should be there, shouldn't it?

Why was he even touching me? Why was he being so sweet and gentle?

Wasn't he disgusted by me?

Alberto's words resonated in my ears and I closed my eyes tightly against the memories, trying to shut them out.

No man would ever want you.

Maybe he was right.

Who would want me?

Not after what Alberto has done. Not after he ruined me.

"Ayla, look at me. Don't cast your eyes away like that."

I shook my head and pulled away from me. "I need to use the bathroom."

I needed to get out of there. Away from him, his sweet words and his understanding eyes.

"Ayla—" I shook my head again.

"Alessio, please," I begged this time, my voice hoarse with tears. He sighed, letting my jaw go. I quickly got off the bed and walked out of his room on shaky legs.

As soon as I was in mine, I closed the door and

went straight into my bathroom, swiping my tears on the way.

I didn't look at myself in the mirror. Instead, I kept my eyes away from it as I brushed my teeth and washed my face, removing the evidence of my crying.

After changing into my uniform, I mechanically combed my hair, feeling strange and weak. After so long I have had a break down. I almost forgot how it felt.

I was so lost in my happiness that I had forgotten the painful truth I'd been hiding from Alessio and everyone else.

I was still the enemy's daughter. Alberto's fiancée. I was an Abandonato.

Shaking my head at my own stupidity, I leaned against the sink as a new wave of tears assaulted me. I was in too deep and now it was impossible to go back now

Even if I tried to forget what I had with Alessio...I couldn't forget. The memories were etched deep inside my heart and soul.

His touches. His gentle caresses. His soft and then possessive kisses. His sweet words. His enthralling bluish-steel eyes. Our moments together...I couldn't forget.

Because I felt it. Every day. Every minute. Every second. I felt it deep inside my soul.

The tears ran down my cheeks and I brought a hand up to my mouth, covering the sob that threatened to come out.

Instead of escaping, I ended up trapping myself.

I cried for the gruesome memories that continued

to assault my mind. And then I cried for the dreams and the future that I desperately wanted to hold on…but they seemed impossible.

After my tears had dried out, I stood up and washed my face again. I quickly braided my hair into a French braid and then stepped out into the bathroom.

But my steps faltered and I froze at the sight of Alessio pacing my room.

He must have heard me because he quickly swiveled around toward me, his shoulders dropping in relief. "You were taking so long. I got worried," he said. He took a step toward me but stopped when I moved back. "Ayla?" His brow furrowed. "Don't do this, Ayla."

"Please go," I whispered brokenly.

He shook his head and took a step toward me again. "I'm not going anywhere."

"Alessio, leave. Please. I don't want you here."

"No."

Growing frustrated at his stubbornness, my head snapped up and I stared into his eyes. "Why won't you leave me alone?" I screamed.

"I'm not leaving you alone like this. I didn't leave you last night and I'm not leaving you now."

"Alessio…please…don't do this. I can't do this now."

Instead of caving in to my begging, he walked forward, stopping right in front of me. Alessio wrapped his arms around me and pulled me into his chest. "I'm not letting you go."

My hands instinctively came up and I grasped his shirt tightly. "Why do you keep doing this?" I

450

sobbed.

"Because I can't have you go back into that dark place. I need you here with me," he replied gently. He bent down, wrapping an arm around my waist and then behind my legs before pulling me up, cradling me into his chest.

I placed my head on his shoulder as he carried me to my bed. Alessio sat down, keeping me into his warm and protective embrace as he settled me sideways on his lap.

"Ayla, talk to me," he said after a few minutes of silence. When I didn't answer, he sighed, his arm tightening around me. "Please."

"What do you want me to say, Alessio?" I whispered tiredly, keeping my face buried in his neck.

"Anything. Just talk to me. Don't shut me out."

"What do you want to know? You already know the truth, but if you want me to say it, I'll say it. I was raped, Alessio. There. I was raped," I said bitterly, harshly pulling away. I struggled, but his hold was tight.

He cupped my cheeks in the palms of his hands, tilting my head up to face him. "Ayla, do you know how strong you are? You are the strongest woman I have ever met. Your strength shines brighter than anyone else."

"Alessio…" Never in a million years would I have thought that Alessio Ivanshov would utter such words to me. He gave me hope.

"I don't know exactly what happened, and I'm not going to push you for more. You can tell me when you are ready. I will wait," he said. "But please don't shut me out. Don't run away from me."

We were both silent for a few seconds. He placed a kiss on my forehead, letting his lips linger there. "I didn't expect you to say anything, but now that you have said it, please tell me who the fuck hurt you, so I can kill the motherfucker."

I stared into his eyes.

They glinted with fury and such ferocious intensity that it took my breath away. I also saw the hurt and pain there.

But what surprised me most was that I didn't see disgust. He didn't look at me as if he hated me.

Remembering his question, I shook my head. His eyes lost the light there and he sighed. I couldn't tell him.

I didn't want this dream to end now. I wanted to continue living in this world.

"Ayla—"

"Please don't ask me about him. I don't want to talk about him. Please, Alessio."

He stared into my eyes for a second before reluctantly nodding. "Okay. When you are ready."

I placed my head on his shoulder again and closed my eyes as his arms wrapped around my waist again. We were both silent for some time. Only our breathing could be heard and I felt his heart pounding under my hand as I laid it on his chest.

We were both content, holding each other in silence.

"Alessio."

"Yes?"

"Do you think of me differently now? Because

of what happened?" My voice was quiet, just a whisper as I uttered the words. My hands were shaking.

Alessio's arm tightened around me and he placed a kiss on my head. He pulled away, forcing me to bring my head up from his shoulder. Our eyes met. *Blue to green.* The world stilled for a moment and he was all I could see.

Palming my cheeks, he gave me a small smile. "No. Not a chance, Ayla. That thought never even came to my mind. What happened wasn't your fault. Rape is never justified. You are a victim and that bastard deserves to die."

Leaning his forehead against mine, he continued in the same soft voice. "Yes. I do think of you differently. But not the way you are thinking. Now, I think you are strong. You have endured this, yet you are still here, fighting. That's all that matters. What has happened to you would never change my mind about you. Never." Placing a kiss on my nose, he smiled. "I don't think anything could ever change how I feel about you."

My cheeks felt wet and that was when I realized that I was crying again. Sniffling, I brought a hand up and cupped his cheek.

He smiled a little wider. I rubbed my thumb over the dimple on his cheek, my tears running down my face.

"I'm no good for you, Alessio," I whispered. "I'm not worthy of you."

My heart clenched at my words.

"Ayla, no!" Alessio said, his eyes widening.

Smiling sadly, I rubbed my fingers softly over

his cheek. "It's the truth. You are too good. Too accepting. You are a good man with a kind heart, but I'm not good for you."

Because I'm not who you think I am, I continued in my head.

"Stop," he scolded, shaking his head furiously. "Don't say that, Ayla."

"I'm not the one for you. You think you know the whole truth, but you don't." I continued, my fingers tracing his eyebrows and then his forehead. "I wish I could be someone else. I wish I didn't have the past I had. You and I...we can't ever be one."

He closed his eyes tightly, his body slightly shaking with the force of his emotions. "Don't say that, Ayla."

"You would hate me if you knew my truth," I whispered. The words flew out of my mouth, my heart shattering in the process.

"What happened to you was not your fault. Don't blame yourself. It doesn't matter to me. All I want is you," he confessed, pressing his lips ever so gently on mine.

If only he knew the whole truth. He wouldn't be saying those words to me.

"I will only hurt you in the end, Alessio," I murmured against his lips.

"I'll take my chances," he fired back.

"Alessio—"

He cut me off with a bruising kiss. Closing my eyes, I absorbed his kiss as my lips moved against his.

Slightly pulling away, his fingers tightened on

my braid. "It's me who isn't worthy of you, Ayla. I have blood on my hands. I have killed so many people that I have lost count. I'm a monster, Ayla. I'm not a good man. But you…you are perfect. You are an angel."

I gasped at his words and slowly opened my eyes.

"You have it in reverse. Whatever you said, it's the opposite," he continued.

"I'm fire. I will only burn you in the end," I murmured against his lips.

He smiled. "The fire is raging, then. I don't know if I'll burn in the end or not. But I don't want to give up on us. If I burn, then I will go with a smile, knowing that I had this little moment with you. Even if it was a little while."

"Don't do this, Alessio."

He kissed me again. I couldn't reject him. I was weak against his words. They were words that I wanted to hear…that I desperately needed, so I hung on even when I knew I shouldn't.

I couldn't push him away. I pulled him toward me, kissing him back with the same fervor. We kissed away all the pain as our hearts came together as one, the pull between us too strong to fight.

This intangible connection…I felt it deep inside my soul.

"I'm not giving up on you, Ayla. So, don't give up on us either," he murmured before claiming my lips again.

And in this very moment, I was thankful that I had gotten in his car.

For he had restored my shattered heart and

broken soul.

Alessio had breathed new life into me.

Chapter 49

Ayla

I was walking out of my room when I saw Alessio limping up the stairs, his face and hands bloodied. "Alessio!" I exclaimed in panic.

He grimaced. "Ayla, I thought you were downstairs," he muttered, his voice laced with pain.

"I was in my room. I was headed downstairs now to help Lena and Maddie with dinner," I said. Bringing a hand up, I was about to touch his face but then stopped, scared that I would hurt him further. "What happened?" I asked worriedly.

"Nothing. I was just sparring with Viktor and Nikolay." He flicked his wrist and shrugged his shoulder nonchalantly, as if it didn't matter.

"Sparring? You are bloody and hurt. What type of sparring is that?" I took his hand and pulled him toward his room. "I'll clean your wounds."

"No. It's okay. You have to help Lena. I'll do it." He tried to pull his hand away but I tightened my fingers. When he hissed in pain, I quickly let go.

"You are hurt, Alessio. Let me help," I said, my chest aching at seeing him in pain. He smiled and bent down, placing a quick kiss on my lips.

"I'm fine. Really. It just looks bad because I'm not cleaned up. I'm not even that hurt."

"But…"

He cut me off with another kiss. "Ayla. Go. Stop worrying so much."

He gave me a wink and walked into his room, closing the door behind him.

Most of the day was spent with Alessio. We ate breakfast together in my room and then went to the creek. After our confessions this morning, we didn't talk about it again.

I thought I could let him go, but I couldn't.

I just hoped that he wouldn't hate me when he learned my whole truth.

After tying my apron around my waist, I strode out of my room but stopped when I saw Viktor and Nikolay standing in front of my doorway, both of their expressions unreadable. They were clean compared to Alessio but I could see the bruises on their faces and hands.

"Can I help you?" I asked nervously.

Nikolay stayed quiet, so Viktor replied. "No. We just wanted to see how you were doing."

Confused, I played with the hem of my dress. "I'm doing good."

We stared at each other in tense silence and then he cleared his throat. "Good. We heard you weren't doing so well this morning. It's good to see you smiling again."

I took a sharp intake of breath at his words and

then nodded. "Thank you."

Just then his phone rang and he answered the call. "Yeah?" He listened for a moment, his face growing frustrated. "Okay. Clean up the mess before the police comes."

"Was that Phoenix?" Nikolay asked when Viktor hung up.

He nodded. "Yeah. There's a mess at the club. I'm going to check it out. Phoenix is cleaning up."

"I'm coming," Nikolay said.

Viktor chuckled and then shook his head. "Let the boy on his own a little. I think he can handle it without you being a mother hen."

Mother hen? Nikolay?

I hid my laugh with a cough.

"I'm not a fucking mother hen," Nikolay growled, glaring at Viktor before sending me a glare of his own. My laughter quickly died but the smile was still there.

"Then don't act like one." Viktor laughed, quickly walking away.

"Fuck you."

Nikolay rubbed his face, making a frustrating sound.

"Is Viktor always like this?" I asked.

"Annoying as fuck? Yes," he replied.

"I think he is funny," I said with a shrug.

"Don't ever say that to him. He'll never stop then."

This time I let out a laugh, while shaking my head.

I saw his expression soften and then he nodded. "It's good to see you like this."

I ducked my head shyly and mumbled a quick *thank you*.

We were both silent and from the corner of my eye, I saw him lean against the wall beside my door. Nikolay sighed and then cleared his throat. "After the incident in the bathroom, we had a few guesses but never asked because we didn't want to push you," he said. "I know what happened."

"I—"

"I'm not telling you this to make you feel ashamed. I'm telling you this because I want you to know that no one would think of you any different just because of what happened to you. We all have a past here. All of us have secrets so we wouldn't judge you. One thing you would find here is that no one is ever going to judge you. We are all fucked up, you know."

His words brought tears to my eyes and I quickly blinked them away. Nikolay proved me wrong every time. I remembered the first time I met him. He was so scary, mean, and rude. He appeared heartless, ruthless, and emotionless. Just like Alessio.

"Especially Alessio," he continued. "He is a good man."

"Did Alessio tell you?" I whispered.

"No. He didn't have to. When he came to the gym and sparred with us, his actions were enough to let us know."

Swiping the tears that had fell down, I looked down at my feet. "Why do you guys fight like this?"

"Ayla, we kill people. We are part of a *Bratva*, feared by everyone. Sometimes, when we can't spill the blood of whom we want, we have to take out the anger somewhere else."

"Oh," I murmured.

"Right. I will leave you to your work now," he said, pushing away from the wall.

"Wait," I called. He turned around and faced me, his face impassive as always. "You said Alessio was a good man…" Walking over to him, I placed a hand over his heart. "You are a good man too."

His breath caught in his throat, but he stayed silent.

"I know the difference between someone who is bad and who is good. And you…you are good. You care even though you try to hide it," I said.

Nikolay was a man who hid behind a mask of anger, just like Alessio. But deep inside, they all cared.

I brought my hand up and placed it on his cheek, right over the scar. He flinched but didn't move away. "You hide behind your scars. You use them as a barrier, thinking that they would keep people away. It worked, didn't it?"

"Ayla," he said, his voice filled with pain.

"You think they're ugly. You think they represent a weakness. But they don't. Your scars represent your strength," I said, Maddie's words rolled off my tongue. I hoped that they would have the same effect on Nikolay as they had on me.

And they did. I saw his eyes soften the slightest bit and he cleared his throat again. "You have a kind heart, Ayla."

I smiled and then let out a small laugh, rubbing a finger over his scar. "You know…your scars don't make you ugly…they make you look…" I paused for a moment, trying to think of the word that Maddie used to describe Nikolay. When it finally came to mind, I quickly said it. "Sexy."

His eyes widened in shock.

Did I just say that?

I pulled my hand away from Nikolay's face and took a step backward. He raised an eyebrow at me.

"That was Maddie—"

"So, you don't think I'm sexy?"

"What? No. You are sexy. Wait, no, I mean your scars don't make you look ugly. They are nice. I mean, you look good with them. Yeah…" I stumbled over my words, rambling as I tried to fix what I said but instead made it worse.

Snapping my mouth shut, I stared at Nikolay mutely. The right corner of his lips twitched in the slightest bit but it looked painful, as if he was having trouble lifting his lips in a smile.

The scar ran down to his lips and I wondered if it was because of it that he couldn't smile.

"Just don't tell Alessio that you called me *sexy*," he teased, his eyes shining with mischievously.

"Right. I should get to work. I've wasted enough time," I said.

"Yeah. Go ahead." Nikolay moved out of my way and I quickly walked away.

As I walked downstairs, I had a smile on my face.

I had just realized I was surrounded with so much love.

Chapter 50

Nikolay

As I watched Ayla walk away, I shook my head. She was too innocent. Too kind and sweet to live in this world. She shouldn't be here.

But Alessio had claimed her. Boss was already too deep in to let her go now. He cared too much.

He loved too much, even if he didn't see it or realize it yet, it was there. In his eyes.

Love shouldn't exist in this life. It was too dangerous. We would only get burned in the end. We couldn't have any weaknesses.

That was Alessio's rule.

No love. No weakness.

But Ayla was now Alessio's weakness.

As she faded from my view, I leaned against the wall again. She said I was a good man. So gullible.

My phone rang in my pocket and I answered the call without looking at the caller ID.

"I need to see you now," a demanding voice said.

"Okay," I replied before hanging up.

Ayla was wrong.

I wasn't a good man. I had done horrible things and I didn't even feel guilty about them.

I was a coldblooded killer. Heartless. Ruthless. A betrayer.

Striding into Alessio's office, I found him sitting behind his desk. He looked up when I came in, and nodded.

"I need to take care of some things."

Alessio stared at me for a few seconds, his gaze penetrating. "Okay," he said. I turned around, but before I could walk out, his voice stopped me. "You should clean your hand."

I looked down at my fist and saw the bloodied knuckles. The same fist that I had just punched into the wall before coming into his office.

"I will," I replied, my voice emotionless.

Closing the door behind me, I went to my room and quickly changed my clothes. Wearing black jeans and a black sweater, I walked out of the estate and got into my car.

When I arrived at my destination, I pulled my hood over my head, hiding most of my face as I stepped out of the car. Two men greeted me. "He is waiting for you in his office."

Without answering, I walked into the club. The door to his office was already open, waiting for my arrival. Walking inside, I closed the door and crossed my arms over my chest, waiting for the man to start.

"Nikolay," he said roughly.

Staring into his brown eyes, I nodded in his direction. "Alberto."

Want to read the next installment of the
Tainted Hearts Series

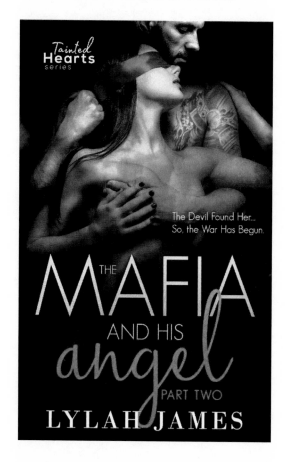

THE MAFIA & HIS ANGEL
PART 2

BY LYLAH JAMES

Acknowledgements

First and foremost, I would like to thank my parents for making me realize that writing is my passion. I was a reader for many years, before they told me one day "You can be a writer." At first, I laughed. And then one day, I wrote the first word down. Without their constant push, The Mafia and His Angel would probably never exist. They are the reason I am where I am today.

To my soul sister, *M.* You hate reading romance books–especially *this* type of romance. But you still picked up The Mafia and His Angel and read it for me. Against all odds, you fell in love with it and I fell even more in love with you. I am so glad you are here with me, supporting, loving and fangirling with me.

A biggest thank you to my Publisher. Thank you for giving TMAHA a chance. I am holding my book right now, because you think it is worth it. So thank you.

To my editor, Rosa–you rock! Thank you for editing this book. I was worried you would have no hair by the end, but apparently you got a lot more hair. Thank God.

Thank you to everyone else who had a hand in making this book–my proof-reader, formatter…you guys are a star.

To Deranged Doctor Design–Thank you for such a kickass cover. I couldn't stop staring at it!

To the bloggers and everyone who took their time to promote TMAHA, you are awesome! My big thanks to you.

And I wanted to leave this for the end, because this is the important part. A huge thank you, to every single one of my reader. My lovelies. If my parents are the reason why I started writing, then *you* are the reason why I am still here. In this moment, holding this book. Your never-ending support and love has taken us on this path. From the first word to the last, you have been here with me. I am proud we took this journey together. Together, we dreamed about holding TMAHA one day, thumbing through the pages. *We* did it, lovelies. Thank you for standing with me, even through my craziness. To all the fan accounts and groups out there, thank you! All the beautiful edits and posters you have made, they are my inspiration and motivation.

About the Author

Lylah James uses all her spare time to write. If she is not catching up on sleep, working or writing—she can be found with her nose buried in a good romance book, preferably with a hot alpha male.

Writing is her passion. The voices in her head won't stop, and she believes they deserve to be heard and read. Lylah James writes about drool worthy and total alpha males, with strong and sweet heroines. She makes her readers cry—sob their eyes out, swoon, curse, rage, and fall in love. Mostly known as the Queen of cliffhanger and the #evilauthorwithablacksoul, she likes to break her readers' hearts and then mend them again.

FOLLOW LYLAH AT:

Facebook page:
https://www.facebook.com/AuthorLy.James/

Twitter page:
https://twitter.com/AuthorLy_James

Instagram page:
https://www.instagram.com/authorlylahjames/

Goodreads:
https://www.goodreads.com/author/show/16045951.Lylah_James

Or you can drop me an email at:
AuthorLylah.James@Hotmail.com

Or check out my website:
http://authorlylahjames.com/

You can also join my newsletter list for updates, teasers, major giveaways and so much more!
http://eepurl.com/c2EJ4z